Reef of Gold

Gary Dale

AuthorHouse™
1663 Liberty Drive
Bloomington, IN 47403
www.authorhouse.com
Phone: 1-800-839-8640

© 2011 Gary Dale. All rights reserved.

No part of this book may be reproduced, stored in a retrieval system, or transmitted by any means without the written permission of the author.

First published by AuthorHouse 3/29/2011

ISBN: 978-1-4567-4471-7 (sc)
ISBN: 978-1-4567-4472-4 (dj)
ISBN: 978-1-4567-4473-1 (e)

Library of Congress Control Number: 2011903418

Printed in the United States of America

Any people depicted in stock imagery provided by Thinkstock are models, and such images are being used for illustrative purposes only.
Certain stock imagery © Thinkstock.

This book is printed on acid-free paper.

Because of the dynamic nature of the Internet, any web addresses or links contained in this book may have changed since publication and may no longer be valid. The views expressed in this work are solely those of the author and do not necessarily reflect the views of the publisher, and the publisher hereby disclaims any responsibility for them.

ACKNOWLEDGEMENTS: As an author, writing can be a lonely endeavor. Therefore, it takes any number of people to encourage you to keep going. For this effort, I am truly indebted. My father, Clifford; brother Steve; Chuck Uber; Kym Croft Miller; Charles Eckert; Danny Ronyak and numerous others who took the time to offer suggestions during my endeavor.

I have had the honor of meeting published authors and asking their opinions. Some have read the first chapter of Reef of Gold, made comments and gave encouragement to this writer. I met them at book signings when they were promoting their own book. My thanks go to Debbie Macomber; Patricia Smiley; and other published authors.

For….Josh, Sara, Sam & Leah

CHAPTER 1

NORTH KOREAN SHIP

She was low in the water.

Whipped by the unusually strong coastal winds of the Singapore Straits, the small blue and red flag of origin mounted on the freighter's stern crackled announcing its arrival to no one in particular. The ocean waves, seemingly coming from different directions, slammed against the rust-spotted ship's hull, bending and twisting the keel, causing the freighter to become less inclined to answer the helm. Enough of the welded steel hull was drawing at least three fathoms to risk running aground if she lost her heading and drifted too close to the barnacle-crusted shoals 200 meters away.

A concealed man, nestled in a dilapidated storage shack at the end of an abandoned pier, watched the freighter through binoculars. He consciously shivered and hunched his shoulders under his threadbare jacket, a futile gesture against the cold wind. His cramped position was tenuous at best. Falling into the freezing sea was not an option. With each pounding wave, he could feel the dilapidated dock shift under his feet. The weather-beaten shed surrounding him rattled and screeched against the few rusted nails holding the collection of bleached boards upright. The abandoned shack, barely four feet by four feet, was storage for a few torn life jackets, hung on the same rusted nails with coils of frayed hemp rope. Finally, he could stand

Gary Dale

the pain of cramping legs no longer. He carefully put all his weight on one leg and ever so slowly stretched out the other, inches at a time, letting the blood flow back into his muscles. Despite his precarious position, he reversed legs and felt instant relief.

Discounting the danger, the man raised his binoculars again to watch the distressed freighter, struggling to make it to port. Painted on the ship's bridge in scarred, yet bold letters was the name, 'Kim Song.' He watched as the North Korean ship plunged and rose in the high swells, trembling briefly at the top of the wave, shaking off the seawater running the length of the ship through her rusted scuppers. The distressed vessel crested on the next wave and then plunged again. The watcher shifted his gaze beyond the ship, to see foam covered waves identifying the razor-tooth reefs just off her starboard bow. It was going to be close.

A small crowd of longshoremen had gathered on the lee side of the old wharf to watch the pitching and rolling freighter in the near distance. One longshoreman, so worried about the ship's crew, wrung his hands constantly. Another, his head downcast, scuffed his sandals at the ancient wharf planks as if reminding himself of the thousands upon thousands of bare feet that had shuffled across the mahogany ribbed dock, unloading ships in all kinds of weather. As the longshoremen talked among themselves, no one alive could remember such a fierce storm at this time of the year. The wind direction was all-wrong for a Java Sea typhoon season.

The North Korean ship had no choice but to make it to the little used, aged wharf. The authorities must not see this particular cargo. A little further south in the same Singapore harbor, calmer waters prevailed. A modernized wharf facility contained a large number of giant lift cranes that moved along on their own rail tracks, parallel to the docked ships, efficiently plucking loose cargo and containers from the ships' holds, allowing goods to be stored in modern warehouse facilities for custom inspections. This was the world's largest cargo handling seaport. Singapore was proud of the tonnage title and wore

Reef of Gold

it haughtily among the shipping companies of the globe. The dirty little secret however, was that Singapore couldn't afford to rip out the centuries old wharf on the northern section of the seaport and rebuild. To do so would make the Rotterdam docks in Holland, the world's largest. Publicly, the Singapore government would lose face and so the thought of tearing down the ancient wharf was inconceivable. A more sinister statement would say the wharf held the headquarters of the Singapore Triad thus completely untouchable.

The North Korean cargo ship rolled and pitched less now as it rounded the point, barely avoiding the dangerous coral shoals. It was as if the wind itself suddenly sought the protection of the harbor moderating enough to allow the ship's rudder to have a little more cause and effect. The freighter dropped her speed moderately as she approached the ancient docks until the force of two large sea-going tugboats promptly took control of her. With great skill, the tugs nestled the ship with the flapping blue and red flag against a familiar berth. Docking lines were tossed back and forth by the waiting longshoremen and relieved crew.

Shaking from the cold wind, the concealed watcher once again moved his stiff limbs in an attempt to keep the blood circulating. Keeping warm was important. His immune system was still not one hundred percent as a result of a recent encounter with the Triad hit men. Strong medication was helping him recover from the slashing knife wounds he had received several weeks ago, but he was still vulnerable to infections and possibly catching pneumonia. In spite of the bone chilling conditions, he watched the North Korean ship with great interest. It was his job to gather intelligence. He switched from binoculars to his long-range Nikon digital camera and snapped picture after picture. As he watched through the camera lens, heavy camouflaged canvases were being winched and pulled by crewmen across cargo hatches covering part of the old wharf, finally giving the canvas canopy a tent-like appearance.

One corner of the heavy canvas was still flopping in the wind

Gary Dale

when a steel hatch opened from alongside the ship's bridge. Several well-dressed men emerged, looking bewildered at the deck activity. They quickly regained their composure, grabbing at their hats and scurrying across the windswept deck, slipping often on the wet deck, and nearly falling with each gust of wind before ducking under the secured canvas cover. Their exposure to the elements was only a brief moment, but it was enough time for the motorized 100 mm long-range camera to snap several incriminating photos.

The moment the camouflage covers were finally secured, the ship's deck hummed with activity. The lighter cargo was shunted under the heavy tarp canopy. Indonesian laborers, carrying staggering loads on their thin backs as thousands of laborers had done centuries before them, quickly moved the lighter cargo from ship to warehouse. For them, walking the plank during the storm took on a new meaning.

"At last," the shivering man in the dilapidated shack muttered to himself. He felt he had solved part of the mystery. The heavier cargo that required the use of the ship's deck cranes must be unloaded at night after the American spy satellite passed over the harbor. After viewing the ship through the long-range camera, the man was positive the deck canvas had been treated with special chemicals to blur the American satellite photos and keep the illicit passengers and cargo secret. What other purposes could the heavy canvas possibly have other than deception? And who were the three special passengers in suits who dashed across the wind swept deck? He hoped the long-range camera snapped enough images to tell him. He ejected the camera disc, palming it quickly into a hidden pocket of his ragged jacket. Uploading the pictures would come later when the atmospheric conditions were more favorable.

He would not delay his departure any longer for fear of discovery. Too much dock activity. Dressed as an unemployed deckhand, he had dyed his hair a light shade of black, added a beak of a nose with actors putty and colored a big, inflamed sore on his lip. He streaked his face with dirt and bunker oil making his eyes hooded like a great horned

Reef of Gold

owl. His old pants and jacket were ripped in places; oil stained, and smelled of continuous human use. The disguise would fit in well as one of the many derelict sailors hanging about the area, desperately looking for a pub willing to let them in to evade the chilling wind. A slight shuffle completed the disguise.

The binoculars and camera were of no value to him now and would only become a dangerous hindrance. He looked down between his legs and found rotting boards. He kicked at the boards using the heel of his shoe, smashing a hole large enough to drop the hindrance into the sea below. He glanced at his cheap watch. It told him it would be dark shortly giving him the cover needed to make his way back to his rendezvous point, only five warehouses away. An old bicycle would be waiting for him to make his escape. He had hidden it among the garbage dumpsters scheduled to be emptied the next morning.

As he hugged the darkest shadows of the dimly lit warehouse buildings, the man moved cautiously. The darkest shadows held his huddled presence intact while he slowly surveyed the area where he had left his bicycle. Squinting, he looked for any object that looked out of place, often looking slightly away from his intended spot to pick out even the smallest suspicious detail. Instinctively, he knew that to look directly at one spot, the cornea of his eye would not focus properly. A natural human physical fault, he knew from previous hunting trips with his Dad many years ago that the human eye could and would play tricks on him.

The sight of a few drunken seamen wandering about in a cold daze suddenly broke his concentration. The four men struggled from being blown off their feet. The nearest pub that might welcome them was several hundred meters away, and each drifter mentally calculated if he would make it safely. Three of the men looking for any temporary shelter decided to turn down an alleyway, eventually disappearing.

The remaining inebriated seaman, drifted on, hunched over,

Gary Dale

head down, fighting the wind, abruptly stopped in his tracks. Facing a gray painted dumpster and using one arm to steady himself, he turned slightly before barfing downwind, ejecting buckets of flying raw beer and rice crackers. He gagged for several moments, before wiping the residue on his sleeve. He leaned against the dumpster to regain is balance before slowly moving on, tracing the containers with his shoulder, trying to find a place out of the miserable wind, if only for a few minutes.

The seaman suddenly stopped before moving to the next waste container and stared at the dark void between the dumpsters. He could not believe his good luck. It was a bicycle. He looked cautiously around to see if anybody would see him steal his newly found prize. With his balance problem, he knew if he tried to ride the bicycle in this storm, he would certainly crash, damaging the bicycle. No, the excited seaman thought, he would push the bike instead until he was out of the windiest area and hide it and himself until morning. Then he would sell the two-wheeled monster to a street vendor. His fellow patrons at the Ding Ho pub would relish the story. Seeing no one, he slid in between the garbage containers to collect his prize.

As the US Commerce Department special agent, Ric Templeton, watched the liberation of his bicycle, he felt like he had just been kicked in the stomach. Now, he had no choice but to get some immediate transportation. He had to upload the photos without haste. Walking swiftly to a weather protected store entrance a few blocks away, he disappeared into the shadows.

Stripping himself of his ragged, smelly clothes, he was left with wrinkled cotton pants, a rumpled cotton shirt, a stained sweatshirt for warmth and a raincoat. He still smelled like a brewery floor but at least he would blend in with the few pedestrians, braving the fierce storm. Searching the discarded foul smelling jacket, he found the camera disc and slipped the film disc down the back of his neck into a specially made shirt pocket, knowing that a hurried body search by any security personnel rarely went as high as his neck. Using the

Reef of Gold

sleeve of his stained sweatshirt and a little personal spit gave him the moisture needed to erase the red sore spot on his lip. The beaked nose was twisted off. He picked at the remnants of his nose as he walked toward a main thoroughfare. Once there, he looked both ways for a taxi stand. Turning left, a half a block away was a hotel entrance with a flapping weather canopy. A rain squall had momentarily moved into the immediate area, dumping a torrent of water. He dashed for the hotel entrance.

A taxi drove up next to the deserted hotel entrance and stopped. A frustrated taxi passenger struggled with his umbrella as he climbed out of the taxi. The hotel canopy didn't quite reach the curb, allowing rain water to cascade down the front of the apron. As the passenger stepped under the dripping canopy, Templeton used that moment to slip into the taxi. Slamming the taxi door, he told the driver to quickly take him to the inter-island ferry dock. The driver scowled, held his nose with one hand and steered with the other. His passenger smelled like a wet dog.

CHAPTER 2

LIAISON OFFICE/SAN FRANCISCO

Hailing a cab, Brad headed back to his hotel to consider the day's events. His confidence in the reef of gold project soared during the meeting with the Chinese seafaring expert, Mr. Wong, and his lovely granddaughter. The grandfather's interpretation of the written Chinese portion of his newly discovered maritime journal confirmed his earlier research. The story of the reef of gold of unimaginable wealth was true and not a fable. According to Mr. Wong's research, a second journal written during the same time period, confirmed details of his journal. The seafaring captains of the early 1400's kept accurate accounts of their journeys and passed on the records to their families. The trading ports and the personal contacts were extremely valuable for continued business. Coupled with the Norwegian translation from a Nordic professor at Stanford University fired Brad's imagination. The keys to finding the fabled 'reef of gold' required both journals. Having access to the second journal rumored to be located in Macau was critical to finding the actual Norwegian Rune stone where the final location of the reef of gold was chiseled.

The more he thought about the adventure, the more excited he became. He knew others would want his valuable journal. He would have to keep one step ahead of them. He located a quiet corner of

Reef of Gold

the hotel lobby where his voice wouldn't echo or be overheard and sat down in a comfortable overstuffed armchair. He would call his parents for financial help and give them a piece of the action. They believed in him. Besides, he wouldn't need any investment money right away. He would use his personal savings for the research time in Australia and then worry about the money for exploration.

Brad shucked his clothes as soon as he walked into his hotel room and ran the shower to luke-warm before stepping in. He disliked the shower water being too hot and besides, he was running through the shower, not soaking in it. He quickly finished and was toweling off when he heard a phone ring. The muted ring, he discovered, was not the hotel phone but his cell phone, half buried under the clothes that he had carelessly tossed onto his bed.

Brad didn't recognize the private number on his cell phone and his hesitation at answering caused him to miss the connection. "Figures," he mumbled to himself in frustration. He fiddled with the phone for a moment before tossing it back onto the bed. "Maybe they will call back." Brad padded around the hotel room in his bare feet, taking his time getting dressed. He watched the Fox Newscaster on television report of another terrorist attack on an American Embassy somewhere in the world. Attacks were becoming common with American embassies especially in foreign countries being the favored target.

Just as he was planning to head out for a sightseeing walk, he noticed his cell phone light blinking at him. He flipped through the settings and found he had an urgent saved message. The voice mail message was from an official at the American Embassy Liaison office. The official stated that his brother Ric had an accident. It was urgent that Brad phone the Liaison office immediately for an appointment. Brad stared at his phone.

"It can't be," he exclaimed. He looked at his watch and figured he still had time to make it to the embassy before it closed. Wait a minute, he thought. What gives here? The embassies aren't normally

Gary Dale

open on a Sunday. He checked the message time on the cell phone call. The call had come in less than a half hour ago.

Without hesitating any longer, he quickly grabbed a few things, locked his hotel room door and ran along the long hallway. Skipping the slow elevators, he bolted down the concrete hotel fire stairs taking two steps at a time, occasionally grasping the steel handrail to slow his headlong speed. He checked the red backpack containing the reef of gold journal with hotel security before jumping into the first cab available. He shouted at the driver to hurry and get him to the American Embassy Liaison office. The driver had a difficult time finding it.

Brad had leaned on the buzzer on the outside locked door of the liaison embassy until a grumbling security guard had let him inside. The embassy receptionist at the information desk was not smiling either when he walked quickly up to her. Her desk was plainly visible in the center of the lobby.

"How can the embassy be of help to you?" she queried, obviously annoyed by his unannounced presence.

Brad quickly told her of his phone message.

"Identification please," she asked. Brad handed over his driver's license. "Typical license photo," she smirked. Barely satisfied, she returned the license and reached for the phone, punching in a few numbers. After a quick conversation with parties unknown, she motioned for an armed uniformed guard. "Up stairs," she said quickly. The security guard escorted him around a corner to a lobby area dotted with heavy steel barriers.

His escort motioned for him to walk towards the heavily armed security guards standing by a metal detector. The Marine guards wore a no nonsense look on their faces. Strictly business, thought Brad. Following instructions, Brad passed through the detector and endured a final pat down. "This way," the guard said. Together, they walked up one flight of stairs, their footfalls echoing on the marble steps. At the top of the stairs, the security guard opened the nearest

Reef of Gold

door with a key and motioned for Brad to enter. It was a small, airless, waiting room with little furniture and no windows.

Brad had barely sat down when a young embassy official dressed in a dark pinstriped suit walked quickly into the room from a side entrance. His pampered hands held a sheaf of papers with a large paper clip attached and a file folder.

"Mr. Brad Templeton?" he inquired.

Brad nodded as he stood up and said, "Liaison officer?"

"Yes, well, ah, Mr. Templeton. I'm Chatsworth Blakely, III, Chief Liaison Officer for the United States Embassy in San Francisco. By the way, we are under a high alert status here at the embassy. If something happens, stay in this room. We know where you are and can protect you."

"That's very comforting to know," said an irritated Brad, wanting to get on with news of his brother.

"Mr. Templeton," the young embassy official said, while sitting down on a worn, chair and indicated to Brad to take the nearest seat. "Let's cut to the chase and answer all your immediate questions. Personally, I'm concerned for your brother."

Brad was beginning to squirm in his metal government chair. The liaison official hurried on, tapping the file nervously with his fingers. "Your brother Ric had in his government file several phone numbers to call in case of an emergency. Your cell phone number was first on the list, and we expected a return phone call. Much to our astonishment, you were suddenly in the lobby of the embassy. In times like these, you can understand that any deviation from the norm unnerves the entire staff," he admonished. "You needed to schedule an appointment with us."

"Pardon me, but I'm here now so can we get on with this?" said Brad testily.

"Yes, well, ah, it seems your brother Ric has been reported missing by our Commerce Department office in Singapore. Apparently he has some high level contacts in that department and they alerted us.

Gary Dale

Any additional information will be forwarded to our embassy here in San Francisco." He took a deep breath. "We have put two and two together and this is what we surmise. The Singapore police have investigated and found out that someone who resembles your brother's description, jumped overboard from the Pulau Ferry into the middle of the Singapore Straits. This person, presumably your brother because there was no body found, was apparently trying to escape from some local gangland thugs, hit men, ruffians, or whatever they are called in Southeast Asia."

"Overboard? Thugs? Hit men? Ruffians?" questioned a stunned Brad Templeton.

The liaison embassy official nodded, looked down at his sheaf of papers, and then continued. "The attack was at near darkness and the ferry captain was quoted later as saying that he had no chance to save the missing person. Apparently, the Chinese thugs threatened the safety of his passengers and crew if the captain tried to look for the victim. The ruffians got off the ferryboat when it docked and disappeared before the police arrived. We recently learned that the Singapore police found some documents belonging to your brother in a shredded shirt left in the crews' quarters, as if he purposely left his identification in his shirt pocket. Unfortunately, the tourists were of little help. We are reasonably certain that it was your brother who was lost overboard. Look, I wish I had better news for you but this is all we have at the moment. So we fear the worst."

The liaison officer took another deep breath. "Much worse, actually. I was informed by the Singapore authorities that no one survives a night swimming around in the Singapore Straits." He nodded his head several times as if confirming his next statement.

"Tiger sharks on their nightly feed," he said. He paused. "I'm really sorry. Since your brother was with the Commerce Department on foreign duty, I felt it was my duty to contact you immediately."

"Is that all?" questioned Brad, still in shock by the news.

Reef of Gold

The liaison official reluctantly nodded his head again. "Finding a body will be remote and next to impossible."

"This is unbelievable!" Brad exclaimed. He leaped out of his chair, pacing around and around the tiny room, wracking his brain of what to do about this preposterous information before finally coming back and facing the embassy official. He forced himself to be calm. He thanked the embassy man for the information. "I think I need to go for a walk before calling my parents. This situation just doesn't make any sense."

"I'm sorry,' murmured Blakely, showing real concern on his face. "Look, maybe you would want to retrace his steps. According to this file, he was based in Kuala Lumpur and had some contacts with the Malaysian consulate here in San Francisco. See the Consulate right away. Check with other embassies as well. Here are copies of all the information we know at the moment."

Brad stumbled outside the Liaison office into the fading sunlight. He started walking first in one direction and then in another, walking in what he hoped was a square so he wouldn't get physically lost, just lost in his thoughts. Finally, he decided to check with the Asian embassies in town the next morning to see if they had any additional information. Someone must know why thugs were after his brother. Then, he would call his parents and let them know what he had learned and not learned.

The hotel manager met him in the main lobby. "We've had an incident here at the hotel, Mr. Templeton. Someone had impersonated one of our security people and gained access to the hotel security room. Several items were taken."

Brad's facial expression froze. An anxious look creased his face. "I had something very valuable stored in there. My red back pack contained something that is irreplaceable to me."

"Better come with me," said the manager, walking towards the storage room. "We need to make sure. A storage tag with your name

13

Gary Dale

on it is in my hand. The matching numbers didn't connect with anything in the storage room."

Brad stepped inside the large storage room. Everywhere he looked, were mounds of luggage of all colors, shapes, and sizes. 'How in world'…. he threw up his arms in frustration. "Mr. Templeton," the manager said, "your luggage would have been near the door as a late arrival. There were several backpacks stored there and all were taken. Look around carefully. Is your backpack missing?"

Brad thought for a moment and then remembered something. "I handed my red backpack to the security attendant, in a rush of course. He gave me a ticket like always. I mean, I've checked this item before. He looked to be a fairly new employee, but he said he would be sure to place the backpack straight away in the security room. Where is he? I'm sure he would remember where he put it."

The manager went to a house phone. In a few minutes, the young man fairly sprinted over to the manager, looking like he knew he was going to be fired. He tried to talk but nothing came out. The manager held up his hand and quietly asked the young assistant if he remembered helping Mr. Templeton here with a checked bag. Nodding his head, words finally were choked out. He apologized for placing the backpack in a temporary storage unit behind the concierge's desk. "The main security room was so full of luggage. I didn't know where to put it. I mean, I never left the desk until a few minutes ago. Sir, your backpack is very safe. I was careful to watch the temporary storage unit. I take my job very seriously." Taking the initiative under the watchful eyes of the manager, the young man opened up the temporary storage unit.

It was like a tiny closet in a small San Francisco apartment. A red backpack with an identity tag on it along with a few other items was stored on a small shelf high above normal reach. He grabbed it and felt its contents. He turned the pack towards the manager and Brad. The numbers matched. "This is mine," Templeton said with a sigh of relief. "Thank you."

CHAPTER 3

MALAYSIAN EMBASSY/SAN FRANCISCO

The Malaysian Embassy street entrance on Clay Street in downtown San Francisco was comparatively small and for a moment, Brad wondered if he had located the correct building on this Monday morning. Once inside, he looked for the customary main reception or information desk usually found in the center of a large, cavernous room. The familiar Government Issue solid metal desk looked like it was bolted to the floor. A line of people of all descriptions patiently waited in front of it. Dutifully, Brad took a number, found the end of the line and waited to shuffle forward on the marble floor like the rest of the crowd.

That's when Mother Nature called.

Brad briskly moved to the front of the line and interrupted the preoccupied embassy official and asked for directions to the nearest men's rest room. He handed her his number to hold his place in line. With hardly a glance at the intruder, she waved her hand in the direction to her left. Figuring the men's rest room was going to be easy to find, Brad took off like any tourist, looking a little bewildered but in a hurry and on a mission. As he approached a stairway at the far end of the building, he began to panic just a bit because the restroom was nowhere to be found. He spun around in a circle for a final frantic look for a men's room sign and then without a further

Gary Dale

thought, bounded past a small restricted area sign and headed up two flights of marble stairs to the second floor. There had to be a men's room close to the stairs.

Hurrying along the long, tiled, second floor hallway, his loose fitting loafers made an annoying slapping sound, adding to his self-consciousness. About half way down the hallway, he began to notice that the muted glass fronts on each office door had what looked like titles and names but in a foreign language. On impulse, he opened a door to an office that had the only English word on the frosted glass window that he could recognize, *Commerce*. Behind a desk was a short, handsome fellow, with a crop of dark hair flipped over to one side. He was wearing a white monogrammed embassy shirt with a light blue tie and looked just a little startled as Brad bolted inside.

Brad introduced himself and apologized for startling the embassy man, and then said, "Men's room and quickly please."

"Ah," the embassy official said, regaining his composure with a slight smile. "This way," he said, gesturing with his arm.

He led Brad out into the hallway, turned right and quickly walked four doors down the hall before opening the men's room with a key.

"Thanks," Brad hollered over his right shoulder, and bolted for the white porcelain urinals with a push button flush.

A few minutes later, Brad returned to the Commerce office and this time knocked before entering.

"Come in and have a seat," the embassy official said. "Your face looks relieved. Are you?" He winked.

"Thanks to you, I can now think."

"Ah, very good," he said, smiling. "What can the Malaysian Embassy do for you?"

After visiting several of the Embassies in San Francisco, Brad was now used to embassy bureaucratic speak. In the private business sector, it was always 'What can I do for you?' but with the embassies, it was always 'What can the embassy do for you?' This was his last

Reef of Gold

embassy on his list to visit as per the American embassy Liaison's instructions and he fully expected to be stone walled again.

'Thank you for seeing me Mr. err'...?"

"Call me Mr. Hiam."

"Mr. Hiam, my name is Brad Templeton. I thought perhaps you might be able to help me since there is the word Commerce printed on your door."

"I can try, but first, tell me, out of curiosity, how did you get past the security guard in front of the stairway? You don't have a visitor's badge pinned to your chest?"

"There wasn't any guard," Brad replied. "I just had to use a rest room and quickly. The embassy person seated at the front desk in the lobby just waved me towards the stairway; at least I thought she did. When I didn't find any rest room along the way, I just bolted up here to the second floor."

"Well, if that's the case, we just had a breach of security and that bothers me. It's not your fault and in a way, Mr. Templeton, I should be thanking you. You tested our security and it failed. I'll take care of that little problem. By the way, you passed the rest room immediately behind the receptionist's desk. Apparently, we will have to make the sign more visible in this old building."

Brad laughed away his embarrassment and said, "When in a great need, the larger the sign, the better. Sorry for the intrusion in your office, but I do really need some help."

"Do you have some identification?"

"Well, yes, I do. Why do you need to see my identification?"

"Since you are on the second floor, it is a security requirement. Perhaps I am a little late with the security request but the embassy needs to know with whom we are dealing with at all times."

"I understand," Brad said, handing over his passport.

"Do you always travel around the United States carrying your passport or are you planning a trip out of the country?"

Gary Dale

"As a matter of fact, I am thinking of visiting Southeast Asia very near future."

"Ah, very good. You may proceed, Mr. Templeton," said Mr. Hiam, handing back the passport.

Brad sighed again, tired of explaining everything for the umpteenth time but this was his last embassy, so he began with "Here is my problem" and then proceeded quickly to explain the circumstances of his missing and presumed drowned brother. He also mentioned that apparently his brother had had several contacts within this particular embassy. Could they be of help whom ever they were? What could he personally do to help find his brother?

Mr. Hiam listened patiently, made a couple of notes on an embassy note pad, and listened some more as Brad traced the events. Brad had experienced the embassy routine before, but this time this particular embassy staff member did not cut him short. It was encouraging to see even a little interest in his problem.

When Brad had finished speaking, including adding his determination to go look for his brother himself, Mr. Hiam sat back in his chair and looked at his notes. After long moments of thought, he wrote down a few more things. He looked up and said, "Let me make a phone call or two." He proceeded to punch in a few numbers and then swiveled in his chair, apparently so he could stare at a world map.

Following his gaze, Brad looked at the map as well but only saw a bunch of brightly colored pins stuck in certain countries.

Mr. Hiam presumably spoke in Malaysian or in a Malaysian dialect. Brad couldn't understand a word of the conversation. Now it was Brad's turn to be patient. He had been disappointed in the various embassies before so he wasn't getting his hopes up just because this guy was making a few phone calls. Passing the time, he gazed around the office noticing that there were beautiful pieces of furniture carved from a wood of unusual grain. He knew from experience it was the quality of the wood that made the furniture enhance a room. His

Reef of Gold

hands caressed the wooden chair he sat in, musing about its origin. It looked like it was Circassian walnut from Turkey with its deep chocolate color, he thought. He traced his finger along the wood grain. It could be a California walnut, which looks very similar to the Turkish wood, but then again, it would generally be lighter in color. Brad's eyes wandered. The rest of the office furniture looked like it came from the hardwood jungles of Malaysia with the exception of a table stand. The stand was too far away to identify the wood grain.

Mr. Hiam actually made three phone calls before swiveling his chair back to Brad.

"Mr. Templeton," he said, "I would like to bring into this conversation a ranking security staff member who has personally dealt with your brother over the past several years. This man is also in charge of embassy communications for all our embassies on the West coast of America. His name is Lee Kuan Yew. He might be able to help you. There was a soft tap on the frosted glass of a side door to Mr. Hiam's office. The door opened and closed in one quick motion. A fit man in his mid- thirties, dressed casually in dark slacks and white monogrammed shirt, slid quietly into the room. His entrance was so quick and smooth that Brad hardly had time to turn in his chair to greet the man.

"Mr. Hiam, is this the gentleman you spoke of a few minutes ago?" questioned the physically fit embassy man. Brad quickly stood.

Keeping with formalities, Mr. Hiam introduced Brad as the brother of the missing Commerce department person in Singapore. Mr. Yew acknowledged Brad ever so slightly. His eyes were taking in Brad, analyzing and calculating. When he was finished with his mental appraisal, he motioned Brad to have a seat. He chose to stand as if emphasizing his position of authority.

"I am Mr. Yew and have some intelligence about your brother that might be of help to you," he began. "I am telling you all of this because of our embassy relationship with your brother. Let me begin

19

Gary Dale

with the factual information. In the past year, your brother Ric has had contact with this embassy in San Francisco and in our embassy in Singapore. As a matter of fact, he was here in this office several months ago. I spoke with him alone, with none of our staff involved. From our morning dispatches, however, we had heard he was missing in Singapore." He paused and closed his eyes as if in deep thought.

"In the past several months, we at this embassy were asked by your brother to get the latest technical material on computer developments in programming and computer firewall protection from several of the high tech firms in Silicon Valley. We sent to him the requested information via our embassy in Kuala Lumpur. He also requested that we contact several companies here in the San Francisco area regarding encryption coding and the programs to break into some sophisticated technology systems. Why, he didn't say but I can assure you that it was a big request in man hours for this little embassy."

"Why didn't he use the American Embassy for all of these requests?" Brad questioned. "Why would Silicon Valley companies just give you his requested information? That information has to be proprietary. There are so many more questions than answers here," his voice raised, as did his agitation.

Mr. Yew remained silent. Brad sat back in his wooden chair and watched Mr. Hiam nervously shuffle paper work on the mahogany desk. Then he closed his eyes to think.

It was becoming clear to him that the Commerce Department was a catch-all term for the various things his brother was doing in foreign countries. Then he remembered reading one article with some concern. High-tech thievery of secrets was on the increase, even among rival American firms, and there was very little that could be done by companies to protect their proprietary technical data. Silicon Valley's answer to their technology theft was to push harder to develop even newer technology that would supplant anything stolen. It was like being on a treadmill. Then again, maybe with his brother's help, American high tech companies attempted to fight back with

Reef of Gold

their own espionage of Southeast Asian and Chinese companies. Having Ric involved would be one way of checking just how much these foreign companies did know and how much they had stolen. That must be it!

Brad felt his neck muscles tightening from the stress. His stomach was becoming a holding tank for the stomach acid leaking from his system. He realized that Ric might have been in deep trouble.

"Mr. Templeton," said Mr. Hiam, breaking the silence. "We worked with an American counterpart of Ric's here in San Francisco to get access to the computer firms in Silicon Valley. We were just the conduits. Sorry we don't have any more information. There is, however, one other thing."

"Yes?" Brad questioned, as he sat up straighter in his chair.

"This is just a rumor," he said, pausing. He looked down at his hands as if he wasn't sure of how to say it. "I think your brother is still alive, wounded but alive."

Brad stopped breathing for a moment. His mouth suddenly became dry. He stared at the embassy official. Mr. Hiam looked up, directly into Brad's eyes. "Look, I don't know for sure, but I believe he is alive. It's just a feeling I have after reading the sensitive embassy reports. From what I know of him, he is a very capable man."

"You're serious?" Brad finally croaked. "He really might be alive?"

Brad's heart leaped. His brother might be alive. Characteristically, he pounded his right thigh in celebration. "Thank you for the information, Mr. Hiam," he blurted. "You have been most helpful and given me some hope." As Brad started to rise, Mr. Yew motioned for him to sit down. Mr. Yew did not look happy, noticed Brad. Was it because of what Mr. Hiam had said, he wondered?

"As head of security for our embassies here and abroad, my information comes from different sources and is most accurate," said Mr. Yew. Brad noticed he glared at Mr. Hiam. "I do not share my colleague's analysis about your brother's survival. I am sorry to say

21

Gary Dale

that holding out hope for your brother's survival and well being is like whistling Daisy."

"You mean like whistling Dixie," Brad corrected, his heart sinking at the new information. "Please get on with this."

Mr. Yew shrugged his shoulders. "I suspect, as others do as well, that the Singapore Straits has claimed his body. The sea in that part of the world is very unforgiving. A word of advice, don't waste your time trying to find out what happened to your brother. You know nothing about the people in that part of the world and will only endanger yourself by asking questions." He glowered again at Hiam. "Now, if you will excuse me," he said, looking once again at Brad. The door clicked shut behind him.

The silence in the room was deafening with the exception of Brad's beating heart. It sounded like a fifth grader pounding off key on a bass drum in band class.

"So," asked Mr. Hiam, returning his focus onto Brad, "have you decided to look for your brother in Southeast Asia?"

"Of course," he stammered.

"I thought as much," he acknowledged. "Your body language said so. That is very good. Look, let me give you some bureaucratic embassy advice. If you go to Southeast Asia *poking around,* as you Americans are so fond of saying, be very careful. Trust no one when making your inquiries, and after making these inquiries, watch out for the Asian bees when you stir up their nest."

"Bee's?" Brad questioned, not sure if he had heard correctly.

Mr. Hiam smiled. "Asian bees are one big family and are known to be very dangerous. They attack without any regard to others and focus intently on the intruder, usually a single wasp. If their beehive is not disturbed, they still watch out for each other. They are constantly circling around their nest in mass, making even larger circles each time, looking for specific pollen, or in your case, trouble makers. This noticeable enlarging circle and their method of attack and defense is what make Asian bees different from other bees in the

22

Reef of Gold

world. A single enemy wasp can overwhelm a colony of European honeybees while waiting for reinforcements. The invader bee simply stands at a nest's entrance as one guard bee after another comes out to defend its home. The invader cuts the guard bee to pieces and waits for the next one. When all the defenders are dead, the invader bee along with his reinforcements strip-mines out the bee larvae. An Asian beehive, however, is heavily guarded at all times and will smoother a wasp, killing it with their combined body heat. The remaining guard bees, though fewer in number become extremely vicious and often act with vengeance towards any intruder."

Brad didn't know what to make of the conversation. Where was Mr. Hiam going with this? he wondered. Noticing the perspiration dripping from Brad's forehead, Mr. Hiam apologized for the stuffiness in his office. "With all the doors closed, the air conditioning has a hard time keeping up," he acknowledged. Mr. Hiam reached behind him and flicked on two more fans and gestured for Brad to flip on the fan pointed towards him. Ticking noises erupted from the fan blades hitting the wire protection cover. He beckoned Brad to lean forward to talk. "My walls have ears, Mr. Hiam said, rolling his eyes. "Personally, I really believe your brother to be alive but hiding out somewhere in Singapore. Having said that, I am going to suggest to you that when you arrive in Singapore, create several disturbances when you ask questions about your missing brother. Be boisterous, obnoxious, and rude. Do anything to create attention to yourself. This act will cause many people to take notice of you, good and bad. The good news is that your brother will hear of your arrival and will contact you. The bad part is that the thugs will also hear of your entrance in the country. Asking too many questions will understandably create unwanted attention."

Brad was beside himself with excitement. He questioned Mr. Hiam again, wanting to but not really believing him.

Mr. Hiam rose from his chair and leaned forward so he was face to face with Brad. "Your brother is probably healing up in some quiet

Gary Dale

hospital or with private nursing. According to my information, he was betrayed by one of his own people. Somewhere in his organization is a mole. Your activity in Singapore just may help to ferret out the traitor by causing him or her to make mistakes. Your brother will be pleased to know that you are coming to his aid." He handed Brad a business card. "Call me if you get into trouble or need my help and keep in touch. Let me know your progress. It is the least I can do for your brother. Keep in mind, the Triad is most dangerous and they are everywhere. Mr. Templeton, in all seriousness, do watch your back."

"Where have I heard that before?" Brad thought.

"One last thing," Mr. Hiam said, sitting back in his chair. "Let me give you a name of an Malaysian embassy employee in Singapore, and an Australian in Perth. Memorize the names and phone numbers and then destroy the note." He scribbled out the names on a piece of small notebook paper and handed it to Brad. It was a nondescript piece of lined paper that included two names with phone numbers. Brad nodded and thanked Mr. Hiam profusely. He handed back the notepaper which was promptly shredded.

Templeton stood outside on the embassy steps, taking deep breaths of relief. Maybe, just maybe, he thought, his brother is alive. And, if I ask the right questions and stir up enough trouble, he might be able to reach me. Brad straightened his shoulders. Suddenly his breathing became rapid. He blew out a deep breath, stored deep from within him. He realized his breathing had been shallow. He blinked his eyes rapidly, trying to eliminate the dryness.

When he got back to the hotel, Brad immediately called United Airlines and booked a seat on the next flight out to Singapore. He packed what he had with him, promising himself to buy the needed accessories after landing. The plane was nearly full but somehow, through a last minute cancellation, he got a business class window seat which seemed large and comfortable enough for the long flight. The pert flight attendant indicated to him that the new Boeing

Reef of Gold

jetliner would arrive on schedule around 11:40 the next morning depending on head winds. Not that it mattered what hour Brad arrived. He would get more than a few hours of frustrated sleep.

As the plane circled and was making its final approach to the runway, Brad noticed a large yacht anchored practically under the approaching plane. "The skipper must be nuts," he muttered. "The screaming engine noise let alone the nauseating jet engine fumes would drive anybody crazy." Brad kept looking down at the yacht, rocking with the tide change until the runway suddenly appeared and the image was stolen from him.

As for the yacht...

CHAPTER 4

SINGAPORE HARBOR

At times, the shrieking noise from an Airbus jet was nerve racking. The Triad enforcer pressed his callused hands to his ears in a lame attempt to block out the irritating sound. The Singapore Airline's plane, spinning its engines to full maximum power before the pilot released the brakes for takeoff was making its scheduled 11:35 am flight to Kuala Lumpur, Malaysia and points beyond. The enforcer was familiar with this particular flight, having taken it often. After the invading noise had subsided, he looked up at yet another plane, lining up a runway approach over the Singapore bay. This airplane was quieter but still had jet exhaust. As the giant Boeing plane landed, an uncomfortable feeling swept over him. It was a sense of foreboding which seemed to settle in his neck and shoulders. He quickly turned away. He hated this noisy, mostly deserted meeting place anyway. Despite what the Lu Yuan Swie had said about tight security against foreign listening devices, there had to be a less irritating meeting place than in a yacht anchored in the bay right in the middle of a flight path.

A crewman of the speedboat, wearing an undistinguished looking floppy hat, shorts, and sun faded deck shoes approached Yang Lee, the Triad enforcer. "We are ready when you are," he said, nodding stiffly.

Flipping the back of his hand as if he were brushing away a fly, the enforcer motioned for the crewman to ease the speedboat away from its berth under the covered warehouse dock next to the airport south runway and make for the anchored yacht, a short distance away. His meeting with his Triad superior, the Lu Yuan Swie was never friendly.

Yang Lee secretly and deeply despised the old man but today he wanted to control his emotions. Too much was at stake. The Shan Chu, who is the head of all the Triad organizations that belong to the Chang family dynasty, had called for a meeting ordering him to attend. "Maybe he personally won't be at this particular meeting," the confident enforcer mused, "but perhaps his representative would be. The fact that the Shan Chu has called such a meeting meant it had to be important."

Lee walked forward to the bow of the speedboat, where the sea breeze tugged at his clothes. He was a large man, broad shouldered, taller than most of his countrymen. In his birthplace of Shanghai, China, it was not unusual to see Chinese men of his size. The British and their merchantmen had made the city an outpost for the illicit and lucrative opium trade in the 1800's. It was common for the Western merchants to avail of themselves in the delights of the local women. The Americans were late arrivals but participated in the trade wars and delights nonetheless. For his own personal reasons, he scorned them all, especially the Americans.

As the speedboat came closer to the anchored yacht, the enforcer recognized several Triad guests lounging on the main deck, waiting for an assignment. Then his heart skipped a beat. Almost in a whisper, Yang Lee muttered quietly to himself. "A rare sight indeed and to think something as beautiful as she is wasted on the old man." No matter how many times he had seen her either from a distance or up close, his emotion was always the same. He wanted her badly and someday he would have her. If he could just be alone with her, without any of his peers being around, he would take the time to

27

Gary Dale

caress her, sensuously from top to bottom, and lovingly explore every little secret place. Using all his senses, Yang Lee would often close his eyes, just to inhale her aura. He would bring up the indelible image of her during his sleep, and would feel exhilarated each and every time. And now, at this very moment, he decided that she was even more beautiful than before.

Closing on the anchored yacht, the high-speed powerboat of Hong Kong registry suddenly slowed to a crawl, reversed engines, creating backwash cavitations behind the propellers as it prepared to dock. The resulting wave gently pushed the powerboat next to the landing. Lines were tossed, tying the ships together.

Timing the rise and fall of the powerboat with the wave action, Yang Lee stepped onto the lowered stairway of the yacht. He made his way up to the main deck where his Triad peers greeted him warmly. He had only a few minutes of celebration before he was ushered into the salon and the Lu Yuan Swie.

There was no one else in the richly furnished and decorated office ship salon.

Disappointed, Yang Lee momentarily ignored the old man who did not appreciate the gesture. It was to be taken as a slight and a sure sign of disrespect.

"It is done," Lee said emphatically, anticipating the first question from the Lu Yuan Swie. "One of the western spies talked rather quickly after our special torture techniques were applied. He suffered greatly. Even you would have enjoyed the torture sessions."

The Lu Yuan Swie's face remained stoic, his hands holding a brown envelope. He did not look up from his ornate teak desk, impregnated with deftly carved dragons. He ignored the disrespectful enforcer and left him standing. A Triad aide walked quietly into the opulent salon and gave his master a three-page document for him to read immediately. The Lu Yuan Swie set aside the brown envelope and opened the folder and read the documents.

Bored, Yang Lee looked out a large porthole and let his thoughts

Reef of Gold

drift. He smiled tightly remembering his enjoyment of the brutal torture sessions inflicted upon a particular spy. What was his name.... Hesan. no, Hsin. That was it.

The wizened old man suddenly looked up from his documents. His stone-like face betrayed nothing. He closed the folder on his desk, leaned back in his padded chair and stared at the young man in front of him. "Tell me about the torture techniques you applied to this spy in order to obtain such information as described in this folder," he said, holding it up for the enforcer to see.

Yang Lee smiled after hearing the request. "Do you remember the ancient holding cells under the dilapidated Singapore wharf," he asked the old man.

"I remember," the Swie answered. "I presume the cells still are retched, dark, damp, and still usable for torture sessions."

"That they are," Lee said, smiling with a great deal of satisfaction. "I have not made any physical changes to the chambers nor has anyone else. Over the years, however, I have instituted some new torture techniques that I myself have thought of and refined during the many torture sessions. I still use our tried and true methods of subjecting the spy to total isolation and lengthy questioning for days on end, depriving him of basic human needs."

"You bore me," sniffed the old man. "You're not telling me anything new."

The younger enforcer brushed off the slight. "I am being a little more subtle on purpose," he snapped. "I wanted this particular prisoner to stay alive until I could get all the critical intelligence from him." He paused for a moment. He was about to issue a cryptic remark about the old man's former reputation of loving the torture of spies for quick information instead of a slower method of gaining every morsel of information, when he thought better of it. The aging man was an enforcer at one time and still was sensitive to overt criticism of his old ways of doing things. He lived for the past.

"In order to get vital intelligence, I held this spy in a single cell,

Gary Dale

deep in the bowels of our torture chambers, depriving him of any sense of light, so he would lose his ability to recognize time and awareness. If he stood up or got on his knees, his balance would become a major problem. With no physical references, his brain had little chance of telling his body up from down. Thus, he would suddenly pitch forward onto the cold cell floor, eventually awakening to a nightmare." Yang Lee smiled at the thought of what was to come next.

"And what is this nightmare?" the old man asked the enforcer sarcastically. "I'm curious."

"Rats. Lots of big rats with bright red eyes and sharp claws were let into the cell to torment this captive of mine. The diseased long-tailed rodents would nibble on the prisoner's ankles, ears, nose, and fingers as if sampling a soon-to-be corpse. In the darkness, the rats would scurry around at all hours, never allowing the prisoner to get any sleep. Their sharp claws made loud clicking noises on the stone floor; a sound so numbing, could drive a person insane. As usual, the stink of fear secreted from the glands of the captive only heightened the rats' activity."

"My prisoner, who ultimately, I discovered, had the knowledge of encryption codes to our computer system, tried to fight off the rats, flinging them off his body in all directions before finally falling into exhaustion. It wasn't long before he began to scream; long, terrifying screams that echoed off the ancient walls." Yang Lee smiled at the thought. "When silence finally came to the cell, my minions noticed the beginning of a ritual of acceptance."

"How so," inquired the Swie, looking at his fingernails before gently closing his eyes.

"The rats too became prisoners," laughed Yang Lee. "Day after day, grains of half cooked rice are thrown by the guards onto the cell floor. The rice would suddenly explode onto the cell floor sounding like a heavy hailstorm frightening the hell out of the prisoner. Immediately, the herd of large rats would scurry around competing

Reef of Gold

with the prisoner for the little grains of rice. They would fight over a small territory. My minions would allow water for the occupant to be provided three times a day by a wet rag thrown into the filthy cell. After what had to be an eternity for the prisoner, the guards would see that he was taken from the filthy cell to a lighted torture room. You remember this special torture room, don't you?"

The old man merely nodded and waited for a huge passenger jet to complete its take off. The engine noise was deafening for an entire minute and then gradually subsided.

Yang Lee's eyes flickered from his intense stare directed toward the old man, involuntarily breaking his concentration. He shuffled his feet for balance. The yacht gently rocked back and forth with the tide change. He briefly glanced towards a porthole and then down at his nemesis, the Lu Yuan Swie, to see if the old man was drifting off to doze in rhythm to the ocean's serene music. The silence between the two men was forced, neither one willing to give in to the other. It was a question of saving face.

The old man suddenly waved his hand. "So," he questioned roughly, "is this special torture technique of yours what made the spy talk? I find it hard to believe that he would break that quickly. I am sure that he has been specially trained to resist torture and knows his personal boundaries."

Yang Lee cleared his throat, dragging up a gaggle of phlegm. He spat on the teak deck as a measure of triumph. "He most certainly did spill all his secrets," he smirked. "The spy did not enjoy bamboo shoots driven into the gaps of his teeth and then wetted and dried. The expansion and contraction caused the spy unbelievable pain. We were not very good dentists. When the shoots were removed, and the pain subsided, he talked rather than have the bamboo installed again."

The old man snapped his fingers and pointed. A deck hand quickly mopped the deck, clearing the spittle and then disappeared.

31

Gary Dale

"And what might I ask did you do after getting the necessary information?" asked the Swie with sarcasm, tiring of the game.

"As soon as the lasting secrets from the spy Hsin were spilled, I ordered my men to surround the rendezvous point and capture his controller, Ric Templeton. Unfortunately, this American spy chose to die. I assure you the computer infiltrator you so despise has met an untimely death with the Tiger sharks on their nightly patrol."

"You are positive that we don't have to worry?" questioned the Lu Yuan Swie, rising slowly from his chair. "I would not want the head of our Triad organization, the ruthless Shan Chu, to be critical of our operations. We have too much at stake to not be sure. You understand that, do you not, Ye Sung?"

Yang Lee's brain was working furiously now. His superior had chosen to use his official Triad enforcer title of Ye Sung for a sarcastic reason. Why? Had he gone to far? Does he know something I don't know? How dare he, he thought, regaining his composure. Eyes raised towards the ceiling, he bowed again slightly from the upper body once again, purposely showing disrespect. "Being a Chang Family Triad enforcer for the powerful centuries old Hung Dynasty," he said, "is a great honor and I take great pride to be at their service. I do my job efficiently and ruthlessly. Why do you question me? When I say the spies are dead, then that is all that needs to be said," bristling at the challenges being thrown at him. The game of insults continued for a few minutes before both of them became tired of the game.

"Yes, yes, I know you, Yang Lee," said the old man, finally. "I am well aware of your desire to become a Lu Yuan Swie like me someday." He paused to wipe away the spittle from the corners of his mouth. "Indeed, I am an old man but," he said, voice rising while shaking his long bony fingers at the disrespectful enforcer, "I will not give up my position until I am ready. I still have the power," he shouted in a gravelly voice, "to have you banished from the organization." Slumping back into his chair, spent from his emotional

Reef of Gold

outburst, he reached for a brown envelope on his desk. "Here is your new assignment," he said with contempt and barely disguised anger, tossing the envelope to the much younger man in front of him. "Fail this assignment and you shall die." The old man snorted.

Picking up the envelope and placing it in his hip pocket to read in private, Yang Lee didn't bother to even make the attempt to acknowledge the Triad position of the old man.

"Is that all?" Yang Lee snarled. Not waiting for an answer, he turned and stormed out onto the open deck, opening and closing his fists in frustration. "One day, one day, indeed, the Shan Chu will honor me as a head of the Singapore Triad organization and nothing will stop me from that honor," he thought, glowering towards the guards who now shrunk back behind anything they could find just to be out of his sight. His eyes flashed with hate and determination. "I am ready now," he raged inwardly, as he continued to pace back and forth along the poop deck. "The old man is standing in my way of upward mobility in the organization and how dare he threaten me, an honored and respected Ye Sung, the enforcer for all of the Singapore Triads." He continued to pace until his rage slowly began to dissipate. He looked back towards the old man in the main cabin and then stalked over to the yacht's steering gear. He didn't care if anyone saw him as he deliberately grasped the handles of the heavily lacquered mahogany helm and gently caressed each wheel spoke. He forced himself to be calmed by his own thoughts, allowing the pent-up rage to ooze out his pores. "It will not be long, old man," he said quietly to himself, "before you surrender her to me. You do not love her as I do. This magnificent yacht will be mine."

Yang Lee closed his eyes for a moment, and heard the yacht's soul speak to him in an ancient tongue. "You will be rewarded with prestige and honor among the descendants of the ancient immigrants of Chiu Chao. It is your destiny."

CHAPTER 5

SOUTHEAST ASIA

It was on the morning after Brad's arrival in Singapore that he decided he must get on with the search. He needed to use this time wisely. He thought long and hard about how he would go about gathering information about his missing brother. Asking the Singapore police would be a dead end, he knew. They would just hand him a computer printout of the known facts and nothing else. He felt he must dig deeper if he were going to find out anything.

The only way he could figure to get any accurate information was to overplay the part of a distraught relative looking for his brother as Mr. Hiam in San Francisco had suggested. He took a deep breath and looked once more into the bathroom mirror in his hotel room. In good conscience, he couldn't stall any longer. He had to do something even if he put himself in danger. He quietly closed the hotel room door, walked down the stairs, and checked his red backpack containing the reef of gold journal with the hotel security staff. He was ready.

By all accounts, Brad did put on a show in Singapore by being the overly concerned relative from the United States, wearing a tattered baseball cap with a Yankee logo, a white cotton shirt, rumpled shorts and a well known brand of black jogging shoes. He made sure he looked frustrated and stressed which wasn't hard to do. He was full

34

Reef of Gold

of questions, shouting when a normal voice would suffice, waved his arms when he talked, darting his eyes from one person to another and generally made a nuisance of himself for several days. He showed up at all the hospitals in the area, hounding the various local police stations, harassing a ferry boat captain when he found him at a corner pharmaceutical dispensary. He even pushed around the newspaper reporters that were trying to get a story for their paper. He made sure he was being quoted saying that his brother is alive. By all accounts, he had created quite a stir in just a few days and still, he had heard nothing from his brother. Back at the hotel, he changed out of his American shorts, shirt and opted for the more comfortable cotton long pants, cotton short sleeve shirt, Nike jogging shoes and a Boston Red Sox baseball cap. He slowed his search to a methodical crawl and began making inquiries politely. A switch of clothes often confused people, he thought. It did.

No one would tell him where the sailors hung out until he started buying a few drinks for patrons in side-street pubs. A drunk finally pointed him in the right direction but slurred his vague addresses. After checking the insides of a few non-descript havens of alcohol dispensaries for the ferryboat Captain, a little street urchin, with dirt stains on his face, scruffy shorts and torn tee shirt, discovered him and for a price, led Brad to a disgusting waterfront pub located in the old part of the Singapore wharf. "Many sailors inside," he had said. The kid himself, observed Brad, looked like a future derelict and definitely needed healthy food and lots of it. Brad thanked the small guide and forked over a ten-dollar American green back. The street urchin kissed the bill and dashed off before others saw him with the money.

Brad looked around. He had not been this section of the city. The alleyway was narrow, several blocks off a main drag. Little sunlight rarely if ever painted the building walls. Several warehouses, opposite the pub, stretched to the wharf's edge. Years of monsoons accompanied by fierce winds had left its mark on the buildings, as

Gary Dale

a constant reminder of the destructive elements of weather. Maybe it was the smell that seemed to hang in the narrow confines of the alleyway that got to him. He suddenly felt nauseated and dearly wanted to throw up. In between the nausea, it occurred to him that the little street urchin might have set him up for a robbery. In this area, the color of money would talk loud and clear. It also occurred to him that no sane person would come near this bamboo walled pub.

He took a tentative first step and then another towards the pub entrance. The wooden planks that sufficed as a walkway were slick from unsightly fungus. His Nike running shoes picked up the grayish-looking crud instantly. He looked down to see the mucus had curled over the soles and into the stitching. He knew he would have to throw away his socks as well as his shoes very soon before the fungus attacked his skin. With the stench nearly overpowering, he hesitated again near the entrance. What if the ferry captain wasn't inside, he wondered? Not only would his efforts be wasted, so would his favorite running shoes.

Another thought occurred to him. Strangers, he was sure, were not welcome. If he created even a hint of a disturbance, would he be able to retreat from inside the pub before someone threw a club at him? He shook his head in frustration. He didn't want to think about that possibility, not after walking through the health hazard. The wharf had settled a little causing him to slide closer towards the pub entrance. The broken door hung ajar, looking like it was held together by only one broken hinge. Was it an exit or entrance? The sign above the door wasn't any better identifying what was inside. If you didn't know where you were, it wouldn't matter. The lettering was weathered and crudely etched in the wood. Brad moved to get a better angle. 'D' something, he mumbled. He squinted, trying to capture any light from the shadows hiding the sign. 'Ho' or 'Ha' was the end of the word, he thought. The rickety door suddenly flew back, banging against the building, loosening the hinge even more, before slamming back into place. At least the spring worked.

Reef of Gold

A figure, resembling human refuse, staggered outside, shielding his eyes from what little daylight remained in the darkened alley way. The drunken derelict paid no attention to the outsider standing near the doorway as he weaved his way towards a main street. The derelict stopped, turned his head towards the pub and shot vomit of green beer and mashed rice crackers against the sidewall. The mucus cascaded down the bamboo walls and slide unceremoniously into the alleyway.

There was no question it was a dispensary of rotgut alcohol, thought Brad, almost gagging at the sight. He looked over his shoulder for reassurance. No one walking on a main street even bothered to look his direction. Returning his interest to the neglected pathway, he slid his feet one at a time, stopping just short of the deranged door. Strange noises came from the piles of garbage near the pub's entrance. He hesitated. Perhaps if he just peeked inside, he thought, he could tell if the Captain was even there.

He pushed open the poor excuse for a door and stepped inside, shutting the door quietly behind him. The stale odors of unfamiliar origin instantly inflamed his nostrils to the point of giving him a severe headache. Not wanting to attract too much attention, he slid his cotton shirt along the back wall away from the entrance while his eyes adjusted to the dark. He stopped after a short distance.

The pub had instantly gone as quiet as a church mouse on the hunt for cheese. Brad was stunned. He sensed he could hear eyeballs clicking in his direction. He stood still, half expecting carefully balanced throwing knives with their finely honed razor sharp points to be thrown at him at any moment, pinning him to the back wall. It was that kind of place, he thought. Several seaman picked at their teeth at the nearest table, while sizing him up for fun and games. Some stared with obvious anger at his intrusion; some smiled as if his presence was humorous, and some cared less. Brad could feel the tension plunder his confidence. His sphincter valve threatened to add more smells and stains to the already vile floor.

37

Gary Dale

What seemed to be an eternity, he made the first move. His shoes responded with slipping and sliding movements on the beer stained wood floor towards the mahogany bar. He asked the bartender as firmly as he could muster, where the Pulau ferryboat Captain was seated. The bartender just stared, looking on with no comprehension. Finally, a shabbily dressed patron, seemingly understanding English, squirmed on his bar stool. He glanced at the stranger and then turned back to nursing his beer. Templeton could only catch a brief glimpse in the dim light. Was it the Captain? From the vague physical description he had been given, it surely looked like him from this angle, he thought. Then he remembered the odd description of the man and others like him. A sea captain always had his captain's cap jaunted to one side mindful that a sudden gust from an offshore breeze had occurred. It was a trademark of the men of command.

Brad fought his desire to run in any direction but towards the captain. Taking a deep breath through clinched teeth knowing it was sure to be his last, he walked slowly past tables of slovenly dressed men to reach the captain. His daring seemed to awe the quiet patrons as he shuffled towards the Captain. It was quiet enough to hear flies buzzing about and one fly in particular seemed to take a liking to his presence by making a dive for the moisture in the corners of his eyes. Brad brushed away the brazen fly several times, thwarting each attempt to suck moisture from him. He used the fly as an excuse to squeeze his nostrils tight to repeal the unfamiliar stink of the men surrounding him. He was painfully aware that all eyes were upon him, watching his every movement.

Reaching who he thought to be the ferryboat captain, something in his gut told him that tapping this man on the shoulder would not be looked upon as a kind gesture, but more of a threat. The last thing he wanted to do was to cause a bar room brawl with him being the target. He wouldn't last two minutes before he would be sliced up and fed to the little fishes schooling under the wharf. Over time, the tide motion had caused the rough floor lumber to rot and crumble,

Reef of Gold

creating large cracks. Clumps of food would often drop from stiff fingers and through cracks in the worn floorboards to the schooling fish below. The fish rarely left the area.

Moving to the man's side to avoid being part of the droppings, he leaned over the beer-stained counter, trying to look the man in the eyes. It had to be him, Brad thought. The bar patron continued to stare straight ahead. Brad directed his questions to the nearby bartender again in a quiet but husky voice about a certain ferry Captain's criminal connections, even accusing him of being an accomplice to the attack and subsequent disappearance of his brother. "But don't worry my captain," he said, speaking with some venom in the direction of the Captain's ear. "I've been told my brother is alive. I just don't know where he is recovering. Did you know he is still alive and recovering?" he asked, pulling away from the Captain. The silence in the pub was deafening. Even the bartender stopped wiping an empty beer glass with his dirty rag. Everyone seemed to have heard the elements of his conversation.

The patron with a Captain's hat turned slightly with an ugly scowl and stared at Brad through blood shot eyes. Although the Captain didn't respond and his face remained stoic, his eyes betrayed him. It was a frightened look. Brad could barely return the stare and wondered if it was a stare of death for him or the Captain, or both. The Captain was now publicly exposed by his accusation. The derelicts drinking near the Captain began to stir. Brad felt the atmosphere change. He was now a problem. The tension in the smoky atmosphere increased to the point that he felt real fear. It was time for him to leave and he knew it.

Brad quickly avoided any eye contact and headed for the door. He did not want them to see the scared look in his eyes. A couple of men started to move off their chairs to block his way. Brad slowed his determined walk. It was only a few more feet to the door. He reached into his pocket, pulling out a wad of American money. He slapped the counter with the pile of bills and announced drinks for all. The

39

Gary Dale

misdirection held the two men momentarily. A sudden cacophony arose as a throaty cheer from the bar patrons erupted. Suddenly, Brad was their long time friend that had come home to port. The would-be muscle let him pass and he was out the door.

Still shaking from the incident at the pub, Templeton slipped and skidded a half block towards a main street before finding solid footing. He grabbed the first taxi that came by. The driver sniffed and scowled. Brad directed the driver to the Malaysian Embassy. When he got there, he had to turn every pocket inside out to get enough money for the fare. In his rush to get out of the nasty pub, he had given away too much money. At the embassy, he found a liaison officer and asked about the name of the person he had been given in San Francisco embassy. Could he see him? he asked politely. The embassy staff person stepped back a few feet, wrinkling his nose and responded that he had never heard of this person. Brad asked to use an embassy phone and his request was granted with the embassy officer being more than glad to get rid of him. He called the phone number he had been given. No answer. The voice recorder asked him to leave a message and he did. Now the question was, had the embassy man in San Francisco given him a wrong name and phone number?

He dropped the thought and left the embassy. He looked up and down the street. One block away was a shopping area. Without any wasted motions, he went to the nearest shoe store for new tennis shoes and two pairs of socks. He purchased the new stuff with his credit card and left the rotting tennis shoes and ruined socks inside the old shoe box. He quickly went back to his hotel room for a long, hot, soapy shower.

On the sixth day, when exiting one of several medical clinics he had visited before, he had an odd awareness of being followed. The back of his neck felt cold yet tingled. He jumped into a taxi to his next destination and once there, the bothersome feeling came back again. Was he really being followed or was it his imagination at play? People in the expected areas of interest should have heard of

Reef of Gold

his brother's disappearance. Either they didn't know or were afraid of telling him. He continued to walk aimlessly, mumbling to himself. He was tired and depressed. The shops were beginning to all look the same. He would take a taxi back to the hotel. He was told by hospital security that enough was enough.

CHAPTER 6

BEE HIVE

On the verge of being arrested for being a public nuisance in a strict place like Singapore, Brad considered his options.

There was no use in staying any longer in Singapore, he thought, despite the nice change in weather from the occasional rain shower to hot and humid. He hadn't confirmed a thing about his brother one way or another. His heart said he was still alive, hopefully recovering somewhere. Reality had said that his brother was missing and presumed dead. It spite of his outrageous efforts to pry loose any information, or planting the seed that Ric was alive, nothing had worked. No one jumped at the bait. He figured he had stirred up a hornet's nest and still nothing. Perhaps his brother's attackers thought of him as nothing more than a buzzing fly meant to be brushed away.

The incessant ringing of his hotel phone interrupted his thoughts. Just as he reached the phone, the ringing stopped. There was a recorded number. He hit the return call button. To Brad, the connection was so strong it sounded like it came literally from the next room. At first, he was speechless. The caller was identifying herself as a secretary from the Malaysian Embassy in San Francisco. Brad was confused. "Hold on," she said.

"Mr. Templeton," said the voice.

Reef of Gold

"Yes," acknowledged Brad, not recognizing the voice. "And who is this calling?"

"We know each other from my embassy in San Francisco, Mr. Templeton. My name is Mr. Hiam. It has come to my attention that you might be in some danger if you stay much longer in Singapore. You have stirred up a major hornets nest and the killer bees are out in force. Why don't you enjoy a good meal at a nearby restaurant and then return to your hotel. You should think about leaving Singapore in the next few days with or without your brother."

"I understand, Mr. Hiam. Thank you. But how did….."

"I am not joking, Mr. Templeton. I am serious about the killer bees being active."

The hotel phone connection disconnected.

It was still early for dinner, so Brad walked down the hotel veranda, found a wicker table and chair, and ordered a Tiger beer. The beer had a unique raw taste qualifying the contents. The beer was also prone to foam and often left a wet mustache. Out of habit, he took a swipe with the back of his hand, erasing the foam. He reached for a napkin to finish the job, just as a waiter appeared and asked if there was anything else he desired.

"No thanks," he replied. "I've got to be going. I'm starved. What's a name of good local restaurant nearby that isn't so tourist oriented?"

"I'll find out for you," said the waiter. "I only know to recommend the tourist ones."

Moments later, he came back with someone from the front desk.

"For you, try the Thai Orchid Restaurant," the hotel assistant manager said. "There are hundreds of restaurants to choose from, but a person can't go wrong with this one. Singapore is a city of wonderful multicultural food. Tell the taxi driver the name of the restaurant and he will know where it is. It isn't far."

Brad nodded, thanked the hotel assistant manager, paid his bar

Gary Dale

bill and left a tip for the information. He hailed a taxi and ended up with a driver with a nervous tic taking him to the Thai Orchid restaurant. Brad was getting good at observing taxi drivers. He rolled down his window to inhale the evening breeze, scented with tropical flowers.

The recommended restaurant was a few minutes off the beaten path, located on a side street with small shops, and fewer cars. The taxi stopped in front of a quaint looking neighborhood restaurant with a marquee awning, brick front entrance complete with flower boxes. He liked it immediately. He reached over the front seat and paid the nervous driver. Exiting the taxi, he accidentally banged the car door on a thick metal post outside the front entrance of the restaurant. Brad didn't even see the black object and quickly apologized to the driver. The agitated taxi driver spouted a mouthful of unintelligible words. He reached over the back seat, pulled the car door shut and drove off, squealing his tires before a stunned Brad could respond.

Inside the restaurant, he signed the guest register announcing his presence to management. The maitre d' was seating another couple, so a waiter nearby looked at the guest register and then guided him to a single table, next to the noisy kitchen. Normally the location wouldn't be his overall choice for a table, but he wasn't in the mood to suggest somewhere else. The taxi driver had upset him, adding to his already overloaded stress level. He was, however, hungry and started to go through the menu items in the dim light when the rather formal looking maitre d' walked over to his table to greet him.

"Ah, Mr. Ric, glad to have you again. I've been worried about you since I heard you had some trouble, but I still reserved your favorite table and your special chair. How's your back tonight? Still having a persistent problem with low back pain and stiffness? You know, you should see an acupuncture specialist I have in mind. This

Reef of Gold

problem you're having has been going on for many months and you need to do something about it."

Stunned for a moment, Brad couldn't fully take in what he had just heard. He looked up quickly from the menu. "Excuse me, but what did you just say?"

Taken aback, the maitre d' stared at his dining guest. He cocked his head to one side as if to get a better look at him in the dim light and then straightened and said, "Very sorry sir. My mistake. I thought you were someone else. Excuse me for just a moment." He left for the front door and then returned with the guest register in hand. "My headwaiter apparently recognized the last name when you signed the register and unfortunately assumed that you were one of our regular customers." He turned to go when Brad grabbed his coat sleeve and tugged him back to the table.

"Didn't you just call me Ric?"

"Well, yes I did," he acknowledged, looking a little rattled. "Forgive me for my error."

Brad took a deep breath, blew some air from his cheeks, and said, "Ric is my brother."

"Your brother?" the maitre de' exclaimed. He looked again at the table guest. "Ric never said anything about having a brother. And to think I thought I knew him well."

"A lot of people have made the same statement," Brad countered. "Actually, he has two brothers."

"Well, well. When I see Ric next, I will have something to hold over him and tease him about. By the way, where has this brother of yours been hiding out? It's been a while. And, ah, what is your name? Just so I can keep you all straight."

"My name is Brad. And you are?"

"Kim," he said. "Kim Louie, at your service."

"Pleased to meet you, Kim," offering to shake hands. Smiling, he said, "You sound like a British guy with a hint of an American west coast accent."

45

Gary Dale

Kim bowed and said, "I attended a university in Los Angeles. Didn't like Los Angeles very much but stayed long enough to pick up the American accent. What brings you to our wonderful city, business, playing tourist, or surprising your brother?"

"Actually looking for my brother," said Brad, keeping to his agreed upon cover story.

Kim looked at him seriously and leaned closer. "I was hoping you were him since I had heard of his disappearance," he said, confiding quietly. "I hope everything is right by him. Some government security people were in here asking questions along with a few others of unknown origin. Ric is a very popular guy especially when he disappears. And now you were going to ask me if I happened to know anything that might be of help?"

Brad nodded.

Mr. Louie smiled. "Ric's somewhat mysterious and when he arrives here, it is always without a reservation. So, I just reserve this table for him and the occasional guest," he said, emphasizing the words 'occasional guest'.

Templeton raised his eyebrows. Then he smiled. "Oh? And what occasional guest might this be? Something along the female line?" he asked with amusement, knowing his brother.

Kim leaned closer and said, "Sometimes a beautiful woman shows up with him. She has dark shoulder length hair, is fairly tall, and wears this wonderful perfume." His eyes twinkled at the remembrance. Brad leaned back in his chair and laughed. "Ric," the maitre d' continued, "could never resist her when she wore this particular fragrant perfume. He would just melt. Then again, sometimes businessmen would drop in on him as if a meeting was already arranged. You just never knew with Ric."

"Have any of the occasional unknown guests shown up here recently looking for him?" he asked, hoping for new information that he could tell Ric once he found him.

"Well, they used to, but lately, no one." Kim turned slightly

Reef of Gold

when one of his waiters signaled him and pointed to the front of the restaurant. "Excuse me for a few minutes, Mr. Templeton," he said, "but I have some hungry patrons to attend too. May I bring you a glass of Australian Chardonnay direct from Perth? It is Ric's favorite."

Brad assured him he would like that and then scanned the menu. It didn't take him long to realize that it was written in Malaysian. He chuckled. So Ric reads and probably speaks Malaysian, he mused. The mistaken waiter must have truly thought he was seating brother Ric when he grabbed the Malaysian menu instead of the English version.

When Kim Louie returned, Brad suggested to him that he bring something that Ric would order only a little less of the hot stuff and more of the mild. Brad wanted to taste his food not assassinate his taste buds.

Later, taste buds still intact, he thanked the maitre d' for the conversation and fine dinner and walked out into the night air. He stood under the canvas awning of the front entrance, enjoying the moment and watching the young people walking hand in hand across the street. "Finally a perfect evening in Singapore," he mused. The maitre d' called him back into the restaurant. "You have a phone call, Mr. Templeton." Brad answered carefully. The caller was Mr. Yew, from the San Francisco Malaysian Embassy. Brad was a little stunned. Now what, he wondered? Mr. Yew was quick and to the point. "Do you remember me, Mr. Templeton? I am head of security for all the Malaysian embassies worldwide."

"Yes, I remember," Brad acknowledged.

"Leave immediately for Perth, Australia, first flight out. You are in great danger. Someone will contact you when you arrive at the Perth International airport main lobby."

"How will I recognize this someone?" he asked.

"No need to worry," said Mr. Yew, "he will find you and when

Gary Dale

he does, he will ask you for a Hoya de' Monterrey cigar. That is your favorite cigar is it not, Mr. Templeton?"

"Yes, but…."

"When you say, 'it is my favorite brand but I don't have any cigars at the moment', he will hand you an Excalibur cigar. That will be your cue. Follow this man and do as he asks. Am I clear?"

The phone disconnected. Templeton thanked the maitre d' again and went out the front door.

He had walked only a couple of paces towards the taxi stand when there was a flash of light followed by a loud bang and a screech of tires. A huge black object hurled itself at Brad, giving him just enough time to react. To avoid being crushed, he threw himself sideways. The grazing impact of the dark object slammed him into the brick wall of the restaurant with a thud. Bouncing off, he landed with his head and shoulders in a raised flowerbed before collapsing in a heap. For a moment, he was conscious enough to hear people rushing out of the restaurant, shouting in confusion. He didn't know what they were saying but the people were obviously excited and concerned. He barely heard snatches of English words "black car, out of control," and "now gone."

Templeton lay still for several moments, wavering in and out of consciousness but when he could think, he did a quick physical check for damage by moving fingers, toes and limbs. The adrenalin receded in his veins long enough for him to take stock of where he was, face pressed against a brick wall and the smell of fertilized earth. 'Maybe I'm dead and being buried,' he thought.

He could hear the crunch of glass breaking on pavement as people walked around and then suddenly a shout from someone as if noticing him for the first time. Brad moved just enough to indicate he was alive. With help from concerned bystanders, he very slowly righted himself to a sitting position on the brick flower box. Several restaurant patrons began to carefully pick off the flowers and brush away the dirt.

Reef of Gold

One concerned bystander looked at the crash victim curiously for a moment and then with a clipped British accent, asked if he had any serious injuries. "Fine shape," Brad mumbled, "if," and he paused and looked down and around, "if I was a flower." He laughed outrageously at his own joke. The bystanders looked at him strangely as if they saw no humor in his comment. Brad squinted at them again. They looked like a double exposure. He began to laugh hysterically.

"Looks like someone didn't like you," said someone with a British accent. "The taxi apparently banged into a metal post in front of the restaurant and caromed off back into the street. Lucky for you the taxi hit the metal post giving you only a glancing blow; otherwise, you might have been a Singapore statistic." The British accent turned and said something to others in the crowd and then gently held the victim carefully around the shoulders and bundled him into the backseat of a parked car a short distance away. Brad remembered bits and pieces of what was said during the trip but he was slipping in and out of consciousness and wasn't sure of anything. Then blackness.

CHAPTER 7

SINGAPORE WHARF

The powerboat knifed through the currents of the Singapore Straits at full throttle. It growled beautifully as the skipper opened her up on the open water, burning out the carbon accumulated in the carburetor jets of the powerful Australian marine engines. The long, cigar shaped hull was designed for speed and was specially built and equipped for the Triad in a secluded and abandoned section of the Singapore shipyard. Her quasi skipper, Yang Lee, known by reputation as the main Triad enforcer, knew the powerboat hadn't been the only vessel built for special customers with a great need for secrecy. He had heard of large deliveries of titanium, Kevlar, and stealth ingredients from China being delivered by surrogate North Korean ships and unloaded into the few remaining sections of rundown warehouses in old town Singapore. Yang Lee wasn't privy to all the business dealings along the ancient wharf, but he knew enough to be aware of the immense power and wealth of the century's old, Hung family dynasty.

The Triad enforcer slowed the craft to half speed and then gave the control to a trusted crewmember as they neared the aged wharf. After another fifteen minutes of yet slower speed, the craft eventually throttled down to a quiet growl before coasting alongside a floating dock nestled under the wharf. The secured powerboat lay hidden

50

Reef of Gold

amongst the docked cargo ships with its sharp bow barely peeking out inquisitively to see if there was any danger lurking about. The Singapore Triad had taken great care to be secretative and secure in their base of operations. No stranger can approach the decrepit wharf from air, land or sea without the Triad's knowledge and approval. The old and decaying wharf along the Northern part of the Singapore harbor was a perfect cover. It created hundreds of passageways for the Triad water taxis to move skillfully and furtively among the tall forests of creosote pilings that helped to support the Triad warehouses above the slack water. Many of the water taxis were carrying sensitive cargo lifted from ship's holds under the cover of repetitive stealth tarps that kept away the prying satellite eyes from above. Special fiber material was threaded through out the canvas, defusing satellite infrared beams. Other water taxis carried passengers of importance, like Yang Lee, to and from various warehouse locations. In the darkest areas under the wharf, some pilings had dim lights attached, guiding boats along the water highway. This was a city within a city with the taxi boatman rarely seeing the light of day as they went about delivering their daily illicit commerce.

A water taxi carried Lee through twists and turns known only to the boatman. A quick turn here or there with silent electric outboard motors and the watercraft would literally disappear in the shadows. Finally, the boatman found the specific slot he wanted, gently nosing the watercraft in docking position. Several guards met the water taxi, their eyes scrutinizing the arrivals in the dim light. Its passenger, Yang Lee bounded up the landing steps demonstrating once again to all eyes how youthful and energetic he appeared to be when compared to other Triad enforcers who were known to have grown soft and were reduced to merely giving commands instead of being involved in the action.

Lee became excited. The adrenalin flowed through his veins. He had been told that this meeting location was where the real gathering of powerful people occurred and it was an honor to be invited to

Gary Dale

such a place. Near the top of the stairs, he was stopped at yet another landing, and received a thorough body search. His weapon was taken and wrapped in a lightly oiled cloth protecting the powerful handgun from salt air corrosion. Salt corrosion was hard on metal. He knew his weapon would be returned to him when he left the meeting. Security for the Shan Chu and his staff was serious business and even the enforcers from their own organizations were not spared a rigorous body search. Being family only went so far.

Yang Lee climbed the last few steps and up through a large trap door which opened into an old warehouse. It reeked of oil and petrol fumes, assaulting his nose, giving him an instant headache. He hated engine fumes and his appreciation for the high-powered meeting place soon faded. He also wondered why someone didn't open up one of the many garage doors to let in some fresh air.

"Yang Lee?" a thick voice questioned from the shadows.

"Yes," he replied.

"Come this way."

With two bulky security men behind him, Lee followed the main security guard in the faint light provided by muted light bulbs through a series of doors and passageways, eventually losing his sense of direction. The passageway was quiet, tomb-like, with only their footfalls echoing along the wood floor corridors. Lee felt a strange awareness of claustrophobia descending upon him like a widow's veil. He did not like the feeling of being closed in and only this meeting with the all-powerful Shan Chu prevented him from bolting. He had never seen the Shan Chu in person. "I must stay calm," he repeated over and over again silently to himself, trying to overcome his anxiety. He took a deep breath. Imagine, he reminded himself, "The Shan Chu." He took another deep breath, only this time; he let the air out of his lungs. "It was an honor to be in his very presence. Very few Triad members had that privilege," he mumbled to himself. He stood a little straighter as he walked, head held up high. The parade of security men suddenly stopped causing the enforcer to bump into

Reef of Gold

the guard in front of him. His security escort opened a heavy metal door leading to a stairway that lead down to a large gambling den, now quiet. A few workers scurried around, cleaning up the place. They were under a time constraint. The Chinese population would gamble on anything, at any hour, anytime, or anywhere. Illicit gambling casinos meant money and lots of it.

"Which way?" he asked when they had stopped in the middle of the casino floor.

A shrug of the shoulders from security indicated that they would know in due time. They were to wait. Although known for ruthlessness within the Triad Organization, Yang Lee knew the penalty for disobeying orders. He felt the pressure and tried to pass this new feeling off as excitement but he knew better. The displeasure of the Shan Chu meant that death was only a whisper away.

Lee looked around and wished he could gamble. He always felt comfortable around games of chance, only the nearby tables were covered with cloth.

Gambling was his favorite vice. Paigow, Baccarat, dice, fan-tan, mah-jongg, it didn't matter. He loved the action. Men would often be packed four or five deep, jostling for a place near the gambling tables, with cigarettes held high above their heads, while their bets were placed on the table in front of them. The atmosphere was one of heavy smoke, rank odors of body sweat, and triumphant shouting of the winners and groans of losers.

Why did he not know of this place? Had he been too busy to notice? Yang Lee shuffled his feet again announcing to his security escort that he was getting bored with all the waiting.

"Now, we go," the escort, said suddenly, as if some unseen button had been pushed. The enforcer had seen no one come forward and give the order.

They walked along a full-length teak bar and then stopped. The security escort gave a quick rap on the back wall. A heavy door, invisible to the naked eye in the dim light, opened on hydraulic

53

Gary Dale

hinges and Lee was escorted inside to a small waiting room, richly adorned, but windowless. He submitted to the security test of a 3-D image of a blood vein match. New security types expertly frisked him again. He winced when he was whacked in the balls to remind him of where he was and in whose presence.

Yang Lee knew. He didn't have to be reminded and he would soon be in the presence of an unpredictable and dangerous man. 'What did he look like?' he wondered. The sweat dribbled from under his arms and down his side. The unknown part was killing him. A door opened and the escort delivered him inside a large air-conditioned room, where continuous walls were interrupted only with closed doors. The entire room was full of Triad computer activity and with men in oversized yellow jackets hovering about like a plague of locusts. Security was tight.

He looked around the room trying to pick out the great man, but no one gave him the slightest hint. He just stood there near the entrance with his yellow-jacketed security muscle on both sides of him. His mind began to play tricks on him with the wait. Everything appeared to be normal, yet not normal. He looked around in amazement.

Maps of the world hung below time clocks indicating the time zones of New York, Los Angeles, Paris, Sydney, London, Hong Kong and other major cities of the world. Banks of computer screens flashed with data and an occasional cell phone would interrupt the otherwise highly charged atmosphere. Yang Lee shifted from one foot to another. This was a different world than he was accustomed too. Mounds of cash were being run through counting machines, bundled and placed in stacks. The casino accounting took up a third of the huge office space. Despite the activity, the room started to close in on him. Windowless rooms, no matter how large always made him feel slightly uncomfortable. He did not like the feeling.

He visibly jumped as a conference room door opened and a stern, tall, muscular man of obvious high military rank strode into the main

Reef of Gold

room accompanied by an unimpressive, squat man. Rotund is more like it, smirked the enforcer to himself. Probably a Triad finance minister. The man had thinning dark hair, wore gold-rimmed glasses to read the fistful of what looked like computer documents.

A third man, well dressed in a tailored brown suit, white shirt and muted tie, walked towards the two men. He was taller than the others, more broad shouldered, giving him a strong physical and self assured aura. He walked like an athlete; relaxed, easy movements, and carried a smug, self-assured facial expression. He stopped along the way to visit with several employees before he joined in conference. The three men conferred quietly in the center of the room, allowing the room sounds to mask their conversation. The men were nodding in agreement with little hand gesturing.

The conversation seemed to switch and suddenly the nodding stopped. Facial expressions became tight with several cuss words spewing outward, loud enough for several nearby employees to hear the words. The employees cringed. The brown suited man was very animated, all the while cracking his knuckles as if to emphasis each point of his conversation. There was a pause in the conversation. Finally all three men nodded their heads in agreement.

The suit smiled and then clasped the shoulder of the military man as a gesture of a successful meeting.

Standing near the waiting room door, Yang Lee watched the impressive suit walk away and close the meeting room door. His shoulders drooped with the thought that his meeting with the Shan Chu just had been canceled. His attention turned to the military man, whose shoulder insignia indicated a high rank. The man quickly handcuffed a brief case to his left wrist, and exited with the yellow-jacketed security escort. He recognized the military insignias stitched to his uniform, 'Chinese army'. That is no surprise, he thought. Finally, the squat man with the computer papers walked over and faced Yang Lee, letting his dark eyes penetrate Lee's soul

Gary Dale

before motioning him to join him at a small conference table in another room.

"You are the enforcer that takes care of my good friend, the Yuan Swie of Singapore and his operations?" he asked.

"I am the enforcer," said a startled Yang Lee, realizing the identity of the man, hoping the Shan Chu couldn't read the remnants of his thoughts. Droplets of sweat appeared on Lee's forehead.

"Good, good," the squat man exclaimed, "I am the Shan Chu, as you must have surmised, leader of the Southeast Asian Triads and all of its organizational branches. You are here in my presence to emphasize the importance of your next assignment. This assignment will not, and I repeat, will not require the enforcer services that you have used in the past, unless of course, I tell you differently." Your previous assignment of ten days ago has been canceled. A distinctive sound, like a muted alarm from another room suddenly caught the ear of the Shan Chu. He quickly held up his hand to Yang Lee as a signal to wait and walked briskly away, leaving the enforcer to momentarily sit alone in the airless small room. A yellow jacket walked over and stood beside the door, waiting for his master to return. Another twenty minutes passed before the Shan Chu walked back into the room. There was a level of noticeable stress and a large frown on his face until he came closer to the table. Then the strained facial lines disappeared. The frown stayed on his face.

Yang Lee rose to his feet.

"We will sit," said the Shan Chu, gesturing to the ornate table. The enforcer quickly sat down, ramrod straight in his chair with his hands gripping the armrests. The Shan Chu continued with the conversation as if he had never left the room. "Your success over the many years in security work in Singapore and recently at the Sterling Mining Company in Australia has brought you to my attention especially after you eliminated the perpetrators who made an attempt to infiltrate our computer security systems here, You are to be given a new assignment of great importance. It has been

Reef of Gold

decided that you will immediately replace a family member as a temporary assignment in Perth, Australia. This man has been taken seriously ill and cannot do the job. He was in charge of several of our espionage cells operating under the guise of legitimate Australian businesses. You will have an experienced staff to help you."

Yang Lee couldn't help himself. "Australia?" he questioned in surprise. He didn't know the Triad had extensive espionage operations in Australia.

The Shan Chu smiled. "You are surprised to find our tentacles go out that far?" he asked, almost more of a statement than a question.

"Well, yes," stammered Lee.

"Actually, Australia is one of our best sources of secret information." The Shan Chu smiled, letting the information soak in the enforcer's brain. "Once their leftist newspapers let the world know that the Aussie secret service had laced the Chinese Embassy building in Sydney with microphones to listen in on every conversation, the Chinese government has doubled their espionage efforts in retaliation. The Chinese military man that you saw leaving this room was in that embassy when the security breach occurred. He vowed to never let Australia do that to China again. That is why he asked us several years ago to help secure national secrets from the Aussies and Americans. He pays us extremely well for our efforts."

The Shan Chu paused as if counting all the money that rolled in from the Chinese government that paid him for his current spy network in Australia and other espionage operations in other countries. It was a cozy and profitable partnership. The Shan Chu leaned forward to emphasize what he was about to say. Respectively, Yang Lee rocked back ever so slightly. The Shan Chu continued the conversation. "The Triad," he said, "operates differently than a government and at times we can use force as a means to an end where a government cannot do the same. On the other hand, the Chinese government, if they could, would publicly thank the Leftist Australian

Gary Dale

newspapers with payment in gold for all their help in recent years in exposing the Australian secret service efforts in counterespionage."

Yang Lee didn't know what to say or think at the moment. He remained motionlessness and let the Shan Chu ramble on.

"Your job will be to again provide tight security at the Sterling Mining Company only this time I also want you to monitor our espionage operation as well," said the Shan Chu. "The legitimate mining business is the cover that allows us to gather information from the imperialist West, especially America. We are able to steal their sensitive intelligence information and secretly send it to Sterling Mines headquarters in Perth and then courier onto us. Our operation is undetected and we plan on keeping that way."

He sighed for a moment to let his breath catch up with his excitement over his great covert accomplishments.

"You will be on a 'need to know basis', Yang Lee, like before. Just understand that the security operation you are over-seeing is very secret. No one must find out what we are doing. You will be working with the president of the Sterling Mining Company who is working for us but not as a Triad member. He should not know about our relationship. We secretly fund his company's mining efforts to give our people a reason to be in Australia. Watch him but let him act naturally. His name is Wong. He comes from an old Macau family of merchants and sea captains. So, when the Aussies check up on him from time to time, he will clear their security profiles. His passion is gold and that is all he talks about. He is a perfect cover for our espionage operations."

The Shan Chu glanced around the room and spoke again. "I know you are not totally familiar with the Sterling Mines operations but that familiarity will come with time. You will be able to reacquaint yourself with the Triad computer staff. Any questions so far?"

Yang Lee shook his head.

"You will leave immediately and enter Australia in a normal manner as a transfer employee from the Sterling Mines Singapore

Reef of Gold

office. A Triad staff member will accompany you and give you more details about our operations. He is our advisor on administration, financial, military and public affairs for the Australian operations. His name is Chi Son Tie, and he is to be your direct contact for any occasion. He reports directly to me. Do I make myself clear?" he asked, rising from his chair signaling the meeting was over. Yang Lee quickly stood.

"Yes, most certainly, Shan Chu," he replied.

"Until we meet again," he said, grasping Lee's shoulders as a farewell gesture. The Shan Chu's black eyes stared deep into Yang Lee eyes, freezing any thought of twitching or nervousness. The man walked quietly away.

This man was no tiger, Yang Lee thought. He was worse. The black eyes of the Shan Chu were those of a viper, waiting to strike.

CHAPTER 8

STERLING MINES......PERTH, AUSTRALIA

The human resource interviewing process at Sterling Mines was going well. Brad Templeton answered the usual 'tell me a little bit about who you are; what are your strengths and weaknesses; and how long do you plan to stay in Australia'? The interviewer also asked Brad about his puffy face, more out of concern than curiosity.

"Road accident ten days ago in Singapore," Brad assured him. "I feel much better." The interviewer nodded as if it was a daily occurrence in that part of the world.

While Brad answered the human resource or "HR" director's questions, they also had a friendly chat about things to do in Perth and the surrounding area. The director was a nice fellow, medium height for an Australian, dressed in a light blue short sleeve shirt and spoke with just a hint of Irish brogue.

"As a consultant," the HR director said, "you won't have any immigration problem. The restrictions for you to work here will be less stringent."

"Why is that?" asked Brad.

"Very simple mate. Perth is a mining town and short on skilled workers. They are in high demand and we pay well just to get them here, especially the sparkies. Unfortunately, the pay doesn't always attract the 21 to 30 year old sophisticated employee. It seems if you are

60

under the age of 30 and the least bit interested in a faster pace of life, then Perth is boring. The perception among the younger Australian population is to live in the big cities of Sydney or Melbourne where the action is taking place. It takes an entrepreneur or someone who likes adventure to live out here in Western Australia. To tell you the truth, I wouldn't live anywhere else but here, even with a million or so souls in Perth."

Brad was about to question the HR person about the term sparkies when he figured it out. Sparkies had to be a slang name for iron and steel welders. He could understand the shortage. It was a special talent that paid well.

Sliding the documents toward him to read, the director indicated where he should sign the originals when they reached the HR's desk.

"I'll give you copies of the agreements you have signed," he said. "It will be just a few minutes while one the office staff finishes the computer entry and generates the rest of the data. As a reminder Brad, this is a short-term six-month contract with renewable clauses for both parties." He smiled. "The mining staff must like your work experience in America. The interoffice memo said to hire you no matter what. That's not unusual for this company."

"Oh, ok," said Brad.

The secretary brought in the paper work, all neatly computerized and compact. Before signing, Brad checked the contract. He realized he was on their computer files forever as an employee number. His contract stated he was a consultant in public relations and marketing. Broad area but he was covering all the bases just to get hired. He was told the company would figure out where he should be placed within the organization and may move him around.

The director rose from his desk and welcomed him aboard. "Now," he said, "make your way to the second floor, using the elevators on the far left, and then ask for Megan McGinnis. She is the Vice President of Public Relations who will get you started."

Gary Dale

Stepping off the elevator onto the second floor was an eye opener for Brad. Before him was a vast semi-open area of cubicles with barriers of strange plants separating one office cubicle from another. From his height of six feet plus, he was barely able to see across the tops of the plant barriers. The low hum of voices of people working seemed to capture the essence of the second floor. It was also a maze of office cubicles with no "yellow brick road" to guide a person if you were looking for someone.

"Now, to find this Megan person," he mused, as he kept looking around. An attractive woman came over to him, realizing he must be lost as he remained in front of the elevators and didn't move.

"You must be new here," she said.

"Yes," he said, "First hour."

"American," she exclaimed excitedly. "This will liven up this dull office. I can hardly wait to tell everyone."

"Ah, and how did you know I was American?" he asked, looking down at his shirt to see if somehow he had an American Flag attached to it.

"Your accent mate. Gives away an American every time. Besides, we watch your American television programming. Say, is the TV show "Ocean View" really filmed on a beautiful California beach near Los Angeles?"

Brad laughed politely. "Sorry to disappoint you," he said, "but camera angles will give the illusion that the beach is quite long and beautiful. Actually, the beach is not that big and only parts of it are beautiful. And the popular show you mention has been off the air for a number of years."

"Rain on my parade will you mate," she said. "We must be getting the reruns. Oh well. That's Hollywood for you, all illusions. Now that we have trashed Hollywood, where can I direct you?"

"I'm Brad," he said, extending his hand. "You are?"

"Alice," she said brightly. "Pleased to meet you mate," shaking

Reef of Gold

his hand with a very firm grip. "I like your American directness. Now, how can I help you?"

"I'm supposed to meet with the vice president of public relations and was wondering just where her office is in this maze"

"Well, Brad, it's like this," Alice explained and pointed at the same time. "Go South along this hallway, turn left by the fake baobab tree, meander along the billabong mural and you will come to a corner office. That will be hers on this floor. She also has an office on the third floor as well, sort of a combat room when she is working with the top execs. At least that is what she calls it."

"And if one gets lost," he questioned, "the procedure must be to hang out near the baobab tree, light a fire and signal for help?"

Alice laughed. "Just shout out, 'Help, I'm an American who has lost his way.' You will have more help than you need."

"Gee, thanks, I think," he said, smiling. With that he pushed off in a southerly direction as per instructions and soon came to the gnarly and ancient looking baobab tree. "This fake tree probably looked just like an original including the height," he observed. The tallest part of the tree in front of him came right through the floor and as he looked up, it went to the high ceilings. It was clear that the Baobab tree would mesmerize any visitor with its gnarly beauty and giant proportions. It looked so real.

Brad finally took a left turn and meandered along the billabong wall scenery actually enjoying his adventure through Australia when he came upon a desk that blended into the background of unfamiliar looking trees and shrubs. He had almost walked right into it. He was looking around for someone to ask for directions when a stunning woman, dressed in a beige, tailored business suit walked through the fake underbrush and stopped in front of him. It was then Brad noticed her beautiful greenish soft eyes that matched her earrings and jade green blouse. For a moment, he was tongue-tied. Then he shuffled his feet and stammered that he was new to the company and was to report to the public relations/marketing area.

Gary Dale

She smiled.

He looked down at the paperwork that he had brought with him and started to ask for the vice president in name when the stunning woman said in a husky voice, "You must be the newly hired chap from America that HR department mentioned."

Brad looked up and nodded, still mesmerized by this trim Australian woman. He stared briefly just to watch her eyes that seemed to change colors with every passing moment. Maybe it was the lighting, he mused.

"Miles will show you where your office cubicle is located and explain what your responsibilities will be for the near future. You will be working for him. His office," she continued saying "is right over in that direction," pointing with slender manicured fingers. Brad's eyes followed the soft feminine left hand and mentally noted there was no wedding band.

He continued to gaze in the indicated direction still stunned by this recent encounter, until he finally focused on the pathway. He turned to say, thanks, but she had gone, disappeared, vanished, exited, or all four. For a moment, he wasn't even sure she had been real except that the slight hint of her perfume was still languishing in the air. He didn't move for a minute or so until his pounding heart came around to the normal beat. Then he remembered that encounters of this magnitude rarely happened in one's life but they occur just often enough to keep a guy excited for the rest of his life. His legs started ahead of his brain as if they knew where to go. The rest of him followed in a daze towards the unknown office somewhere in the fake bush along the pathway.

"Over here, mate," said a male voice from a nearby cubicle. .

"Excuse me," the American said, "but I'm looking for a fellow by the name of Miles. Public relations sent me. This Miles person is supposed to help......"

"You're at the right place," he said, interrupting. "Name's Miles Donnagan. Megan sent you over, right?"

64

Reef of Gold

"I don't know," said Brad. "Whomever I met was dressed very professionally with dainty ear rings to match her beautiful eyes. She could have been a secretary."

"Ooh, are you in big trouble. That was most certainly Megan. She is our Vice President of Public Relations and a secretary she is not. Fact is, you might end up as her personal assistant. Have a seat."

"I didn't know," he exclaimed, feeling more than a little embarrassed as he slid into the guest chair.

"No worries mate. Now that you have seen her and know who she is, what do you think? You know your first impression of her."

"Well," said Brad, while making himself somewhat more comfortable in the uncomfortable chair, "I must admit I was so taken with her beauty in that brief moment of introduction, that I probably made a fool of myself." He took a deep breath. "Actually that's not true. The truth is I really did make a fool of myself. I didn't mean to be so tongue-tied, but she totally caught me off guard."

Miles started to laugh and continued to laugh his lungs out. His whole body just shook and his laughter boomed all over the office. Finally, to Brad's relief, he slowly stopped laughing, brushed his eyes to catch his tears and then said, "Mate, every male in this building has had the same reaction when meeting Megan for the first time. In fact, you will get used to her beauty, as she doesn't let it get in her way. By the way, what is your name? You didn't say."

"Brad Templeton."

"Ok mate," he acknowledged. "She is very likeable and one smart lady. She has all our respect. However, Megan is sort of an enigma around here."

"Really. What's the mystery?" asked Brad.

"The enigma," said Miles, "is that when she leaves the office at night, no one knows where she goes other than home. She doesn't hang out with any of the office staff after work and certainly doesn't date any one from the office. God knows we single guys have all tried

Gary Dale

to get to know her on a more personal level, but as you Americans always say, we struck out. I am now hoping you, being a Yank, will be able to crack the barrier. Maybe there is still time if you can learn how to talk when around her."

"Thanks a lot."

"No worries mate. Look, we can shoot the breeze later over a couple of beers. The company needs to get you up to speed right away. Since your assignment for now is to replace staff who are starting their holidays, you will have to learn on the job."

"Excuse me, but what does all of this have to do with my consulting contract?" Brad asked, handing him the stack of paper work from the HR department.

"Ah," said Miles, "that consulting contract just gets you on board and away from immigration. Your consulting talents will come later. Replacing staff members on holiday is just a good way for you to learn what the company is all about."

"Ok, with me. When and where do I start?"

"You start straight away. Here is a list of people who will be on holiday shortly. Talk to them if they are still here and their co-workers about getting involved in their projects and keep on schedule for completion. There are secretaries and assistants to help you, and besides, we all pitch in around here to help each other. Just ask and someone will help. Start with Clayton's desk over there," he said, pointing to a nearby office.

Miles paused in his rapid-fire instructions with a word of caution. "Having said all of this," he said in a quiet voice, "be a little careful about asking questions of why, whom, what, etc. about any of our Asian staff and their contribution to the company. We have Asian management and employees from the third and fourth floors wandering around on our floor every once in a while and they are rather quiet about what they do upstairs. Just don't get too inquisitive; otherwise, I'll hear about it. By the way, here is your temporary security badge. You will need to get a photo taken today by security for your permanent badge. The security office is just down…."

He stopped suddenly. He looked at Brad sort of funny and then asked very seriously, "Are you ok? You look a little under the weather. Your face looks a little puffy."

"It's just some swelling left over from a disagreement with a car in Singapore. I was in a hospital for observation for a several days. Except for the occasional headache and soreness, I'm fine."

Nodding a response, Miles pointed in a general direction, telling Brad to go down the pathway to get his photo taken, puffy face or not. "Notice," he said, "I'm not wearing a security badge because on the first and second floors, we don't really need one, except when we arrive and leave. You will also need the security badge to enter the building on weekends and after 6:00pm weekdays. And," he said, "I hate to tell you this because I don't like it myself, but be prepared for random pat downs by security as you exit the building. Management just started this new security only a little while ago. Miles paused.

"There is more," he sighed and then said, "Sometimes we have a total search of every employee leaving the building. Why, I don't know and I don't ask. I can only surmise that it has something to do with the third and fourth floors insecurity. Sterling Mines is also involved in many other projects besides the gold mining. Theft of computer secrets, documents, etc. has happened here before; at least those are the rumors. I think our Asian management gets a little paranoid and goes overboard in security measures. Anyway, my advice to you is to do your job and put up with the security. No worries, Right?"

For a moment, Brad was a little stunned by the security measures. He had pegged this Australian company to be pretty well laid back. All he could do at the moment was nod his head in acknowledgement.

"And, if for some reason," said Miles, "someone on the upper floors wants to see you, put on your security badge. On the fourth floor, they do have a palm print security system in place and maybe

Gary Dale

even retina scanning security. Most likely you will never see the third floor, let alone the fourth floor. Good luck, and if you need anything, come to me. We can always talk about our vice president of public relations."

Brad didn't know where the time went but the office staff melted away around 5:00pm. During the lunch hour, however, he had accomplished something. He had rented a townhouse from a retired Australian Army officer. It even had a shop in a lower level-parking garage. The rental had been a referral from work mates, which had eased all the unnecessary paper work that a real estate firm would have required. His leased furniture would arrive the next day and then he would be able to move in. He was looking forward to it.

CHAPTER 9

WADDLING DUCK PUB

The next week turned out to be easier for Brad because of his familiarity of the office work and expectations. Alice, who was the first person whom he had met standing at the elevators on his first day of work, turned out to be a conduit for organizing the Wednesday and Friday night after work pub gatherings. Drinking beer is an Aussie national pastime and heaven help the unsuspecting American.

The favorite pub of a number of the office staff was the Waddling Duck. With its long mahogany bar, fireplaces, high ceilings, and padded chairs for the table crowd, it was no wonder the place was popular. The pub was busy during the week and packed to the walls on Friday nights. Patrons made their own salad, chose their cut of meat or favorite fish from a refrigerated glass case, and then cooked their own selection on 6-foot x 20-foot gas barbeque. The grill obviously became a friendly magnet for people to get to know each other while they cooked their own dinner.

The after-work office gathering was also an opportunity for Brad to listen and gain some knowledge about the management of Sterling Mines. The office staff seemed more open with their conversations at the pub without the security constraints at the office. On a Wednesday evening, the few office staff that remained at the

69

Waddling Duck talked company gossip for the most part. Brad hung around feeling like a damp bar rag. He didn't have anywhere else to go except to his lonely townhouse and worry about his brother. Then it was back to work the next day.

For the Sterling Mining employees, the recent speculation at the Waddling Duck Pub centered on the comings and goings of security personnel and the fairly recent changing of some of the Asian executives. The headquarters building had a heliport on the roof and it was being used every day this week. Usually the helicopter came only on Tuesdays or Fridays. The consensus of those gathered around the table was that something was up. After hoisting a few more glasses of beer, most of the employees decided to leave for home, just as Brad was hoping to satisfy his curiosity. He walked over to the few remaining office mates and joined in the group discussion.

"Maybe it's a gold strike," Brad jokingly volunteered, which was his first real venture into the conversation. Alice had re-introduced him to Michael, from the engineering department, as they were now the only ones left at the table.

"Ha," snorted Michael. "We search and search and nothing yet, just like the others."

"Just like the others?" Brad questioned.

"The other mining firms haven't had a significant strike lately either. Finding new mineral deposits, especially gold isn't that easy. Deposits are usually found in the roughest country where no mining engineer in his right mind would look."

"Speaking of searching," said Brad, "and this might sound like a miners' story, but I had heard of a reef of gold being discovered in Australia a long time ago. Do any of the mining companies have claims even near the approximate site or have they actually discovered the reef already?"

Both Michael and Alice looked at each other. Finally Alice spoke up. "Funny you should ask. The President of Sterling Mines has this mysterious reef of gold as one of his pet projects. He has batted

Reef of Gold

around this theory of actual location for quite some time, at least as long as the company has been in existence. Sterling Mines has had their mining engineers looking for it periodically. An old miner named Lassiter did find a reef of gold somewhere in the outback in the 1930's and actually mined it, or so he said. He came back a few hundred miles to town for supplies, showed the gold, and told everyone about it. Then, he took off again to mine it. Well, naturally, everyone in town had seen his gold ore, so many of the shopkeepers closed up shop and followed his trail for some time. They found him under a rock overhang, delirious from no water or food, talking about his discovery only he couldn't find it again or so the story goes. The secret 'reef of gold' location died with him. Apparently, there never was a map. Some still wonder if Lassiter's mine actually existed even with the evidence of gold he brought back to town. The history books say he was quite a character."

"Where did they find him before he died?"

"Michael, do you remember where?" asked Alice. "You have more access to the claim maps than I do."

"Well," said Michael, "one of our engineers who still goes out on these wild goose chases for our president did tell me that scuttlebutt has it that there was another rumor of a reef of gold near the ocean in the Kimberley's region of Australia; maybe even in the Northwest Territories. That's up North, Yank, way up North. The Lassiter's lost reef of gold is supposedly hundreds of miles south of the Northern Coast of Australia. Who knows, maybe there are several gold reefs. At one time, the entire continent of Australia was covered in water, so the theory is possible. No one seems to know much about our President's theory or where he got his information, if there is any actual information. Maybe he has the gold fever bug and just made it up with wishful thinking. If a person wants something very badly, one can visualize anything by changing the details to fit his or her fantasy."

Brad quickly refilled the glasses with beer, trying to keep the

Gary Dale

interesting conversation going. He was hoping more peanuts or bread sticks would be delivered from the bar during happy hour. He needed something to soak up the Aussie beer that was beginning to catch up to him, at least that was what his bladder was telling him. The nickname 'four oz.' from his buddies in the states always seemed to apply when drinking beer or diet soda pop.

Changing to a structured British accent, Michael said, "Of course, no respected mining engineer worth his salt would start spouting the Northern Territory theory let alone the Lassiter's mining claim out in the Gibson Desert. But that doesn't stop the horde of people from looking for Lassiter's lost mine, including our own President Wong."

"Wong?" questioned Brad as if suddenly struck by lightening. "Wong?" he repeated again as the name finally connected. "Is that a common name or a unique one? I mean, how many Wong's are there in Australia?"

Michael smiled. "In this part of the world, the last name of Wong is like "Smith" or "Jones in America." There are a million of them."

"Oh," said Brad, a little deflated by the news. He thought he had something going. He had remembered the Wong's in San Francisco.

"Anyway, you just need to hope you don't get sent on one of those searching expeditions. The outback is very unforgiving even under the best of circumstances." Brad hadn't heard Alice's high-pitched voice and was still working on the Wong mystery when Michael spoke.

"We do have mining company competitors, all three hundred of them," said Michael, in his heavy voice. "We search within the boundaries of each of our claims, hoping to tap into the tailings of the mother lode all the while not touching or encroaching on the other claims. Sometimes the engineers' fudge on the boundaries and like

Reef of Gold

young kids in the backseat of a car, we fight over any encroachment of space. The backseat was never big enough for the three of us.

Snapping out of the trance, Brad rolled his eyes and said, "I remember. It drove my parent's nuts."

Michael nodded. "Having said all of that, gold is still elusive and it takes persistence to find it. Sterling Mines has enough mineral claims to keep us busy, but we all would like a bonus check from a new gold discovery. It's been a while."

"That's an understatement," said Alice, with her tone of voice flaring. "Those pet projects of Wong's and the constant redoing of our computer systems sucks out the company profit and our bonuses."

Brad was startled with the venom displayed by Alice. He hadn't seen that side of her before. Not wanting to get trapped in that dialogue, he continued with the previous conversation direction.

"Do you think the fourth floor people have found something because of all the comings and goings?" he asked, changing the subject. "I could hear the helicopters landing on our building rooftop."

"Hardly mate, as we," gesturing to include Alice, "would have known just by reading the computer printouts and watching for increased activity in the engineering department," said Michael.

"If it's not a new gold or mineral claim that is causing the sudden activity at Sterling Mines, what is causing it?"

"Careful mate, lower your voice a touch." Michael looked around carefully, adjusted his chair, sipped his beer, and then opined on the consequences of talking too publicly about the company.

"Really!" Brad exclaimed. "In here?"

Finally Michael said, "Look mate, you're new with the company. Our conversation here is office knowledge and some gossip, but it stays here. Right?"

"Fine by me," he assured them both. "I hardly even know anyone."

Michael smiled. "We wouldn't be discussing all of this with

Gary Dale

you if Alice and I didn't trust you. I just wanted you to know the importance of keeping our conversation private. It's ok to vent, just keep it on the quiet side. If we are too loud, our discussions always seem to get back to the company brass."

The conversation paused to allow ordering one more round of beer before calling it a night. Brad politely passed. It was time to leave.

CHAPTER 10

SWAN RIVER YACHT CLUB........
PERTH, AUSTRALIA

The secluded table with a white linen covering was nearly perfect. While overlooking the myriads of expensive yachts of sail and marine power, yacht club patrons could enjoy a good meal and name drop. The club was one of many along the Swan River and now had become one of the most popular private yet public gatherings. The new club rules separating private members from the public were firmly in place.

The old facilities had burned down in a huge fire late one Saturday night during the summer, blackening nearby buildings, docks and scorching many boats, especially a few of the fast Three meter sail craft. A spilled barbeque with its hot briquettes was blamed for starting the accidental fire, but many questioned it. Even so, it was thought that alcohol had something to do with the carelessness. The yacht club, because of years of neglect and abuse, actually needed the cleansing. As a result, a modern, upscale, yacht club rose from the ashes. It was at this particular club that Yang Lee liked to entertain and to hold important meetings.

His chosen secluded table was near the large windows on purpose. He preferred the outside deck with umbrellas where one could hear seagulls squawking a 'tally ho' as they, with amazing accuracy, dive-

Gary Dale

bombed anyone unprotected who wanted to go out on the pier to enjoy the scenery. His outside table would have to wait until another time. He was meeting someone.

This was Yang Lee's newly adopted life style. Being a yacht club member made him feel important and prosperous. He enjoyed the powerful feeling that came over him when he walked into the club restaurant in his perfectly tailored white jacket. Still, his stoic face and penetrating eyes made people wary of him. His presence often became a topic of conversation among the restaurant staff. Presenting a proper public image was new to Lee. Before, he had been in the shadows as an enforcer, but now, he was recognized as a part of corporate management of Sterling Mines. He liked the usual trappings that upper society offered.

Lee stared out the window over looking the yacht basin once again. His dream yacht would be docked in front of this very window some day, he quietly reminded himself. It was his destiny.

He gazed out of the window letting his thoughts take over. He had received a terse message from the Triad this morning. A coded e-mail from the Singapore office had told him that an administrator was requesting a special meeting and would arrive shortly by plane. Lee immediately sent his minions to pick up the important Triad leader to bring him to the yacht club instead of the Sterling Mining office. It was a matter of timing. The yacht club was several miles closer to the airport and both men had things to do that couldn't wait.

"Why is this administrator late," he hissed. The dining room continued to fill.

This sudden meeting with Chi Son Tie, 'the Triad administrator', however, worried him. His confidence had been shaken several times during this learning process of overseeing the Sterling Mining espionage effort. Little things seemed to always go wrong and Yang Lee knew the distractions would call attention to him. The Triad administrator did not like mistakes and made mention several times

Reef of Gold

of his lapses in sound judgment. He signaled for the annoying waiter, complaining about the soap spots on the silverware. The waiter quickly apologized and brought several new polished sets. Lee had the fresh flower vase removed leaving only the hot tea service remaining on the otherwise sterile table.

The enforcer impatiently drummed his fingers of his left hand on the cloth-covered table. He disliked waiting for anyone for any reason. His right hand with its distinctive Triad tattoo was hidden under the table. The waiter appeared several more times asking if he wanted anything and each time, the Triad enforcer would brush him away in annoyance like brushing away a pesky fly buzzing around food. He was staring out the window when Chi Son Tie walked up to him.

"Here?" said Tie, looking around. "This is most unusual."

"Why not?" asked Yang Lee, rising to his feet. "Please be seated." Lee recognized the man immediately. This administrator was very high in the Triad hierarchy.

"How secure can this be?" Tie questioned. "Our conversation is to be private."

Lee smiled, confident in what he was about to say. "What better place than to be in a popular restaurant with a lot of people around. The acoustics disguise our voices well enough," he said. "I have a financial stake in this place and consequently, I had specially treated windows installed to deflect any microwave beams that would try to pick up our voice vibrations from the outside. In addition, a computer system of white noise is being broadcast every time I make my presence known in this place making it impossible for any one to pick up our conversations even with the latest listening devices. Each employee is checked and rechecked for loyalty. My staff has electronically swept this location for listening devices in anticipation of this meeting. There have been no problems thus far."

The administrator reluctantly nodded in acceptance and sat down with his back to the window. He signaled for the waiter and had him

Gary Dale

remove the now cold house blend of tea and asked for an English tea. The waiter nodded and glanced at Yang Lee, expecting an order before leaving the table. There was silence instead. The waiter quickly left.

"Things are going well?" Tie asked, pleasantly.

Lee nodded and said, "Just a few minor problems that occur occasionally, usually due to weather."

Tie looked carefully around before speaking, analyzing each restaurant guest. Each patron looked like a businessman on an extended lunch. The waiters were busy bringing drinks to accompany the bread and cheese boards. None of the businesspeople seemed to pay any real attention to Yang Lee's table. Then his gaze caught on the table in the center of the dining room.

There were two couples at the table, pleasantly talking amongst themselves. One couple looked like parents of the other two. The younger man sat with a military bearing and his young lady companion seemed to talk with her hands. She was very animated almost to the point of being nervous. What was it about her? Tie wondered. Was it familiarity or just a distraction? Something about the body posturing, maybe? Or was it the other couple that triggered his suspicions? Something was not quite right. Tie looked away and then back again. He noticed that the couples were positioned to view every table in the room and its occupants. Interesting, he thought. Were they rookie agents planted to make sure I saw them, a distraction from the real watchers. The experienced ones' would be tough to spot, if at all. Those agents would blend in with the dining patrons. They wouldn't do anything that would cause them to stand out. They would be subtle in their observations. They are here, thought Tie. He could feel their presence.

With his left hand, he held up the wine list brochure in front of his mouth to partially obscure the movement of his lips. He didn't feel comfortable with the occupants at the center table and he really wasn't confident of the dining room's electronic security. "Yang

Reef of Gold

Lee," he commanded in a voice, slightly above a strong whisper, "regarding this security system of yours. I need to remind you that electronics have a way of intercepting each other. When you trust your system, it is time to distrust it. The Australian security people are not stupid." The outburst momentarily unsettled the enforcer.

"We have little time," Tie continued, keeping the wine list brochure close to his lips. "What I am about to tell you is extremely important. Enough time has passed for you to now be aware of at least some of our espionage involvement in this country. Our gathering of sensitive information comes from many sources and in different forms. It is a continuous process. Our conversation together will be verbal, with nothing written down between us. Understand?"

Yang Lee nodded and wondered where was this conversation going. He thought he had been thoroughly briefed about his company's espionage efforts. What more was there to discuss?

The waiter approached the table unannounced and left a pot of hot English tea. Tie fiddled with the teacup contents for a moment before enjoying the wonderful aroma. He paused while he gingerly tasted the tea for warmth, blowing on it as if deciding it was too hot for his liking. This careful act hid the movement of his lips.

"Exactly how we get the information that comes to your office is not your concern nor is who sends it to us," he said. "The agent's name or names you will never know. What I can tell you is that the Americans have satellite intelligence centers all grouped together in the middle of the Australian outback. Alice Springs is the main town, and besides being the only source of recreation for the American personnel manning the satellite sites, it is actually a major tourist hub for bus trips to Ayers Rock. All the tourists fortunately head south, away from Alice Springs and the satellite facility the Americans call Pine Gap."

He smirked. "Pine Gap is actually a nice secure facility if you like cold winters and 120-degree summers. Not much in the way of a change in the extreme weather seasons. It is one extreme or the other.

Gary Dale

There is a streambed called Laurel Creek that runs full during a rare torrential rainstorm sliding down from the North but it's mostly dry for long periods of time. For obvious reasons, the American base was built where the sky was free from obstructions like mountains and the cities with all their electronic devises."

"Sounds like you have spent some time there?"

The Triad administrator ignored the question and placed his teacup back onto the saucer. He just stared at Yang Lee. Eventually, his eyes released him.

Stirring his tea, Tie became quiet as if in deep thought. Finally he raised the teacup to his lips and spoke again. "The Pine Gap base," he said, "is manned by Americans and Australians, who share the technical and maintenance requirements of the facility. The arrogant Americans make a show of sharing the satellite intelligence with the Australians, but they really don't share everything. This rubs the Australians the wrong way as it seems as though nothing of major importance is passed to them. This conflict is an on-going problem."

He paused to set his tea down and observe the newly arrived restaurant patrons. Nothing unusual about them, he concluded, except for the beautiful ladies. Must be magazine models, he thought. They walked like they had some runway training. He glanced at the center table. They barely noticed the new arrivals. "Hmm," he murmured. "Everyone else in the restaurant at least turned a head in the direction of the models."

Picking up his cloth napkin to dab his lips, he continued. "We, of course, have capitalized on this Australian and American discord. The main computer building in Pine Gap is one of the world's largest. At least 5,600 square meters and growing. The many Radome buildings, which look like cracked eggshells, contain the satellite dishes that capture the satellite information and send the lot to their main dissemination and assembly room. From there, bits of information are directed to other departments."

Reef of Gold

He paused to look around the room before continuing the lecture.

"Special information gathering satellites overlook China, Russia, and all of Asia, intercepting military traffic as well as microwave transmissions and eavesdropping on every conversation. The Pine Gap computers are programmed to look for certain key words, tendencies, etc. to find out who is calling whom and what is being said. The computers also pick up naval ship communications. All of this makes it very hard for our Chinese client to do business in all of Southeast Asia. So, with our client's permission and encouragement, we have infiltrated the Pine Gap satellite base and now receive direct satellite information on a regular basis. As a bonus, we also read what the Russians are up to as well."

"Two for the price of one," said Yang Lee, warming up to the intrigue. He liked the cat and mouse game with the Americans. It made him feel superior. He also knew better than to ask too many questions. He had been warned by the Triad council several times not to interrupt.

"Yes, that is so," said Tie, "two for the price of one. Very good." He signaled for the waiter again and asked for a small serving of crumpets to go with his pot of imported English tea. When the waiter had left, Tie turned back to face Lee who remained motionless the whole time. He gestured towards the English teapot with a quick pointing of his hand.

"Only the exceptional teas of the world reach the English royalty and the wealthy. My desire for the very best tea is a left over habit from spending too much time in Hong Kong," he winked. "The English habit of drinking tea with crumpets imposed on me by their government bureaucrats is hard to shake." He smiled broadly this time. "Tea became my cover years ago when I started to import the finest of the fine tea and sell it to the British at a monstrous price and therefore got me into places that wouldn't have otherwise been made available to me. His face suddenly changed. "In their eyes,"

Gary Dale

he continued, "I had become one of them, if only on a business basis, which was all they would allow anyway." There had been no bitterness in his voice, only his face showed any contempt.

The waiter returned with a fresh pot of tea water and toast, quickly informing Tie that crumpets were not available. As if purposely adding color to the tray, lemons, sugar and a crème server surrounded the serving tray. The waiter carefully poured hot water through the porcelain tea strainer. Satisfied, he turned and left the table, ignoring the enforcer, Yang Lee.

Sipping and blowing on the tea occasionally, Tie pressed on. He talked over the top of the teacup again, disguising his conversation. "Now, for the computer part of this discussion. This information does affect you and how you will continue to handle the couriered information to Singapore. Our client has indicated to us an urgent need to receive the satellite information much faster. Apparently there are some hot spots in the world that might foster some America military action. The American satellites in the Southern Hemisphere transmit encrypted telemetric information from their embassies and military ships to their Pine Gap satellite base, where the Americans re-encrypt it for different uses, sending the information back up in space to bounce from one satellite to another and finally to their homeland where the information is redistributed. Are you with me so far, Yang Lee? I don't want to have to repeat anything."

The enforcer nodded and leaned forward once again to make sure he heard everything. He was really paying attention now.

Tie placed the delicate teacup on the saucer with a clank as if to emphasize his point. He picked up his cloth napkin, dabbed his lips and again talked through the napkin.

"This encrypted information has been a stumbling block for our client to decipher," he continued. "It didn't help when the Americans used a one-time pad. Numbers are easily coded in Binary or Gray codes because it is a simple matter to change them, making it nearly

Reef of Gold

impossible to decode the telemetry in such a short time without special computers. We had to find a way around the time obstacle."

He put the napkin down and sipped his tea. Satisfied with the taste of the warm liquid, he drank sparingly.

"Now, Yang Lee," he lectured over the top of the tea cup, "I know this satellite language is probably way beyond what you ever wanted to know, but in reality, there is a simplistic answer to a very complex set of circumstances." He carefully placed the teacup on the saucer.

Carefully cutting his toast into eight small squares, he picked a square and slowly chewed. The enforcer stared at him in confusion. "Chewing food while trying to talk makes a person mumble," said Tie, slowly, not worrying about enunciating each word carefully. "Therefore it becomes difficult for someone to read my lips. I do take security precautions do I not," he said, looking directly at Lee. Without waiting for an answer, he looked down at his plate and picked up another small piece of toast.

Chewing, he said, "You have a lot of responsibility on your shoulders, Yang Lee, in receiving and couriering the stolen satellite information. Do not disappoint us."

While the enforcer remained stoic, his mind was racing. They hadn't finished their conversation, he thought. What had happened? Tie didn't share with him how the information got to his computers. He didn't know what to think.

Tie leaned forward to get closer to Lee, letting his necktie drag across the table and almost into his warm tea. He quickly caught himself before disaster occurred. Chi Son Tie was a meticulous dresser. He whispered this time to Yang Lee for emphasis, barely moving his lips while attempting to take a bite of toast. "As head of security, you must make sure nothing interferes with any computer disks containing satellite information. I will not tolerate any excuses. "You must courier the computer disks faster when we require immediate delivery. No delays. Courier immediately to the

Gary Dale

Singapore office and I mean immediately. He stared at Yang Lee. Am I understood?"

The enforcer nodded. He was confident of the newly installed computer system. He had been assured that it would handle electronic traffic at all hours and would let him know if the signal was lost, garbled or broken in transmission. But how and in what form did he receive the satellite information? He could only guess and he wasn't very good at that. He had a blank look on his face.

Yang Lee slowly shook his head. Even this little bit of espionage information almost overwhelmed him. He felt the tightness in his neck and shoulder muscles building as a result of the increased responsibility being placed upon him. His mouth felt dry.

"I also want to congratulate you for your foresight in dissolving the Sterling Mines security issue of many months ago," said Tie. "The Triad council believes your new security methods have eliminated the employee theft problems and outside interference we had in the past. It was very smart of you."

"Thank you. You are most kind," said Lee, quietly.

Chi Son Tie looked curiously at the young enforcer for a moment and then ignoring him, looked out the window. His mind drifted, not even noticing the yacht basin in front of him. Beneath that tough exterior, he thought, Yang Lee is a smart man, street smart if nothing else, and yet he still makes small blunders. I must remind him again of this fault.

The Triad administrator turned his head back to the center of the room to observe the diners and then back to the windows as if looking at the tied up three-meter sailboats mirrored in the plate class window. He saw nothing; he was merely refocusing and thinking. 'It's too bad,' he thought, 'that Lee is not aware that our espionage operation might suddenly blow up in our faces. The embedded agents in the bowels of the American secret Pine Gap satellite base were facing increasing danger on a daily basis. If it weren't for that American agent, Ric Templeton, snooping around, things would be

84

Reef of Gold

much safer.' Tie cleared his throat and took a sip of tea. 'On second thought, it couldn't be him. He is supposed to have drowned in the straits of Singapore. His ghost, however, lives on. I must solve that problem. It has become a huge distraction.' Tie looked blankly around again at the patrons, watching for things out of the ordinary. He returned to his thoughts of the current situation.

Yet, there was nothing Chi Son Tie could do about it at the moment, nor could his embedded agents, he realized. He sighed involuntarily, letting himself relax and erase the sudden fierceness from his face.

He refocused. The calculated risk was always going to be at Pine Gap and there were going to be tense moments. His agents would just have to be extremely careful and prepare for the worst. A rare smile broke out onto his face when he recalled the past events causing Yang Lee to lean forward for a moment as if expecting Tie to say something; and when he didn't, Lee sat back in his chair. Tie continued to be lost in his thoughts as he revisited his memory.

The planning and execution had been going on for several years to make the current espionage effort so different and so simple that it was ludicrous. "Silly Americans," he mused. "Always looking at the obvious for intruders and always looking up instead of down. Their security people are totally unaware of the compromise of their satellite information." Yang Lee sat passively.

Tie barely noted the departure of several groups of businessmen but did cast an eye on the center table occupants. The older man, dressed in a pinstriped business suit, excused himself from the table. He immediately left the room.

Tie sipped his tea and revisited his thoughts. He congratulated himself once again for the successful espionage effort going on in Pine Gap. He had taken over the spy operation of many years when he solved the one-time pad problem. While it was still his area of responsibility, he made time to plan another espionage effort.

85

Gary Dale

Why not? His closest advisors knew he was restless and needed new projects to keep him happy where the Triad could not. He smiled.

He had learned a great deal from the Pine Gap operation and was ready to apply the learned knowledge to a new adventure. He had decided that two of his three newly arrived agents from the North Korean ship would concentrate on stealing the engineering plans for the 5,000 mph supersonic combustion scramjet engine. The technology was under development by the University of Queensland research department in the South Australian state capital of Adelaide. The agents were aerospace engineers and would understand the terminology and what to look for when embedded in the University research program. This espionage act would be an on-going project.

Tie smiled. What a coup that would be for China to have near final engineering plans for the scramjet engine in hand first before the Americans, especially since Japan was working with the Australians on the research. The duties of the third agent, he reasoned, would be in communications using laser technology. This man was incredibly smart. He had already made plans for the embedding of this agent. The thought excited Tie. Success again, he thought. He would keep his cover as an extremely well paid Triad administrator and use that position to establish the new spy operations for his country as soon as possible. It was the challenge that kept him going. The bulging Swiss bank numbered accounts didn't hurt either.

Tie closed his eyes and slowly shook his head from side to side at the unbelievable success of the Alice Springs spy network. It was all so very simple, he thought. The critical intelligence from American embassies; military bases; ships at sea and the numerous intelligence-gathering agencies traveled down routine bandwidths from the satellites. When his espionage agent would purposely scramble one of the many regular channels within a broadband width, computers automatically bounced the frequently fouled up channels of satellite information to a clear maintenance channel

Reef of Gold

until repairs were made. Sunspots, bad weather, other satellites often interfered with the signals. Unknown to the Americans, the agent would download information from the maintenance channels, thus temporarily by-passing the routine of others to de-encrypt and reassemble downloaded information from the regular channels. The agent had just enough time to de-encrypt and reassemble. The Americans and Australians, rarely if ever, monitored a maintenance channel for outside intrusion. Only the regular communication channels were monitored 24-7 by the Americans. The plan was perfect, but for some reason the Americans suspect something.

CHAPTER 11

STERLING MINES........SINGAPORE OFFICE

The elevator moved very slowly. By the time the snail-paced lift reached its destination, Brad had concluded that this was one special elevator, with its video camera and specially built steel doors. Most elevators shake and rattle a bit when moving but not this one. Only humming here.

An Aussie staff member had cornered him with an urgent message. 'Go back to your desk and put on your security badge." The yellow sticker left on his desk didn't give him much information. Someone from the fourth floor had summoned him. It was just a name, time, destination, all underlined from a red marking pen marked URGENT and nothing else. He wondered what he had done wrong. His desk area was being rotated almost weekly as those on holiday would come back and bounce him from his current base of operations. Maybe he had dropped the ball along the way and didn't know it, he thought. Unfortunately, Miles wasn't around to ask.

When the heavy elevator doors slid open, the reception committee was one very large muscular Asian fellow, with a slight bulge under his left armpit and a stoic expression chiseled on his disease scarred face. He stood in front of Brad, literally blocking his way for a moment. The security guard finally backed up and let him step out of the elevator. The guard motioned for him to raise his hands while

88

Reef of Gold

he was quickly and professionally patted down. The guard was not only scary but his breath smelled of old shoe leather. Straightening up, the burly guard tugged at Brad's security badge before directing him to a receptionist around the corner.

She was not just an ordinary receptionist but also a young and very beautiful Asian woman in a well-fitted silk dress standing beside her ornate office desk. As Brad approached, she moved behind her heavy wooden desk using it as a barrier. Brad wasn't looking at her as much as he was staring at her desk. The teak wood desk, he concluded was probably made from wood harvested from Southern China or the Northern Vietnam jungles. Beautiful, he thought.

Brad finally raised his eyes and focused on the secretary. Her startling dark eyes glanced at Brad's security badge and then scanned him from top to bottom like a hospital x-ray machine. He thought he saw a flicker of interest in her eyes. After a few moments of hesitation, Miss Silk Dress gestured for him to follow her. The guard was literally in his hip pocket as they walked over to a small table surrounded by four chairs. A small instrument adorned the sterile table. The guard pushed Brad into a chair, grabbed his left hand, separated the fingers, and stuck the middle finger into an opening. Instantly an infrared light came at unusual angles to scan the finger. The light was partially absorbed by the blood in his finger allowing a camera to capture a 3-D finger vein profile for future authentication. The latest and most secure form of identification was over with in seconds. During the scan, Brad felt like a little of his soul was drained from him without his permission. He was now profiled whether he liked it or not. Why, he did not know.

Miss Silk Dress motioned for him to follow her once again. Still perspiring from the stress of being on the fourth floor, Brad decided that it was a relief from the guard's intimidation to just follow her curves. Once through the tall, double Jarrah wood doors, he suddenly slowed and gazed around the beautifully decorated foyer.

"Wait here," she said, in a commanding voice.

Gary Dale

"Be glad to wait," he responded, a little startled. "Take your time. This collection is terrific." The guard still remained in his hip pocket like a lead paperweight. Brad would have to drag him along just to see the stunning works of art in this huge room.

What limited knowledge Brad had of oriental art came from a couple of well taught college courses many years ago and was reinforced through a traveling art exhibition from the Chicago Art Museum. The office foyer did not hide the security showcases, full of delicate vases. Not the type of vases you'd see in the lobby of an American insurance company but only in an extraordinary global corporation. The ornate vases seemed to be of the Ming Dynasty era if he remembered correctly. In spite of the visible heavy electronic security surrounding each work of art, he was mesmerized by the display cases as he casually walked around. He wondered if the guard was even interested.

Hoping he had more waiting time, Brad looked even closer at the stunning display near the back of the room. Could some of these vases with the eggshell porcelain and distinctive Imperial Blue coloring be of the Emperor Yung Lo reign during the Ming Dynasty? he asked himself. He turned around for another look at the Ming Dynasty vases near the door and then back again. These ornate vases in front of him looked to be different from the rest. Not quite as florid. He turned and walked back to the Ming Dynasty vases from different time periods. On closer inspection of the detailing, he realized that these stunning vases had pencil thin lines carved into the white strains of clay with a sharp instrument. Embellishing the line drawings with three colors, enamels filled and flowed in a beautiful violet blue, a turquoise green color and finally a distinctive yellow color. Then the pictures had been carefully painted in colored enamels onto the white glaze outlined by the thin lines. The vase would be fired in a kiln at relatively low heat. He looked at a third vase and noticed that gilding had been applied with a brush. The fourth vase had gilding in leaf form to make the vase even more distinctive. The colors were as beautiful today as they were eons ago. Then he remembered that all vases had a final kiln firing, making the vase impervious to destructive elements of sea and land. He looked back at the other vases for the visual differences. The collection of Chinese history was almost overwhelming, he mused.

One vase was centered in the room. Brad had missed seeing it the first time because he had darted randomly from one pillar to another. He stood quietly for a moment, just staring at the vase. Other than the fantastic beauty, he wasn't sure why he was drawn to this particular vase. It seemed to tug at him, almost like a karma trance. What was it about this particular vase that took his breath away? Had he seen this vase somewhere before? He was smiling inwardly, trying to answer his own question when a man of diminutive features slid quietly into the room along with Miss Silk Dress.

"Ah, Mr. Templeton, I am President Wong's assistant, Au Chen. Welcome to the fourth floor. The vases are of the Ming Dynasty."

"Ming Dynasty vases are very beautiful," Brad acknowledged with a wave of his hand illustrating the entire collection. His gesture hopefully would give the impression that, in reality, he knew something about the collection. He didn't want to make a bad impression the very first meeting.

"Thank you for your observation. Come this way please." She nodded to the guard to leave them. The lead weight was gone from Brad's back pocket.

Brad reluctantly followed her, leaving behind the rare vases he had never expected to see in his lifetime. He wasn't stressed now about why he was on the fourth floor.

Au Chen lead him into a large conference room, decorated professionally, with expensive matching couches, coffee tables, lamps and ash trays that gave only a hint of cigarette use. He realized that the room was not only a conference room with a well-attended library but a place of geography. The room was loaded with maps and world globes. This was his kind of room.

Gary Dale

Before Au Chen could get started with the meeting, a faint beeper signal went off and he excused himself. Two minutes later, Au Chen came rushing back into the room looking a little pale. He cleared his throat and said "There has been a change in plans and Mr. Lee has a special assignment for you. As an employee of Sterling Mining Company, you are going to be required to travel as a representative of the company. We have a Singapore office and we want you to ...."

"Excuse me," said Brad, interrupting Mr. Chen, "I don't mean to be rude but I have been with the company for only a few weeks and hardly know what is going on let alone know any details about Sterling Mining. I'm supposed to be filling in for those staff members on holiday. How can I represent the company with so little knowledge?"

"Mr. Templeton," Au Chen said emphatically, "things change pretty fast in this company. We feel the best way to have someone learn about the company is just to *"Fei bu gu shen."* That is the Chinese interpretation for *just jump into the fire.* Something has come up; and with so many employees on holiday; we need someone immediately to act as a courier to our office in Singapore. It is your duty to go. Now, will you pay attention please? Here is what you are going to do. First..."

Brad arrived in Singapore later that afternoon. He had flashed his Sterling Mining credentials as instructed, easing through an almost non-existent Customs and security screening. He did not have to go through the public screening but through a special passage way. He was more than a little surprised at the no-look-no-delay custom inspection. He stopped at an airport kiosk for a bottle of water and a snack. The line was long but Brad needed the energy boost. As he exited the airport terminal, the humidity pulled at his lungs. The cotton shirt immediately stuck to his body making his appearance looking less than corporate. Brad felt like the disheveled servant that he was. His only immediate remedy was to signal for a taxi, hopefully

92

Reef of Gold

with air conditioning. A new but slightly dented taxi rolled to a stop in front of him. The driver cracked open the back door. The rush of cool air beckoned an entrance and once inside, Brad felt better with each passing minute. The taxi ride was pleasant enough despite the heavy rush hour traffic.

His thoughts drifted to his instructions from Mr. Chen. "Your stay in Singapore will be short," he had said. "No delays. Make sure you release the briefcase to Mr. Chang or one of his appointed staff members. He is an investor in our company and runs the Singapore office for Sterling Mining. I must remind you again, Mr. Templeton, no one else is to take possession of this briefcase under any circumstances. You must be prompt for your meeting. There will be instructions for you at the hotel front desk when you arrive. In case you are wondering why such security, it is because of competition. We are in different kinds of business other than mining. Competitors will do anything to take advantage of our businesses."

One question Brad had insisted in asking Mr. Chen "Why me? In reality, you could have asked any employee to go to Singapore."

"Ah, Mr. Templeton," he had said with some frustration, "you are new with the company and available, so as a courier for us, no competitor will recognize you for a while. Eventually, our competitors will be aware of you and then we will send someone else. You leave immediately. Enjoy your stay in Singapore."

The air-conditioned taxi approached the Goodwood Park Hotel. He had asked Mr. Chen if he could stay at the famous colonial hotel and after some discussion, Mr. Chen reluctantly agreed even though he had another place in mind.

The doorman grabbed Brad's luggage and together they marched directly to the registration desk. "Mr. Templeton checking in," the doorman announced, having glanced down at Brad's luggage nametags. He knew his business.

"Ah, Mr. Templeton," the registration clerk acknowledged, "Welcome. Sign here please. We were expecting you."

Gary Dale

Brad's signature honored their guest register.

"Your electronic room key and room number are here in the envelope," he said directly. "Third floor. Take the West elevators over by the kiosk. Please put all your hotel expenses on your room number. Your company pays everything during your stay. Oh, and you have two messages," handing him a hotel envelope. "Enjoy your stay here in Singapore."

Brad felt like a new man after a cool shower and a change into a new tropical white polo shirt, which fortunately was all cotton, as were his lightly colored tan slacks. Luckily, the hotel kiosk had his size. He didn't have the proper clothes. Perth, Australia was not known to have heavy humidity. His watch told him that he still had time before visiting the Singapore office to go down to the lobby bar for a refreshing drink and read the messages. According to the bellman, the Sterling Mining office was located only a few miles away from him.

The hotel veranda, with its stunning display of numerous varieties of orchids among the white rattan chairs, enjoyed a cooling breeze circulating the lobby noise. The veranda offered Brad a relatively quiet place to read his messages. His briefcase with the office documents occupied the nearest chair in plain sight. He still had not clicked on the handcuffs from the briefcase. He did not want to attract any more attention than necessary. The briefcase should be no more than two feet away from him at all times as requested by the home office in Perth. Follow procedures to the letter, Au Chen had said. So, Brad pulled up a chair next to him and set the briefcase on it, two feet away.

An Asian waiter, dressed in all white cotton uniform took his order: bottled water with a lime twist. Brad lit a Dutch cigar, one of several different cigars he had purchased from the hotel kiosk, and read the first message. It was drafted as a routine message from the Perth office but had a personal message at the bottom: 'Keep in touch and be careful, signed Megan.'

Reef of Gold

Now that was interesting, he thought. He had seen her in passing many times around the office and spoke with her only at office meetings. Was this a personal touch from Megan or was it just wishful thinking on his part, he wondered? 'And be careful of what?' he asked himself in between puffs of his cigar. That part of the message concerned him.

The next message was about Brad's meeting instructions with Mr. Chang, including how to get to a new destination and a new appointment time. Staring at the message, Brad knew he would have to ask for directions from some hotel employee even though a taxi driver would probably know how to get there. But for safety's sake, he wanted to know in advance and trace his route on his city map. It was a fetish of his to use a map wherever he traveled in order to know the city on more intimate terms, for his own protection. A business trip to Atlanta, Georgia, several years ago had convinced him of caution.

"Mr. Templeton?" asked a voice in a clipped British accent.

Startled, Brad looked up and turned to face what appeared to be a hotel staff member. He squinted at the name badge, trying to pronounce the Asian name.

"Just call me Max," the staff member said, noticing his dilemma.

"Yes, Max?"

"I have a package for you. It's marked urgent."

"A package?" Brad inquired, wondering who would send him a package. "I just got here. Are you sure you have the right person? My name is Brad Templeton but I just arrived at the hotel not over an hour ago," he said, looking at his watch.

"You are in room 310 is that not correct?" the British accent asked.

Gesturing with his hand to hold on a second, Brad stood up to reach in his pocket for his room key and then remembered that the hotel used electronic cards instead of keys. He sat down again and

95

Gary Dale

looked at the blue ink markings on both arms. There, he had written the address of the hotel on one arm and his room number on the other. Max looked at him curiously.

"So I'm forgetful," Brad muttered. It was one of his idiosyncrasies.

"Room 310 is correct," he acknowledged finally.

"And you have arrived from Perth, Australia."

"Yes, just a few minutes ago."

"Then, this package is for you. It was hand delivered by a very pretty lady. Apparently you were delayed from the airport so she left the package with me. I thank you for your late arrival." Max winked.

"Max, you old dog you," said Brad, his eyes twinkling. "Hand delivered, you say, and by a pretty lady. Wonder who would do that?"

"I take it that you don't know anyone here in Singapore let alone a beautiful woman?" questioned Max. "Too bad."

"I think I know who sent it," he said smiling. "It was probably a co-worker named Miles from the office playing a trick on me. He got me this time. Too bad I missed seeing the delivery person. Miles will be disappointed. He would want a full report."

Thanking Max and tipping him for the delivery, Brad looked at the pocket-sized package and turned it over looking for a return address. There was none. "That is strange," he thought. "No company office label, either."

He relit the cigar, which had uncharacteristically gone out, sipped his bottled water, before ripping open the package. A country music CD slid out onto the table. It was *The Best of Toby Keith,* which included his favorite song. Why a CD? Why the hand delivery? And why here?' he wondered. Brad shook the packing envelope for a note or a letter of some kind. It appeared empty until a tiny bit of blue paper floated out with the bubble plastic protection. He quickly

96

Reef of Gold

glanced at it and then again. The message didn't make sense. It was a warning of some kind about a taxi driver and a tattoo.

"Excuse me, sir. Can I get you anything more from the bar? From the kitchen?"

Brad looked up. It was the friendly and attentive waiter, Max. Brad felt comfortable enough with the waiter to banter some more.

"No, nothing from the bar or kitchen," he said. "Thanks for checking with me Max. Here, look at this," holding up the music CD. "This was what was inside the package."

"Well, well. Somebody either knows you well or made a mistake."

"I didn't think anyone knew of my arrival in Singapore, Max. Second time in this country and already unexplained things happen."

Max laughed. "You were here in Singapore before?" he questioned. "I take it you didn't allow enough time to meet any beautiful Asian women while you were here or at least thought you didn't? Maybe it's bad Karma or then again, maybe…"

Flashing a quick smile, Brad interrupted. "No offense but tell me, where did you get the name 'Max'? Your name tag suggests something else."

Max shrugged his shoulders. "My British mates gave me the name and it just stuck. My real Asian name is rather complicated and not very memorable." Max hesitated and then continued. "My father was British and in the Foreign Service. My mother is Malaysian/Chinese heritage and because of my father's career with the Foreign Service, we moved around a great deal. I was educated in England and migrated back here. Obviously I missed the wonderful high humidity and torrential rains of Malaysia."

Brad laughed. "And there is a bridge for sale down the street." Max looked at him a little on the incredulous side. "A bridge for sale?" he questioned.

"Sorry about that Max. Just American slang that means you were

Gary Dale

kidding me about liking the high humidity and monsoon rains. Sometimes my mouth gets going too fast with flip remarks."

"Actually," said Max, shrugging. "I do like the change in seasons, from the wet season to the dry season. In England, the weather always seemed to be cloudy, drizzling, or foggy. And in the winter, a person has to add the bone chilling damp cold to the mix. So what's to miss there? I sure don't miss it."

Brad glanced at his watch again for the umpteenth time and finally realized he had to break away. He would have preferred to stay and talk to him, but he had to deliver the briefcase on time.

"Well, Max, hate to break up this gathering but I have a meeting to go to soon. Will you have someone prepare my bill please? And, thanks for the conversation. I'm going up to the room and relax.

Brad dropped his shoes on the carpet and undressed. He hung his meeting clothes to dry out if they could. Stretching out on the cool sheets, he listened to the Toby Keith CD, letting his anxiety drain from his brain. It was the fifth song that awoke him from his dreamtime. It wasn't Toby Keith singing a hot country western song. It was his brother Ric speaking directly to him. Yes, he was alive. He still had lots of pain from the knife cuts he received during an ambush by Triad hit men and a subsequent dip in the Singapore Straits, but that wasn't going to stop him from accomplishing his mission. He was back on the job. There was something Brad could do for him. A mole had penetrated his organization and he had to find out who it was that had betrayed his entire group. "Brad, trust no one and don't tell a single person that I am alive. Listen carefully to any conversation you have with anyone, with the knowledge that a mole exists. I will have someone deliver an encrypted cell phone to you sometime soon so I can talk to you. Don't worry about me. I'm fine. Watch yourself buddy. Like it or not, you are now involved with some nasty people. I'll try to protect you. Get out of Singapore as fast as you can and back to Australia. It will be safer for you. Love you, Bro. Oh, one last thing. Did you like the beautiful messenger? She is

Reef of Gold

something else. Oh yes, she is a nurse. That should bring back some memories. Be sure to break up the CD and drop it into a wastebasket by the hotel kiosk. See ya, Bro."

Brad sat on the bed, stunned. He couldn't move at first until the realization finally set in that his brother was alive. "I can finally sleep again," he thought.

He looked around his hotel room before focusing on his clothes. The meeting, he reminded himself. I have got to make that meeting. He took a deep breath. "I can't believe it. Ric is alive." He characteristically slapped his thigh. "I knew it. I just knew it," he shouted. He changed back into his clothes, broke up the CD into pieces, grabbed the briefcase and dashed downstairs to the bar.

Glancing at his watch again told him it was more than soon. He unfolded his city map he had purchased from the hotel kiosk, smoothing out the creases on the table. The time factor was finally registering in his mush for brains, he berated himself. He had to hope the taxi driver would drive fast to this new location if he could find it.

Standing up, he put a newly purchased Singapore emergency cell phone in the left pocket of the light yellow jacket that he wore for the expected evening rain. The rain shower was sure to come, as regular as midnight. He had programmed the hotel phone number and a hospital number just in case he got stranded. A nagging but vague question kept creeping forward in his brain but he just couldn't come up with the thought.

"Your bar receipt, Mr. Templeton."

Lost deep in his thoughts, Brad literally jumped at the sound of the familiar voice.

"Any trouble, Mr. Templeton? Can the hotel be of any service?"

"No, it's nothing really. I was just thinking. By the way, where do I sign the bill?"

"I checked with the bartender and he said you don't have to sign.

Gary Dale

It will go right on your hotel bill. He knows you by sight now. This is just a confirmation receipt."

"Thanks, Max. Say, I could use your help with some directions. Apparently, I have a new meeting place. The city map doesn't show the location of this unfamiliar address. At least I can't find it. I would like you to trace my route on this city map."

"Certainly sir, I'll do my best. It shouldn't take but a moment. I'll get a marking pen."

After a few dismal attempts at drawing lines, marking points of interest, and distance, they finally had a reasonable map showing the general location of the meeting place, in the old wharf area of the Singapore docks. They both hoped the taxi driver would know the dock area well enough to find the meeting place. He thanked Max again and agreed to have a drink with him when he returned if he was still around.

"I'll walk with you to the taxi stand," said Max.

Brad grabbed his briefcase, snapped the handcuffs on his left wrist as instructed by the home office and walked quickly to the hotel taxi stand. The doorman gave a shrill whistle for the next taxi in line. Suddenly a black taxi bolted from out of nowhere, cutting in front of the taxi line and screeching to a halt amid curses from other taxi drivers waiting in line. Brad and Max exchanged glances. The driver cheated just to get the fare.

Brad slid cautiously into the backseat and handed the driver the handwritten note from the office containing the address change.

He gave a sigh of relief as the taxi route was more or less on the same direct line on the hand-traced map although the driver made some adjustments due to traffic. The taxi driver kept up a decent speed until he neared the harbor area. At that point, Brad's map meant nothing, as there were no address markings on any of the old storage buildings, just what looked like Chinese symbols painted on a building corner. In fact, there were no other markings of any kind. He had no clue to his final destination.

Reef of Gold

It was dark now, as it always is after 7:00pm when near the equator. There were no lingering sunsets. The streets seemed deserted and the time for Brad's appointment was rapidly approaching. "It wouldn't be good for me," he thought, "to keep Mr. Chang waiting or worrying if a delivery was going to be made at all." He personally liked being punctual. It always made a good impression.

The taxi kept going through seemingly endless intersections before the driver made a right turn off a main street and drove slowly for several more minutes. The taxi finally stopped for a moment at a deserted street corner, its motor remained running, quietly belching exhaust fumes. The driver said nothing. With the subdued harbor lights barely casting their beams in the cab's direction, Brad could see the driver's eyes looking for something. Brad was getting nervous.

"Why aren't we going?" he demanded.

The driver sat perfectly still. The only movements were the whites of his eyes, searching back and forth.

Brad sat back in the seat. This situation had a distinct odor of not being right, he thought. Instinctively, he put his hand on the door handle, ready to bolt from the taxi. It was locked. Little driblets of sweat were beginning to form on Brad's upper lips and behind his ears. His breathing became labored. It was then that Brad noticed the taxi headlights were turned off. The taxi had become another dark object next to an old building. Silently, Brad muttered a cuss word. More silence. Just great, he thought, a perfect setup for a robbery if there ever was one, leaving no survivors. He could feel the squeeze of his buttocks coming on.

Suddenly the driver slipped into first gear and released the clutch, driving slowly with no headlights and keeping in the shadows. The taxi seemed to have eyes of its own as it crept forward. Since the steady light rain had briefly slowed down to a mist, Brad rolled down his stubborn window as far as he could for some needed fresh air. He breathed in deeply several times, trying to regain his composure. He suddenly realized he could hear what sounded like wooden planks

Gary Dale

of the dock creak underneath the tires. It was so dark now that as the taxi angled away from the lighted cargo ships, it looked like they were traveling into a deep cave.

The driver didn't touch his brakes but coasted almost to a stop before pulling his hand- brake; avoiding any flash of taillights. Suddenly, out of nowhere, several men, dressed in dark clothes, padded silently past the taxi to push the vehicle through a large garage door and into a dark building. The door immediately closed behind the taxi and then silence.

"Someone is going to a lot of trouble to be discreet," thought Brad. By this time, he was drenched with sweat and reeked from the musty smell of fear of impending trouble. Unconsciously, he checked the security of the handcuffs. They were tight on his left wrist. He sat still, barely breathing. There wasn't a thing he could do but sit tight.

A few dim lights suddenly came on, casting surreal shadows on the walls and ceiling. Releasing the electric door lock, the taxi driver snarled and gestured with his right hand for Brad to get out of the taxi. When he got half way out of the taxi, a sudden awareness struck him. The muted light had cast a beacon of light showing the driver's right hand with a tattoo with an arrow pointing to the little finger.

Brad's breathing slowed and he silently cursed himself. He had been in too big of a hurry at the hotel to notice the taxi driver and had disregarded the warning of the two-line blue note. He closed the taxi door quietly and slowly turned around to observe the inside of a large parking garage. There were many expensive cars and oversized limos parked in a helter skelter manner. No parking garage attendant worth his salt would admit to creating this chaos, he speculated. As his eyes adjusted to the darkness, he noticed there were more exit doors than he had realized and all the windows of the old building were painted black to keep the garage lights from escaping.

Finally, a bulky Asian wearing all black clothing, moved from the shadows, walked over to Brad and quickly frisked him. He found

Reef of Gold

the urban cell phone in the rain jacket pocket and kept it. He frisked Brad again, a little rougher this time. The Asian muscle forcibly grabbed him by the arm, lifting his feet nearly off the ground to get his attention and said in broken English to come with him to the waiting room. "Someone will meet you and will take responsibility for the briefcase and its contents. Keep your eyes riveted to the floor. You are to say nothing and you will leave the room immediately with your guard. Is that understood?"

Brad nodded and dutifully followed like a puppy dog about ready to release his sphincter valve on the nearest tire. The muscle bound guard opened a big sliding door with a key and then lead the way, proceeding down several long, dark hallways, twisting and turning before finally approaching a guarded door. "Well, this is it," Brad thought. He took a deep breath and slowly let it out.

CHAPTER 12

TRIAD COUNCIL

Just before sunset, a Bell helicopter landed on top of the Sterling Mines building, mindful of the nest of bristling communication antennas taking up a good portion of rooftop space. The air was cooler, allowing for a stable landing in downtown Perth. The heat of the day had warmed the concrete streets and sidewalks below to nearly unbearable levels. Escaping heat waves would spiral upwards along the sides of steel and concrete buildings creating unstable air. Touching down in a helicopter on top of a tall building during the Australian summer heat often made for interesting landings.

Yang Lee jumped from the four-passenger helicopter, just missing the ankle twisting skid rail. With briefcase in hand, he instinctively ducked under the whirling blades and ran for the top floor stairwell. His minions waited for him and gave him a quick greeting before all disappeared down the stairs. The walk gave him time to reflect.

His superiors had called him to a high level Triad meeting in Singapore. Some of the ruling council apparently had misgivings about his commitment to the Triad. He was surprised at this announcement until he found out who was the accuser. It was the old man, Lin Yuan Swie, his former Triad boss that had caused the dissent among the leadership committee.

The council heads demanded an explanation of the circumstances

104

Reef of Gold

surrounding the supposed death of a particular CIA agent in the Straits of Singapore. With a nervous tightness in his voice, Yang Lee had approached the council and told them briefly about the torture of the captured Asian agent and the information retrieved. The American agent in question was cornered on a ferry, sustaining several deep knife wounds. The agent broke away bleeding heavily. He threw himself overboard to escape.

There was an instant up-roar from the council. Yang Lee could sense the venom spewing from the members. Failure in espionage was not an option. After much heated discussion, the chairman motioned for quiet. In response to a hidden signal from the chairman, security muscle moved next to Yang Lee.

Beads of sweat ran like driblets down the back of Lee's neck. He could hear a little rattling sound coming from the mouth of one of the guards. It was the sound of the ancient tongue clicking, common among those who dispensed death.

Yang Lee stepped forward several feet to look the chairman directly into his flashing eyes. He spoke quickly, knowing his life depended on his answer. "The tiger sharks in the Singapore Straits would have made short work of him," he said confidently.

The chairman slowly rose from his padded leather chair launching into verbal condemnations of Lee's failure with only a few angry showers of spittle hitting Yang Lee directly. "There have been reports of the CIA agent in your territory that did not die as we ordered. You had assured Lin Yuan Swie that the CIA agent had died in the Singapore Straits, and yet we have heard reports from our agents that he is alive. What do you have to say?"

Instead of saying anything, he stretched out his arms and opened his palms as he offered: "No excuses. I am the enforcer and I promise you, and the council, that I will double my efforts to see that he will not live another day."

The council considered his reply. Their conversation was brief but heated. Finally, the head of the council spoke up. "We will take

Gary Dale

care of this little problem for you, Yang Lee. Your current assignment is too important to let you run off on your own and try to find this elusive CIA agent."

Yang Lee remained silent but committed to redeeming himself. His eyes did not mask his embarrassment from the council.

"Now tell us about the operation in Perth, Australia," the council head asked, changing the subject as he sat down again. Yang Lee dared to breathe again.

"There have been no security breaches within Sterling Mining computer programming for a long while," he replied, breathing normally again. "However, I asked for and convinced our Singapore computer experts to come in and double check the security firewalls." He paused to gather his thoughts. "As a precaution, I have also instituted a top-level security system within our corporate headquarters for employees. We have a file of identity prints on everyone internally. We also have the latest 3-D finger vein profile for even non-employees who come to see us on the fourth floor and for those who are supposed to be near our sensitive areas like our computer and encryption departments. This allows us a few moments to do a database background check on any and all visitors."

"Is that everything?" asked the council head.

"We have been very careful about not calling attention to ourselves. As you are aware, we are receiving encrypted and de-encrypted messages quite often now. These messages are couriered to our Singapore office several times a week, sometimes even several times a day and then carried to you." A number of the leadership council nodded their heads several times in agreement.

Yang Lee paused and thought carefully about what he was to say next. He wanted to ask more about the internal espionage effort and how it all worked but he knew better than to ask. "There is one other thing," he said. "Security has been recently heightened in Australia as a whole because of a strange explosion in the middle of the outback.

Reef of Gold

There has been nothing in the newspapers about it in any great detail. Apparently it was a surprise even to the Aussie security force."

The chairman stood stoically for a few moments. Then he glanced quickly at the other council members before replying. He chose his words carefully. "There was an explosion as you said. After the Saran gas attacks in Tokyo subways years ago, international pressure forced the terrorists to go into hiding. The cell had been dormant for many years only to surface once again. Apparently, a violent and dangerous rogue element of one of Japanese criminal gangs has taken things into their own hands. This, of course, can dangerously affect our own operations in Australia, and we made it very clear to our Japanese friends that this rogue element must be permanently stopped. These gang members apparently continued to make Saran gas in their small manufacturing plant in the middle of the Australian outback, thinking that no one would know what they were doing. Of course, they were correct. The outback is so vast and empty, that discovery was remote. In an effort to speed up the making of Saran gas for the next attack, they got careless and accidentally blew apart their manufacturing plant. The explosion concerned us greatly as it called attention to the outback in general. We do not need that kind of scrutiny from the Australian authorities."

The chairman stared at him. "Do not cause us any worries, Yang Lee. Our espionage effort is yielding rich results for the Chinese Government for which they pay us very well. Do not fail the Triad. You may go now."

Still upset as he reviewed the earlier meeting, Yang Lee paced back and forth in the 4th floor hallway before he bolted into his office and strode to the windows overlooking downtown Perth. He felt a wave of relief surge through him. He had momentarily passed a test of confidence in front of the council with the exception of the embarrassing mistake with the spy. He had lost face in front of the council because of this despicable CIA agent. This elusive agent

Gary Dale

would continually be a thorn in the side of the Triad hierarchy unless he was found and killed.

He pressed the security button for Au Chen, President Wong's assistant, to come into his office. It was time once again, he thought, to activate the *little eyes* within his former command structure. He would redeem himself with the elimination of this elusive CIA agent. The *little eyes* would track him down and kill him this time.

Yes, indeed, the *little eyes*.

CHAPTER 13

MR. CHANG

There was a faint roar of voices that became increasingly loud as Brad and the squat, well muscled Asian guards stepped through the door. The guards guided him down a flight of wide stairs to a balcony overlooking a huge room. Brad's mouth dropped open. The faint roar became a cacophony of boisterous people in evening gowns and tuxedos appearing to be having fun. Before him was a miniature Las Vegas gambling casino with all the bright lights, the obnoxious sounds of the slots, laughter and shouts of winners and groans from the losers from the craps tables. The cigarette smoke from the patrons gave the scene a surreal look. In a far corner, away from the evening gowns and tight fitting tuxedos, Brad could see a smaller room, cordoned off from others, packed with sweaty Asian men, dressed in common street clothes, smoking heavily, and shouting encouragement to the roll of the dice. The traditional Chinese gambling methods were apparent although Brad hadn't a clue as to what they were betting on.

Another Asian security guard met them at the bottom of the stairs. They moved through the mix of well-dressed gambling patrons before reaching a full-length bar. A Caucasian man of medium height, tanned complexion, and dressed in all his evening finery, confronted Brad and said in a working class British accent, "Welcome courier. I

Gary Dale

can see you are slightly surprised by all the activity. Do you like it?" he asked, nodding towards the casino floor's party atmosphere.

Brad must have looked very bewildered because the British host calmly asked him if he wanted a refreshing drink.

Brad nodded his response.

The British host said something to the bar tender, and Brad's drink appeared in a split second, a glass of soda with a lime twist.

Brad slugged it down quickly, while surveying the room in a stunned silence.

"Nice," he finally said, finding his voice.

"Nice?" the British host questioned, in a slightly irritated voice as if not understanding Brad's answer. "You must be a Yank," he said disdainfully. He stared with cold, hostile eyes.

It caused Brad to think that this is where cultures seem to clash and misunderstandings occur. If they were government officials, this could have lead to war.

"Well, yeah," Brad said. "Now that you mention it, this is really something. I'm still a little overwhelmed by it all." He smiled, rolled his eyes mischievously, and said, "Looks like a cocktail party for the down and out," as his eyes paused on two beautiful women in long and revealing dresses standing at a roulette table. Their pile of chips was substantial in front of them.

The smile on the British man's face was finally one of understanding. "You Yanks and your slang are often confusing to us Brits," he said.

Brad laughed guardedly, breaking the tension even more. "We developed slang on purpose to revolt against your English King and your proper usage of the Kings English. No big deal anymore. We like you English now for the most part."

"Thank you, 'courier' for that bit of history. It answered many of my questions regarding Yanks. Would you like another soda and lime or shall we see Mr. Chang straight away?"

"Mr. Chang, first. I don't want to keep him waiting."

Reef of Gold

"Good thinking, mining courier. He is waiting for you. Come with me, please. I see you have your rain jacket on. It may get a little warm where you are going. When the handcuffs are off, perhaps you will want to remove it."

"No thanks. I feel a little more dressed up with it on."

They walked around the corner of the bar and then ducked behind a fake beachcomber façade, which helped dissipate the noise from the casino patrons.

The British guide softly knocked several times on the painted mural. While they waited patiently, it flashed through Brad's mind that this place looked like a *speakeasy* from the 1920's. A series of hallways and entrance doors just to get in the casino and now an apparent hidden door so cleverly camouflaged that even if one looked carefully for the opening, it still might be missed. It all seemed straight out of a gangster movie.

The British host knocked lightly again on the mural painting of a Tahitian native girl adorning a coconut bikini when a tiny peephole opened for visual inspection. At a nod from his escort, the peephole closed and a thick Burmese hardwood door opened up. The inside door hinges took on the heavy weight smoothly.

"In you go," he said. "We will have a real drink when you come out, a dollop of Blue Sapphire Gin."

As Brad entered, he had a gut feeling that all was not right. He still had no idea of what was happening. What's all of this got to do with Sterling Mines? he wondered. Diversification of business was one thing but mining to gambling? Then again, maybe cash flow has something to do with it, he reasoned. Casinos were known to generate huge amounts of cash.

The guard motioned for Brad to step over to the familiar small box for the 3-D finger vein print. He had expected the sophisticated biometric system security check so this didn't bother him. He had come to realize the extent of office security. The latest technology

111

Gary Dale

had virtually eliminated the scanning of retinas and fingerprinting. Then he was instructed to sit.

The silence was deafening in the small, windowless waiting room. There were no magazines, tabletop books or flowers to view. The word 'barren' came to mind, he mused. A twist of the door handle startled Brad. He quickly stood in anticipation of something happening. Two square looking men with buzz cuts fairly bounced into the room. Brad was professionally frisked again, before he was allowed to walk through a sliding steel door that scraped the floor because of its immense weight. He stepped down into a sunken, sparsely furnished, but nicely decorated spacious room. There were several men in conference when one of them excused himself and walked over to him.

"Sterling Mining courier I presume?" questioned the overweight but well dressed Asian man in his mid fifties. "I am Mr. Chang."

Brad quickly offered his hand as a greeting, more out of nervousness than anything else. The handshake was rather limp from Chang's end. Brad felt a very strange sensation of apprehension.

The man quickly released his noodle-like squeeze and beckoned the courier to follow him into another air-conditioned office.

The office area in the back corner of the room was elegant with a rather large desk, complete with side chairs, and several computers. Brad was a little too far away from the desk to identify the wood grain. While there were no live potted plants in this sunken, windowless room, the area was adorned with muscular bodyguards, each the size of a freezer, dressed in tailored yellow sport coats with black ties.

"You have the briefcase I see," said Mr. Chang, gesturing to the courier's handcuffed left hand. The instructions from the main office had been to wear the handcuffs with the briefcase when leaving the hotel for the final destination meeting. To do so earlier would draw attention to him. One does not openly walk around a strict place like Singapore handcuffed to a briefcase.

Reef of Gold

Mr. Chang unlocked the briefcase from the courier's wrist and handed him the key. While Brad was fiddling with the cuffs, the overweight man placed the briefcase on a small conference table, spun it around so no one but him could see inside and opened it. He stared at the contents briefly, apparently reading a message included with the material. He looked at his mining courier for a moment and asked if Brad knew what was in the briefcase he had carried all this time.

"Haven't a clue," said Brad, looking up from tinkering with the cuffs still on his wrists. Finally, with a loud click, the cuffs dropped from his wrist. "I was told mining documents and computer disks and the contents were important and for your eyes-only. By the way, do you want me to make a courtesy call on our Singapore office before I leave? It just occurred to me that maybe you might have something going back to Perth."

Mr. Chang smiled at Brad's apparent innocence and then replied, "No, that won't be necessary. You have done your job well." He looked at the briefcase contents once again. The hurried note from Yang Lee had described this courier very well, he mused. It was true, a total innocent stood before him. This courier knew nothing. Chang ran his tongue over his lips as if taken a reading of the air surrounding him. It's a good thing, he thought. Yang Lee had taken a great risk, a calculated risk to rush the documents to me. But, due to the immediacy of the secret satellite intercepts printed on a one-time message pad, Yang Lee probably had no choice but to send the least identifiable courier.

Chang nodded to one of the "yellow jackets" before he locked up the briefcase. He sat down in his office chair, picked up a phone, and then swiveled around in his chair facing a far wall. The courier's meeting with Mr. Chang was over. A quick escorted walk through the anteroom, a rap on the disguised door, and Brad was guided back to the bar to meet again with the British host.

"You don't have to rush off," he said, while handing Brad a shot

Gary Dale

glass, filled with British Gin. "If you would like to gamble a bit, I can provide you with some chips. It's all part of the extra benefits of being a courier."

"No thanks. I'm not much of a gambling man. I work too hard to lose my money by gambling, so the game doesn't really excite me." Brad took a sip of the gin and handed the shot glass back to his host. "I do have a quick question for you, though. It's a historical question."

"Good on you, courier. Test my Oxford learning. It's been some time since I read history books, but then again depending on the question, perhaps I am living the history."

"Good point," Brad acknowledged. "My recollection of the laws of Singapore stated that it was illegal to spit on the streets; to throw away your gum on the sidewalks; to cuss; and to gamble." He said the last word with emphasis.

"Ah, you are very observant of our Singapore laws and customs," the British accent exclaimed. "What you have said is true. There are many laws in Singapore that keep the masses in line. For the wealthy," he shrugged, "there is a different set of laws, or at least laws that are not regularly enforced. Gambling is technically illegal and has been for a long time, but it is tolerated and mostly over-looked by the authorities especially this place. We even have government officials and judges that gamble here because of the casino's obscurity. The 'look the other way' tradition is a left over from the days when we British ruled Singapore. The government lets the Chinese have their small and private gambling dens for the most part."

"So, are you ever raided?" Brad asked.

"Oh, once in a while but we know when the harassment raid is coming several days in advance so we have a certain number of employees who act as patrons and get arrested without incident. We are open the next day. The masses learn of the raid and think the police keep gambling by the rich in check. After all, the wealthy have to have some fun in secrecy."

114

Reef of Gold

Brad shook his head at the double standard. It's the same the world over, he thought. The double standard exists even in America, especially in politics.

"Something troubling you?" his British host asked.

"No," he said, "just remembering a few things of the past. By the way, my taxi driver was very cautious about coming here. Was that because of the security requirements of the casino?"

The British host thought for a moment and then nodded the affirmative. "You probably figured out that the limos and cars are parked for an easier egress through the multiple garage doors."

"I thought you said you knew several days in advance when the police raids were going to occur."

"That we do know, but the clinker for this gambling casino and others like it is when the Singapore security agents get involved with a raid. Then we have to really clear out in a hurry and lock everything up as we leave. Raids rarely occur but happen enough to warrant special precautions for some of our guests. That is why your taxi driver probably took the precautions he did to make sure the area was safe and not being watched. Besides, it adds an element of danger and privacy that our guests seem to enjoy. Human nature, I suppose, but I am only guessing."

"Really," Brad acknowledged, as if something wasn't quite right with the statements. "Well," Brad countered, "you have impressed this Yank with the secrecy and all the gambling tables and the lovely decorations that occasionally walk by."

"Thank you for your history questions and your astute observations of our female guests," said the British accent.

"You're most welcome. Perhaps I will come again. Nice talking to you but I would like to get going. It's been a long day."

"Understood," the host said, putting his arm around Brad's shoulders and walking him to the staircase. "Look forward to your eventual return."

They shook hands at the bottom of the stairs. Brad paused.

Gary Dale

"By the way," he asked, "just curious, why do some Asians have a simple tattoo of an arrow on the back of their hand while others have a colored tattoo? I've noticed it on several people including Mr. Chang. His tattoo had a unique coloring."

The British host froze. His eyes suddenly turned cold and very penetrating. He gave Brad's hand a bone-cracking squeeze, roughly twisted his arm and said with some vengeance in his voice, "Don't inquire too much, my friend, about the activities you see before you. Asking questions is not part of your job description nor is the place to make inquiries. Now leave."

The taxi driver didn't seem to be aware of any of the problems from the casino. He eased his taxi out the back door of the garage and slowly made his return along the dark wharf without headlights. The driver turned left onto a well-traveled street, flipped on his headlights and raced back to the hotel with no conversation, running a few intersections, sliding in and out the flow of traffic. He knew.

The taxi barely slowed as it approached the hotel's circular drive and finally pulled into the taxi stand. The driver snarled at Brad to get out immediately, which he did, although left-handed. As soon as Brad shut the car door, the taxi spun its tires in leaving, nearly running over his toes. It occurred to him that on neither occasion was he ever charged for the taxi fare. He smiled and then muttered, "Then again, I didn't tip him, either." He smiled.

As for Brad's future.............

CHAPTER 14

GOODWOOD PARK HOTEL

"Ah, Mr. Templeton, you have returned from your meeting already?" a voice asked.

Brad turned at the sound and there was his waiter, lounging to one side of the hotel's swinging doors. "Right you are, Max. Still up for that drink, because I need one?"

"Been waiting all evening for it," he exclaimed. "I'm off work now. The hotel has several quaint bars located on the veranda. Shall we find one to our liking?"

"Lead the way," Brad mumbled, "anything to kill the pain in my hand and shoulder."

"Did you say something? Mr. Templeton, you look a little peaked, if I dare say so."

"Tell you later."

The white wicker bar chairs scraped the cool tile floor as the waiter pulled them out from under the table and seated both of them. "Quiet crowd tonight," observed Max.

Brad nodded, sitting quietly for a few moments, familiarizing himself with his surroundings. He had felt a subtle atmosphere change as soon as they had entered the hotel bar. Pairs of eyes seemed to be interested in him for some reason. He didn't like the feeling of being scrutinized, especially after the earlier confrontation. Then

Gary Dale

again, maybe it was his awkward appearance that made them look carefully at him.

Max broke the silence. "Probably the cooling sea breeze blowing in shore tonight is having a subdued effect on the evening crowd." he suggested. He waited for a reaction. He noticed Brad's facial muscles were stretched tight. "Then again," he continued, "perhaps there is a lawyer convention going on in the hotel and the locals have scattered to other bars." The comment broke the tension. Brad cracked a smile.

"Well," asked Max, "what will you have to drink?"

"It's been a while since I've downed good American whiskey. Think they will have some handy?"

"Perhaps," said Max. "Personally, I'm not a whiskey drinker so I don't know. Must be a bottle stashed somewhere behind the bar."

The waiter came when beckoned and Brad asked for the availability of several brands of American drinks. The waiter couldn't recall any of them but reassured Brad that he would check. "Ok," said a disappointed Brad. "Well, then, maybe you bring me a couple of good cigars, Hoyo de Monterrey Excalibers if you have them. The waiter nodded and turned towards Max who ordered Boodles, with a hint of tonic water and a plate of bread and cheese. The waiter spun around on his heels and walked briskly back to the bar.

"My guess is that this American whiskey request is going to take some effort, Brad. I should tell you that since Singapore was a British possession for so many years, Boodles is the best-known brand of gin, and gin is a very popular British drink. Good American whiskey might be rare."

"I can order something else. It's just that I wanted a familiar drink. What ever I finally end up drinking, I'm going to make sure it's neat and a double."

"Oh, tough day?" Max inquired.

Brad merely nodded.

The waiter walked a little slower towards the table this time

118

Reef of Gold

carrying several drinks on his tray with the cigars wrapped in a cloth napkin placed as far away from the drinks as possible. "Compliments of the bartender," he said, as he put several small neats in front of Brad. "I'm supposed to tell you that these are the most popular drinks we have behind the bar and you will recognize the quality."

"This will be fine," said Brad, shrugging his shoulders. He just wanted a drink. The waiter breathed a sigh of relief and headed back to the bar.

Brad scooted his chair closer to the table. "Tell me, Max, is working here at the hotel your main job or is it a part time thing?"

Max smiled. "It's temporary at best. I enjoy the concierge bit because I like people but other than that, I could leave it tomorrow. My days are generally not being filled anyway, so I opted to work some hours as a fill in. It helps to know the personnel manager here at the hotel. So, how was your meeting a few hours ago? It must have been a tough meeting if your first response was to order a double."

"Max, did you know that for certain people, gambling is a big deal in Singapore?" Max raised his eyebrows at the question, wondering where it was leading. "We have a large Chinese population here in Singapore and gambling is their passion. Why is that such a surprise?"

Brad stared off into the night for several moments. "When I left the hotel, my map worked for part of the way. When the taxi left the main street for side streets, I was completely lost. The map didn't help at all. The crazy part came when the taxi driver drove me along the docks. It was dark as a cave wandering around those warehouses. Gave me the creeps. Finally the taxi stopped, and from the shadows several men emerged to escort me into a warehouse. I couldn't see what was going on, but I thought I could hear the obnoxious sounds of slot machines. Now I think the whole setup was rather strange. What would slot machines be doing in a warehouse? I asked several yellow jackets what was going on, but they remained silent."

"What do you mean by yellow jackets?"

Gary Dale

"You know the silent security guards. I don't know about the gambling patrons, but I was escorted from the moment I arrived to the moment I left. Hardly anyone said a wordto me. I found out it was a casino. I walked through it to get to my contact. "

"Quite the adventure," exclaimed Max, taking a moment to enjoy his Boodles. "Let me ask you another question. How did the guards know it was you? I mean, did you announce your appointment with this Mr. Chang."

That question stunned Brad for a moment. He reached for one of his kiosk cigars lying on the drink tray. "Want one?" he asked Max.

"Sounds good to me. What brand are they?"

"You now have in your hand, my favorite cigar, a Hoyo de Monterrey Excalibur, a number two. I think I remember reading where the cigar people hand rolled Excalibur's in Honduras and imported from the USA, the Connecticut wrapper leaf. It's been said that the wrapper is the most important part of the cigar, giving the cigar the last bit of flavor. Some people call this particular cigar a 6 x 48."

"A 6 x 48?" questioned Max.

"Means the size of the cigar will give you an hour smoke, give or take," he acknowledged, while cutting the butt end of his cigar with a cutter just above the cap line and then lighting the tip with heat from the lighter and not the flame. He slid the cutter and gas lighter across the table to Max and watched him analyze the proper approach to cigar cutting and lighting technique.

In between puffs, Brad asked him a question. "Max, who in the hell are you really?"

Max fidgeted a little in his chair as if his leg muscles had cramped, before ceremoniously cutting the end off of his cigar and lighting it. He held up the cigar in the air and looked at it thoughtfully. The cigar seemed to hold a fascination for him as he slowly twisted the cigar, allowing the smoke to lazily drift in the light breeze. He made

Reef of Gold

the moment last. Brad watched the ritual and suspected that the preoccupation was a device to give Max time to think about his next words carefully without appearing to do so. Finally, Max placed the cigar on the ashtray and leaned forward.

"Why do you want to know?" he asked.

"Max, you are playing games with me. I never told you whom I was to meet tonight. And yet, you had asked if I announced to the guards my appointment with Mr. Chang. How did you know about him?"

Max let out a sigh and sat back in his chair. He picked up his cigar, lighting it again and drawing a few long puffs. "I was planning to tell you in a few minutes," he said. "I wanted to drag out of you everything you could remember before the alcohol caught up with your adrenalin flow. I wanted you to be clear headed as much as possible."

Max took another puff on his cigar. "I didn't mean to deceive you." He leaned forward and said very quietly, "At the moment, all I can tell you is that I work for the Malaysian government, authorized by the same government to investigate theft of computer software. The Triad is involved is some way. The government has classified me as a computer expert. Please keep this to yourself as my future may depend on it."

"Ok," Brad said, somewhat amused by the theatrics. "Things are now making a little more sense. Do you have any identification?"

Max hesitated.

Brad used the hesitation to think. He let a few questions circle around in his head for a moment but he let them go until another time. He really wanted to find out if Max knew his brother.

"Is my brother alive?" he asked, knowing full well that he was walking around.

"I know your brother well. Remember, he likes to stay in the shadows. The hand delivered package could have been from him. Someone gave it to me to give to you."

121

Gary Dale

Brad nodded at the thought of the pretty delivery lady. He hoped that Max hadn't lied and waited for him to continue.

Max toyed with his cigar in the ashtray.

"Now that we have danced, Brad, maybe we can lay some cards on the table. Ric has been in this game for a long time. He is too resilient to let the Triad guys kill him. So, I have to believe he is holed up somewhere. We miss his brazen style and dedication to getting the job done. In the past, he would leave little droppings here and there, like a forest animal to let me and others know things. Until we hear from him, all of us will continue to investigate the Triad." Max took another puff of his cigar.

"Now, as to the question of my identification. Over a glass of wine, Ric said something about you and he playing football as kids in your front lawn. You were going to be tackled, so in a bit of panic, you turned around to escape and ran right into a cherry tree. The result was a bloody nose if I remember the story correctly. He said even to this day your sense of direction is suspect." A delightful crinkling appeared in the corner of his eyes. He arched his eyebrows to form wrinkles on his forehead. "Was any part of the story true?" he asked.

Brad smiled, momentarily lost in thought. Max did know Ric personally. Only his brother would have known about the front yard football story. The cherry trees always got in the way of a touchdown. It was like having extra defensive linemen.

Max continued. "Back to your original question of identification, is this conversation enough or do I need to continue?"

"You're fine. Sorry. I've had a very unusual experience tonight, and I'm still a little apprehensive about the whole situation. What concerns me is that I'm only a courier of mining documents. How important can that be to attract all of this attention?"

"Tell me about where you met this so called Mr. Chang? Was his office part of the casino operation?"

"Yes, well, his office was physically attached to the casino operation. A few people came and went from the gambling area carrying trays of cash and chips. Piles of cash in bundles were lying around. It felt like being in a bank vault. I couldn't tell what the rest of the staff was doing in the main office area. He had what looked like a regular business operation to me. His office was located in a separate area of the room. I do remember...hold on. Here's the waiter with our bread and cheese. Shoot, and we just lit our cigars." Brad fiddled carefully with his cigar and said, "If we lightly stub them out by using this method I'm showing you, they will still be good a little later on."

Max looked at Brad to see if he was kidding or not.

"Trust me on this one, Max."

Max watched the technique and then stubbed out his own cigar very gently in the same way.

The waiter put the tray of cheeses on the table and gave each of them a loaf of freshly baked bread, hot out of the oven. Its aroma swirled around them like intoxicating French perfume. They each dove for the cheese tray as if they hadn't eaten in weeks. Lucky for the both of them the tray contained two knives.

"Now, you were saying?" asked Max.

"I was saying," Brad said, with crumbs dropping from his fingers, "that my contact had a tattoo on his right hand. Looked like an arrow pointing to his little finger. Do you know what that means?"

Max stopped with the hunk of bread and cheese in mid air. "Would you repeat that mumbling sentence?"

Brad chewed and swallowed. He took a sip from his bottled water. "There was a noticeable tattoo on my contact's right hand. Do you know what that means? Is it a religious thing?"

"Did you notice if anyone else had a tattoo on their right hand?" probed Max.

"Well, it wasn't like I looked at everybody. If I noticed, my brain didn't pay any attention. I was too busy trying to make sense out of all of this secrecy. This Chang person that came to get the briefcase

Gary Dale

off my wrist did have a distinctive tattoo on his right hand. I felt that something wasn't quite right when we shook hands. He became very uncomfortable. I don't think he wanted to or intended to shake hands."

Brad barely shrugged his shoulders before a sharp muscle spasm ricocheted throughout his neck and shoulder area. He winced. "I was just nervous. Later in the casino when I asked my escort about the tattoos, things got real intense."

Max suddenly stiffened in his chair. "My friend," he warned sternly, "it's time for your immediate return to Perth. You don't want any more involvement with Mr. Chang and his associates here in Singapore. It will be safer for you in Perth."

"Safer for me?" Brad questioned, while reaching for his cigar. His appetite was suddenly gone. After relighting and taking a few puffs, he asked, "Why would I need to worry? I'm done with the courier thing. I am going to refuse the next trip."

"This Mr. Chang or whom ever you met is somehow involved with the Singapore Triad. With all that cash lying around, he may be running a money laundering operation for them. I suspect the Sterling Mines branch office is just one of the many businesses he probably manages." He paused. "Brad, I want you to think and I mean really think hard. Do you remember what the tattoo looked like and if it was in color, like faded blue, black, green or red?"

"The tattooed arrow pointing to the little finger was obvious to me when he pulled his hand away." Brad hesitated for a moment. "I'm pretty sure the tattoo color was more like a faded red color."

Max was silent for a moment. He took a deep breath. "Brad, if the tattoo was indeed reddish in color then the people you were meeting came from a very ancient criminal society who has their roots, or family ties if you will, in Macau. Hate to tell you this but if this setup is what I think it is, you have just been in the nest of the most feared warlords of crime not only in Singapore, but also in all of Southeast Asia. The guy who relieved you of the briefcase probably was using

124

Reef of Gold

Mr. Chang as a code name. He wouldn't have been the real warlord of the Triad because they would never see anyone like a courier, but this guy had to be up there in the Triad hierarchy."

Brad choked on his cigar smoke and briefly turned from the table to control his coughing. After a drink of water and clearing his throat, he faced Max again. He didn't touch the cigar. He smiled weakly. "Please continue, Max," he croaked.

"You ok?"

Brad nodded but didn't say anything.

Max continued. "These Chinese secret societies had criminal businesses going for them all over the world and have remained active for centuries upon centuries. Remember the time line of history. The Great Wall of China was being built some 200 years before Christ. On simpler terms, the Chinese had a wheelbarrow a thousand years before England even thought about it. The ancient Triads have survived all this time.

"No kidding," Brad whispered, still choking slightly. "How did you learn about all of this history?"

"My father was in the British Foreign Service. So, history discussions were a big thing at my home. Most of the time, I just listened with one ear to the adult conversations even though some of the most knowledgeable historians alive were at the dinner table. As a kid, I used to sneak into our library where the men smoked their cigars and talked about world events and politics. They visited my father on their business travels around the world, and by half paying attention, I picked up on some of the details that really interested me."

Picking up his cigar, Max relit, drew a few puffs, winked at Brad as if to say, this is a good cigar, and continued the conversation. "The Chinese developed a culture that promoted international commerce before the time of the pharaohs of Egypt." He paused to tap the ashes from his cigar. "With commerce and trade, came established trading ports. The Chinese criminals established massive empires within the

Gary Dale

trading commerce routes from as far away as the east coast of Africa, the coasts of India, to the Spice Islands and along China coasts, all commerce eventually directed by criminal activity in some way. Global business was really invented by the Chinese sea captains and taken to a new level by the secret societies. The local organizations are now called 'Triads' in today's vernacular."

"I've heard of the term Triad when I was in the states," said Brad, finally finding his normal voice, "but this is the first contact I've had with them on any level. Who are these Triad people?"

"It's a long story," acknowledged Max, "but I'll make it short as I can. You did say this was an hour long cigar, didn't you?"

"I did. But in the meantime, I might drift off to sleep."

Max smiled. "Large amounts of stress will do that to a person. I'll make the story even shorter. The term Triads or Triad societies applies to several groups but one ruthless organization in particular is called the Hung dynasty, a very ancient Chinese criminal society. It's like having, as you say in America, an old mafia family with Sicilian roots and having lots of fingers in every major city in the USA. The ruthless and brutal Hung dynasty directs all its Triad Societies in cities all over the world. There are other smaller Triads vying for the crumbs.

"Is the Singapore Triad particularly violent?" asked Brad.

Max hesitated for a moment. "That might be an understatement," he said quickly.

"What you seem to have run across is a branch of the Triad from the Hung dynasty. Your Mr. Chang with his unique tattoo coloring apparently is part of the Hung dynasty leadership. He may be and probably is, a Shen Chu, which is a big leader of all of the various branches of the Singapore Triad or then again, he could be just a leader of a division, which the Triad calls a Lu Yuan Swie. To show their Hung family loyalty, they go through a rigorous initiation and as part of their identity among other Triad members, they have a special tattoo on their right hand. This is a badge of honor. The

Reef of Gold

Triad tattoo is often distinguished even further by the color of the tattooing."

"So," said Brad, "when I questioned my casino host about Mr. Chang having an unusual tattoo, that might have put me in danger, not just a little danger but as in life threatening." He paused. "Think I just answered my own question about Triad violence."

Max nodded. "The Triads, we figure, are involved in extortion, gambling, prostitution, narcotics trafficking, human smuggling, high jacking of cargo ships, smuggling of computer chips and lately, computer espionage. Because their activity creates huge amounts of money, these criminal societies all have the best high tech computer stuff in the world available to them, more sophisticated than the police or even governments. They launder and stuff cash in bank accounts everywhere. I do know that the Singapore security agents have tried to follow the main computer trail to the criminal's lair but haven't really come close except on one occasion and even then, they didn't succeed in breaking into the computers. They wanted and needed the encryption codes. The Hung Society in Singapore most likely has their computer system set up so that any physical intrusion into their computer premises like a raid from Singapore Security forces will automatically transfer files to another computer in another country to another computer in another country and so on. Then it proceeds to destroy itself in Singapore and the original file content. The Triad doesn't mess around. That's why we have had a difficult time trying to stop them."

"Look, I don't want to be involved any more in this Triad business, Max. This is way above my pay grade. How do I get out of the mess I'm in now? I mean, they really did get offended; at least my British escort did, when I asked about Chang's tattoo. And, I'm sure he reported my inquisitive question. My right side is still hurting from that encounter. Now, the pain is even in my forearm and neck area.

"So, that's why you keep squirming around in your chair, trying

Gary Dale

to ease the pain in your neck. The nerve that runs down your arm must have been crimped badly. Frankly, it was lucky they let you live. Maybe the Triad hierarchy views you as being an innocent and therefore would continue to have a cover as a Sterling Mines courier."

"Max, I need to know something. Well, actually a couple of things. One, can I get out of their clutches right now? And two, who in the hell are you really? I think you know too much about the secret Triad Society for the normal computer investigator. And your father couldn't have been that knowledgeable about the Triad operations and still have been alive when you were growing up if he was just an ambassador type, now could he."

Max smiled and then sipped his drink. "First question first. No, you can't get out of their clutches for the moment. You are a courier for a company they own, and they probably will continue to have contact with you as a courier until you are no longer of value to them or eventually just lose interest in you."

"And the answer to the second question?"

"Let me answer the second question this way. I had to dispose of your Malaysian Embassy contact here in Singapore. He was not whom he represented."

Brad gulped his drink as if he hadn't heard correctly.

"In spite of the unsavorily contact, I have covered your back most of the time while you were previously here in Singapore and I was tempted to contact you directly, but you were doing such a great job being nosey that I'm sure Ric would have wanted to let you continue. You just never know what a person like you might stir up."

Max shrugged his shoulders and continued. "This was as good a time as any to contact you. To answer question number two, my father worked for a special services branch of the British Government, which was an information-gathering department. He was killed several years ago. It had to be Triad involvement although my own government won't confirm it even to me. When that happened, I

Reef of Gold

arranged for my mother, my wife, and my children to live in London when I joined the British secret service. I wanted revenge. With that kind of desire, I became expendable in the eyes of the service so they sent me here to Malaysia. The special services department that I work for is the computer section. Consequently, I work with your brother." He looked up at the ceiling for a brief moment and then back to Brad.

Brad felt the stress slowly leaving his body. His confidence in good people was rising. He had been carrying the burden of helping Ric all alone. But, despite Max's credentials, Ric's being alive was still a secret. There was still this mole thing. He would tell Max when he thought it was appropriate.

"Geez Max, wish you could have told me sooner that you were my contact. Look, what more can I do to help my brother?"

Max thought for a moment. "The thing for you is to get out of Singapore immediately. Then, once back in Perth, you will be safe. I know you have more questions than answers. But we are making progress against the Triad as never before. At the same time, it is helping me by giving us some inside information."

"You mean," Brad asked, "that not one of your people has ever been on the inside?"

"Not one," said Max. "We have tried to infiltrate, but it is nearly impossible. The Triad has so many layers of family hierarchy with very little moving up the ladder at the lower levels. If you are recruited as an ordinary member, you are a Sey Kow Jai forever.

Brad looked around the veranda for a few moments suddenly worried. "Max, I'm new at this game. Aren't you the least bit concerned that you might be seen talking to me here at the hotel for such a long time?"

Max looked strangely at Brad trying to figure him out.

"Sorry, just nervous, Max. My brain has too many questions that need to be downloaded. Hard to keep up with all the stuff you've been telling me."

Gary Dale

Max waved him off. "You aren't under any serious suspicion from the Triad, at least not yet, and my cover is fairly safe. If someone saw us, they would probably try to figure out who I am. Besides, we did establish a rapport earlier in the day and to anyone that would be watching, it would look like we are just having a drink and discussion. I could be anybody."

"Ok, so you want me to just go back to Sterling Mines and be normal. Heck, I'll never be the same. I know what's going on now."

"Actually, you don't. You only know the surface stuff and for a reason. You are a fast learner, Brad, but the less you know, the safer it will be for you. Look, go back to Perth, do your job at Sterling Mines by keeping your eyes open for any irregularities. I would suggest that you keep a tight lip in talking about Mr. Chang and the Triad ties with Sterling Mining Company."

"This isn't going to be easy," said Brad while stubbing out the last of his cigar, "Part of me gets very nervous and things just pop out of my mouth. Can't help it."

"Well, maybe it is all about luck. You have a tub full. Still, you'll have to be careful. I'll try to be available in Perth if you need me. I do have a security agent contact there that can be of help and between the two of us, we can watch you and cover your back."

'Where have I heard that before?' thought Brad. He sat forward in his chair. "Will this Australian contact of yours reach me, and does he or she have a name? I know now that it won't be the same name that Mr. Yew in the Malaysian Embassy in San Francisco gave me. Am I correct or not?"

"Right you are my friend. Your new contacts will identify themselves at the appropriate time."

"Anything else I should know?"

"My cigar is about as short as I can make it. It's been great to work with you Brad. Take care and thanks for the cigar. I'll be seeing you."

Reef of Gold

Max abruptly left the table and disappeared into the hotel lobby as if he had sensed something a miss.

"My pleasure Max," mumbled Brad to himself. He sat in his chair for a while, trying to absorb much of the conversation. It didn't take long for fatigue to overtake him. It was like a switch being turned off. He slowly rose from his chair and made his way to his room. Maybe he would sleep tonight. Maybe he would even dream about finding the reef of gold for a change.

CHAPTER 15

THE LITTLE EYES

The place stunk.

After centuries of neglect, the wood plank floors were stained with blotches of dried blood, spittle, and green beer. Cobwebs hung from one isolated light bulb to another suppressing the dimly lit room. Little black things with wings dotted the webbing announcing an enticing feast tonight for the big tropical spiders. The bamboo walls were dirty from soot, diesel fumes and Turkish tobacco smoke. Floorboards were weak and rotten in places caused by the harbor water moisture ravaging the wood from below.

A stranger sat alone near the back of the pub, unusual for this dive. The regular pub drinkers, grubby themselves, tended to group at tables for their own protection. It was in reality an illusion. While the derelict patrons tolerated each other, there were no loyalties except when a stranger walked into the place. Then all the blood shot eyes would turn towards the intruder with suspicion. The stranger might have looked like most of the men, smelled like them, and talked the same language, but all the same, an intruder, who immediately would become the subject of mutterings and idle gossip. All the pub patrons were all out of work for the time being. No interisland rust buckets were in need of unscrupulous seaman during the months of the nasty

Reef of Gold

typhoon season. Ships of the sea including naval ships stayed in port. Even the pirate season was temporarily on hold.

Straining the raw beer though his teeth to keep out the dead flies when he swallowed, the stranger slowly sloshed a mouthful of beer around in his mouth before setting the glass down on the stained table. Then he spat a long stream of liquid onto the floorboards, a sign of acceptance in this place. He sat alone at an unsteady table and for amusement, watched the pub flies skate across his stream of liquid while attempting to land. These were tiny ones making quick flight paths in and out, scooping up the liquid before the big ones arrived and started hogging the air space. It didn't take the big flies long to smell a feast. A smile barely creased the corners of the stranger's mouth. A nasty-looking fly had sucked up a full load and had trouble taking off. The insect finally made it with a long and arduous takeoff.

Someone shifted in a chair, drawing his attention back to the patrons. He glanced at the entrance through hooded eyes. The urgent meeting with his agent was arranged a few days ago. There were things to discuss and only a face-to-face meeting would do it. The agent was late. Where was this guy? he wondered. Losing his agent Hsin was bad enough. He didn't need another agent disaster. Head down, resting on his left arm, he carefully slid back layers of clothes on his wrist. Cupping his right hand to cover the partially exposed wristwatch, he took a peek through the cracked plastic watch cover, determining to wait only another five minutes. The scarred watch was the only item that wasn't a legitimate part of the disguise. Derelict seamen usually didn't wear watches.

His table was next to the thin bamboo outside wall. The bamboo matting was rotten in places and so weak that one could fall against the wall matting and end up outside. But the bamboo wall did breathe. The sea moisture from below the floorboards created a cooling sensation despite the high humidity outside the bamboo walls. It seemed the walls themselves flexed with the changes of

133

Gary Dale

humidity. The table was in a dark location but the cautious stranger could still see anyone who entered the pub. He suddenly jerked and then scratched under his arm as if another damn flea bit him. It had. The movement was another common sight among the patrons sitting nearby.

Out of the corner of his eye, he caught a flash of a street lamp, swinging in the wind. A side door had opened and closed quickly. Another shabbily dressed derelict patron had entered the pub, standing still to let his eyes adjust to the dim light before meandering to the dilapidated bar. "It could be my contact," he thought, putting his head down on the table as if he were tired or sick. The derelict bought a glass of beer from the scraggly one-armed bartender, and then moved slowly around the pub. Few paid any attention to him. The unemployed regular stumbled for a brief moment slopping beer on the floor but caught himself with a hand on the bar. He looked around for a table and found one near the back. He staggered over, mumbling to no one in particular, before he kicked the chair with the apparently sleeping occupant in an attempt to wake him up. The stranger stirred, barely looking up. Shrugging, the newcomer pulled out a stubby wooden stool with two of its legs partially sawed off. This part of the plank floor had a slope to it caused by the moisture from below. The shortened stool fit the table just right if one liked to lean forward, elbows on the table. The derelict sat down and punched the stranger in the shoulder in an attempt to create a conversation.

The stranger slowly raised his head to stare at the derelict, then mumbled something quietly. This new tablemate raised his glass in a salute. The man nodded and barely raised his glass to return in half gesture before he returned his head to the table.

Contact was made.

There were fewer drinkers now who even paid attention to them. In a couple of minutes, no one would care and all would lose interest. The stranger would occasionally raise his head and then reluctantly put his head down, cradled in his arms. He used the ploy to talk

Reef of Gold

quietly so no one else could hear. The agent would lean over to the man's ear and whisper back. Each time, the agent would lean back in his chair and laughed as if he had told a joke to the sleepy stranger. The bar patrons paid no attention.

The agent tilted back on his stool and talked while he sipped his beer, disguising his conversation. "Word has it that another North Korean cargo ship is due to arrive soon with special cargo. That makes two ships in as many weeks."

"Must be special cargo to risk it during the typhoon season," said the stranger in a hoarse voice, hacking from the foul air.

"The cargo has to be important or why the great hurry?" asked the agent, rocking forward once again. "I haven't been able to find out what is on board yet that could be so vital. The Triad is keeping tight security on both ships. Fortunately, several of my contacts are part of the Indonesian labor unloading the freighters. From them, I confirmed that the Triad has small watercraft under the wharf to transport the ship's cargo including human cargo. Near as I can tell, what ever happens under the wharf is a city onto its self. A ships' cargo is moved around in small craft under the ancient wharf and then is dumped onto various landings and stored in the warehouses above. We're sitting above a landing right now. Ironic isn't it?"

The stranger encircled his arms on the table and cradled his head. He raised his voice a notch. "Keep working on this under-the-wharf city. This could be a big break-through for us. The department has heard rumors of water passageways under the Triad wharf but some how the interest waned from lack of attention. Maybe our reports will get some action. Good job." He hesitated. "The North Korean ship that will dock soon must be our focus. I want to know what is in the cargo holds. We will meet here again. I will contact you in the usual way with the date and time."

There was a pause in the conversation while a scarred face drinker, beer in hand, staggered close by before being shoved back to the bar by the patrons at a nearby table.

Gary Dale

The agent leaned close to the man's ear. "What else is new?" he asked quietly.

The stranger almost smiled. He raised his head and wiped his nose several times with his forearm. "The whole Triad computer thing is going to blow up soon. We'll get to watch the pieces fall from the sky. I can feel it," he said.

The agent snorted. "With only bits and pieces of information, I can hardly picture any real success," he whispered. He leaned back away from the table before he let out a long sigh then a big belch. The raw green beer was upsetting his stomach. He leaned forward. "But I know you will tell me when it's appropriate." He looked around for a moment. "Keep your head on the table," he hissed. The stranger did as he was asked. There was a noticeable pause before the agent said something. He leaned down to the stranger's ear. "Did you pick up a tail? I checked my back trail several times and found no one."

The stranger stiffened. "Not that I know of. I was careful. Why?"

"Something is going on. I can sense it. A little street urchin dressed in rags snuck in here from a side door. He can't be more than 12 years old. The kid is looking closely at all the patrons. Little bugger even has a cell phone. He is using it now. What the hell is he doing with a cell phone? He can't afford an evening meal."

"Think it has something to do with me?" asked the stranger.

"Has to be. You are the only stranger here. He is looking in this direction. I may have to move on and quickly if he comes over here so it appears I'm not associated with you."

"You got it," said the stranger. "Good luck."

Abruptly, the agent got up from the table and staggered over to the sagging bar and ordered another beer. He slugged down a couple of big swallows and then left the half filled glass on the bar and headed for a side door exit before exiting. The stranger kept his head down, eyes just above his coat sleeve. "A street urchin with a cell phone?" he muttered to himself. "That's odd."

Reef of Gold

Suddenly, there was a loud splintering of bamboo behind him. Instinctively, the stranger lurched forward from his chair, knocking over the cockeyed table. A long bladed knife stabbed at him through the splintered outside wall. He had moved fast enough to avoid the wicked blade slicing past his kidneys. Spinning around, he grabbed the thin arm that held the knife, jerking hard enough to force a muted grunt of surprise. A shoulder and head stuck through the enlarged hole in the bamboo wall. It was another filthy looking street kid. Even in pain, the kid's eyes showed hate. The stranger gripped harder and twisted the skinny arm forcing the knife to drop, kicking it away. He jerked again, pulling the squirming urchin more than halfway through the splintered bamboo wall and onto the floor. A cell phone was in the left hand. A quick stomp from the stranger's foot released the grip from the phone. The street urchin yelped with pain. In one quick motion, the stranger leaned down and grabbed the cell phone, stuffing it into his jacket pocket. He started to stand upright then instinctively ducked. He heard the familiar swishing sound of a Rotan club passing swiftly over his head. Using the scarred faced derelicts forward momentum; he staggered under the attackers weight briefly, adjusted his footing, and then flipped the heavy out-of-work sailor over his shoulder, slamming him to the floor.

The rest of the red-eyed pub patrons sat still and watched with amusement, knowing this fight may be the only entertainment for the week. The stranger didn't waste any time trying to get out of there. He scrambled through the debris and suddenly stopped. A long, curved knife in the hand of a pre-teen street urchin had something to do with the stranger's hesitation. It was the kid who had just walked inside a moment ago. The only way out for the stranger was by the kid and through the side door at the end of the bar. Grabbing an unclaimed half full glass of beer off the bar, he threw it at the street urchin. The kid ducked the glass but took the beer full in the face, temporarily blinding him. The raw beer stung his eyes making him squeal with anger. Wasting little time, the stranger stiffly vaulted over

Gary Dale

the bar, grimacing in pain from his healing wounds. The patrons were cheering. He rushed towards the bartender who put up his only hand to indicate he wanted no part of the fracas.

Reaching the side door, the stranger burst outside into the dusky night. By the next city block, the man had thrown away most of his disguise and become Ric Templeton.

CHAPTER 16

COMMITMENT TIME

Brad reported back to Miles, mentioning the temporary change in engineering procurement staff responsibilities and that Michael would have the updated equipment inventory list shortly. Miles nodded and then reminded Brad to see the operations manager because the company was now in a frenzy to get things done. Brad's path down the green carpeting took him towards the enormous fake Boab tree, which Brad had now dubbed the ninth wonder of the world.

Passing the tree on his left, Brad slowed just a little to get a closer look and then went back to his hurried executive pace. While turning right, near the Billabong Mural, Brad ran into Megan. Literally.

"Pardon me," Brad stammered. "You're not hurt are you?" he asked, still holding Megan upright, albeit in an awkward position. "I wasn't looking, well, I was looking but at the Billabong scene, I mean the Baobab tree and didn't see you."

"My apologies to you, Brad. I wasn't looking in front of me either as my mind was on something else. It happens a lot around here. Look Brad, we can stay in this awkward position, but eventually your muscles are going to give out. I would recommend that you straighten me to more of an up right position."

"Oh, sorry." he said, gently releasing his grip as he eased her upright once again.

Gary Dale

She straightened out her pin stripe suit and stood more formally, as if the wreck had never happened.

Brad cleared his throat, giving him a moment to build up a little courage before speaking. "You know, there is a better way to get to know another person other than crashing into them. Would you allow me the pleasure of buying you a drink after work?" He quickly held up his hands in a gesture of partial surrender. "This is not a come on, Megan, just an offer for a pleasant social get together."

Megan smiled.

Brad could sense the wheels turning in her head, mulling his offer. There were probably a million reasons for her to say no and the reason she would give him probably would be very logical and kind. Brad braced himself for a negative answer and tried to rationalize his asking her as nothing ventured, nothing gained.

"Ok," she said. "But there is a catch. We have to do something first. Meet me at the YMCA on Douglass Street, in the main lobby, at 6:00pm tonight. Dress in exercise clothes and bring some type of cross training shoes to change into. You can help me with something and then we will have that drink."

As soon as Brad nodded his head as affirmative, she waved at him and with a flash of movement, rushed past the massive Baobab tree and disappeared.

De'ja'vu swept over him as a hint of her perfume lingered. He was still a little perplexed and in shock from the past moment. Damn, he thought, she said yes. Unbelievable! He swept his tongue over his parched lips, blinked his eyes several times in an attempt to refocus, and tried to breathe normally. Once he got himself under control, he looked around; and for the life of him, he couldn't remember why he was even in the area. He thought about it for another moment and still couldn't remember why he was heading in this direction. "Retrace my steps," he concluded, "it's the only answer."

His retracing took him past Miles office and Miles stopped him with a "back already" comment. Brad turned around.

140

Reef of Gold

"Sorry, Miles," said Brad, "where was it you wanted me to go and for what reason?"

Miles looked at Brad. "Must be losing it, mate," he said. "Take a day off or something. Too many hours of work will dull the mind."

"Actually, Miles there was a reason for my forgetting and you aren't going to believe my answer."

Miles smiled. "Try me," he said. He leaned back in his chair and folded his arms across his slightly rotund stomach. "Have a chair, mate. For some reason, I have a feeling this is going to be good."

Brad sat down, crossed his legs in a relaxed position and put his hands behind his head, and said, "Megan."

Just that one word started Miles belly laughing in his loud and boisterous way. He truly enjoyed Brad's discomfort with that woman and it never ceased to amuse him.

Brad let him have his way for a few moments and then raised his hand in a futile gesture for Miles to stop laughing. Brad uncrossed his legs and leaned forward, pausing for a moment, and then said, "I have a date with her." That stopped Miles' laughter immediately. He raised his eyebrows.

"Say that again?" he questioned in disbelief.

"I have a date with Megan. I asked her out for a drink." Brad said. He shrugged his shoulders.

Miles rocked forward in his chair. "Unbelievable mate," he exclaimed. Wagging his finger at Brad, he said, "Every bloke in this office will want a minute by minute report on everything that happens. It's your duty, you know, to keep us males informed. Oh, this is going to be good."

Miles grinned like a Cheshire cat.

Brad knew that asking Miles to keep quiet about this date with Megan was impossible as the word of his accomplishment would be all over the office before quitting time. The subject of Megan would create a good deal of discussion of where they would go and

141

Gary Dale

the results. The imaginative scenarios would run from a formal meeting to carnal depending on who was talking. It was all based upon personal experiences and dreams. Brad concluded it was tough being the source of male envy.

. The YMCA building was close to downtown Perth and yet on the way to Freemantle and the suburbs. It was a two-story affair and occupied a good portion of the city block. The main street in front of the building was tree lined, giving the YMCA a look of tranquility. Maybe that is how people felt when they ended their strenuous workouts. It was something to look forward too.

"Thanks for coming," Megan said to Brad, as she stood in the brightly lit foyer, holding onto her oversized gym bag.

Brad gently squeezed her arm in acknowledgement and knew there wasn't a chance in hell that he would miss out on this opportunity. She looked at his cross training Nike's as well as exercise clothes stuffed in his tote bag and beckoned him to follow her. "Change clothes in the locker room and meet me back here," she said. It didn't take long for Brad to change. Megan greeted several YMCA staff members by name as they walked through several corridors to a main door that had very familiar wording painted on the door, Gymnasium. Pulling open the doors, they were greeted with plump white volleyballs flying all over the gymnasium in no particular direction. Groups of screaming teenage girls were playing a wild form of free-for-all volleyball. A screech of recognition immediately stopped the circus atmosphere.

As they watched the groups get organized, Megan turned to Brad. "This is what I do a couple of times during the week," she said, "coaching these young girls in the art of volleyball. We have games on Friday and Saturday nights. Keeps them busy and out of potential trouble. We also travel some, competing with other teams outside of Perth. There are many small towns nearby."

"Where do you get the energy for all this teen activity?" asked Brad. He smiled.

Reef of Gold

"Sometimes I wonder myself," said Megan. After an hour of volleyball drills and a short game, she whistled and instantly the players stopped what they were doing. "Time to stop and put away the gear, she said. "Your parents are anxious to get you home for dinner. Have a nice evening." The girls reluctantly put white balls on the cart and headed for their waiting parents.

"Where to," Brad finally asked Megan, "now that all the volleyball players have left with their parents?"

"There is a cute, quiet place called O'Bannions not too far from here," she offered. "I would suggest leaving your car here and go in mine. You could get lost at night as the pub is a little out of the way."

She was right about the pub being quiet but cute wasn't the word Brad would have used. The floors were covered with discarded peanut shells, which Brad found out were part of the regular fare. A fine shell dust covered everything in sight but no one seemed to mind. They found a table for two in a corner near the long mahogany bar and each pulled up a wooden water barrel as a seat. "Unique," Brad commented, while rocking back and forth on the barrel to find a smooth place among the peanut shells on the floor. "Do they serve anything else besides peanuts in here?"

"Funny man," she said.

Interestingly, they didn't once talk about work or the company staff. No gossip left Megan's lips and since she didn't socialize with others in the company, Brad doubted if she even knew about the department level Wednesday and Friday night pub gatherings. Instead, they talked about the young girls on the volleyball team and how much they were developing into pleasant young adults. With only a couple of weeks left in the volleyball season, Megan voiced her apprehension about missing the camaraderie developed with the teenagers. Brad could tell how proud she was of them. Then they shifted gears and talked about their immediate families.

Anticipating Megan's question, Brad wasted no time. "Yes, I've

Gary Dale

been married before, but no children. It ended several years ago as amiably as a marriage could. I dated fairly often since then. Nothing special. As for dating here in Perth, you are it."

"So, do you have any brothers and sisters?" she inquired.

"I have two brothers. My older brother Ric has a job with the US Department of Commerce and my younger brother Jon works for the Air Force. My mom still complains about no girls in the family. My brothers and I still feel to this day that we needed an older sister to knock us around a bit and teach us about the ways of women. We are rather deficient in that area. Our Mom tried her best but we still don't get it."

Megan laughed at that point. "Forget it, Brad," she said. "It's best not to even try to understand us."

She looked at Brad for a moment as if sizing him up and then nodded her head in a positive way. "I can see you being a soft shoulder to lean on in times of crisis," she offered. "You have that 'love of life' outlook that attracts women."

"Now, what about you? Any brothers or sisters?" he asked.

"One brother and he is younger than I am and lives near my parents in Canberra. Geoffrey is a government worker and travels back and forth from Canberra to all parts of Australia. It seems he is never in the same job description every time I talk to him. How he does it in the bureaucratic system, I'll never know. Whenever he is in Perth, we get together, only I just never know in advance when he is going to arrive and neither does he. You would like him as he has the same outlook on life as you do. His lovely wife works for a group of attorneys as a legal assistant, which gives her the flexibility of time so she can spend it with their two children. Won't be long before Geoffrey figures out that by traveling so much, he is missing out on too much family life." Megan glanced at her watch and was startled by what it said.

"Listen Brad, it's getting late for a week night, and I have a busy schedule tomorrow so we better pack it in. Thanks for the evening

Reef of Gold

and volunteering to help the girls in volleyball. I could tell you made a hit with them. Of course they are very impressionable at 13 and 14 years old." They walked out together holding hands.

The next morning, Miles was waiting for Brad in front of the main floor elevators.

"Couldn't wait for me to arrive, I see," said Brad, barely stifling a laugh. His eyes were dancing with delight.

"You got that right, mate. So, was it a ripper?"

Brad gave him a questioning look, and asked, "Come again?"

"You know mate, was it a terrific evening?"

"Oh, absolutely, Miles," said Brad, giving him a big Cheshire cat grin as he walked into the elevator. Miles stood speechless, and then before the doors could close, he bolted into the crowded elevator.

"Come on now mate, don't leave me hanging," he said, whispering, hoping that only a few people would hear.

The doors opened before Brad could answer. Brad knew that he had held Miles off long enough. "Let's wait until we get to your office," he suggested.

It didn't take too long before he had Miles laughing and offering some suggestions about where Brad could take her the next time they dated. Brad was a little vague about his next date and told Miles that they hadn't set a date for dinner. Miles didn't care as he now had solved the mystery about where Megan went after work and what she did on weekends. He now had enough scuttlebutt to last a month or two. He would divvy up the information in bits and pieces. He relished being the main conduit of gossip.

Megan had Brad busy the next couple of weeks with her volleyball team, mostly with transportation, setting up the nets and officiating. In America, Brad would be called a volunteer assistant coach. He was having fun so he didn't really mind the running around for Megan. Their friendship grew with each meeting, so much so that Brad even discussed with her his 'reef of gold' research findings from the Perth library. It also wasn't long before the teenage volleyball players

145

noticed how their mannerisms had changed as they were making more eye contact and finding excuses for light touches when they were standing together.

Just when Brad thought feelings between them had grown, the relationship suddenly slowed to a crawl. He was perplexed. Then, an invitation was accepted by both of them for a Saturday afternoon birthday party for Michael's daughter, Melissa.

With Melissa's decision to move her friends into her bedroom, it left the adults time to have a casual sit down dinner. They discussed every topic and solved all the world's problems with a light banter. There was one occasion at dinner where office gossip got going for some reason, and Brad probably hit a nerve with Megan with one of his questions. She wasn't angry, but Brad could tell she was giving him information the way she would to people on a tour of the company. Perhaps because she wanted to let Brad know she didn't approve of office gossip. That is, until the subject of President Wong and Yang Lee came up.

"Sterling Mines," she said suddenly, "through Yang Lee's efforts has re-established exploration and survey ventures far beyond the normal borders of our own current claims in the Gibson Desert area. If any of our own mining engineers knew through the grape vine what we were up to, they probably were scratching their heads in wonderment and embarrassment, Yang Lee continues to send teams into very remote areas. Occasionally he has sent out our company helicopters with purely Asian consulting engineering teams from Singapore. Sometimes a private consulting team of all Australians would go out, but they never seemed to find anything either. The only common thread was that Yang Lee went with all groups of consulting engineers to the outback on the pretense of supervision and training. He doesn't know much about mining by his own admission. President Wong knows more about mining than Yang Lee, and you would think he would be out there exploring if anybody."

Michael chimed in with, "That's a surprise."

Reef of Gold

"What is?" asked Megan.

"Those private consulting teams," said an exasperated Michael. "Our department was never asked to be a part of this effort. We didn't even know about it."

"Never occurred to me that you didn't know," remarked Megan. "We did have a company representative go with one of the consulting teams. The expedition was reported to the mining commission as required. I checked. How accurate was the information is the real question. Also, the data wasn't submitted in a timely manner."

"The fourth floor decisions never cease to amaze me," said Michael. "I suppose they were looking for some lost gold mine again."

"Wait a minute," asked Brad. "Who was the company representative? Couldn't you get more information from that person?"

"I would," answered Megan, "if I could find him. He is never around for me to ask."

"Don't tell me," suggested Michael. "It has to be our famous disappearing character Ian Downs. He is the only one I know that just shows up out of nowhere, and then he is nowhere to be found."

"He's the one who signed the log," admitted Megan. "He is upper management's problem." Everyone took this moment to stretch. It was like a five-minute break between speakers at a conference. When everyone returned to the kitchen table it was Megan that brought up the topic of the reef of gold and Brad's ship captain's journal, surprising Brad.

"I'd like to see your ship captain's journal some time, Brad," she suggested. "Especially if it has something to do with a long lost gold mine. I accidentally overheard President Wong talking with his assistant, Mr. Chen, about sending an exploration team to have another look at finding Lassiter's two billion dollar lost gold mine, but Mr. Chen said that Yang Lee wouldn't stand for it. After they broke up their conversation, Mr. Wong called me into his office

147

Gary Dale

for a rare visit to discuss the mining commission's decision to take parts of each mining claim for the Aussie government. He was upset, as it appeared to all the mining companies that the take-over percentage was really an additional tax. Anyway, it was in his private office that I noticed a book under a high security glass case. He saw my interest and said that it was a sea captain's journal and was a family heirloom going back hundreds of years. The journal was his pride and joy. For a moment, he broke from his stoic facade and mentioned that his family came from a great line of seafarers. Some were merchantmen but more were sea captains that had established many ports of commerce all along India and Africa coastlines. Like all Chinese sea captains President Wong had said, each sea captain had a written journal of their voyages, but this particular journal under the glass case was special. He walked over and actually stroked the security case. I immediately thought of your reef of gold journal, Brad. Maybe it is similar."

Brad didn't quite know what to do with Megan's information. He was stunned, frankly. As a result of his conversation with Alice and Michael, he had written off any connection between Wong and the journal. Now, with Megan's revelation, it immediately reminded him that a certain Wong family from Macau did have at one time, a journal similar to his, according to the ancient Chinese gentleman from San Francisco. Was this the same Wong family? Sure, the name Wong was akin to Smith, but could it be the one he was looking for? There was no way at the moment to check out Megan's information if the Wong's were related unless he wanted to lose his job. Miles had warned him about asking too many questions. As a result, he didn't think President Wong would approve of his questions and interest.

"Ah, just wondering Brad," questioned Michael, "are you going to tell the rest of us about this reef of gold journal in your possession?"

Megan suddenly realized that Brad hadn't included Michael and Maggie in the need to know circle. Her face turned beet red.

148

Reef of Gold

As he thought about what to say, he unconsciously brought his hands together touching his lips. "I'll make this short for now," he said. "In my possession, is a rare ship captain's journal that describes an ancient reef of gold, perhaps located somewhere in the Northern Territories of Australia, I think. The Chinese ship captains were apparently familiar with the coasts of Australia during their sea voyages in the early 1400's and they kept journals as a business record of sea routes and contacts. Sometimes, my research in the Perth library revealed that sea captains often went exploring on their own accord, with the promise of gold as a way to avoid the crew's boredom. This journal seems to point out a way to find an ancient reef of gold. Long story short, I'm trying to find that gold reef."

"So, that's why you were so anxious to explore the Wyndham gold strike area up North," remarked Michael. "I can understand your passion and reasoning."

"You found out this additional sea captain stuff from the Perth Library?" asked an amazed Maggie.

"Well, yes," said Brad. "There is a special section in your library where rare books are stored behind a big glass case. It's all locked up, of course, but with my international research card, they allowed me to retrieve certain books, journals, maps that they had on file. The whole section is quite fascinating. I just love to sit in a chair and look at all the books and try to visualize all the adventures the authors had been on in their time. I could sit for hours."

They all looked at Brad in stunned amazement.

A glazed look had come over Brad's eyes for a moment and he was barely breathing. He snapped out of the trance when he noticed everyone at the table staring at him, waiting for him to continue.

"Sorry," said Brad. He took a deep breath. "Anyway, the town of Freemantle, just south of us was at one time a big seaport for ships arriving from England where unloading of the unwanted from the jails of the crown occurred. Ship captains built homes here, established commerce, and often went exploring for new markets

Gary Dale

on their return to England. Fortunately, they left a record of their voyages. Also in the library's special collection of books were journals written by sea captains voyaging into the unknown waters leaving bits and pieces of gossip or stories about other sea captains hundreds of years before them. There were rumors of the gold reef even in that time period. It is quite fascinating."

"By the way Michael, if you are interested, there are a number of journals on gold mining efforts in Western Australia. These journals talk about ancient gold discoveries to the present day mining efforts. Several documents mentioned an ancient crack in the earth that has some unexplained enormous boulders trapped in the bottom of what I would call a canyon. Apparently, according to one theory, Australia was at one time attached to the continent of Africa. It broke loose and floated about until it ran aground at today's location. The unusual boulders that were trapped on the Australian Continent had to come from Africa. It's the only other place in the world where they are part of the landscape. The reading is a bit dry but the subject matter is all part of history. In any event, where ever that ancient crack is located, I'd like to explore it someday if I can find it. In the meantime, I want to head to the outback and look at some of Sterling mining claims in area five. I'll have to wait until I have saved up some vacation time unless the company closes down for a few weeks."

"Oh, you mean the long week company holiday," suggested Michael. "We never know when that might occur if at all. The decision is entirely up to the president of our company."

"If it does happen," said Brad, "I want to definitely head out to the mining areas."

There was a significant pause until Melissa and her friends walked into the dining room, reminding them of her birthday party. This was her moment.

150

CHAPTER 17

OUTBACK TRIP PREPARATION

It wasn't but a few days later that President Wong sent down an official memo to all employees announcing that in one week, the company, including the engineering department, would close down and honor the long week holiday. Mining efforts were slowing down.

Brad smiled when he read the announcement because he knew that Michael would be celebrating. Everyone was just plain tired from working on the same everyday stuff and even the Friday pub gatherings had dwindled in attendance to where most employees had even stopped meeting after work.

As promised, Michael helped Brad prepare for his expedition and loaned him several copies of the mining department contour maps to study, showing where the company had been spending some of its time searching for gold on known claims and what to be looking for in landscape. The outback was full of bumps, humps, and canyons and the towns of Kalgoorlie and Laverton were the centers of the most famous gold strikes of all of Western Australia. The area was the focal point for all the company maps. It was a huge region.

With further study, it looked to Brad that gold also had been found in the fringes of the Gibson Desert as well as the Great Victoria Desert. Sterling Mining had mining claims in both areas. He took the charts back to his office to analyze and decide just where he wanted to

Gary Dale

start his exploring in hopes of finding an ancient canyon, overlooked by mining companies. He had just a few clues. He made some circles on one of the maps with a crimson marker indicating Sterling Mining claim boundaries and in royal blue marked the approximate areas that hadn't been thoroughly explored yet by company engineers. One map made reference to the competitors and their area of exploring. There were a lot of claims, but each claim seemed to fade away the further one went deeper into the Outback.

Brad carefully rolled each map back to the proper size, rubber banded each and then placed them into protective tubes. He had borrowed ten maps from Michael's engineering department but only needed the one map he had marked for the journey. He went to roll up the chosen map when he noticed it was rather thick compared to the others. He held the map up to the overhead lights. It looked like a double exposure against the bright lights. Examining the corners of the map, he took a penknife from his desk drawer and peeled back the corner edges. Two maps had stuck together. Hand written at the bottom of the map was Yang Lee's name and the names of the survey crew. In one corner of the map was penciled a large question mark.

Brad stared thoughtfully at the map. So, he wasn't the only one wondering where Lee traveled on his outback trips. He walked over to the copy room where he duplicated the suspect map. He would let his brother Ric know about this discovery and all the other stuff he had learned at their next meeting. The suspect map could be important or it might not, he thought.

Leaving the chosen maps on his desk, Brad walked over to Michael's office, past the Boab tree, and found him frantically pulling off computer data while simultaneously on the phone. Brad pointed to the marked up chart he carried under his arm. Michael nodded and held up his finger as a one-minute pause. The pause sign was accurate within the minute. He was off the phone and computer.

Brad quietly asked him about the accuracy of the map he held

152

Reef of Gold

of Yang Lee's latest secret foray into the outer fringes of the Great Victoria Desert.

"Hmm," said Michael, "good question. Let me see the map again." He paused for a moment, as if gathering his thoughts. "These are nothing, really. Just my guesstimates from Megan's conversation," he said, as he casually stuck the map into a round paper tube and stuck it back into the map rack. "More like doodling. You don't need this map, as it would just throw you off."

Brad felt like he was being politely brushed off. Now he was intrigued.

"Did the exploration trips by Yang Lee take place in the same general area as recorded by your engineer reports?" asked Brad. "Just curious."

"From Megan's description, it is possible. But probably not," Michael concluded. "They may have started out on our claims but eventually moved in another direction. If you remember, we never did get a printout or maps from the fourth floor expedition. If you're thinking what I think you're thinking, forget it. You won't be going that far into unknown territory. It would be very difficult to track you. It's very rough country in the Great Victoria Desert. Besides, your expedition will be heading for Area Five, in the Gibson Desert. That's rough enough. Don't be pushing me, Brad," he warned. "Stick to the plan we agreed upon. No straying off course."

"Why do you keep referring to my trip as an expedition?"

"Brad, when you go out into the outback for any reason, you must prepare for an expedition. Your life may depend upon your preparation. It doesn't matter if it is only for a day or an extended stay of weeks at a time. Things happen in the Outback that you can't even imagine. Sources for water and food are non-existent unless you are an Aborigine. Their ancestors have lived on this continent for thousands of years and obviously know where to look." Michael shuffled some paperwork around before pulling out a list three pages

153

Gary Dale

long entitled, 'The American's Adventure.' It had lots of red marks on it as if it was a college theme paper.

"You're still determined to explore during the long week?"

Brad nodded in the affirmative.

"Merely checking. No offense." Michael smiled. "Well then, the good news," he said, looking at one of the three pages in his hand, "is that since you plan to head for our claims near Laverton, I can let you use company equipment. We had it all set up for future expeditions so you can just about drive away today if you want. I can have the equipment supervisor load fresh water, and petrol. You will have to provide any extra food that you will want that fits your particular palate. But Brad, please use the basic food list I gave you. It will save you future problems out in the outback."

"You can get a company rig for sure?" asked an excited Brad.

"There is a precedent. Most often, the mining vehicles are used by our own engineering department staff on their days off or holiday time. No one has asked for the company exploration gear for the long week this year, probably because we have been working on speculation projects. Therefore, a mining rig is all yours."

"Just what Sterling Mining equipment do I need?" Brad asked out of curiosity. "I want to see how close I had come in my own estimations for one week of exploring."

"Go get the map you will be using. I'll show you stuff that will answer some of the questions."

Brad quickly returned with the main map and handed it over to Michael who started making circles with a black grease pencil. While marking the map, Michael noticed compass markings were marked in green rather than the standard GPS system grid marks marked in red. He shrugged. Then he handed Brad the list of equipment.

"Ha, this list will boggle your mind." Michael crossed off the fancy rented rig with all the extras. "I can tell you that our big stuff includes a specially modified 4 x 4 rig for mining exploration. It's loaded with all the spare parts, like fan belts, extra tires, oil and just

154

Reef of Gold

about everything else possible. It will tow three tag-a-long, two-wheel trailers, with bladders full of petrol and water, some dried emergency food, and all the tools you need to make any repairs."

"What are bladders that require trailers?" asked Brad.

"Bladders hold your water and petrol. Drinking water is drained into soft tube-shaped plastic and covered with a special canvas that breathes. Helps to keep the water cool. The fuel is pumped into big truck tire-like inner tubes, which are specially lined with an anti-corrosive material and are wrapped with tough canvas." Michael paused for a moment.

"Follow my marker. On your map, I have approximated the distance for each drop-off point for the trailers." He pointed to the selected area of exploration before making a few more circles. "Each trailer contains food, water and petrol to make sure you and others can get back to the next trailer and eventually civilization. Most of the established drop- off points are clearly marked with the company logos. That way, we are less likely to lose people, especially new engineers, and equipment. If, for some reason you can't find the established drop off, then find your own area, pinpoint it with the global positioning satellite system and mark it on your map for future use. Does that make sense?"

"Does for me," Brad exclaimed. "It's a little overwhelming to say the least, but I guess I can understand your reasoning."

Michael looked thoughtfully at Brad and said, "We have a tendency to over-protect our employees anyway. With the office GPS, we can find you if you are injured and you will have phone communication."

"Ah, Michael, my cell phone cuts out sometimes in Perth, so how will it work hundreds of miles in the outback?" Brad persisted.

"Mate, the mining phone you will carry is a special satellite phone that will have the range you need. It bounces the signals off several satellites to reach me in Perth. These phones are very powerful unless you have a low battery or find yourself under a rock overhang

Gary Dale

or a canyon with steep walls, then, you will have problems with the satellite phone. I'm repeating myself to make a point. If you get in any trouble, contact me and I can call our own search and rescue."

"That is what I'm afraid of and look at all the ridicule I'd receive from the staff."

Michael laughed. "There is no question that we all would give you some static about getting lost or stuck in some sand hole. But, nothing ventured, nothing gained."

"Just how many company people have to know about this trip of mine? I'd like to keep the catcalls to a minimum when I return. Especially don't tell Miles what I'm doing. He would dole out this information for months."

"Oh, probably four or five including the supervisor from the equipment building and his loader, who will know you took out the equipment but not where you are headed. As far as your known destination, just Alice and I will know your true whereabouts. Oh, and Megan too. I'll give you a signed authorization form, but you will still have to personally sign out for the equipment when you pick it up. You should go over to the equipment building in a couple of days so they can show you how to release the trailers from each other. They are very heavy, so dropping the trailer stand correctly is pretty important. Just be sure to find out how late they work on the last day before the long holiday because when they are gone from the premises, that's it. They don't come back in to work. Oh, I did see our wandering soul today. He shows up just as the company goes on holiday. Can you believe it?"

"You mean 'Ian? He must be incredibly lucky. Wish I knew how he does it."

They both laughed. They agreed that every company has at least one like him.

"Guess I'll return my rented dent proof 4-wheel rig," said Brad. "The rental guy wasn't too thrilled to be renting a fairly new 4 x 4 Nissan Patrol Man to me anyway."

156

Reef of Gold

Michael laughed from the gut this time. Just like Miles, he enjoyed Brad's discomfort. He gave Brad the three page survival list of needed items to gather before he left.

A couple of hours later, Michael walked quickly into Brad's tiny cubicle and handed him the various lists of equipment. "You are all set up," he said quietly. He looked around the cubicle and then snapped his fingers. "You left your map on my desk. I forgot to bring it with me. No worries, I'll bring it by or will have someone drop it off to you shortly. As soon as you can, go see the equipment guy at the warehouse. He is expecting you. He is leaving early. Be sure he goes over the driving and handling characteristics for towing the trailers. Oh, almost forgot. The rig you are taking is one of our more 'experienced' off road vehicles. Meaning it doesn't have all the bells and whistles that our newer ones have, and it has personally met a few rocks. Unfortunately, I can't let you have one of the newer rigs. It's company policy. It is a matter of seniority.

Perplexed for a moment, Brad asked him what he really meant by an experienced rig.

Michael chuckled. "Brad," he said, "your rig just returned from the service shop. The certificate said it is in good repair, but it has a lot of dents and worn spots. Mechanical things happen with any rig, and that is why you carry all the necessary spare parts. This particular rig can overheat especially if you use the air conditioning extensively. So use the cool air only when in great need. Oh, yes, it doesn't have the on board GPS system. That part is still in the repair stages. You will get a hand held version. Someone will drop by your desk to show you how it all works."

Brad shrugged his shoulders. "I'm ready," he said.

It was Friday before Brad knew it and time to leave. Michael had come by to wish him good luck and reminded him that there was a special place in the rig for the company laptop computer. The special place kept the laptop from being damaged when bouncing around on the rough terrain. Brad would just have to remember to strap it

Gary Dale

down tight each day of travel. Brad argued that he didn't need one, but it was a requirement by the mining company that all rigs carry one in case of mineral discovery. "Lot of good that would do me," Brad thought, as he didn't even know how to run the complicated computer mining programs. He sighed. Then again, he could check his email with it.

He wandered over to Megan's work area. Fortunately she was in her office and at her desk.

"Hi," he said. "I'm heading out on my adventure. Just wanted to say goodbye."

She looked up and smiled. "I think you will do fine out there," she said encouragingly. "Michael told me that he has planned your trip well and will be plotting your every move. If he is confident, then I am as well. I understand from Michael that you are going to Area Five, Northeast of Laverton."

"Yes," said Brad, "That's the plan. According to Michael, Area 5 would be the closest to an unexplored Sterling mining area that I could get to and still get back during the long week. He said it would be a good test for me."

"I agree," said Megan. "Besides, it will be loads of fun."

Back at his desk, Brad found someone had dropped off a satellite phone and his map. Unfortunately, there were no instructions for the piece of communication equipment other than a post-it-note to check with the warehouse supervisor. He forgot about the GPS unit that was supposed to be delivered to him.

He passed the time by reshuffling mindless paperwork and watching other staff members clean up their desks in preparation for the holiday. Brad knew he was a bit nervous about the expedition, but anxious to get going. He was all packed. His travel bag held the company map and communication gear. He looked at his driving schedule once again. Driving the mining rig to Area 5 would take several days. Dropping off the trailer caches deep into the outback would probably take another couple of days of rough travel. He

Reef of Gold

would take it slow and enjoy the country. He was in no hurry. After unloading the trailers, he could begin his actual exploration.

The sudden noise and vibration from a large helicopter landing on the roof of the office building vibrated the window panes. The office windows seemed to track the noise from floor to floor. It didn't startle Brad anymore as he figured it was the usual Friday flight. It probably would have several of the Singapore staff disembarking, and a few minutes later the helicopter would take off for the airport or some destination that only the Asian management knew about. Then President Wong would leave the office for his home in Dalketh, one of the more secluded and wealthy areas of Perth. The scuttlebutt in the office had the 3rd and 4th floors working off and on during the long week. Maybe the Asian management didn't honor the Aussie long holiday, or more likely, their work was entirely different than the rest of company and may demand working during the long week. In any event, Brad wasn't going to hang around to see if they needed a courier. He turned off his computer and placed his chair under his desk. He was now on holiday.

As for the secrecy of his trip...........

CHAPTER 18

OUTBACK

The taxi dropped Brad along warehouse row, on the docks of Freemantle. He found the warehouse supervisor had already left for the long week, leaving only the young warehouse loader to show him again the routine of unhooking his heavily loaded trailers. Brad noticed there were now four trailers and not three as previously planned. He asked the warehouse loader about that.

"Sorry, mate, don't know. I just load the stuff. I know the last trailer is loaded with only about a third the weight so you can still pull the trailers with the rig. It's going to be your first drop-off cache anyway so someone must have figured that you or the next mining expedition might need the extra fuel bladders. Maybe it was the mate that was here earlier that made up the extra trailer. He checked out your rig thoroughly including the trailers."

"Who was the last guy?" asked a curious Brad.

"Don't know," the kid answered. "Anything else? If not, good luck mate. I'm leaving for the nearest pub to water me down."

Brad slowly eased the rig and the trailers out of the warehouse area and onto the main highway. He went through the gears roughly. He couldn't help it. He was driving a rig with the steering on the right side and shifting with his left hand. To any driver following him, it looked like a snake moving down the highway. Cars behind

160

Reef of Gold

him gave him a wide berth. It was hours before he reached the first town of any size, finding parking in a motel back lot.

After spending the night in a 'slippers only' motel room, Brad carefully started his caravan of trailers again down the highway, by-passing many small towns. Traffic was light. It took him three hours of steady driving before he spotted the turn off marked by a big Sterling Mining sign. It was tipping backwards. Probably because of the wind, he thought. On further inspection, it looked like the sign had been propped up recently and rather hastily.

Turning right as the big Sterling Mining Company sign indicated, Brad followed the previous tire imprints that led away from the main road and had him generally following a south by southeast direction. He was expecting to circle around eventually returning to a more northerly direction. He found driving on the so-called mining track was really just a minor imprint on the floor of the Outback. The earth was sporadically covered with gray-green brush, Spinifex, occasional small Eucalyptus trees, and a few scattered Ghost Gum trees, all growing in reddish soil and as far as Brad could see in any direction. He was reminded by Michael's travel notes that navigating through the rough landscape was going to be the toughest part of the trip. While he had planned on having a well-worn track to follow for a good portion of the way to the last Sterling Mine boundary, he knew it wasn't always a given.

Brad wasn't apprehensive when the track started to get a little faint and then disappeared. So had the ghost gums. Luckily, he came to his first company drop off point. It was entirely by accident.

Without too much maneuvering, Brad added his smaller trailer to the ruminants of previous cache dumps. He would pick up any empty trailer on his way out. The unmarked cache looked like it had been there a while making him curious if any of the dust-covered bladders still had any liquid in them, be it gas or water. He lifted the covering tarp and gave the bladder marked with white paint that said water, a weak kick. The bladder flexed enough to indicate that

161

Gary Dale

fluids were still inside. How good the water would taste was another question. He called Michael's office just in case he showed up on a weekend, leaving a cryptic message on Michael's voice mail that he had made it to the first cache and was proceeding with his trek. He said he had been lucky to have found it.

What had been a track very early on was now indistinguishable from the rest of the reddish sandstone fine gravel-like landscape. He stopped the rig after only a mile and stared at the foreboding Outback, desolate as far as the eye could see. Brad's heart was pounding now and his breathing becoming rapid.

'Do I really want to do this?' he asked himself. He blinked his eyes forcibly a few times and then rubbed the rough stubble of his beard. Unconsciously, he slipped gears into first and let the clutch out. The rig moved slowly forward almost as if it was on its own journey, accepting the challenge even if the driver had reservations. The jolt from hitting and bouncing off the first large rock with his front tire broke his trance.

Sweat continued to bead across his brow and his lips were becoming cracked as the heat of the day accelerated. The constant wrestling with the steering wheel to dodge rocks and brush drained his energy. With each torturous kilometer, the same boring appearance of the Outback went on and on. The compass directional needle on the passenger side of the rig kept swiveling back and forth. Nature's obstacles made it nearly impossible to read the compass accurately when he was driving. He hoped his compass would provide him an accurate direction because that was all he had in his possession.

He skirted the edge of a long rip in the earth, letting his rig drift kilometers away for safety reasons. At first, Brad would occasionally stop, check the compass, change course with a line of sight, record the angle of the sun and the time with a little characterization drawing in his pocket notebook and drive off. Now he was just driving with only a suggestion of where he was going, dropping off an occasional trailer at the appropriate mileage making it easier on

Reef of Gold

the rig's engine. He must have completely lost track of time when it dawned on him that the sun was sweeping to his right and reflecting off the rear view mirror. His concentration had been so strong on the terrain ahead of him that lunchtime had apparently come and gone. Exhausted and hungry, he finally gave up and stopped. He was becoming light-headed.

Brad struggled out of the rig. Each body limb was stiff and painful and he felt groggy. The muscle strain from twisting and turning the steering wheel over the rugged terrain was becoming a problem. Downing a slug of water made him feel a lot better, so much better that he figured that from now on, he would take more breaks to stretch and drink water. He realized that he was finding out some things the hard way.

When he was through stretching his tired muscles, he chomped down an energy bar before spreading the map across the scorching hood of his rig. He quickly revisited the approximate circled locations of several caches, anticipating the mileage where he was to drop off the next trailer. Driblets of sweat dropped from his nose onto the map. He watched the moisture dry up almost immediately.

Brad suddenly leaned back, gazed at the landscape and then looked back at the map. He muttered a few chosen words. The map in front of him was the wrong one. This was a map from Michael's desk indicating Yang Lee's supposed exploration trips. Now, he was in unexplored territory whether he liked it or not. He recorded his notes from his notebook on the top left hand corner of the map. Then he climbed into the left seat where the passenger usually sat, checked the laptop computer security straps to make sure they were holding tight, and leaned over to read the compass heading this time from a different angle. He went back to the map and marked an arrow where he thought he was located. It wasn't pretty.

A headache was beginning to appear above his left eyebrow. He drummed his fingers on the hot metal hood lightly as if the tips were on fire. More sweat dropped off his nose in little driblets. It took him

Gary Dale

a few moments to realize the implication of his finding. He was a long way from his first drop off point both in terms of distance and time. Yang Lee's map didn't indicate any company trailer drop sites. His route had been by helicopter in unexplored territory.

He looked around in a 360-degree turn, slowly taking in all the landscape. He didn't want to go back to the highway because he wasn't even sure if he could follow his own trail back. The steady wind had brushed away his tracks. Subconsciously, he knew he could be in real trouble. He wasn't going to admit it even to himself.

Brad sat down on the ground leaving the rig door open for needed ventilation. His dinner was packed in a cooler and it didn't take long to eat the meat sandwiches that the restaurant had made for him earlier. He washed it all down with warm water, rested as best he could in a little spot of shade provided by the rig until it was nearly dark and then crawled into his swag. He slept like the dead.

The rising sun didn't pay any attention to the rig and driver. It popped up on the horizon and stayed there like a red furnace. He left immediately after a quick breakfast. After an hour of rough travel, he finally stopped, drank some water and called Michael on his long-range satellite phone. It was his second attempt with this powerful piece of equipment. Michael was in his car when Brad gave him the mileage locations of the various caches. Michael said he thought the caches were spaced about right. The compass readings were relayed. He paused and then Michael started to laugh.

"Ok, Michael, what's up?" asked Brad, seriously.

"Aw, not to worry. It is not what you think." He broke out laughing again.

"Yes," asked Brad, waiting for a response.

"I have a message for you from Alice. She asked me to read it to you but I can't read it to you without laughing, so I will have to paraphrase it. Here we go." He laughed some more. "Sorry," he said. "She has feelings for you. Now that you are gone, she realizes that she should have been more direct with you. Bottom line, big guy,

164

Reef of Gold

she wanted to go exploring with you. Would you please consider coming back to get her?"

There was silence on both ends of the satellite phone.

"I'll pass," said Brad. "Tell her I'm too deep in the Outback. Thank her for the offer and tell her that the lure of adventure has become my mistress for the moment."

"Ok, Brad, I'll let her down gently. I'll tell her that her offer will keep you warm at night." He laughed again.

"Some buddy you are. Geez, Michael, let's not get carried away here." Brad could hear Michael's laughter echoing from the satellite phone even as he held it away from his ear.

Brad quickly changed the subject and talked to Michael about a big rip in the earth that he had placed on his left shoulder, as a temporary visual guide. He explained that this particular crack in the earth seemed to go forever and was there a name for it?

"Of course there is, Brad. We have a name for everything and in most cases two names. Take your pick." Michael began by telling him all about the Shelby ravine, which was a substantial crack in the vastness of the Outback and subsequently a major obstacle for some of the mining companies. It divided a few mining claims in half and most companies only worked the northern side. It should be on your map and marked...." Then Michael stopped in mid-sentence.

There was an empty silence at the other end of the phone from Perth. Finally Michael said he would check Brad's position coordinates when he got home and would call him back.

Brad protested. "Wait," he shouted in the phone. "I have the wrong map." He was too late. Michael had already dropped the signal.

True to his word, Michael called back in an hour. The ringing of the satellite phone broke Brad's focus. He stopped the rig immediately.

"Brad, this is Michael. I'm looking at my map showing the ravine location. This little deviation of yours is more serious than I had

165

Gary Dale

thought. Are you sure you took the compass readings accurately? What about your GPS handheld device readings?"

"No one dropped off a GPS unit on my desk. I left without one. All I have is a compass attached to the rig. I mark every reading on my map, which brings up a good point. I have a different map, Michael. It's not the Sterling Mining map of area 5. I have a map showing the areas where you thought Yang Lee had explored. I remember you had made big circles on it."

"I'm stunned," said Michael.

"I didn't even look at this map until I'm out here in the wilderness. Once I left the main highway, I followed a track for a while. I thought it was the correct one until the track disappeared."

There was a long pause on both sides while both of them thought about the situation. At last Michael broke the silence. "Keep on drifting away from the ravine for safety reasons and check in periodically. Since you are already out there, might as well stay. I know about where you are, at least within a couple of hundred miles. I'm here in case of an emergency. I can send helicopters after you if necessary."

"I'm not laughing," replied Brad, and clicked off.

After making a slight compass adjustment of two degrees to the southeast, Brad had only been bouncing around in the rig for about an hour when he stumbled upon a strange sight. He stopped the rig and after a drink of very warm water from his water bottle, and walked up for a closer inspection. Line-less telephone poles were stretching as far as he could see in either direction like a zipper running across the landscape. When he rubbed his rough hands along the crude scrape marks on the poles, he knew immediately that they had been peeled by hand. These weren't telephone poles; these were very old telegraph poles probably from the 1800's. They had to be, he reasoned. Telephone poles were machine made and thick. This pole was rough hewn, skinny in comparison and not nearly as tall.

Reef of Gold

He walked around the pole again and then stared off into the distance to make sure he wasn't seeing things.

Yet, here the telegraph poles were still standing, solid in the ground like so many soldiers on parade. Obviously the poles were not being used anymore, even by nesting birds, which Brad thought a little strange. Brad looked around at the nearby landscape. If he didn't know he was already in Australia, he could have been in Nevada, he reasoned. It looked the same to him.

As he drove along, Brad realized the telegraph poles were heading in the general direction of his new heading so he decided to keep within eyesight of them. The poles would be a reference point for him and keep him away from the dreaded crack in the earth. The longer he paralleled the abandoned telegraph line, the more his mind pondered the source and ending. Could the line have stretched as far as Alice Springs, which was in the center of Australia and in a straight line all the way to Perth?

Following the telegraph line made his driving easier. The concentration required to stay on course, however, had changed to being mesmerized by the monotony of seeing mile after mile of poles. He was nodding off more now, and struggled to stay awake. Suddenly, an awareness of something different broke the dullness. He stopped the rig. In the bright sunlight, he could see something perched near the top of one of the poles. It was a saucer shaped dish about three feet in diameter. Curiosity getting the best of him, Brad drove closer to the saucer. He studied the strange object. One saucer seemingly pointed in the direction of the next pole and another pointed in the opposite direction towards the previous pole. Brad walked around looking for wires of any kind and yet found none. "What the heck is this?" he muttered to himself.

Walking away from the telegraph poles gave him a different angle of viewing. On the very top of the pole and in between the saucers was a weather-scarred black box about the size of a small suitcase. From this new vantage point, the whole thing now looked like each

Gary Dale

concave dish was sticking out on each side of the pole. Kind of like his ears did when he was a kid, he mused.

Walking back to the rig for his binoculars, Brad surveyed the dish setup and discovered that there was some wording on the sun-bleached metal. He could barely make out *Property of Australian Communications Co. Ltd.*

Shaking his head in disbelief of the many mysteries of the Outback, he climbed back in his little oven of transportation to sweat some more. He was a little disappointed. He still hadn't discovered any ancient streambeds nor any of the giant boulders he had hoped to find.

About 50 kilometers away from the first sighting of the saucer communication dish, Brad came upon another dish setup, just like the first. It looked somewhat weather beaten and had old telegraph lines dangling to the ground. Since it looked the same, Brad didn't hang around to reason why. His rig's engine didn't need to be cooled, so he slipped it back into first gear and moved on, determined that he would find an ancient streambed sometime soon.

The mind numbing dullness of the landscape, mile after mile, kilometer after kilometer, mesmerized his brain once again. He just kept on bouncing around in the rig, in a rhythm of side-to-side, down and up motions. Bleary eyed, he was barely keeping the line of telegraph poles in sight as the rig was ever so slowly drifting away to the South. His breathing became shallow as if he was holding his breath. Brad was nodding off from fatigue when some vague warning, deep in the recesses of his scrambled brain made him suddenly slam on the brakes.

Light dust swirled all around him in a big cloud and then gently settled. Brad just sat there for a minute, with the engine idling, brake fully depressed, wondering why he stopped. His breathing was faster, as was his heart rate. Without thinking, he pulled on the emergency brake and switched off the engine. He ran a roughened hand over his dry and dusty face. The silence was overwhelming except for

Reef of Gold

the vibrations of his body. He opened the door and stepped down. Leaving the door open for ventilation, he walked a few steps along the front fender. Suddenly, his knees buckled. He grabbed at the front fender keeping him from pitching forward and gasped at the sight before him. A huge drop-off of hundreds of meters lay before him. A string of swear words peppered the air. He had nearly driven over the edge of a cliff.

Shaken, Brad slowly got to his feet and with a little more foolish courage, ventured closer to the edge of the cliff, just a couple of feet away. With his left hand firmly grasping the metal fender, he leaned ever so slightly over the edge to look down. It was enough to make him slightly dizzy. The canyon was deep. Brad let his eyes follow the widening canyon rim to his right. The mouth of the canyon was less than a half a mile away or so it seemed.

Brad inched backwards to the rear of the rig. He checked the trailer to see if it could be backed up without jack-knifing on him. The position looked all right. He grabbed a water bottle, swallowed several gulps of water and splashed his face. The little bit of water helped him to think clearly. He climbed back into the rig. Why couldn't the rig have been an American 4-wheel drive where all the gears were familiar to his right hand? he complained, mumbling to himself. He knew that one slight, uncoordinated act on his part, and the rig would roll right over the edge with him most likely trapped inside despite taking the precaution of leaving the driver's side door open.

That thought worried him. The fact that the terrain indicated a slight downhill slope towards the edge of the cliff didn't help his waning confidence. He took a deep breath, blew it out, started the engine, slipped the gears in reverse, and gave the engine a steady feed of petrol. He gradually released the hand brake, barely letting out the clutch at the same time and slowly backed up, an inch at a time, navigating the rig about 50 meters from the edge of the cliff. Only then did he start to breathe again.

Gary Dale

Swinging the rig around, he could see the terrain sloped gradually downward towards the canyon mouth. Using first gear, Brad eased the rig down the slope and onto the canyon floor, full of hope, and expectation of what he didn't know. As a guardian to the canyon entrance, a very large Boab tree stood tall and menacing like a Sterling Mining office security guard. Beneath the rare tree, it was mostly devoid of vegetation and interest except for a patch of shade. Boulders seemed to guard the tree. While the tree provided some immediate shade beckoning him to stop, he opted to find better protection from the sun. He drove the rig a little further into the canyon until he found a rock overhang carved out by Mother Nature and backed in the trailer. The shade dropped the temperature immediately. Blocking the tires, he remembered to drop both jacks before unhooking the remaining small trailer from the rig.

Released from the confines of the trailer, the rig responded with a newly found quickness. He continued into the canyon before finding a large overhang offering a huge amount of shade. He maneuvered the rig underneath and turned off the ignition. Still vibrating, his muscles felt numb from all the driving. His ears were ringing from the engine noise. He had done it.

CHAPTER 19

PERTH…..MISSING DISK

Things were not good.

Yang Lee paced back and forth in Wong's office, snapping in half any pencil he could find, leaving wooden shards to stab the carpet. "What had gone wrong?" he muttered to himself, his mind seething with frustration. Large, grotesque veins throbbed in his neck with each beat of his heart. He seemed oblivious of his surroundings. President Wong observed his behavior from behind a sizable mahogany desk. Lee continued to pace, trying to work out his problem. "My courier arrived in Singapore without the proper disk," he hissed through clinched teeth. He slammed his fist in to the palm of his other hand shattering the few pencils remaining. He showed no pain as he removed the splinters from his hand. What he really wanted to do was to physically attack someone or something to ease his escalating frustration and fear.

President Wong shifted positions from one leg to another. Noticing the movement, Yang Lee whirled around and stared right through him. Time seemed to stop for Wong. He felt like a cornered rat, waiting for the deadly viper to strike.

Yang Lee turned his back to Wong and continued to pace the office from one end to the other. Lee's mind raced with possibilities. The original disk was missing. So, where was it? Who touched it

Gary Dale

last? How did the fake disc get into the courier briefcase in the first place? He suddenly paused in his pacing. Is it possible that someone from his own staff could have stolen the disk? He grabbed at his cell phone and called his security chief. "Search again," he demanded, his fingers almost crushing the cell phone. "I want to know who has been in the building over the past 48hrs. Check all the records. Find who was here over the weekend and bring them here for questioning. I want to know those names now." He snapped shut the clamshell cell phone, looked up and noticed Wong as if for the first time. "You," he said venomously, "are causing me problems."

A frightened President Wong shrugged his shoulders as if he didn't know what was going on. He realized that Yang Lee had suddenly focused his anger and frustration on him. Wong instantly knew he was in the wrong place at the wrong time.

"Your pursuit of this gold reef has now become a major concern," Yang Lee shouted at Wong, spraying spittle onto the mahogany desk. "You were to keep your special gold reef search project to yourself and not attract any unwanted attention. Who is this associate of yours and why is she here?"

President Wong froze. This emotional outburst was almost too much for him. He did not like confrontations under any circumstances especially with someone as dangerous as the enforcer. There was only his desk between the madman and himself.

"Answer me," commanded Lee.

"She is a relative," croaked Wong, quickly plopping down in his oversized leather chair, "an American from San Francisco."

"I already know that," snapped Yang Lee. He leaned forward, placing his gnarled hands on the massive desk and stared at Wong, challenging him to continue. Like a reptile, his tongue constantly swept over his open mouth as if testing the air.

President Wong averted the stare and quickly looked on his desk to find some moisture to wet his dry throat. The water glass trembled

Reef of Gold

in his hands as he sipped the warm liquid. When he finished, he held the glass in both hands in his lap in case he needed more water.

"As a family," Wong stammered, "we have been searching for the fabled reef of gold for many centuries. There are two known journals. One is in my possession, but it does not give the exact location of the gold reef. The other journal belongs to an American who happens to be here in Perth right at this moment. My cousin believes the American journal contains a map that has the location of the reef. She recognized the person who has it. He, in fact, is a Sterling Mining employee. She has been watching his residence for nearly a week now to see when and where he is planning to search for the reef of gold. He comes home after work with maps and charts in his arms and often spends hours alone in the Perth maritime museum. He is up to something."

"And you jeopardize our position here," sputtered Yang Lee, "because this adventurer might have this diary? Wong, this is the Triad that you are upsetting with this nonsense."

"But this is the reef of gold location we are talking about discovering," Wong argued passionately. "These are riches beyond our imagination. With the two diaries in my possession, I can discover the reef and privately mine the gold."

"Wong, I don't care about chasing after some foolish dream," Yang Lee shouted. "Your relative has to stop asking Sterling Mining employees questions about who does what in the mining company especially who goes out on expeditions. And she cannot use company research on any gold discoveries in the Northern Territories. Employees are suspicious of what we are doing on the third floor as it is, and we certainly don't need any more animosity or curiosity developing. What is wrong with you?"

President Wong's brain was working furiously now. Lee's statement may have offered a way out of this confrontation. "My deepest apologies, Yang Lee. As a precaution, I will yield to your

Gary Dale

advice and have my relative immediately disassociate herself from asking questions from the office staff."

Yang Lee glared at him like a shark eyeing its victim and then abruptly turned, walking out of the office and through the double doors of the waiting area. The elevators down to the third floor would not move fast enough for Lee.

President Wong forced himself to move from his chair and closed his office door. He started to breathe again, but his trembling continued. He felt exhausted. He sat down again and closed his eyes, letting the raw emotion drain from him. It had been a long time since he had faced an adversary in a life-changing situation. He shifted positions in his chair. "Yes," he said to himself, "it had been ten years ago, almost to this very day. The discovery had changed my life."

With his eyes still closed and breathing deeply, he let himself drift into the memories of the discovery of the original *reef of gold* journal. His mother had arranged a meeting with her brother, so her son Wong could explore any possibilities for employment in her family's shipping business. She knew that her brother would disapprove of this direct approach, but she needed the money her son would bring home. She wanted to live again in a nice apartment and socialize with the upper class. Besides, her brother had his sons already working in the family shipping business. Why not her son? After all, he had some experience in international trading by working for other companies even though he was placed in low-level administrative jobs. That wasn't his fault.

Wong had tried to convince his mother that he would someday succeed and avenge his father's premature death, which had placed them lower in the economic ladder. But coming from a father-less family, his employers expected little of him. They had told him that he was smart and clever when it came to business figures but he lacked the killer instinct to handle his business adversaries. They would shake their heads as if disappointed in him. Wong hoped his uncle would teach him to be stronger in the face of others. His

Reef of Gold

mother was confident. His uncle wasn't so sure and said so to Wong during the interview.

A cousin of Wong's had walked into the room, interrupting his uncle during their conversation, with questions about the company board meeting due to start in an hour. "Some cash," the sharply dressed cousin in a brown suit said while handing his uncle a slip of paper, "is needed for several of the board members." His uncle nodded in response. He stood, turned his back to Wong and opened a wall safe cleverly disguised behind a Ming Dynasty vase mounted on a plain wooden mantel.

Wong tried to ignore his cousin who stared at him. He tuned his attention to the wall safe recognizing the vase immediately. He had seen the same vase being hawked by the street vendors. One touch by any street vendor would have known it was a fake made for the unsuspecting tourist. Wong could only surmise that the cheap vase replica must be of some personal significance to his uncle. What significance he didn't know. His mother had not said. Wong watched in awe as his uncle spun the dials opening the wall safe. He did not know of anyone who had a wall safe.

Several items of importance and personal effects were taken from the large wall safe including a heavy book. His uncle carefully set these items on his desk before retrieving several stacks of American and Australian currency.

Wong's eyes got very large. He had never seen so much money in his life. He had occasionally seen American money in small wads but nothing compared to the stacks of green money in front of him. His uncle arranged the currency in neat piles on his desk before counting out the required amount. Satisfied with the count, he tied each bundle with a silk ribbon and immediately stacked the money in a metal brief case. He handed the case to his son who immediately quit his annoying habit of cracking his knuckles and left the room immediately.

As his uncle was placing the rest of the money and his personal

175

Gary Dale

effects back into the safe, Wong asked his uncle about the significance of the thick book still on the desk. Wong knew his uncle was not a university educated man and thought it was unusual for him to have something like a book of this magnitude.

His uncle ignored him.

Undaunted, Wong stared at the book. All he could see was the beautiful cover. It had a Ming Dynasty vase drawn upon the cover surrounded by a gold trim. He couldn't remember ever seeing anything quite like it. Just as he was about to inquire as to its contents, his uncle had whisked it away into the confines of the safe, closing it securely with a loud click. The interview ended abruptly with the acknowledgment by his uncle that Wong would work in the international trade department located one floor below. His responsibilities would be in export/import area with the filling out of documentation and shipping forms with accompanying letters of credit and drafts. In addition, he would be helping the marketing and sales staff with the buying and selling of contracts for Australian mineral shipments.

Wong was stunned for a moment. He wasn't comfortable in the sales part of these areas of business.

His uncle's face showed no emotion. "Your salary will be nearly the same as my youngest son. You start tomorrow morning. The department head will be expecting you and he is to be your boss from now on. You will have no need to come up here again unless invited by me."

Wong knew he wasn't going to be part of upper management anytime in the near future.

His uncle cracked a thin smile. "Be sure to tell your mother of your new job. She doesn't need to call me anymore."

Wong walked quickly out of his uncle's building after meeting with his new boss. He was excited about his job and could hardly wait to get home to share his new adventure. As expected, his mother was pleased that her son was now part of her brother's

176

Reef of Gold

establishment, especially with the good salary. It would take them out of his mother's definition of middle class. Wong retold his mother every bit of conversation about the meeting with his uncle including his encounter with his uncle's oldest son. Wong knew he would be watched. The son was also an enforcer for the trading company.

She slowed her pacing. "Did your uncle say anything else?"

"No. He said I wouldn't visit him in his office while I worked there unless invited, but I did see something that father had told me existed for hundreds of years."

His mother's face fell at the mention of her deceased husband and then blossomed into excitement. "You saw the journal," she exclaimed. She pressed him for more details and then, clasping her hands behind her back, she fretted and paced back and forth in their small apartment. Wong kept silent. He knew she was in one of her moods. She stopped and motioned for Wong to sit with her on their tiny bamboo couch. She carefully outlined her plans for their future.

A knock on the office door snapped President Wong back to reality. He slowly got out of his executive chair. The nerve-wracking confrontation with Lee was still running through his veins. He started to say enter but his dry throat wouldn't let him. He grabbed at his glass of water, spilling a little on his chin before he could swallow the liquid. Another knock at the door occurred before he could respond. The door opened and in walked his American cousin, Sue Wong, looking very pale and stressed.

The look on his cousin's face told him that she must have met up with Yang Lee on her way to his office. What was once a beautifully sculptured face was now sagging around the eyes and mouth under the weight of stress. She didn't look well. President Wong nodded and motioned her into his office. "You must have encountered Yang Lee," he suggested, knowing full well she had faced the demon.

She tried to glare at him but she couldn't get her face muscles to

Gary Dale

work. "Who was that creature?" she demanded. "I thought you ran this company? You are the president, are you not?"

President Wong motioned for her to take a seat in front of his desk. She rearranged the scattered chairs back to their accustomed imprints in the carpet.

"Cousin," he said, "the man you encountered is Yang Lee, an enforcer. He runs a secretive division of the company and has the final say in our overall operations. It is very profitable for Sterling Mines to have his people here in the same building. I only run the mining company and it takes a back seat to his operations. We rarely are at odds but occasionally we butt heads as you just experienced. Watch out for him and please stay out of his way while we work on our own project. He is very dangerous and so are the people that he represents. Do not ask employees any more questions about our company expeditions and especially about this Brad Templeton person. We don't want to attract any more attention from Yang Lee at this stage. He is very unpredictable. And stay away from company research in the Northern Territories."

"Yes, cousin," said Sue Wong, still shaken from her encounter with Yang Lee. I will honor your wishes." She took a deep breath and changed the subject. "We are making progress. I now know where Brad Templeton lives and the little things about him. I also know he has left on some kind of mining adventure during the long week and when it is confirmed that he has entered the Outback, we can steal the journal."

"How do you plan to do that?" asked President Wong.

"He arranged for an exploration trip in Area 5."

"Area 5," exclaimed President Wong. "Why there? My company has already mapped and explored the entire area. He might find some gold nuggets that have traveled a long ways but the find won't amount to much, I am certain."

"This is his practice trip, cousin. Remember, he has little knowledge of the Outback and his friends in the company have

Reef of Gold

made plans to know where he is at all times. He has it all arranged with a support group and borrowed company equipment. This will be a fairly low risk trip for him or so he thinks. He has briefly been in Area 5 before with one of your survey crews as a non-working participant. He wouldn't even remember where he had been. Things look far different from a helicopter than from ground level."

President Wong was momentarily lost in thought. He looked up. "What do you mean, 'so he thinks'?"

Sue Wong smiled. "Area 5 is what everyone knows to be his destination," she said. "He will be confused when he checks his maps against his compass. Someone conveniently forgot to drop a GPS unit off at his desk so he has to rely on using a compass. I found a way to throw off his compass headings with a specially placed magnet. Hopefully, he will end up deep in uncharted areas, uncomfortably lost and very discouraged with his efforts."

"And you believe this will give you time to thoroughly search his residence and office for clues to the whereabouts of the journal?"

"I do. The only problem I see so far is his nosy neighbor. She watches his townhouse like a hawk."

"Do you think he will take the journal with him?"

"No, I don't think so, at least not on this trip. There is no need. He won't be in the area that the journal suggests, not even close. That means he will have left the journal somewhere safe in his townhouse or perhaps with someone, which I doubt. Regardless, this still means breaking into his residence for clues. We will enter his townhouse in the evening when the snoopy neighbor will be out playing cards. I am glad he is gone for at least a week. We might need the extra time for our search if the journal is not found in his townhouse."

"Ah," said President Wong. His acknowledgment let her know that he was beginning to get the drift of her diabolical plan. So simple and yet well planned. He also figured that the break-in couldn't be backtracked to him. He could plead innocence if she were caught. After all, it was her plan to steal the journal by any means possible.

Gary Dale

He would, however, have to watch this one carefully as she could be too clever for her own good. He did not want to anger Yang Lee.

Sue Wong smirked. "I have hired some rough Aussies who will search his home thoroughly for clues to the journal. The Aussies will be well paid for their expertise and continued silence."

President Wong looked down at his hands, briefly lost in thought. "Our family will soon have the riches they deserve after centuries of being one of the 'have nots'." He looked up into her sparkling eyes.

She winked and said, "Revenge will indeed be sweet, my cousin."

CHAPTER 20

OUTBACK CANYON

It was a cool morning with the sun barely awake.

Shouldering his heavy pack of mining tools, food, water, digital camera and satellite phone, Brad's feet gathered themselves for the journey. Even though the heat of the day was escalating, Brad walked at a steady pace, excited at the prospect of finding gold on his first day of exploring. He had slept like a log last night, and his brain was clear. Walking felt good after days of bouncing around in the rig. After the first fifteen minutes, he slowed down. 'Why hurry'? he thought. 'There's lots of time.'

The terrain now looked different than it had from the top of the canyon with the direct rays of the sun penetrating the landscape from a different angle. He continued to walk slowly, criss-crossing the canyon floor like a wandering ant in search of food. The silence in the canyon was intense. Only the crunch of his boots on the surface made any sounds in this seemingly barren area.

Brad stopped and stared across the canyon. An ancient track or trail, carved out from the steep sides of the canyon, found its way from the canyon floor to the top of the escarpment. He walked closer and realized that the closer he got to the trail, the more it seemed to disappear. Was this really an ancient 'track' as the Aussies would say, or was it the heat of the day playing its usual tricks? He retreated and

Gary Dale

sat down on the nearest rock to allow his eyes to examine each foot of the track as high as he could. Then the track suddenly blended into the background. Brad stared at the canyon wall for a few minutes to see if the rising sun would give up the secret.

The track had disappeared.

Amused and yet mystified from the sighting, Brad continued to walk further along the canyon floor, intently examining possible sites of gold bearing beds of gravel created by a rare flash flood. Each site looked plausible to him, but he still was uncertain with his choices. What if his digging turned up a dry hole? All he would have to show for the effort would be a sore back. If only he had more mining experience to simplify the search. He marked each possible dig by stacking rocks like a gravesite. By his count, he would have more than enough work.

Walking to the end of the canyon didn't take long. The landscape had changed again to a rock strewn area with pockets of small scraggly looking trees and scrub brush. Each pocket seemed to have its own little oasis of life. Insects of all kinds were active as were the feasting birds. The chattering flocks of birds ignored him completely, so intent on their feeding. This area of the canyon had come alive.

Brad sat down in a tiny shaded area. During his exploration of the mouth of the canyon, he observed little life on the desert floor. Now, right before him, the cycle of life was being played out. As he watched the burst of activity, he realized why this area was different. Water. That was it. There had to be an abundant water source nearby to support this multitude of life.

Getting to his feet, he looked towards the narrowing end of the canyon. Standing guard were huge boulders that looked like they had toppled over the edge of the escarpment. "Where did those boulders come from?" he wondered. "Are these the boulders that I have been looking for from Africa?" Brad reached the huge boulders and let his hands slowly trace the girth of each one. The feeling was like attempting to hug a giant Redwood tree in California without

182

Reef of Gold

receiving splinters on his nose. "What was the geological time-line of these boulders?" he asked himself. "And, what was on the other side of these boulders?"

Further examination indicated a space in between the wall of the canyon and the boulders, enough room he figured for a determined person to slide behind. The only danger might be getting stuck. Dropping his pack and mining tools on the ground, Brad slid behind the boulders to see how far he could go. It took only a minute or two of scraping his back against the wall, sucking his stomach in, and shuffling his feet to make it through. The passage wasn't much, but it put him near an unusual overhang. He scrambled up some of the smaller fallen rocks almost as if they were stepping-stones forming a crude staircase. Reaching a resting point under the overhang, he looked out in amazement to a carpet of tall grass-like reeds, reaching the height of six feet or more.

Brad suddenly realized that the huge boulders and a few scrub trees on ground level had formed an almost impenetrable screen from the rest of the canyon. Whatever this reed filled area was, it was hidden from view because of the boulders. He climbed up even higher on one of the numerous rocks that had fallen from the ceiling of the overhang eons ago and had planted themselves at their present location. He looked out over the landscape of reeds. No more than 50 meters away, he discovered something he had never expected to see; a precious body of water simmering undisturbed in the heat. It was about the size of a city lot, surrounded by tall reeds and grasses on three sides with the canyon wall flush with the small body of water.

Against the backdrop of the canyon were several black and gray mineral streaks cascading down the sides of the rock walls like a water-less waterfall. The more Brad stared, the more his brain began to consider how over time, rushing floodwater from the monsoons up north, must have repeatedly flushed and refilled the lake. He knew from a previous hunting experience in Nevada that beneath the tiny

183

Gary Dale

pebble strewn surface would contain a clay-like reddish sandy soil that would only absorb so much water before the rest of the water would run freely on the slick surface. Any rare cloudburst, even miles away, would funnel the rain runoff to this crack in the earth, flooding the canyon floor below.

Brad slid down the rock perch a little faster than he wanted and crashed to his knees. While scrambling around on all fours looking for his dropped water bottle, he noticed something unusual. Rock paintings were tucked up and under the back portion of the overhang. Fascinated, he stretched out his lanky frame flat on his belly and crawled along the confining back edge of the overhang, examining each and every one of the ancient Aboriginal paintings. Some of the paintings were of a spiritual nature, deformed humans, wild looking creatures with spears and crude drawings of ships with sails. The rock canvas also illustrated rodents, fish, snails, turtles, small game animals and a huge snake. He craned his neck to see more of the drawings. He felt like reaching out and touching prehistoric art but thought better of it. He turned his head slightly to remove the neck muscle strain. Enough of this mystical place, he thought. He backed out, careful not to disturb the surrounding dirt any more than he had too. He found his water bottle at the same time.

With adrenalin still pumping though his system, he squeezed through the giant boulder passage way and moved on down the canyon floor back towards camp. He was taking deep breaths when he discovered that he had a heightened awareness of his surroundings. With great clarity, he started to notice things that he had missed hours before. Instead of the big picture, he was noticing little things. Following a hunch, he walked down the middle of the canyon floor searching for dark shadows against the canyon walls that indicated outcroppings, irregular rock formations and tailings from rockslides. Each fan-like disturbance from the mundane canyon wall could indicate a previous earth tremor of some kind or a result of a flash flood. He worked the tailings hard, shoveling the gravel onto the

Reef of Gold

screens. Using the large opening screen to corner the debris and the fine screen to sift out the smaller particles, Brad looked for any nuggets.

He was glad he followed his hunch.

With diminishing daylight becoming a factor, Brad left his screens, shovels, and a couple of water bottles under a rock next to the junction of an arroyo funneling into the main canyon. This was the same little crack in the earth that had branched out from the main canyon he had discovered upon arriving to the area. He had remembered driving around it. He would cautiously explore the small arroyo for gold ore bearing alluvial fans tomorrow.

Brad's evening meal, cooked on his propane stove, consisted of prepackaged Australian bangers, semi-thawed under the shrinking dry ice in his cooler. Brad enhanced the Australian version of German sausages with a can of baked beans, a few bruised tomatoes and freeze-dried prunes for desert. Somewhere in his readings of the old American West stories, he remembered that prunes were the cowboy's favorite fruit. Being regular as the sunrise each morning was the basic idea. Unfortunately, his dried prunes tasted a bit like sawdust and gave him the same feeling going down. He could hardly wait until the next morning of exploring.

As the sun was fading rapidly, he set out two camp butane lanterns for extra light since sunlight had a habit of disappearing in the bottom of a canyon rather quickly. Since it was a little too early to sleep, Brad fussed with making his campsite comfortable until it was time to call Michael and tell him the good news about the canyon discovery. Using his flashlight, Brad walked cautiously down a narrow trail that he created from his comings and goings. Once away from the overhang, he called Michael at his home.

"Brad," answered Michael, "good to hear from you. How's the reception? You are fading in and out."

"Ok at this end," Brad acknowledged. "I'm in the bottom of this great canyon which normally shouldn't be a problem for the satellite

185

Gary Dale

phone according to you, but this is sort of a mystical area, so I'm not surprised at the fading in and out. I've got some exciting news to tell you. Are you sitting down?"

"No, but perhaps you had better sit down."

"Why?"

"You should know that the third and fourth floor people from the office have been trying to find you and a few other employees. President Wong's office people have been asking everybody specifically when and where you went on holiday. I assured them repeatedly that I don't know exactly where you are other than near Kalgoorlie, and that you just asked for the mining equipment and signed the release forms on Friday. Since no one else knows really where you went, you are probably off their radar screen for now. But they are serious in their search."

"Why do they want me," Brad asked, a little stunned by the event.

"I don't really know. But more importantly, Yang Lee is really upset...something about a missing disk."

"Michael, I don't know a thing about a missing disk. I don't understand. What's a missing disk have to do with me? "

"Probably nothing," exclaimed Michael. "Maybe I got some of the particulars wrong but the gist of Yang Lee's anger is the missing disk. They have certain people under suspicion for a variety of reasons known only to them. You may be just in the mix because of being a courier. All I know is that it's getting nasty from Mr. Lee's end of things. Remember, he's the tough guy from the fourth floor. And that's not all. Megan needs to talk to you straight away. She is coming over here in an hour or so. Apparently she has been under a great deal of suspicion herself. Yang Lee had the entire third floor swept from top to bottom looking for the 'missing disk.' You may be able to claim your innocence but with Megan, she has a problem. She has been the only person from the mining division to even have access to the third floor. Wong liked to see her when she was away

Reef of Gold

from the rest of us. He arranged for her to have an office on the third floor. Apparently, this last weekend, she worked in her war room office as she calls it, to catch up on paper work before she went on holiday. You know Megan; being 'Miss Conscientious'. Well, it has caused her to be a suspect. She called me from a pay phone because she is so scared."

"Whoa, wait a minute, Michael! What can be on a disk that is so important that employees are scared?"

"Beats me, mate. I'm grasping at straws. Maybe a new gold discovery is in the works in an area that hasn't even been fully explored by our company let alone any other mining company. But this is too soon for any leaking of information. We don't even know what's going on with our claim. So, I haven't a clue as to why all this turmoil. In any event, Megan can stay with us as long as she needs if she chooses to do so."

"It's very strange," said Brad. "Tell Megan I'll keep my satellite phone on and will sit tight until she calls me."

"Sorry this all has to be brought to your attention, Brad. Management is very, very determined to find what ever was lost. So, watch your "back trail" as they say in the old western novels."

Brad filled in the time by pacing back and forth while smoking a cigar that he didn't even enjoy. The cigar was just something to fiddle with while he waited.

The jarring ring of the satellite phone made him nearly jump out of his skin. Brad scrambled closer to the lantern to make sure he hit the right buttons and then moved away from the overhang in order to make the connection. It was Megan and her trembling voice indicated her fear.

"Brad, I'm so glad you answered the phone. I don't know where to begin. There's this....".

"Slow down Megan, It's hard to understand you when you speak so rapidly. Take a deep breath or two and start from the beginning. I'm here for you, so take your time."

187

Gary Dale

Brad could hear her take a deep breath and when she spoke again, the edge was gone from her voice. .

"Brad, something is going on with Mr. Lee and his third floor people. They have gone totally berserk. I was in my war office over the weekend and everything was fine. Then, on Monday after lunch, I mean, today after lunch, I got an urgent phone call at home from President Wong to get back to the office. He wouldn't tell me over the phone what was wrong, just to get down there. I thought maybe the mining board was after us for some regulation we didn't follow on some part of a gold claim operation. There is a lot of money riding on the prospects of a new claim up north and the mining board controls who does what up there. That mining claim development is still in its infancy. Are you still there, Brad? You're fading in and out."

"Go ahead," Brad said, "I can hear you."

"Ok. When I got to my office on the third floor, a bunch of larrikins were in the process of destroying both my offices, turning everything upside down, ripping my book shelves apart...."

"Whoa, slow down Megan. Who or what are larrikins? I'm not familiar with the term."

"Larrikins are awful people who wouldn't even think twice about hurting someone if they were told to do so. They are under Yang Lee's control. Now you know why I'm so scared."

"Go on."

"They wouldn't answer my questions or even speak to me. When they did talk, they spoke to each other in Chinese. They pushed me out of my own office so I ran down to my second floor office and it was torn up as well. Yang Lee was there. He shoved me into a chair and demanded to know about some computer disk that was missing. I had no idea what he was talking about and told him so. He told me that they knew I was in the office over the weekend and suspected that I'm somehow involved. Apparently they had a courier leave for

188

Reef of Gold

Singapore early Monday morning and it wasn't but a few hours later that panic ensued here."

There was a catch in her voice that meant she was becoming frightened again.

"Brad, they are watching my house and have been following me where ever I go in my car. My neighbor called me to ask about the strangers parked outside my house. Now, she is afraid."

"Ah, Megan, do they know you are at Michael's house?"

"I don't think so. I took some precautions. I left my car in plain sight at my house, gathered a few things, and snuck out the back door. I know it sounds silly." She took a couple of deep breaths. "If you remember, I mentioned to you that there was a patio in my back yard that is sort of private but it has a gate to my neighbor's yard so we could visit easier. Well, I told my neighbor that my car broke down and I needed a ride. She gladly gave me a ride to a neighborhood train stop. I called Michael to see if I could stay at his house. He told me to come over right away. I caught the next commuter train and got off a couple of stops later. From there, I took a taxi to Michael's house."

"At least you are safe for the moment. Do you think this will blow over soon?"

"I don't know. I'm sure Yang Lee wouldn't hesitate to harm people if he felt the need. He was very hard on the company couriers in the past and they didn't last long with the company. That's why I worried about you when you were a courier. Brad, I don't know for sure but it's almost as if Yang Lee is running things and not President Wong. Yang Lee is convinced that I have the missing disk or at least know who has it."

"Where is President Wong during this crisis?"

"I don't know. He saw me briefly on the third floor, but when I walked over to talk to him, he just put up his hands as a gesture as if to say this wasn't his idea. He turned around and went back to the fourth floor elevator and probably his office."

Gary Dale

"All right, Megan. Let me think for a moment."

Brad took the satellite phone from his ear and looked up at the Southern Cross in the sky almost for guidance. He alone knew that Yang Lee was a Triad member and a threat to her safety. Brother Ric's message on the music CD had warned him about Lee. Until the larrikins found the disk, Megan's life could be in danger and perhaps Michael's and his family as well. Anybody, including family members that had any contact with Megan would be under constant scrutiny. She had to leave town and quickly.

"Megan, are you still there? Ok! Look, here's what I think we ought to do. We don't want to put Michael and his family in any more jeopardy. According to Michael, all they know is I'm in the Outback near or on their Kalgoorlie gold claim doing some exploration. Fortunately, they don't know my exact location. Frankly, I don't either but that's beside the point. So, here's the deal; I'm coming in to get you and bring you out here. They will probably be watching the airport and highways leading out of the city to make sure you don't leave. You will be safer in the vastness of the Outback until things cool down. I'll leave tonight and arrive at Michael's late tomorrow evening or early the following morning. I will be tired."

"Brad, you can't drive in the Outback at night. You might run into something or drive off a cliff."

"Tell me about it. I already know about cliffs. Look, no worries. I've got my compass sightings and I've got some landmarks to keep me going in a straight line on a minimal track I'll just have to retrace my route."

"You will stop for some sleep, won't you?"

"For sure. Look, Megan, another thought would be to call your brother. Let him know what is happening. I'll be there at Michael's place as soon as I can. So until then, try not to worry." He paused a few moments to look at his satellite phone. "My battery is beeping a low charge for some reason so I'll have to sign off shortly." Brad's

Reef of Gold

voice dropped an octave or two and became very soft and caring. "Megan, I ah, ..."

The battery lied. It wasn't just low, it was dead or at least it had just enough power to cut him off with a click. "Just can't trust the company stuff," he muttered. "The phone should have been fully charged when it was left on my office desk." Brad stared at the satellite phone for a moment, finally cursing it.

The Southern Cross star became his guiding light as he pulled out from the bottom of the canyon. The high beam headlights of his rig finally spotted the telegraph poles and their straight line. Following the abandon telegraph poles for endless miles cut off hours of twist and turns through rough terrain on his previous track.

After driving all night and most of the next day with a few snatches of sleep, he stopped for petrol and water at the next to last drop-off site according to his map. Brad's escape from the outback finally ended at the main road about 5:45 pm. A friend once said to him, "mostly you gotta have luck". It was pure luck that Brad came out just west of Laverton, far enough away not to be seen by anyone. His rig, with the Sterling Mines logo, was like driving a moving billboard.

With Megan's safety on his mind, Brad kept a steady pace with a careful watch on his fuel gauge. It wouldn't be long before the arrow would point to the near empty mark. The miles now clicked by with regularity and according to his memory, Kalgoorlie was not far. It was a big mining town, he remembered, and his plan was to avoid it all together. It had an airport and well established service industry, so any stops on his part, coming or going, would be noticed. Yet, he was still going to need fuel.

The dust covered headlights cast a ghost-like beam as he passed through the towns of Manzines and Goongarrie without finding any out-of-the way petrol station. Smaller towns had few if any businesses open at that hour giving them an eerie, deserted feel. Now, he was getting frantic. His last chance to fill up before Kalgoorlie would

Gary Dale

be the wide spot in the road called Bardoc. "Bardoc," repeated Brad to himself. The sound of his own voice made him jump. The reaction seemed to take him out of a trance. He liked the town's name immediately and figured there just had to be a petrol station open at this late hour. Since he didn't know what was going on at the office, he wasn't going to take any chances with Yang Lee's larrikins watching the obvious places.

Avoiding the all night highway convenience store with brightly lit petrol pumps, Brad took what he thought was Bardoc's first street off the highway. He was so tired from driving that he allowed his rig to actually pass in-between two buildings that really wasn't a street. Looming up nearly in front of him was an enormous stone statue of some war hero or early explorer, surrounded by a park-like setting. By taking an Aussie left turn at the statue roundabout, the street actually became straight like the bottom of the letter "T". Brad drove slowly. The small town, with its few street lights displaying a ghostly halo effect, was still quiet, almost too quiet. This is not good, he thought.

Brad needed to worry because in two minutes, he was quickly at the bottom of the "T" and a dead end. There were several minor side streets that had possibilities so he turned around and headed slowly back the way he had come. At both street intersections, he stopped and looked both ways for any sign of a flashing neon petrol sign.

That was his mistake.

In a small Aussie town, it was like being back in the 1950's where everyone knew where the petrol station was located. So, common Aussie logic suggested why waste the expensive electricity on lighting or even modern neon signs. Turning around again, Brad headed slowly back down Main Street. On a side street, the last building had what looked like an old-fashioned petrol pump out front. If he had blinked, he would have missed it.

Colin's. That's what it said on a faded red and white metal sign stuck in a dusty frontage window, highlighted by a weak street

Reef of Gold

lamp. *Petrol and garage* read the other faded sign in smaller letters. Brad pulled in under the garage overhang to the lonely petrol pump. The lights were so dim that for a brief, heart-stopping moment, he thought the place was deserted. The screen door screeched when it opened and an old-timer shuffled out with a tinny in his hand. He took a swig.

"I'm a little zonked tonight mate, but I'll help you if I can," he said. "What do ya need?"

"Just some petrol," Brad answered, relieved that gasoline was even available. His American accent did not go unnoticed.

"You got it, mate. Fill'er up?" he questioned, as he began pumping with a steady hand, filling the large glass jar on top of the petrol pump.

"By all means," answered Brad, watching the strange gas pump methods. "What are your hours anyway, just in case I make a return trip tomorrow night?"

"I don't have regular hours, Yank. Sort of stay out back and listen for rigs that pull up to the pump."

"I've never seen a petrol pump like that before. How does it work?"

The old man looked at Brad for a moment wondering if he was putting him on.

"Easy," he said. "Hand pump the petrol up from the storage tank into the glass jar that you can see above your head. It has a gauge on it so you can see how many gallons and then let gravity do the rest. I know it's old fashioned but so am I. It was the best pump in town in the 1940's when I was a young boy. I bought the place '*as is*' twenty odd years ago to have something to keep me busy in retirement. I'm still keeping sort of busy."

"Mind if I look around?"

"Av-a-go, mate. You'll find the, what is it you Yanks say, ah, oh ya, bathroom facilities are in the back. Through the garage and near the back door. Mind your step."

193

Gary Dale

"Thanks, appreciate it." Brad could feel some of the tension ease out of his shoulders with each passing moment. He needed this stop in more ways than one.

The screen door screeched again as it opened and Brad walked inside. His nostrils were assaulted with smells of used motor oil, welding fumes, engine grease mixed with petrol, and just a hint of engine fumes. Just guessing, but Brad figured the garage hadn't been cleaned up in years. Anything attached to the walls had an outline of black crust formed by oil and grease mixed with dust. Tools were scattered about on the floor with empty part boxes thrown in a heap near the waste bin. Going to the bathroom was a great need, but first Brad had to make it through the littered floor without hurting himself. He wondered what the conditions of the bathroom facilities were going to be if the front of the shop was any indication.

Surprisingly, his mother would have been proud to use this restroom. A fairly new roll of toilet paper, paper hand towels, and hand soap were available. The toilet seat, bathroom sink, and floor looked and smelled like an operating room in a hospital. Brad could actually wash his face in cool water with soap. What a treat.

Brad paid for the petrol and complemented the old man on the cleanliness of the bathroom facilities.

"It's the Sheilas," he said. "They buy petrol from me. I do it for them. They always smile when they come out from the loo and say thanks. For an old guy like me, it's a pleasure to have any Sheila say thank you."

Brad smiled. "What's your name?" he asked.

The old man looked at him sort of funny, and said, "Colin."

Colin's garage. "Of course," Brad exclaimed with embarrassment. "Sorry about that. My name is Brad, nice to meet you. I'm tired and under a bit of stress," he said ending with a sigh. "I have an occasional brain fade. Maybe I need to get some sugar in my system, like a donut or something. I ran out of them yesterday."

"No worries mate. Happens to the best of us. As far as the donuts

194

Reef of Gold

go, I'll slip upstairs to my kitchen. Surely, I have some I can spare. Besides, the convenience store donuts will be stale."

"Ah, before you go, Colin, I have a question, well, actually a request of you. I might be passing this way tomorrow night rather late or early in the morning, and I was wondering if I could get some petrol from you without drawing a lot of attention. I mean, sort of quiet like. I know you will have some questions and I owe you some sort of an explanation, but you will have to trust this Yank. I'll explain when I return, but it is important that I buy petrol from you rather than the all night convenience store. I won't have enough to get where I want to be without your help. I'll have my lovely Sheila with me, and I'll be pleased to introduce her to you, Colin. If I don't show up by ten o'clock the following morning, then don't worry about me. My plans would have changed," Brad mumbled, as his voice quietly trailed away.

Brad looked directly at Colin. He could see the wheels turning on the trust factor, with Colin probably wondering just what sort of trouble this Yank was really in, whether or not it was illegal, and did he want to get involved. Colin looked at Brad for the longest time, then to the dusty rig with Sterling Mines plastered in big letters on the door and finally spoke.

"I've trusted a few Yanks in the past and you seem to be a good bloke. Come around to the back whenever you get here. I'll hear your rig anyway, so no worries. I'm a light sleeper. Besides, meeting your Sheila will be interesting. Looks to me like you need all the help you can get."

They both laughed at that one, and Brad assured him that she was smarter and definitely prettier. Munching on a couple of homemade donuts, Brad quietly drove out a back way on a side road and out onto the highway, out of sight from the highway convenience store. His fingers functioned, as they should, around the steering wheel, instead of in a death grip. He planned in his mind to be in Perth after nine hours of steady driving from the Kalgoorlie cut off and

195

Gary Dale

onto the Great Eastern highway heading due west. There would have to be a few 'nature stops' along the way and another petrol stop in the outskirts of Perth. He figured to look just like another mining engineer driving a dirt clod until he could get the rig washed thoroughly before driving through downtown Perth.

The long drive was beginning to be a contest of wills for Brad, such as "will he make it without falling asleep" or "will he crash the rig and not even know it" or "will he fall asleep and not remember the last fifty miles." Fatigue was becoming a very real factor. Using every ounce of will power to stay awake, Brad finally emerged on the outskirts on the East side of Perth proper. Suburbs were beginning to appear and finding a petrol stop on any of the criss-cross roads was relatively easy except for finding one that was open in the wee hours of the morning.

It was barely daylight and not a whole lot of traffic. Brad curled around a roundabout towards Freemantle on Leach Highway. Just where the Leach highway and the Albany highway cross each other, all four corners had what he needed. "Figures," he said to himself. "Drive for hours looking for just one open petrol stop and not finding any and then suddenly, four petrol stops show up at one time and all open for business." Getting petrol was easy compared to the time spent washing the dirt and grime from the rig. Brad thought he would never get the grime off. A dirty 4-wheel driving in the suburbs would attract attention while a clean one would be just another neighborhood rig.

Finally giving up on a half-baked job of washing the rig and accepting the results, Brad eased his aching and reluctant body back into what felt like his prison, waved to a petrol station attendant who looked at him curiously, and drove to Michaels house in the Cottlesloe suburb, a ten minute train ride from Freemantle. Cottlesloe was near the ocean and Michael had told him it was a great place to raise kids with the ocean in their backyard. His house was a block off Ocean Drive and in amongst the sea trees. The front yard was of

196

sea grass and wind driven sand piling up at the garage near the back of the house. Brad quietly pulled into the driveway and under the carport before switching off the engine. He could hardly move, let alone open the rig door as the vibrations from the extended travel were continuing to rattle his bones. As he staggered out of the rig, the back door opened and Megan stepped out of the house to greet him. He could see the bags under her eyes from apparent lack of sleep and stress. She hesitated for just a brief moment. His face probably was unrecognizable until she got closer.

"Brad, you made it. Oh, thank God."

She threw herself into his arms almost toppling him from her excitement. Under different circumstances, that moment would have been a funny grand entrance. Arm in arm, they made it into the kitchen before the rest of the household descended upon Brad with hugs all around.

Michael's wife, Maggie, quickly made some breakfast for Brad and pumped him full of orange juice. While there were a million questions and few answers, Brad's adrenalin was running low as he started to drift and couldn't stay focused on the conversation. Finally, Marge suggested a halt to the conversation to let him get some sleep. Everyone agreed. She showed him to the spare room in this three-bedroom home and pointed to the yellow bath towels carefully laid out on the bed. He took the hint and picked up the towels. She gently took an arm and guided him towards the bathroom for a shower.

"Wake you in eight hours or so?" she asked.

Brad nodded and gave her a big hug of thanks. She quickly backed away, smiled, and then pointed once again to the shower.

"I get the message," said Brad. "See you in eight hours." He smiled.

The warm water from the shower made him feel like a new man. Brad couldn't get enough of this luxury. After slipping into a borrowed pair of Michael's pajamas, the bed and cool sheets quickly put him into a deep sleep. The next thing he knew, he felt a shaking

Gary Dale

of his body and thought for a moment that an earthquake had hit the region.

Brad opened one crinkly eye at a time, struggling to awake from the dead. It was Melissa, Michael's daughter, trying to wake him. She kept saying "wake up Uncle Brad, wake up." Brad finally tried to acknowledge to her that while not awake, he was alive but his voice was gone. He must have grunted somehow and Melissa took that as an 'ok'and before he knew it, she was back with a glass of orange juice and some plain wheat toast. Brad rose up on one elbow and croaked out a thank you. She watched him eat and made sure he drank the orange juice before taking away the tray. Then he fell back to sleep.

It wasn't long before Brad felt his shoulder being gently rocked back and forth. His eyes opened to see Melissa staring at him.

"It's time to get up," she said looking a little perplexed.

"Any thing wrong?" groaned Brad, while rubbing the sleep from his eyes. He could use some more sleep, like another day.

"Do you always have a smile on your face when you sleep?" she questioned, her face perplexed.

"Only when I'm really happy. Is everyone waiting for me?"

"Yes, they are."

"What time is it, Melissa?"

"About 4:00 o'clock in the afternoon."

His body must have jumped, as Melissa suddenly backed away.

"Melissa, I have to get up now. Would you excuse me, please? Tell the others that I'll be right out. Deal?"

"Deal," she said, closing the door behind her.

Brad dressed in record time. Maggie had washed all his clothes and then had them dried, folded and neatly laid out for him.

"Well, you look a whole lot better," exclaimed Michael, as Brad walked out into the cheerful kitchen.

"It helps to have clean clothes to put on. Thanks Maggie."

Reef of Gold

"You're welcome, Brad," she said with twinkling eyes. "Maybe now we can hug each other without a clothes pin on my nose."

"That bad, huh."

Maggie rolled her eyes.

While the others ate sparingly on the afternoon meal, Brad ate heartily. They discussed the increasingly dangerous situation developing before them and what they could do about it. Michael reiterated that he had repeatedly been asked questions by Yang Lee's staff about Brad's departure with the mining rig and where he was headed. All he could do was to repeat the same story, each time. The pressure was mounting for some clue.

"Why the increased interest in me?" Brad asked Michael.

"Seems like more and more of the staff are being questioned about their relationship with you. Management seems to be unsure of something. Maybe it had something to do with your trip to Singapore as a courier. I really don't know. Alice called me from her home in a bit of panic because she had received a personal visit from one of Yang Lee's assistants asking some questions about her relationship with you."

Brad looked in Megan's direction quickly to see any reaction. When there was none he looked back again at Michael.

"If they asked Alice about me," Brad said, "then they must know that all of us are friends as well. Looks like our Wednesday and Friday night company gatherings were not as private as we thought. It also means they might make a stop here."

"I know," agreed Michael. "What really bothers me is this entire inquisition of all of our acquaintances. I've explained to Megan all about our conversations regarding the company gossip of computer problems and etc. She has confirmed all of that and more. The mystery still exists as to what all the new computer equipment on the third floor is all about. No one from the third floor has said a thing."

Gary Dale

"Brad, do you know anything about microwave?" asked Megan.

"A little," Brad said. "Radio and Television stations use microwave transmissions and isn't the transmission/receiver dish on the roof of our office building for KXYU Radio/TV?"

"Actually, there are several transmission dishes on the rooftop of our building," added Michael, confident in his observation.

"What does that have to do with our problem?" Brad asked.

"Nothing, I guess," remarked Megan. "It's just that my brother Geoffrey called me back finally, and I told him about what was happening. I think he was more than a little scared for me. This whole thing sounded so bazaar. He asked me about microwave transmissions being received at company headquarters. I told him that I didn't think our company had a microwave system in place to receive microwave, at least not yet. The leased roof top space is by a local radio station for their microwave transmissions and receiving.

"Are you positive?" asked Michael.

"The computers on the third floor download a lot of stuff, but I don't know where the information originates other than from our Singapore office. Anyway, after telling Geoffrey about all that office turmoil, he suggested I get a hold of you Brad. He thought you could think of a place for me to get away for a couple of weeks until the company found the so called *lost disk*."

"He is probably right," agreed Michael. "It's foolish for you to stick around when you have been threatened by the company. Have you thought of a place to go to hide out for a while? I mean, Megan, you probably have some relative or some friends out of town to hang out with for a couple of weeks, right?"

Megan started to speak but Brad interrupted her in mid-sentence.

"My opinion is that we can't endanger anyone that we know including you Michael and your family. I've suggested to Megan that she and I leave right away, meaning tonight to the Outback where

200

Reef of Gold

my camp is located. You know the approximate location Michael. Don't you think that would be a good place for us to hole up for a couple of weeks?"

Michael was cautious with his answer.

"If you could get out of Perth without being detected, then your mystery canyon might be the best place. You could stay lost out there until I contacted you. Who would think you would come all the way back into Perth and then head back to the Outback again."

It was Maggie that reminded everyone of the cold fact that if the disk was so precious to Yang Lee, he would stop at nothing to get it back. "What are the odds of him figuring out where you were in the Outback and send out a party of larrikins to do you in? Your bodies would never be found."

"Wait a minute," chimed in Michael. "We might be overreacting a bit. If Megan doesn't have the disk, why would they harm her?"

"The thought has occurred to me," said Megan with a deep breath, "that they may have thought that I might have downloaded and emailed the entire content of the disk to someone like the Mining Commission in Canberra. I did email the mining commission some data last Saturday but it wasn't that important. Yang Lee would know that I had sent something just by checking my computer. He would also find out that I had told the mining commission that more data was being sent to them." She paused for a moment as if remembering something. "Occasionally, I send a blind copy of a joke with an attachment to one of my friends on the commission staff just for fun. I know it's against company policy but sometimes working on a Saturday, I get a little bored. Its possible Yang Lee might see that sending a blind copy as one that could have contained something about the missing desk. It would take some time for one of his larrikins to peel the sent email information off my hard drive. They could do it if they wanted too. His technicians are that good."

There was a definite pause in the conversation as if no one knew

Gary Dale

what to say next. Coffee was poured while everyone toyed with the remains of their dinner. Finally Michael broke the stalemate.

"Megan," he asked, "do you know what is being sent to the Singapore office when they send a courier?"

"Well," she answered, "I am aware they use one-time pads for their multitude of company operations. Some time ago, I was told that a one-time pad was hard to decipher without a special code. I thought that was pretty silly until I realized how serious they were." She shrugged her shoulders. "The other possibility that I can think of is that they didn't use a one-time pad for some reason this time and put their hard copy on a regular disk. That would make the information vulnerable."

"Whoa," said Brad. "You could be right. Maybe that is why there is all this attention and energy being paid to finding the disk. Apparently, it's a security breach of some kind and they don't like it."

"Does it really matter?" asked Michael. "They are after the both of you and for all we know, probably others as well."

Brad glanced at the kitchen clock on the stove front and called a halt to the discussions.

"Look," he said to everyone, "the idea of hiding out in the Outback is the route we should take. Megan and I won't be putting anyone in jeopardy out there. I'm almost positive that Lee's men are watching the airport, train station, bus station, and all along the highway petrol stations going out of town. Knowing the money and manpower resources they have, they probably have everything covered. I mean, there are only three main highways out of town and the rest of the roads lead into the Outback and eventually disappear. Our only hope is to get out of Perth as soon as possible and out there," gesturing with a sweep of his hand.

"You mean, out there, there," Michael laughed gently, as his sweep of his hand was in another direction.

"Right," Brad said with a bit of strain lingering on his smile.

Reef of Gold

"What do you think, Megan?" asked Michael.

Everyone looked at Megan. Finally, she smiled and said, "Let's get on with it."

Brad looked at Michael's family with all his admiration visible on his face and then gave them a heart felt thanks of appreciation for all the things they had done for him and Megan.

"It's nearly dark outside, so if you can get your stuff packed Megan, we can sneak out of town," Brad urged. "I have more than enough supplies for two, at least for awhile anyway."

"Hold on, Brad," remarked Maggie. "We have all kinds of small water bottles and food for you to take with you. Melissa and I will pack what we think will help you. You can spend your time thinking of how to get out of town safely. Come with me, Melissa."

The conversation turned immediately to their options about getting out of town without being seen. The ideas were bouncing around like a volleyball for the next several minutes. Then the conversation stopped as if at a dead-end.

"Megan, before we go, is there anything you absolutely need from your apartment?"

"You mean, if they haven't already trashed it looking for the disk, then is there anything I could not do with out? The answer is no. Maggie and Melissa went shopping for a few clothes for me this morning, so I'm fine for a a few weeks."

"Well, there is a problem for me, I'm afraid. My red backpack with the ship captains' journal is in my townhouse. I don't think they would have broken into my place, at least not yet. My next-door neighbor is better than having a security alarm. The last thing President Wong or Yang Lee wants is for the authorities to be asking them questions. But I have to take the backpack with me. It is too precious to let Wong have it without a fight."

"Will you be safe from prying eyes if you go back there?" she asked.

"Maybe," said Brad. "That is a concern. As a matter of fact, I

Gary Dale

didn't tell you or anyone else this but ever since my return from Singapore, my place is being watched. My guess is that they want to see if someone in particular shows up to see me at home. Maybe it's my brother they are after and hoping he will show. Then again, maybe I asked too many questions at the office? Who knows why?"

"How did you find all of this out?" queried a shocked Megan.

"My neighbor lady put me onto them as she noticed strange cars showing up at odd hours and parking near our townhouses. A car would stay awhile and then be replaced by another. She's a night person and probably suffers from insomnia. Me, I'm usually asleep by 11:00 pm., so I never really noticed. After talking with her, I started staying up really late watching for any unusual activity. Sure enough, someone was observing my townhouse across the street. Sometimes it was a car a half a block away. They changed locations off and on."

"Well," she sighed, "it seems to fit a pattern."

"I'm worried that Lee or Wong will eventually order a thorough search on my place. I just want to get the backpack out and in my possession before President Wong or Lee gets his hands on it.

CHAPTER 21

HILTON HOTEL/SINGAPORE

The Singapore Hilton seemed to gather Americans like bees to clover. Familiarity was the key. All Hilton hotels had basically the same floor plan anywhere in the world. American travelers, particularly businessmen, stay at a Hilton because they want to feel like they are coming home after an exhausting day. With the time zone changes and shortness of stay, they really had little time to adjust. Recognizable lobby, bar, rooms, hotel services were big marketing tools for hotel management. Americans weren't the only business people traveling to Asia. The hotel's lobby was packed with international business people and visitors from around the globe. One could hear a dozen different languages being banded about. It's like waiting for arrivals at LaGuardia airport international terminal in New York.

A good-looking, man with an expensive black leather briefcase walked through the large turnstiles and headed for the crowded front desk. He was dressed impeccably, wearing a tailored light wool suit blended with a hint of rayon, adorned with a light blue shirt and muted tie. He looked like all the other American businessmen going about their daily preparation for appointments with emerging Asian companies in a world economy.

The man moved like an athlete. He looked every bit like he belonged to the business fraternity. Noticing the man acknowledging

Gary Dale

the business fraternity in the hotel lobby, the desk clerk gave him a cordial smile as the man approached the counter.

"May I help you sir? the clerk inquired. "Checking in now, I presume. Do you have any bags?"

"Actually, yes and no," the man replied. "Yes, you may be of help to me. Where is the business center? I would like to email something to my company. The answer is no to the second part of your question. I will be checking in later after my business appointment."

"Yes, of course," said the clerk. "The Singapore Hilton is in the process of remodeling the first two floors of the hotel, including the area of the business center. Because of the disruption, I'm not sure exactly where it is located. Perhaps, one of the bellman would know.' He pointed discreetly, almost like he was embarrassed to be seen pointing. "See the bellman standing next to the luggage trolley. I would suggest asking him for directions."

"Will do," acknowledged the tailored suit. Meandering through the multitudes of hotel guests and their peers, he found the bellman, looking absent- mindedly at the throngs of foreign people. "Excuse me, could you tell me or show me where the business center might be located?"

The bellman looked puzzled. "Sir, my English not so good. He thumped his chest proudly. I speak other languages much better." He looked away momentarily and then said, "Ask that man." He nodded towards the express elevators.

The elevator man wasn't much use and rather curt with his answers. He spoke some English but was little help with directions. He didn't know where the center had been relocated. "Besides," he said, "I'm too busy running the elevators for impatient hotel guests. Please try another employee in the lobby."

The tailored suit politely said 'thank you' and walked in the direction of the front desk. He was going to ask for the hotel manager this time.

Seeing the perplexed man in a suit muttering to himself, a hotel

Reef of Gold

bar employee walked over to him. They had a brief discussion, with the employee waving his hands in several different directions. Finally the tailored suit agreed to follow him.

The employee did not speak until well out of sight of others. "This way," he whispered. Up the stairs and making two right hand turns, the tailored suit and the employee stumbled into the business center, torn up with construction. There were no computers because of no power cables, just holes punched into the walls, waiting for the wire. One wall was not torn up. It had been sheet rocked and painted blue. The employee turned towards the wall and used a key to open a solid hardwood door. The employee opened and closed the heavy door. It was a storage room. He walked towards another locked door. This too was opened but with a different key. The door gently closed behind them with a loud click.

"Ric Templeton," exclaimed the bar employee, "Good to see you. Some of us had heard you were dead. It is a bit of a shock to have you standing next to me."

"It's not that they didn't try, Roger." He grimaced and placed his hand against the wall for balance, letting the wave of pain subside. He took a deep breath and sighed. "Hate these little inconveniences. What have you got, Roger?"

Roger suggested they sit down before Ric fell down. "Wait a minute," he said. He took both keys and quickly ground off the key code, tossing them in a receptacle. "I'll change the lock pins after you leave and make new keys. We are moving new equipment and personnel in here next week. This hotel will be our new safe house. What better place to hide than in plain sight. The wardrobe expenses will go up to look like the businessmen that stay here, but oh well."

Ric merely nodded.

"I think we have spotted two of the three Chinese men that secretly disembarked from the last arriving North Korean ship," said Roger, "but we are not sure. Since highly skilled engineers are in

Gary Dale

short supply, these two had little trouble hiring on with an Australian company. Both men apparently have an aerospace engineering specialty in metallurgy, and since their employment, they have been pestering the regional manager to transfer to corporate headquarters in Brisbane. If they are who I think they are, then in my opinion, that transfer would get them closer to the development of military airplane engines. Seeing how this new scram-jet revolutionary technology is the thing of the future, it's no wonder they want to be a part of the development. Just think a scram jet engine that propels a plane at 5,000 mph or more. Absolutely amazing." He paused thoughtfully and then reached into his pocket.

"Here are some recent photographs of the two suspect Chinese. They arrived early at the Singapore branch office in a dark Mercedes and parked in the underground garage. These photos of the men were taken through their office windows. A little grainy but isn't technology wonderful. Couldn't imagine doing this a couple of years ago."

"Will you run these photos of yours through computer imaging and see how they match up with mine," said Ric, handing him a small camera disk. "If they are the same men, then you will have to alert the Brisbane staff to start a file on them. What happened to the third ship's passenger? Where did he or she go? Any ideas."

"Big mystery," said Roger, as he busied himself with the computer imaging. "We are trying to find the elusive passenger. When the three of them evacuated the North Korean ship, one of the longshoremen hauling their luggage to a small boat under the pier, overheard one of them use the word, laser. He mispronounced the word but at least he remembered it and only because it was spoken in English. He didn't know what the word meant."

"I think I know what that means," suggested a concerned Ric. "There are all kinds of laser experiments going on in different fields of study, but a hot subject for an experimental communications project would be sending and receiving messages via a unique laser

Reef of Gold

beam. There is an Australian firm located in Perth who has made tremendous strides in this kind of research since they have access to a satellite base in Alice Springs. They are partnering with United States military and Australian military who have the funding to carry-off such a monetary commitment. It may take a while to manufacture but from what I hear, development of that technology would eventually change everything we now use in communications."

"Right," said Roger. "The most pressing need will be to prepare the laser technology Australian firm of a potential threat of espionage even if we don't have all the evidence. Let me know when you plant someone on the inside to watch for an intrusion. Now, is there anything else going on that I need to know about, so we won't cross paths in our investigation?"

"Since we haven't located the third passenger dropped off by the North Korean ship, he or she presents a problem for us." said Ric. "The real question might be who is running these three people. I'm working on this problem in addition to my other investigations in hopes of a tie-in. There may be a connection with the current espionage efforts in Perth. When I find out something, I'll contact you."

"Watch yourself," warned Roger.

CHAPTER 22

THE GET-A-WAY

Brad and Megan quietly loaded the rig with additional water and food just in case they couldn't find the trailer drop offs and two carry-on bags with Megan's recent possessions. She ended up with more clothes, shoes, and jackets from Maggie, as they were somewhat the same size. Megan was a little thinner so the clothes hung on her a bit, but she didn't give it another thought.

As a final security check, Michael and Brad looked up and down the street several times just to be sure there wasn't a strange car lurking about watching the house at this hour of early darkness. Michael took the moment to counsel Brad about his direction in the Outback. "You are way off in your headings to area 5, Brad. So, retrace your route carefully. Remember, I know your approximate location. But approximate could mean a hundred miles difference in any direction in the outback. It all looks the same. That is one reason why the city bred Aussies call the Outback the 'Big Empty'."

Brad agreed.

After a flurry of hugs, Brad then eased the 4-wheel drive rig out onto the street and headed southeast on various side streets and then turned onto Mulberry Street, a main road.

They didn't talk for a while as both were concentrating on any car that came up beside them during and after the roundabouts. They

210

Reef of Gold

furtively glanced at any of the occupants for any sign of recognition. Finally Megan broke the silence by asking Brad what his plan was going to be to rescue the red backpack from his townhouse since watchers were sure to be there. She knew from the direction they were going that he planned to make a stop. He had made his decision.

Brad motioned for Megan to open up a bottle of Bonner's Spring Water for him, as his throat was unusually dry. After a slug of the cool water, his voice decided to work in normal tones. He explained to Megan that his townhouse was located near the King's Garden area on Fourth Street. The front entrance to the townhouse and the entrance to his one car garage were on this quiet tree lined street. The garage had several small windows built into the flip up door, so a person could see inside if they wanted too. His speculation was that President Wong and or Yang Lee's watchers had checked out the garage to see if his car was still inside, which it was. With his indoor security lights coming on at irregular intervals, the place would have some semblance of someone being inside.

"How are you going to get by the street watchers to get inside?" she questioned guardedly.

"What they hopefully don't know, Megan, is that directly beneath my kitchen is a mechanics shop. It was built partially under my townhouse with an entrance on Fifth Street. It's strange, I know. There is a side door entrance to the shop and once inside, I can get into my townhouse. The old guy I'm renting from used to restore old cars in the downstairs garage as a hobby. He had an entrance with stairs built so he could enter the basement from the inside of the townhouse. He told me it made it easier for him during the winter months when it rained or got cold. When he decided he was too old to climb stairs, he sold his cars and moved. I rented the fifth avenue garage as well for my wood furniture hobby."

"Ok," questioned Megan once again, "so what's the plan?"

"So," Brad said after a big sigh, "I plan for the both of us to enter the lower level basement entrance, climb the stairs, and with a little

Gary Dale

luck we could be in and out of the townhouse with my backpack without the slightest hint of discovery."

"That's the plan?" she said, aghast.

"Short of creating a disturbance to misdirect the watchers, I can't think of anything else that might work," said Brad. "As we approach the townhouse on this hill, I'm going to drive slowly and see if we can spot the watchers first before I make the final approach on the backside which is just about now." Brad downshifted into second gear to slow the rig down on the curve ahead. The road straightened before sloping to a downhill descent to where the road split into Fourth and Fifth streets resulting in a V shape.

"Here we go. Look up and across Fourth Avenue for any watchers. You will only have seconds to see anything. I'll use the hand brake to slow us down instead of alerting the world with my red tail-lights. He quickly shifted into neutral and quietly coasted downhill. He had learned something from the tattooed Singapore taxi driver.

They watched for any movement or strange cars that didn't belong.

"Brad, there," she said, quickly pointing to a car, dark in color, facing away from them. The car door was open obviously for air circulation. It was parked two houses up the street from Brad's townhouse. All others cars were parked in their respective driveways.

"I see them," said Brad. That's the car. I have seen it parked out there numerous times late at night."

About half way down Fifth Street, Brad turned into a parking space and pulled on the emergency brake, stopping the rig on a down hill slope. He cramped his front wheels toward the curb just in case the rig had a mind of its own before switching off the engine and headlights. They sat quietly for a moment. They were now out of direct sight, and the darkness would shield the parked mining rig.

Breathing a little more normally now, Brad cautiously opened the rig's door on the right side and got out ahead of Megan. Both quietly

Reef of Gold

closed the passenger doors. Fortunately he had remembered to turn out the dome lights. The neighborhood was quiet.

Keeping to the dark background created by the tall shrubs and using their left hand to brush against the prickly branches for kinesic awareness, they etched their way down the sidewalk, stopping for any unusual sounds, before finally making it to the lower garage. Brad was worried as much about curious neighbors as the watchers themselves, sneaking about like they were. The outside security door lock was an Australian snap spring lock. It worked as it was supposed too. Brad couldn't make the key work in the lock. He turned and looked at Megan. "Some realtor I'd make," he whispered, "can't even open a lock. Here," he whispered again, handing her the key. "Take this key and give the lock a little of your magic to see if you can get the thing open."

Megan had nimble fingers and a computer mind that seemed to understand the lock's peculiarities. The spring lock popped open this time with a loud snap. Her annoyed look towards Brad said it all.

"Forgot to tell you about the tension in the spring," hissed Brad through gritted teeth.

They quickly maneuvered themselves next to shrubs dark background and let the moment fade into the night sounds before venturing back to the opened door. He beckoned Megan inside while carefully closing the door behind them. With no workshop lights on, Brad whispered that they were going to have to feel their way across the basement garage. He couldn't exactly remember where he had left things. After taking off their shoes, Brad's toes stretched and folded in his socks as he inched his way across the floor, feeling ahead for any obstruction in their path. Megan followed closely behind holding onto his belt with one hand and clutching her shoes with the other hand.

As Brad's eyes adjusted to the dim street light shining through small windows that cast isolated beams on the garage floor, several obstacles loomed in front of them. The obstructions were tree stumps

Gary Dale

from a housing development that Brad had rescued before the stumps were to be burned. He had recognized the beauty and had planned to make some furniture out of the rare Jarrah wood. Brad wished he had moved the stumps into a corner. His toes and shins became very familiar with each stump, and it's a wonder that they both made it across the darkened garage without planting their faces on the concrete floor. Brad found the stairway. Leaving their shoes on the bottom step, they tiptoed up the flight of stairs.

The stairway door to the first floor of the townhouse was closed as it should have been, and Brad knew it would be stuck in position. The weather had swelled the door tight at the bottom and it was always a challenge to open it up. They weren't sure if someone was in the townhouse, so Brad took all precautions against unnecessary noise.

Megan turned the door handle while Brad forcibly pushed on the bottom of the sticky door. It took a couple of rocking motions on the door before it popped open. Brad quickly held his hand on the bottom of the door, stifling the vibration. He brushed past Megan to be ready for any encounter. Stopping to let the noise of their entry pass, they both cautiously slid their socks along the cool tile floors. They discovered his place hadn't been trashed but a feeling of being uncomfortable in his own home was disturbing. Brad sensed something was amiss, but he couldn't put his finger on it. Everything looked normal but it seemed to him that there was a left over 'essence' of someone having been there since he had left several days ago. Then again, maybe it was just him, overreacting to preconceived events. Brad took a deep breath and slowly let it out.

There was enough light coming through the lace living room curtains from the street lamp outside to let them wander around the room without knocking things over. With Megan in tow, Brad pointed to the front window. With pantomime motions of peeking through the curtains to see if there was any movement outside,

214

Reef of Gold

Megan understood and moved along the shadows to the window, brushing back the curtain ever so slightly so she wouldn't be seen.

While Megan was spying on the watchers, Brad carefully made his way upstairs to his bedroom where he had a small desk and work area. This is where he had been doing some of his research into the newly discovered Northern Territories mining areas. The company had scant information on the new claims other than where they were situated well in relation to the new gold find by another firm. His borrowed mining charts were on the desk but where was his red backpack? It should have been on the floor next to the desk for reference. Turning a light on would have been helpful but that was out of the question. Searching his bedroom by 'Braille' brought no results even when he carefully repeated the performance.

'Where did I put the backpack?' Brad silently questioned himself.

He walked quickly down the steps to Megan.

"Any movement outside?" he whispered.

"Yes," she hissed back. "Two men just got out of their car. I can't identify them. It's too dark. There're just standing around, as if waiting for someone."

"Keep watching," Brad said hurriedly while moving into the dining room and then rummaging around in the hall closet. He found nothing. He moved into the kitchen.

Megan suddenly whispered in a terse voice. "Brad, another car just drove up with its headlights off. They are getting out of the car. There are four of them now, and they are conferring with each other and one is pointing up here. Hurry up," she said urgently. "They are crossing the street heading our way. We have to go now, Brad."

Brad spun around in the darkness, trying to recreate the scene where he might have put the backpack. He concentrated harder and kept turning around and around in one place as if searching for a visual clue. Megan moved away from the curtains to the kitchen and

Gary Dale

confronted Brad, this time issuing a demand to leave. "They are at the street entrance."

In Brad's townhouse complex, the front door on 4th street opened up to a shared hallway that was common with the other tenant next to him. From the hallway, each tenant had his or her own entryway. Brad's entry was at the end of the hall.

Megan's warning gave Brad only precious few seconds to search one last time. "Under the kitchen sink," he remembered. He pulled open the doors not caring if he made a little noise. The squeaky hallway floor the intruders would be walking on would mask any sound he made. His hands quickly ran over tops of dishwashing soap bottles, cleaning solutions, plastic garbage sacks, sink brushes, but no backpack. Brad sat back onto his bent knees in stunned silence as he closed the kitchen sink doors. Where was the backpack? Did someone already have it?

"What?" gestured Megan with her hands. Brad stared at her, uncomprehending her gesture.

"The pantry. That's it." Brad suddenly remembered that the kitchen sink had been his first choice, as burglars usually didn't search under a kitchen sink. "Bad idea," he remembered. His insurance agent had warned him against leaving anything valuable on floor level. Water pressure breaks in kitchen sink pipes were common. If the pipe broke because of water pressure, then his backpack and its valuable contents would get soaked and probably ruined.

Brad quickly crawled over to the pantry on his hands and knees and jerked open the pantry door only to have it snap back into place. He'd forgotten about the rubber bands holding the door shut. While he fumbled in the dark shadows with the rubber bands, Megan came quickly to his side.

"The entry door is being fiddled with," she whispered. "We will be trapped if we don't go now. Please, Brad," she pleaded.

"Just one more second," he whispered. The pantry door popped open with the release of the rubber bands and Brad reached in and pulled the large sack of potatoes out onto the floor. Behind the potatoes, sitting on a case of soup was the red backpack with a bad zipper containing the Ship Captains Journal. Sliding the slightly opened backpack onto the kitchen floor and out of the way, he didn't notice a Perth Library special access card slip out from the backpack and land on the floor. Brad crammed the potato sack back into the pantry, and closed the panel doors. Grabbing the backpack with his left hand and leading Megan with the other, they half ran and half slid their way across the tiled kitchen floor to the downstairs door.

Brad closed the door and locked it just as he heard the tinkling of the entry door chimes. He heard a curse in English as the watchers tumbled into the living room.

A muted voice could be heard echoing in the stairwell commanding a search in every nook and cranny. "Wong wants every document and personal effect in this bag. Be quick about it," and then the commanding voice faded.

At the bottom of the stairwell, they stopped to listen once more. There were heavy thuds above them.

"We still have to keep the lights off," he whispered while shouldering the pack. "Hold onto my belt if you can and stay right behind me. Let my shins take the beating."

"All right," she whispered, gathering up their shoes in her arms and juggling them for a moment.

Brad's memory had something to do with their quick retreat through the garage. So did his shins. Then again, maybe their eyes were more adjusted to the darkness now, as they made it through the tree stump minefield in record time. After slipping on their shoes and peering outside for any movement, they exited. Megan quietly placed the spring lock back into place and locked it. They both headed for the shadows along Fifth Street, walking swiftly without looking over their shoulders.

They climbed back into their rig. The strain of the events was etched into their faces.

Gary Dale

"That was close. Now, for the next part of our escape," Brad whispered. They silently closed the rig doors.

He slipped the gears into neutral and turned on the ignition part way. Not enough to start the engine but enough to get the power steering to work. Straightening the wheels away from the curb, Brad released the hand brake. There was enough of a downhill on Fifth Avenue to coast for a ways before he would have to engage the engine.

Brad concentrated on using the hand brake to slow them down. He didn't need to broadcast their departure with flashing brake lights or headlights. Neither of them said a word. They didn't breathe either.

At the bottom of the hill, Brad made a left turn onto a main road. Within a minute, they were out of sight of the townhouse and its unwanted occupants. He started the engine and flipped on the headlights. He purposely headed in the opposite direction for a few miles before making a couple of turns toward the eventual goal of driving on the Great Eastern Highway towards Kalgoorlie and beyond.

"We can talk now," said Brad. "No more whispering." He smiled like he meant it.

"I don't know about that," she said. "I rather liked the change of pace. It made me think before I opened my mouth."

"Well, you do have a point." It took just a moment for Megan to process the comment. "Just kidding," Brad said hurriedly.

They both laughed just enough at his lame attempt at humor to release the tension a bit.

The kilometers rolled on and on in a straight road of nothingness. Little traffic impeded their way. While they made good time in stretches of the road, there were times where the animal population was added to the road kill. Animals had a nasty habit of hanging out alongside the road in the cool of the night feeding all along the grass-covered swales. Then for no particular reason, the animals often

218

Reef of Gold

decide to dash across the roadway only to be crushed underneath a tire. Megan grimaced with every bump.

They took turns driving and cat napping to insure they would endure the long hours of driving. Brad had to stop, stretch, and visit the side of the road several times when he drank too much water. He figured they would hit the town of Bardoc very early in the morning and hoped that Colin would awake at their arrival. Since they couldn't get far enough into the Outback before sunrise, Brad wanted to spend the day hiding out and then travel at night. He told Megan of his plans before he drifted off into another dream about her.

They were approaching the outskirts of Kalgoorlie, a good-sized town in the Outback, when Megan nudged Brad in the ribs. He was immediately awake and alert especially when Megan suggested they take a back road and go around the main highway intersection. The Great Eastern Highway branched off at Kalgoorlie, going onto Laverton and the gold mining claims or heading the opposite direction for Adelaide, a couple of thousand kilometers away. They both figured it would be at this crossing point that any of Yang Lee's larrikins would be watching for any white painted mining rig. Megan was way ahead of Brad.

"I'm going to turn on this auxiliary road," she said, "which will take us south for bit, paralleling the Great Eastern Highway towards Adelaide. I'll drive for about 5 kilometers and then according to the road map, the auxiliary road will cut under the highway and circle back East of Kalgoorlie. That way, we miss driving through the town."

"Sounds like a good plan to me. You make a good companion," he added. Megan stole a quick questioning glance from him as they passed under the main highway and onto the auxiliary road.

"It's going to be light soon. Are you sure you want to stop?"

"We need a place to hide out for most of the day," he replied. "We don't want the watchers to see us head out into the Outback

Gary Dale

from the highway during daylight. Besides, we need petrol. We are going to stop at Colin's garage. He is expecting us. Besides, I'm not positive I can locate my petrol and water drop off sites."

"Well," Megan said, "I'm glad we talked about your latest plan because that little string of lights up ahead is Bardoc. Must be a really big town you're taking me too. Probably has a nice five star restaurant for dining."

Brad smiled.

CHAPTER 23

THE THIRD AGENT

The little Chinese tailoring shop was non-descript among all the glitter surrounding it. The brightly lit storefronts were adorned with twinkling lights and in front of each entrance, shouting pitchmen encouraged shoppers to come inside immediately for a bargain of a lifetime. In this section of Perth, customers were at the mercy of a hard sell.

The cacophony of voices dwarfed this small place of business. The store's name, Kim's was painted in big gold letters in English and Chinese, spreading across the front window. Small signs proclaimed the best tailors in the world were inside crafting the finest custom made suits. A sign for the ladies that said alterations was tucked down in the corner of the window. Prices varied, said another sign.

During the hot summer months, the owner's business was slow. But now, after taking a picture of his latest customers grouped together like a bunch of grapes including a number of nearby hotel staff who were not customers, the advertising flyer proudly proclaimed that seven out of ten people in this picture had their suits tailor-made at Kim's. As a result, the proprietor was suddenly overwhelmed with business. It seemed everyone wanted to be one of the seven and have his picture proudly taken for future flyers. And, if you asked any of the three who did not have their suits made at Kim's, they would tell

Gary Dale

you they were one of the seven who had their suits tailor made. No one wanted to admit to being a non-customer.

The shop was busy making a perfect cover for the arrival of the third agent from the North Korean ship, docked in Singapore. The shop owner, Kim, would hide the agent in the back of his store in his mother-in-laws apartment when he arrived. Kim knew nothing about this third agent. His job was to provide a safe haven as ordered. Kim was worried. Where was this agent? He was really late in arriving. Had he been discovered? If so, would Kim be implicated? He would lose his store if he was implicated. That he could not allow. He would contact his controller at the Chinese Embassy. The controller would know what to do, Kim thought.

In the meantime, Kim made suits as fast as he could, capitalizing on his sudden fame as a businessman. He owed the handsome American who had walked into his establishment recently for suggesting the seven out of ten advertising flyer idea. Maybe making the American a fine suit of high quality light wool, blended with a hint of rayon was not enough of a trade-out. It did help to send the tall American to his cousin's specialty store to find the perfect light blue shirt accented by a muted tie. The fine leather briefcase the man had wanted was not available. The customer would have to try a shop at the Hilton Hotel, a few blocks away. The worry over the third Chinese agent was forgotten.

The third agent, however, knew he was behind schedule because of the storms at sea. He would be late in arriving at a safe house. The helicopter would only make so many tries to pick him up at the appointed spot along the coast before canceling the attempt. The spy would then have to make his own way into Perth. He had to hurry.

The fishing crew had been hired from the same village on the island of Lombok, south side. Fishing was non-existent because of the typhoons sweeping across the Timor Sea at this time of the year.

The small Indonesian coastal men manning the sails were

Reef of Gold

financially poor, and their families depended upon them for survival. These sailors had experience in sail craft of this small size for many years. They took few risks with typhoons and purposely did not sail unless paid an outrageous amount to deliver an unknown person to the Australian shore. The trip could take many days, depending upon the weather.

Arriving at night and anchoring off a tiny island close to the northern mainland coast of Australia, the crew and passenger found a few hours of sleep. The breaking of dawn at 6:00am equator time allowed the sailors to hoist a small sail to catch an irregular puff of wind, driving the craft towards a safe anchoring close to the partially submerged island, before jumping over the side and dragging the vessel to the shallowest part of the shore.

The fishermen had been here before, even their ancestors. The island was small, barely a barnacle-encrusted rock pile at high tide. At low tide, the reef rarely, if ever, shared its second reef ledge, supporting a diverse sea life. The two tiered reef had at one time, been a part of the main continent of Australia; but as the seas had risen the past several hundred years, it had become an island. With a slow current sweeping around the mainland bringing nutrients with it, an area on the leeward side of the island provided a haven for sea cumbers; vast quantities of them covered the shoreline at different times of the year.

This time, the fishermen were lucky. The highly prized sea cumbers called Trepang were littered all along the shoals. While waiting for their passenger to be picked up, the fishermen were delighted at being at the right time to harvest a great number of the Trepang, rich in protein and inherently delicious after being slowly cooked in pots, as their ancestors had done before them. The fishermen would feed themselves first before filling the rest of their containers with as many cooked Trepang as possible and sail for home when the passenger was picked up.

The boat captain hollered to one of the crew to finish tying up

Gary Dale

the craft. The crewman carried a stout rope tied at one end to the bow and secured the craft to an exposed large rock with strange markings, almost like the aboriginal art that graced the many caves in the area. The crewman wasn't interested in art or strange markings. Neither was the rest of the crew. The scratch marks on the large boulder were of an unknown language to them. It wouldn't have mattered. The crew was illiterate and couldn't even read their own language. The familiar rock acted like an enormous land anchor that happened to be handy for securing their boat. Tides fluctuated greatly in this part of the world.

The passenger huddled under a tarp, avoiding the splash from the waves hitting the side of the boat. Lifting a small portion of the covering tarp, he watched the anchor rope being wrapped several times around a large rock before the thin fisherman secured a small pick deep as possible into the pebble-encrusted shore. With the boat doubly secure, the passenger threw the tarp aside and stiffly crawled forward to the bow. He couldn't wait to get off this tossing and turning cork of a boat. The man took off his shoes, dropped them into a waterproof bag, before placing his feet into a pair of black, knee high rubber boots. He straddled the boat gunnels, dropping one leg onto the gravel bar.

It was a mistake. The man struggled with his balance. The boat rocked with the new distribution of weight, causing the passenger to hobble along, one foot caught on the gunnels and the other, firmly on land, carried all his weight, his boot filling with cold seawater. Hopping on one leg, the landlubber was uncoordinated in his efforts to get his one leg off the gunnels. Making a splash into the sea was not the passenger's idea of a good time. He raised his right hand in an effort to signal for help. The waving hand did not attract any attention. He finally screamed for help. Two crewmen dropped what they were doing, rushed over and lifted the struggling Chinese man's stiff leg off the boat and onto the gravel bar. They steadied the landlubber who was still trying to get his leg muscles under control.

Reef of Gold

He gestured towards the boat. One of the fishing crew grabbed his briefcase and waterproof bag. Together they made for shore. They emptied his rubber boot of seawater, sat him down next to the anchor rock and out of sight.

The Chinese agent took a deep breath, relieved to be off the moving monster. He had wanted to vomit, but since he hadn't eaten since the previous day, nothing would come flying out of his upset stomach. He had traveled with unpleasant seasickness on the North Korean freighter, briefly found his balance again on the Triad's wharf before he was whisked aboard a Singapore ferry that hugged the shoreline to avoid the heavy seas until forced to cross the straits further to the south. Finally, after a terrible ferry crossing, he arrived at the magical island of Bali, sick and discouraged. He rested the night, hidden in the storeroom portion of a local kiosk before being sent immediately on a high-speed ferry motoring an hour across the strait between Bali and Lombok Island. Upon his arrival, he was taken to a prearranged fishing boat that would carry him for the long sailing journey across the Timor Sea.

The sun had set at 7:00pm as it always has on the equator, giving the passenger cover for his boarding. With little or no electricity on this rice-growing island, pitch dark meant very dark, almost as dark as the sea. He would be invisible leaving Lombok Island and with luck, arrive on the northern coast of Australia the same way in secrecy.

Now, sitting out-of-sight beside a very large rock, he waited patiently for the Sterling Mines helicopter to pick him up where he would be whisked off to another secretive landing, ending with a long ride in a four-wheel drive mining rig to Perth. If all went well, another agent dressed as a crewman coming off the North Korean ship would meet his contact at Kim's tailoring in Perth, distracting the Australian authorities while he would meet secretly with a Triad administrator. The spy stretched his legs and found a better backrest. The exhausting trip had been worth it, he thought.

Gary Dale

He had avoided customs and any scrutiny by the Australian security service. So simple was the plan, no one would know he was in the country. The pick-up helicopter suddenly swooped down from out of nowhere, startling him. The blowing sand limited the visibility for all until the blades retreated to neutral mode. The machine barely had room to land. The Chinese man struggled to get aboard, stiff and sore from his voyage. Helping hands dragged him aboard. He never looked back as the helicopter rotated itself into the sky. He was off the water finally.

The Lombok island fisherman had taken all day to harvest their load of sea cumbers, stopping a few times to enjoy their find. They gutted the sea cumbers, tossing the entrails into the sea and slowly cooked the Trepang. They ate with relish, juices running down the sides of their mouths. They laughed and talked of their adventure. What would each one do with all their money earned by dropping off their passenger on this deserted rock, they wondered in unison. They laughed again at their good luck. Finally, one of the crew suggested they keep the money a secret, spending a little at a time. No use in alerting the army or police with extravagant purchases. The authorities would confiscate all of it for themselves and then put them in a lockup. Fearing for their safety and their families, they all agreed. Then, with an incoming twenty-foot tide, and a full stomach, the fishermen loaded their harvest and sailed for home, leaving nothing behind except for the Trepang entrails, hugging the bottom of the Timor sea.

The tide covered the evidence of their arrival and departure. The rock pile of an island and its second reef soon became invisible once again.

CHAPTER 24

PRESIDENT WONG'S OFFICE

Wong called his American cousin into his office. "And?" he questioned. Sue Wong fidgeted. "We did not find the red backpack containing the journal nor the journal itself. He must have taken both with him. I don't understand his fixation with carrying the journal around with him. Unless he senses our presence, why would he risk taking the red backpack into the Outback? He could die out there, and we could lose the secret of the reef of gold forever. How stupid of him," she hissed.

"His townhouse contained no clues?" he asked.

"Only a scrap of paper from the Perth Library was discovered. It was an international permit to research in a special area of the library. I have someone in the library now, posing as an international researcher. Maybe, with a little luck, we can find the same books and maps that he was using to help us locate the reef."

"What are you going to do now?"

"I will wait to hear from my people at the library. Since our mysterious Mr. Brad Templeton is currently and conveniently lost out in the Outback, we will do nothing to alert him of our search."

"This is all very nice," President Wong snorted, "but I feel we are no closer to learning the whereabouts of the reef than we were a few weeks ago. I am disappointed."

Gary Dale

"Hold that thought," she snarled, "my cell phone is vibrating."
"Yes," she said. "You have what? I see. Bring it to me immediately.
What do you mean; they won't let you take it out? Since when has
something like that stood in your way?" She snapped the cell phone
closed.

"My people have used Templeton's library permit record of
selected documents to find several maps that have been reportedly
copied by our intrepid American researcher. There was an additional
oceanographic map that could not be photocopied. It was too large
for the library copiers. According to the librarian, Mr. Templeton
traced certain sections and then cobbled the pieces together. He
wanted to copy another document from a special reserve file but was
not allowed to do so without special permission from the museum
director. Unfortunately for him, the director was not available. Since
Mr. Templeton wanted the special reserve file so badly and didn't
get to see it, my people will steal it. Maybe we will learn something
that even Mr. Templeton doesn't know." She swung about and left
the office in a hurry.

President Wong sat back in his chair. This has been such an
elusive journey, he thought. He fiddled with a broken stub of a pencil
he found lying on his desk. What am I missing here? What am I
missing, he asked himself again and again? Without thinking, he
flipped the yellow stub into the wastebasket. He rose from his desk.
He looked up at a ship's model of a 14th century design, like the one
used by the Chinese sailors when they found the reef of gold. He was
proud of his country's sea heritage. He analyzed each special feature
of the model. The treasure ship was truly of unusual design. Large,
single sails made of bamboo rattan, that could be raised up and down
to collect or spill more wind, crowded the deck. The massive rudder,
was located seemingly amidships, although in reality only 20 feet
from the stern, making steerage easier than the European ships of the
time period. The rudder had holes cut into the reinforced wood to
allow the release of water tension when changing directions. Wong

Reef of Gold

was amazed and delighted each time he revisited the model ship. The detail in the wooden model was exact and beautifully carved.

He carefully lifted the model down from its perch on the shelf. Walking carefully to his desk, he lowered the two-foot long masterpiece onto the flat surface. The model ship was made in two large pieces and one small component.

He took a deep breath of excitement. He lifted the entire ship's deck out of the hull and placed it on the table. Inside were the vessel's inner workings, reproduced in exact detail of the time period. Each storage hold was compartmentalized, water tight, making the ship difficult to sink. Crews' quarters were miniaturized to the extent of tiny bamboo hammocks. Cargo of ivory were packed into several holds and tied down. Spice bags made of rough cloth were stacked tightly against each other for balance. Wong reached inside the hull and pulled out the remaining section located in the bow of the ship. This showed the ship's ballast storage, the heavy, mineralized rocks that lined the keel. Without ballast, the ship would flip over in the slightest breeze. The ship's design allowed for tons of carefully placed weight, stretching the entire length of the ship, for maximum speed and safety.

In the anchor compartment, just above the massive ballast was a small notebook Wong had placed there, containing the security alarm codes of all the glass pedestals in his office and waiting room. The most complex code was for the pedestal in his office containing his copy of the reef of gold journal. His mother's one and only family heirloom, a rare Ming Dynasty vase that was passed on from generation to generation, was under security like the others in the lobby. Wong cracked a smile of confidence at his insistence of unusual security for his prized possession. The security company had never installed such a system. It demanded careful maintenance on a regular basis and Wong paid dearly for the security. Only he knew the codes and only from the codebook.

President Wong rose from his desk, codebook in hand, walked

Gary Dale

over and stared at his prized possession. His mother would have been so proud of him, he thought. He walked around the journal pedestal, caressing the codebook with his thumb. If the coding sequence was not properly entered for the reef of gold journal inside the pedestal, the malfunction would trigger an instantaneous canister release of a fine fog-like mist, attacking the journal with microorganisms, eating at the journal and within minutes, leaving a pile of dust in its wake. The rare porcelain vases on the rest of the pedestals would be spared. Wong bragged to everyone about his unusual security system encompassing all the items.

Wong had to install such a drastic system. His cousin in Singapore was finding the time to be aggressive in his pursuit of the journal stolen from his father. Wong called him the "brown suit" with distaste and venom. The brown suit relative also had the irritating habit of cracking his knuckles while he was forcefully gesturing a point of conversation as if violence would occur.

The master code in the codebook was Wong's only connection with life as he knew it. It was his only hold over his brown suited cousin. In spite of the security arrangements, he knew it would be only a matter of time before his cousin from Singapore would make his move to get access to the journal pedestal. Wong would never give him the proper code. He would die first. Fingering the codebook as if it were his nighttime security blanket, Wong flicked open the small book. He stared at the numbers and then closed the book. He walked back to his desk and placed the codebook back into its hiding place in the model ship. He must find the other journal now, he thought, and claim the reef of gold. Time was of the essence. He could wait no longer. His deceased father and mother were counting on him.

CHAPTER 25

TROUBLE

When there was still enough daylight left of the day, Brad took Megan for a walk up the gorge. He pointed out to her the beautiful walls, dotted with a growth of brush and holes where small boulders had fallen out, littering the floor of the gorge. In his excitement, he shared with her the alluvial fans that had resulted from a rare cloudburst bursting with floodwater. He also showed her the giant boulders, stacked against the side of the gorge like guards to an ancient tomb.

Her face showed amazement. "Where on earth did these boulders come from? How did they get here?" she asked.

"You haven't seen anything yet," Brad said. "Follow me. I have this little water pond to show you. You won't believe it." She didn't, at least not at first. All she could do was to shake her head in amazement.

Back at camp, they discussed the ancient drawings and the pool of water. The overhang itself had obviously filled in eons ago from the ceiling dirt. If the Aboriginal lived under the overhang as the drawings suggest and above the pool of water for 10,000 years, the question becomes how did they survive? The ideas danced about in their conversations. Finally, they concluded that although Outback animals had to be aware of human existence, water was still vitally

Gary Dale

important to their survival. The animals must have entered the gorge edging their way along the gorge wall on the far side, away from the Aboriginal family living under the overhang. If they didn't find human scent at the waterhole, then they would drink. Because of natural predators also wanting a drink of water, the animals wouldn't retrace their steps but traveled through the middle of the reeds and into the canyon. The Aboriginal must have figured out a way to attack the returning animals for their major source of protein.

"That meant," said Brad, "that young Aboriginal children couldn't swim in the pond, period. Otherwise, the human scent left would scare off the animals. Imagine, children having to obey their parents." They both laughed at the thought. They sat for a while, just absorbing the moment and letting the stress leak out of their bodies.

It wasn't until Brad wandered over to their make shift office area under the overhang that he saw the laptop. It suddenly reminded him to call Michael and let him know that they had made it to the canyon. How could he forget to call?

"Megan, want to talk to Michael and his family?" he asked, as he walked away from under the overhang.

"By all means," she said.

Brad punched in the numbers and waited for Michael to answer his phone. Nada, zip. Punching the end button, he hit the redial once again and no one answered. Finally after ringing and ringing, Michael's voice mail came on and Brad left a brief message about their mining success.

"Well, maybe they are out for dinner or visiting someone. Want to check your email while we have the phone set up? Maybe your brother has a message for you?"

With a quick nod, she hooked up the satellite phone and the company laptop and punched in her codes. They shared a joke that the expensive satellite phone bill was on the company tab so who cares at this moment.

Reef of Gold

Her email log was full with a lot of the usual mining stuff from the mining commission not withstanding the demands from Yang Lee to contact him immediately and to quit hiding out. "**I WANT THAT DISK**," he demanded, in big bold letters. Lee's stoic anger and determination gave Megan an instant headache. Her stress level began to rise rapidly.

"What's the date of that email?" asked Brad.

"Today's date," she answered. "Looks like the mystery of the missing disk is still a big deal to Yang Lee."

"We've never really discussed this in detail before," Brad said, "but why does he think you have the missing disk. He has to have some reason. What did you do last Saturday that would have put you in this predicament?"

"I really don't know. I went in on Saturday morning, actually mid-morning, just to clear my email and finish organizing one of our massive documents for the mining commission. The documentation was taking longer than planned because the engineering and exploration departments were more focused on the long week than doing paperwork on our current mining claims. I wrote the mining commission an email telling them we would miss the deadline and would have documents for them after the long week. After several hours of mind numbing inputting the data of our research, I got tired and went home for lunch. I came back later in the day and found I needed some documentation that President Wong was supposed to supply me from his 3rd floor research department. Apparently, some of Yang Lee's own people went out again exploring in some of the outer reaches of our claims including looking into new areas. The mining commission wants each company trip to be thoroughly documented as to where they were and what they found, if anything. Guess our first explanation didn't satisfy the commission."

"What about my trip? Does it have to be reported?"

"No, yours is a private trip of one person, so you were ok. When

233

Gary Dale

Yang Lee sent out the Asian exploration crew in a helicopter this last time, no one in the company received a single document."

"Yeah, I remember now, Michael told us about that. He was a little upset. No maps were drawn for his department nor were any documentation sent to him. Big mystery."

"Well, Yang Lee's exploration crew was spotted by one of the mining commission aerial survey planes. The commission made a note of it and our last report didn't contain any documentation of that exploration. A natural inquiry followed."

"Where were they?"

"You mean Yang Lee's crew?"

"Yes."

"At the most southeastern corner of one of our claims or so President Wong explained to me. That's not awfully far from here, I think. Anyway, from that point on, there were no records. They could have gone on for hundreds of miles in any direction and no one would have known about it. President Wong had promised me the documentation so I could add itto the mining commission report. Since the documentation wasn't on my second floor desk, I went up to my third floor office to see if it was on my 'war room' desk. No one was up there except Charlie, our cleaning guy."

"Charlie? That's not a typical Aussie first name, is it?"

Megan shook her head. She paused while Brad processed the answer. She continued. "No, it's not a typical Aussie name. Actually Charlie is a displaced American war veteran who became a citizen. He was recuperating in a hospital here and then stayed on in Australia after the war in Nam, and since he had been severely wounded, sweeping and cleaning is all he wanted to do. The company hired him on a couple of years ago and gradually he has worked on every floor. Besides me, he is the only one that has complete 3rd floor security clearance. Sometimes, he cleans on the 4th floor but only during the day when others are around to watch him."

"Hold that thought while I throw some wood on the fire," Brad

234

Reef of Gold

said. Scrounging for a couple of larger sticks of sweet scrub wood gave him a chance to reflect on the company and its security. "Continue," he said, and sat down again and stretched out his long legs.

"Anyway, we talked some, like always, while I was doing paperwork at my desk. Except for the lights on at my office, the rest of the office areas were fairly dark with only some wall track-lighting. Charlie prefers, or so he says, to work in the semi darkness. Then again, maybe that is all the light he is allowed to work with on the 3rd. floor. Keeps his prying eyes off the desktops would be a security guy's answer. There are security people always walking around 24hrs. a day. Anyway, he was dust mopping the floors with an oil treated sweep when I heard a big crash in another office. I ran out and asked if he was all right. He muttered something that I couldn't hear. When I got over to him, he was on his hands and knees picking up pieces of pottery. He had cut himself on his hand and had put a handkerchief around it to stop the blood flow. I had a first-aid kit and lead him to my desk. A security guard showed up and helped me with the bandage."

"How bad was the cut."

"More than my first-aid kit would handle if he kept on working. Band-Aids weren't enough to hold the gauze pad in place and the nature of the cut would bleed profusely again. He said it wasn't the first time he had badly cut his hand. I could tell because a previous cut hadn't healed yet from a few days earlier. We fixed this cut straight away, but he was most concerned with the broken vase, especially the cost of replacement. He had bumped a coffee table with this vase on it. He went back to sweep up pottery pieces after he assured me that both bandages on his hand would hold if he was careful. I told him security would have some larger bandages to help him when he left the office building."

"Whose office was he in or does it matter? A vase can be replaced."

'Unfortunately, the office was one of Yang Lee's assistants, who

Gary Dale

works in a real secure area. Most of the time, the poor guy lives in fear from Lee's presence. I had a piece of the broken pottery at my desk and from my desk light; it appeared to me that the vase was from one of the Chinese collections that abound on the 4th floor, probably on personal loan from President Wong."

"Uh, oh," Brad grunted, "that probably wasn't a good vase to knock over. Charlie's probably in more than a little trouble."

"He could be, but I don't think serious enough to lose his job, but someone will climb his frame, especially with all the tension from the missing disk." As the conversation waned, they both sat quietly for a few minutes.

Brad interrupted Megan's thoughts and asked if she had considered that maybe Yang Lee's people had asked Charlie if anyone beside himself had been on the 3rd. floor. "I mean, they probably figured you worked on Saturday just from the security records, but they wouldn't know how long you were on the third floor and where you went."

"Oh, security would know. Once a person clears the main building security people, they would have to wear a security badge and have a pass code screening to get to the 3rd floor. The security system recorded my entry and the time. Rarely does anyone work on weekends, at least when I've shown up. Besides, the security guards search you pretty thoroughly on weekends especially if my security record shows I've been on the third floor."

"Only a conscientious workaholic like you would show up on a Saturday." Brad laughed and then said, "Maybe that is why they believe you have the missing disk. Think about it. Charlie breaks something in one of Yang Lee's offices, cuts himself, you bandage his hand, and leave. Maybe that's the office area where the disk originated. Lee's security guys probably checked Charlie out pretty thoroughly which left them with your exit."

"Oh boy. I never thought of that. That is a possibility. But I never

Reef of Gold

saw any disk, and if I had it on me, the security guards would have found it," she said defiantly.

"Well, maybe they think you somehow slipped it by security," suggested Brad. "They're grasping at straws since they don't have any answers. Lets hope they find the disk."

"Brad, you better read this," she called out in alarm.

He jumped up and laid his newly lit cigar down on the nearest rock. What he read on the computer screen was very disturbing. The email message was from her brother. He did not know or at least wasn't aware of the seriousness of her predicament until he had called Michael. He was now concerned that her situation was becoming more alarming. Michael had told him that Yang Lee had launched a major search for her, putting in far more effort than anyone had realized. She was to get back to him immediately by email or phone. He needed to know exactly where she was."

"What do I send?" she asked. "I don't want to sound desperate."

"Start with my picking you up at Michael's and our arrival out here. Tell him we have enough food and water, and that we are concerned Yang Lee is looking for you. Just so your message doesn't sound like such a desperate message, ask him an innocuous question, like 'what about the telegraph poles with the communication box every 50 kilometers that we discovered in the Outback'? It would give your brother a better idea of where we are. You might consider giving him our compass readings, inaccurate as they might be, because it might help your brother feel better knowing about where we are located.

"Sounds good to me, Brad." She sighed. "I just wish this nightmare would end."

"We'll make it," Brad assured her, squeezing her shoulder. "This is as good a hiding spot as there is anywhere. No one knows precisely where we are, including us."

She emailed back a fairly long message including the rough

Gary Dale

compass coordinates and then switched off the laptop and the satellite phone. She looked at the low battery power indicator on the satellite phone showing red. She was going to ask Brad about it when she got sidetracked. "Are we having dessert?" Brad had asked. The flashing red indicator light was forgotten.

After a while, they both seemed to sense that they were tired of conversation for the moment, and it was time to prepare for bed. The awkward moment would come soon enough. It always did when the decision came to decide whether or not to sleep in the same room or sleep with someone for the first time. Unless two people made it a spontaneous reaction, a romantic interlude could have all kinds of pitfalls if there was any thinking time allowed between them.

When Megan finished washing her face and the rest of the things women do before bed, she looked at him hesitantly as if to say, 'what's next?' She didn't move.

Brad stood still, not saying anything. He had been in situations like this several times with other women and handled it well. But this time was different. Megan was really, really special. He didn't want to mess up this relationship. Megan broke the ice and walked over to him.

His heart immediately started pounding like the sound of kettledrums in a community orchestra. It was so loud that Brad was sure she could hear its beats echoing off the overhang walls. He thought she looked terrific with the firelight casting a reflection on one side of her face, accenting her high cheekbones and hair. She was absolutely stunning. His mouth suddenly became dry as sun bleached bone in the Outback. If there ever was to be a time where his fantasy honeymoon would come true, then this nature-made setting had to be the place.

"Brad, I, ah," she started to say until Brad bent down and gently kissed her on the lips. Not once, but tenderly several times before they fully embraced. When they surfaced for air, they were both smiling and seemed eager for more although Megan had tensed

Reef of Gold

and then relaxed her body during the embrace. Everything seemed to have stopped in time for Brad with no thoughts, no worries except for the moment at hand. A bomb could have gone off and he wouldn't have paid any attention as they continued to look into each other's eyes.

Finally, out of nervousness, Brad felt he had to say something. "Megan," he said carefully, ever so gently releasing her little by little from their embrace, "I want to hold onto you like this for a long time."

She kissed him again, even more passionately and then broke their embrace. Still holding his right hand, she looked into his eyes and said "thank you." With a gentle squeeze, she released their emotional attachment and crawled into her own Aussie swag.

Slowly Brad moved towards his own swag. Reminding each other to put their shoes in the sleeping bag with them to keep the critters away from them during the night, they drifted off into frustrated dreams.

The next morning, they were up an hour after daybreak doing the morning chores before heading out to the promising mining dig area half-way up the gorge. Things were pretty well organized from the night before, but water bottles had to be filled and lunch still needed to be prepared. Brad worked on this while Megan fiddled with some of the outreach mining programs already installed in the computer, more out of curiosity than anything else. She plugged in the satellite phone and quickly checked her email again to see if her brother had contacted her. He was her only link with the outside world.

Her brother had emailed sometime during the night and said he would email again later in the morning. He had to check out a few things first. While he couldn't be there to protect her, Brad would have to do. Megan had a good laugh at that one. "Typical, overprotective brother," she said to Brad. "He also asked for a favor from you, Brad. Could you email him with more specific information

Gary Dale

about the boxes on top of the telegraph poles, describing them in more detail, as in size, markings, and etc. as soon as possible?"

"I'll give it a shot," said Brad.

"While you email him, I'll finish with making up the sandwiches." She smiled. "Then," she said, rubbing her hands together, "we can get on with the digging of more of those beautiful gold nuggets. I would like to have a couple of pairs of gold earrings."

Brad did his best for her brother with the description of the communication boxes with ears facing each pole direction and how every 20 or 30 miles, another box with ears appeared directly in line with each other for a long ways in both directions; east and west. How far they went, he didn't know. He pushed the send key and then punched a few more keys and buttons with his gnarly fingers which were bruised and swollen from the previous days shoveling efforts. Nothing worked in the shut down computer category. He probably messed up all ready, he thought. He decided he would let Megan do the final closing. With these mining computers, Brad knew there were always special shut down program procedures that had to be handled with care. That's why he vowed never to touch the computer programs in the first place. Michael wouldn't appreciate his clumsiness.

Brad helped her pack the food and water bottles in each backpack and then left her to gather up a few remaining personal items. While she was busy, he walked down to the rig to check the tires and make sure all was secure. The tires still had air. Returning to the nest, he hoisted his backpack and grabbed the handle of his favorite shovel, which now was as smooth as a baby's bottom. He had forgotten the shovel yesterday and had to settle for a dinged up version of a mining shovel at the site itself.

"Let's go," he said, "we are burning daylight."

"Wait a minute," she said, noticing the computer screen. "You didn't shut down the computer properly."

"I know. I wanted you to do it because you know more about

Reef of Gold

the mining programs and their procedures than I do. Don't forget to unhook the satellite phone and bring it with you."

"No worries," she said. "I'll only be a minute."

Brad tested the weight in his backpack, adjusting a few items for better balance. He turned around for a last minute look for any forgotten gear when Megan asked him if he had left a disk in the laptop.

"No," he said. "I never put a disk in it. No reason to. The disk must be left over from the previous trip."

"Brad, come look at this!" she said with some puzzlement.

Shedding his pack and gear, Brad walked over to Megan.

"Look at the screen. I opened up the disk that was in the laptop. Its pure gibberish until one looks at it closely, and then it seems it is some sort of encoding or program language. Maybe it is encrypted."

"So, what's the question?"

"Have you ever seen anything like this?"

"No. Have you?"

"I don't see all of the raw computer mining stuff. It's mostly filtered by the time I receive the material. Michael might recognize the data program or perhaps the mining commission."

"It's got to be in your mining language," he said. "The company mining engineers had to have been the last ones to use the laptop."

She scrolled up and down looking for some clue as to the identity of the disk. Finally, she dropped her hands and leaned back from the laptop. She turned with a stricken look on her face.

"Oh boy, you think this is the disk Yang Lee is looking for?" questioned Brad.

"Look at the screen Brad, it's pure gibberish."

"If it is the disk, how and why is it in this particular laptop? And, why do I have it instead of you?" asked Brad nervously.

They both stared at the screen again without saying a word. They both knew there is a fine line between overreacting or brushing it off as a forgetful employee.

Gary Dale

"Look, my gut feeling indicates nothing happens without a reason and that's what bothers me," said Brad.

"Let's take each question one at a time, Brad, and try to filter through possible scenarios. If my memory serves me well, there have been several Sterling Mining exploration trips in the past to the same unexplored area at Yang Lee's orders. His Asian crews on the last trip are the ones that came in question with the mining commission. Remember I told you about the survey plane flying around and spotting the Sterling Mining survey crew near our mining claim borders? The crew didn't report their trip for me to send into the mining commission. That caused us some problems, especially since our company had determined several years ago that the area Yang Lee and his crew were inspecting wasn't of commercial value. Not enough gold to mine it profitably. But Yang Lee still sends mining teams out. A possible scenario might be that they used this same laptop and accidentally left the disk. Maybe they found something and didn't want to disclose it."

"Ok, so we have a mystery. Next question. What if Yang Lee's group didn't leave a disk in the computer? How did the disk get into my laptop if the last exploration crew didn't leave it in there in the first place?"

They both thought about it. Then Megan asked Brad who gave him the laptop before he left and why.

"My memory is a little fuzzy on this due to the rush to get out here. I think Michael said at one time that a laptop was part of the required equipment and that no exploration trip went without it. The rig had a special protective place set up for the laptop so it could take the pounding and bouncing around from the rough driving conditions in the Outback. I wasn't even planning to use it except to email because I don't know the programs."

"How did you get the laptop?"

"It was already in the rig. I thought Michael had decided against giving it to me, but there it was. The only equipment that I grabbed

Reef of Gold

at the last minute was a satellite phone. I don't remember if Michael handed it to me or someone else from his department or if I picked it up from my desk. It wasn't fully charged, because it cut off our conversation yesterday in mid-sentence. I've recharged it from the rig's battery several times, but the new charge only gives the satellite phone less and less of a temporary boost and not a full charge to engage in any long conversations or sending of documents."

"Do you remember anything else that was unusual or last minute that wasn't what you expected to find?"

"No, not really, but the equipment loader who helped me with the trailers did mention something about a last minute trailer being added by someone. He was talking about the small trailer that I first dropped off at the first company cache, just off the road from the town of Laverton."

"Ok," said Megan. "Another question and it may be the toughest. What is all this gibberish on the computer screen? I've been searching on the computer, but I can't find anything that would give us a clue. What do you think we should do? Any ideas?"

"Well," said Brad. "First, I think you ought to email the gibberish to the mining commission and let them unscramble it. Maybe the information was something that needed to be reported to them in the first place. That way you are protecting yourself in case Sterling Mines tries to do something funny with your final report since they are rather upset with the both of us. My other thought would be to email your brother the document and ask him. You told me he is a computer nut. Maybe it's some kind of computer program language written in some code for one of Wong's other businesses. I remember reading a technical magazine article on the computer industry a couple of years ago about high tech companies interviewing people for jobs. This article said that the company hired this young kid as a programmer because he dreamed in code at night. You and I might find that a bit strange, but apparently the company doing the hiring loved it. Somebody like that could probably figure this out."

Gary Dale

"Well, one thing is for sure," said Megan, "the file information doesn't do anybody any good just flashing on the screen here. I'll send it as an attachment to the mining commission first, then Michael and if we have the battery power, my brother will get a copy. If it is harmless, then no worries, right?"

"Right," Brad sighed, "then we start looking for gold. We just can't sit around for two weeks and do nothing except worry. We may not find any gold to speak of, but at least we can keep busy."

Megan hooked up the satellite phone once again and emailed the document to the mining commission with a short note of explanation of how they came across the information. Her note to her brother was more of a personal one; and when she was finally through, the satellite phone battery indicated they were very low in power. Despite the low battery charge indicated by the flashing red light, they agreed to take the phone with them in case of emergency, figuring they could hopefully get a couple of short messages out if they got hurt. The flashing light was a concern but there was nothing they could do about it.

CHAPTER 26

DISCOVERY

It was mid-morning before Megan and Brad finally left the camp and headed for their undiscovered gold claims. Already the heat of the day was making a statement. The heat waves were simmering off the rocks and the dust laden brush leaves seemed to hibernate, waiting until the coolness of the coming evening. A near constant wind had swirled away the short lifetime of their boot prints. It was almost as if the foot prints never existed.

They were serious rookie gold miners now, and they both agreed that teamwork was better than competition to find the biggest nugget. They both knew that the digging kept their minds off the office turmoil. Even though Brad's neck and shoulders would spasm on him from the heavy sifting effort, he volunteered to do the heaviest work. He wanted to have a good dinner prepared for him each night, and it wouldn't be good if he pushed the camp cook too hard.

They had just reached the ribbon of green brush from the ancient streambed spilling out of the canyon wall when the satellite phone rang. The sound came in spurts as if the satellite couldn't make up its mind to make the connection or not. They both stopped and Brad tried to find it by rummaging around in Megan's backpack. She quickly told him to stop rummaging and to move his right hand

Gary Dale

down the left side of the pack. It was still spurting electronic signals when Brad finally retrieved it and pressed the receive button.

"It's your brother," Brad said, "at least I think it's him."

The voice message was sporadic at best, with words being cut off let alone a complete sentence. Brad looked up at the towering edge of the cliff and realized that the satellite triangulation signal was having a hard time making a triangle with the phone even with several satellites doing their best to pick up a signal. As Brad moved away from the edge of the cliff, the unidentified voice was able to repeat part of the garbled message again.

Brad wished he hadn't.

"Megan," he urgently called over to her while shutting down the connection. She hadn't been listening to the phone call but preparing to dig near the green bushes.

"Come here, quick."

"Yes, what is it," she said, laying down her shovel and running over to Brad.

Before he could answer, they could hear the sound of a helicopter frantically beating the air in the near distance. The whoop whoop sound from the blades became more distinguishable with each passing moment.

"Oh, oh," said Brad. "They are here faster than your brother thought they would be."

"What do you mean, faster?" she asked. "And who are they?"

"Look, we don't have much time. Grab your pack and shovel. I'll tell you on the way."

In between gasps of hot air during their half run pace, Brad told Megan of the phone call from her brother, at least he thought it was her brother. The message was garbled most of the time. The best that Brad could figure out from the conversation was that the satellite cell phone had an emergency transponder to it, and when the battery was really low on power, it sent out an identifiable distress signal giving a GPS location. It was standard procedure for all the mining

Reef of Gold

satellite phones, but no one had taken the time to explain to Brad the idiosyncrasies of the phone before going on his exploration trip.

"Bottom line," said a worried Brad, "is that the Sterling Mining office must have traced the satellite phone signal to this area and now Wong or Yang Lee and his staff has sent people after us, right now. I'm not sure how your brother knows about the distress signal but his phone call at least alerts us to the arrival of some bad guys."

There was a shocked look on Megan's face.

"The helicopter we heard a minute ago has to be somebody's musclemen. What did you call them?"

"Larrikins, but the name is not that important now," she snapped, thoroughly frustrated and scared.

"Sorry," said Brad. "Anyway, they have figured out that I'm somewhere around here. Maybe they don't know about you. Just in case, I want you to hide in a cavity under the giant boulders where we have stashed the extra food and water. You will have to climb the ledge without my help."

"What about you?" she asked in a strained voice. "What if they find the camp? All our remaining supplies including the rig are there. If they got all of that, we wouldn't last but a day or two. Brad, what are we...."

"Hold that thought, Megan. Just crawl under the rocks." He pushed the satellite phone into her hands. "Take the phone. I'm going to climb to the top of the gorge to see if it is really people looking for us or rescuing us. If they are the larrikins, which they probably are, I'll lead them away from you. If they don't know you're here, maybe they will only look for me. One of us has to escape to get the word out for a rescue attempt."

"Be careful Brad. I'll be with the water supplies under the rock cavity until you return."

"Back before you know it," he replied. "If for some reason I don't return in a couple of hours, use the satellite phone and call for help. There may not be enough transmission power left but you have to

Gary Dale

try. Your brother should answer. " Brad grabbed a couple of half filled bottles of water and slipped away as Megan vanished.

Picking up a fallen branch from one of the near dead shrubs, Brad carefully brushed away their tracks near the boulders, scratching at the surface until he had reached a gravel part of the ancient streambed. He couldn't do anything about their tracks along the floor of the gorge, but they were few in number and it wouldn't be long before the wind would repair the damage. Brad just didn't want any indication of tracks to lead them back to Megan. The next obstacle was how to get to the top of the cliff to see just who the intruders were. To go back to the camp would take too much time and even with his small binoculars, he wouldn't be able to tell who these unknowns were from that distance. He would have to get closer.

Gunshots rang out echoing in the walls of the gorge. Brad ducked instinctively and scurried behind a large bush that barely hid him. He looked around frantically and realized he couldn't stay very long in his exposed position. Were the intruders shooting in his direction or were the gun shots a signal? He took a swig of warm liquid from his water bottle to calm himself and thought for a few moments. Most likely the unknowns would gather on the east side of the gorge where the sun would be at their backs if they were to look down into the canyon, he concluded. Looking into the sun to find someone wouldn't be that pleasant nor productive. They couldn't be that stupid, he thought.

Subconsciously, his fingers stroked the binoculars while he remembered that he had seen the track tracing the gorge wall to the rim just a few days earlier if he could just find it. He took one of the half empty water bottles and sloshed water in his eyes, clearing away the grit. Squinting his eyes against the bright sun, he looked for a track of any kind. The sun-baked gorge wall gave no secrets. He looked down at the ground to give his eyes time to refocus. Then he cursed. He quickly brought the small binoculars to his eyes and glassed the hillside up and down. He could barely make out a

Reef of Gold

discolored slash along the side of the canyon. The track didn't appear to be much. It didn't even look possible for an animal to use. Was this the same track he had seen earlier only to have it disappear?

He dashed to the gorge wall. Above his head was a rock ledge exposed by undercutting floodwaters. Putting his left foot in a branch of a bush for support and using the wall for leverage with his right foot, he was able to claw and scramble onto a rock ledge.

In between the droplets of sweat now cascading from his face, Brad leaned inward towards the sloping dirt wall of the gorge for balance and picked his way along the track with his shoe heels often hanging out over the edge or so he imagined. Brad couldn't look down. He hated heights. He would get vertigo. In fact, he would get vertigo just standing on a sidewalk curb. One misstep and he would slide, bounce and roll to the bottom. Every little bush was a handhold. Every rock was an obstacle. Breathing in the hot air in gasps, Brad would stop and look up for a perspective, and then push forward on a slightly widening track. His climb seemed to be an eternity. He was so high up the face of the gorge wall that he dared not look even sideways for a fear of dizziness. The top of the canyon rim was near when he heard another disheartening sound, the one of a 4 wheel drive rig laboring in the sandy soil.

He carefully scrambled another ten feet to a small hole where a big rock had taken residence before it had loosened and tumbled down the gorge. Controlling his breathing and vertigo, he climbed the last few feet and cautiously peered over the top. Two crewmen stood next to the helicopter watching the 4-wheel rig approach them. Four occupants crawled out of the dusty rig dressed in desert mining fatigues.

Blowing the dust from his binocular lens, Brad glassed the intruders who were busily greeting each other. The men gathered around in a circle when one of them finally walked over to the rig and switched off the engine. The silence was noticeable. Brad could even distinguish their words.

Gary Dale

"Well, what do ya think, mates? Is he around here?" one of the big larrikins asked no one in particular.

A chopper pilot, with his distinguishing flying cap pulled down over his eyes and slightly off center, stared at them through his pilot sunglasses. As Brad watched, he spoke to one person only, a thin guy with a baseball cap and dark glasses. He was the one who had crawled out of the passenger side of the 4-wheel drive rig.

"Searched all along the telegraph line," the pilot said in a thick gravelly voice, "and found no tampering with the boxes nor saw anyone else for that matter. We landed at each communication box for eighty kilometers in both directions and every site seems to check out." His flying partner elbowed him in the ribs. The pilot grimaced and then quickly corrected himself. "We use the communication boxes sort of as survey markers. In answer to your question, there were no ground disturbances we could see. With the wind blowing out here daily that doesn't mean much."

"Why did you stop here?" asked the baseball cap in a shrill voice.

"We got a radio message from the office to be on the look out for you. I'm a survey pilot, not a search and rescue helicopter. This just happens to be a convenient place to check up on your party."

"What about the satellite signal the company recovered at the office?" asked the shrill voice? "How close are we to the readings that were intercepted from this area?"

"We don't know anything about intercepted satellite signals from the office," said the pilot.

The shrill voice looked frustrated. "We need your help with a search for a camp. It's possible we are not in the right location, and therefore we aren't sure of anything."

"What do you mean, you aren't sure? Look, Yang Lee's office radioed us to land and meet you in this general area if we had enough fuel left." said the helicopter pilot. He stared at her. "We spotted your rig heading this direction. You want to tell us what's going on? No

Reef of Gold

one has told us what you are doing out here or whom you are looking for in this place. I know we work for the same outfit, but Yang Lee hired us to do a particular job and we are doing just that. He is not a man to cross. We shouldn't be here, and we sure don't have to be a part of your search party. You are on your own."

The conversation had turned quiet as the person answering his question was turned away from Brads hearing. 'Definitely Larrikins,' thought Brad. Then one of the smaller men made some smart remark.

The pilot turned to him and snarled a cuss word. Then he turned back to the others. "For one thing," he said in a disgusted voice, "do you know what compass setting he is using in his rig? It could mean four different locations. Well?"

"What do you mean?" the baseball cap asked in a shrill voice.

"Did he set his compass to Grid North; True North; Magnetic North or False North? Was he using his on board GPS system or doesn't his rig have the system. Was he using company maps to help him?" he asked.

The shrill voice said nothing.

The pilot continued. "You said he wasn't a mining engineer so he probably didn't set the compass according to the company's specifications. Unless he knew company procedures, he probably wouldn't be accurate with any of his readings."

After the statement sank in, there were several explosions of cuss words and exclamations penetrating the silence of the Outback. Finally after some discussion, the baseball cap made a decision for all the rest of them. "We will search this area because we are here."

With a nodding of a head or two, an agreement seemed to be reached among the group.

Shaking his head with disgust, the pilot reminded the thin one that he had to report back to Yang Lee.

There was a heated discussion going on between the thin one and the pilots as they walked to the helicopter. The thin one suddenly

251

Gary Dale

turned and yelled in a high pitched voice at the remaining three larrikins to get on with the search.

Two of the searchers didn't waste any time and walked towards the edge of the canyon. They came so quickly that Brad barely had time to slide back down the track a few feet and out of sight. Looking at his surroundings on this narrow track told him that he would be found soon if he stayed where he was. Brad carefully backed down the track a few steps at a time, mindful of not creating any dust. He moved sideways along the edge rim away from the track.

After what seemed like ages, he found a small overhang about five feet from the top of the track. He could barely crawl under it. He quickly dismissed the lack of comfort as he maneuvered even further under the overhang by tucking his knees against his chest and curling his toes back against the back wall. Then he froze in position.

The voices from two larrikins sounded like they were practically standing on top of him. Both were discussing the merits of drinking water and shade while glassing the eastern slope across the way as well as the bottom of the canyon. As they moved about a bit, a little trickle of reddish Australian Outback dirt cascaded down the side of the canyon wall, curled around the lip of the rock overhang and drained onto Brad's face. The fine dust almost made him gag while the heavier dirt with small pebbles gathered momentum and just kept on going down the canyon wall as little dirt balls.

"Look at that will ya," said one of the searchers, as he kicked even more dirt over the edge. "Stuff goes clear to the bottom of the canyon. That's got to be over a hundred meters drop. Think this guy we're looking for is around here?"

"If he is mate, he'll be like a rat in a maze with big cats pursuing him. There is hardly any cover down there, and he'll run out of water if we keep pressing him."

By this time, the cascading dirt buried Brad's face, and he dared not move and brush it away just yet. He held his breath for as long as

Reef of Gold

he could before quietly blowing the air out the corner of his mouth creating a little air pocket to breathe.

"Come on, mate, it's bloody hot out here. A lousy 130 degrees Fahrenheit if anything," he said in a loud voice with the sound echoing across the canyon. He wiped his brow with the back of his hand, smearing the dust across his forehead.

"Why did you use Fahrenheit instead of Celsius?" the other larrikin asked cautiously.

"Because, if he is around, I wanted the American to know how hot it was right now and any further escape effort on his part would be futile. He'll realize that the heat and sun will kill him if he doesn't give himself up soon. Hell, I'm even ready to croak. Cussed dry season anyway," he snorted. "Look, there's some shade under the desert oak trees further down the gorge floor. Maybe there is a way down if we walk along the rim. You never know."

"Wait a minute," the other larrikin said. "Hey, Neville," he hollered, "you wakka. This way. Walk along the gorge on this side, not on the other side. You can't see anything by looking into the sun. We're going to get the boss and try to find a way down to the gorge floor. Watch from over here where we are and see if we scare something out of the bush. Got it?"

The decreasing sound of the voices told Brad he could move his right hand and brush away the dirt from his face and create a larger breathing pocket. Then he heard the whomp, whomp, whomp, of the helicopter blades biting the arid air for a lift off. As soon as the obnoxious sounds faded in the distance, Brad could hear the laboring sound of a 4-wheel drive engine towing a small trailer, heading in the southerly direction towards the mouth of the gorge.

That didn't sound promising, thought Brad. It would put the larrikins rig uncomfortably close to the camp and his supplies. If Megan stayed put, she would be safe until dark, if they didn't find the rig and if they didn't find the camp. A lot of 'ifs' Brad concluded. He was about to reach for his water bottle when above him were

253

Gary Dale

scraping sounds of feet scuffing the hot surface, and the clanking of metal broke his thirst for water. He froze. The sounds stopped just short of his location.

The one they called Neville made himself comfortable for the long haul with a folded lawn chair and umbrella. It was obvious he wasn't going anywhere for many hours. The larrikin just sat and spat.

Brad was beginning to get leg cramps in his curled position. He couldn't stretch without being discovered. As the hours passed, his throat became parched from the lack of water making swallowing and breathing difficult. Neville, he could tell, was getting bored. He started moving around just above him, constantly stretching, spitting now and then, before taking a leak over the edge of the gorge. He was drinking water all the while cursing to himself that his umbrella was too small to ward off all the sun's rays and that his folding chair was uncomfortable.

Every time the larrikin moved around away from the edge, Brad sparingly took a sip of water until the precious liquid was gone. As the hours crawled by, he started to doze. God help him if he snored.

Neville's loud voice suddenly startled him.

"What did ya find down there?" he hollered, his boisterous voice echoing off the canyon walls. The reply barely made it to the top of the gorge. "Oh," he said, "so there was someone down there." Then Neville started to laugh. "Hey, bring the water bottle up here. He won't need it." Neville continued to pace making snorting and spitting noises before finally sitting down in his folding chair.

Brad was stunned. A water bottle left behind. His confused brain couldn't comprehend his mistake. The larrikins knew he was here. Occasional sweat driblets ran down Brad's face creating little ticklish rivers tormenting him just like the insufferable heat. The rock ledge had become an oven, trapping the heat in his little cavity of space. With his water gone, the heat was slowly but surely sucking the life out of him. The dirt had become so hot that his exposed body parts

Reef of Gold

felt like they were being burned completely through. Yet, all he could do was to lie quietly and blend in with the landscape.

Both larrikins retraced their steps from the bottom of the canyon and met up on top of the rim with Neville once again. Brad was able to hear their conversation, sometimes only catching bits and pieces, and sometimes full sentences before falling in and out of an exhausted stupor. He still couldn't change positons.

"I'm tired of this heat," exclaimed Neville. "You didn't chance even a rabbit at the bottom of that gorge?"

"You aren't the only one who's hot. So shut up, you wakka."

"Enough bickering," the big fella said in his deep voice. "It's going to get dark soon, so Neville, you go with Billy and help set up camp. You two can bitch at each other all the way down to camp but no tinnys until I get back. I'll wait here for a while and watch. We know he is down there. The small amount of water left in his water bottle we found hadn't even evaporated. We will find him in the morning. He won't be wandering around in the dark."

Sometime during the night, a night breeze had swept across Brad's hot face like a cool washcloth. Awakening, only one eye barely opened. It somehow gave him a sense of not being alone. He blinked his left eye several times, trying to focus. He could vaguely see tiny objects moving every once in a while and finally could sense that something was crawling about his neck. The sensation of one suddenly became hundreds. Little ants came prancing by, sometimes tickling his eyelash. One after another they came with their golden behinds reflecting off the moonlight. As the army of ants passed by, Brad could sense them climbing on his roughened face, one whisker at a time, leaving little ant tracks and composite on his dirt caked face.

Golden ants. Something stirred in him. He remembered that Alice, his friend of Sterling Mining fame, had enlightened him a little bit about the Aboriginal Outback. Since there was little sugar in the Aboriginal diets, they took to biting off and dissolving the golden

Gary Dale

behinds of these particular ants. The behinds held small amounts of sugar for satisfying one's taste buds. It was the Aboriginal desert in the Outback.

Brad must have briefly dozed again, because he awoke a second time. His subconscious was letting the ants crawl into his mouth, onto his tongue making his involuntary response to slowly retract his tongue lizard-like, carrying the golden behinds with the ants attached. How many ants he swallowed was uncountable as the ants kept marching onto his swollen tongue triggering his swallowing response. One part of his brain told him that he needed more. The ants with their sugary golden behinds seemed accommodating. Then he slept.

The shadows were disappearing quickly along the canyon rim and were being replaced by brilliant yellows and antique bronze colors unique to the Australian sunrise in the Outback. It was the brilliant colors dazzling the retina of his left eye that finally woke him up. He tried to lift his head and failed on the first attempt. His head felt it was on fire and every muscle in his neck ached from being stuck in the same position for so many hours. The cold morning didn't help either.

The morning birds were singing in concert below him feasting on the multitudes of insects. With natures' music blasting away, Brad knew the larrikins would be awake soon. With a great effort, he managed a slow roll over into a semi-sitting position, feet dangling above the gorge floor.

Balance seemed to be a problem for Brad until he figured out that only one eye was barely working. His right eye was encrusted with dirt, mucus and closed tightly along with a numbing feeling on the same side of his face. It was the side that had been buried in the dirt for hours. Brad's tongue was still swollen so much that his mouth was permanently open inviting a multitude of flying insects.

"Water, I need water," he told himself. Slowly, one muscle movement at a time, Brad dragged himself upright, muscles quivering

Reef of Gold

from the lack of electrolytes that only water could give him. He leaned forward, pressing his face and hands against the side of the canyon for balance. Dizzy from a massive headache, he felt like an old man on his last legs. Somehow his brain told the rest of his body to get it in gear. He knew he couldn't go down the steep trail unless he wanted to roll to the bottom and injure himself. That left the option of staying put or climbing up and over the rim and then staggering along the edge of the gorge itself. He chose to wobble. His only hope was that this early morning hour, the larrikins would still be asleep.

Brad didn't know how long it took him to make the last few feet or so up the steep canyon wall to the rim, but finally he rolled over the top and kept rolling for several more turns. In his condition, he was afraid he might lose his balance if he suddenly stood up. A fall over the edge would not be good.

His light-headedness kept him flat on his back until the moment passed and with one final roll, Brad was able to get to his knees and then stagger to his feet. He didn't even have the strength to look for the larrikins' camp. His brain said just keep away from the edge of the gorge. He wobbled downhill like a drunken sailor, keeping the sun on his left side as a guide. Dehydration was a major factor now. He had little body reserves left and let his wobbly, stumbling gait keep bringing him closer to water stored in his rig. He looked down at the gradual sloping landscape near the mouth of the gorge where his rig had so carefully negotiated the first time. It was a momentary thought as Brad failed to pick up one of his feet, which in turn caught the top inch or two of the reddish, wind blown, pebble strewn soil and over he went. The sensation of falling was more like a quick thud and a cloud of dust and then he rolled and rolled down the incline to the bottom. He lay there for the longest time. Finally catching his breath, he rolled over once again to his knees. The survival mode had kicked in gear once again. He needed that life saving liquid stored in his rig.

Gary Dale

It wasn't until his subconscious told him to find some shade to escape the morning sun and stop for a brief rest that Brad recognized something familiar. It took some rapid blinking of his good eye and some real concentration, but there it was. A shady spot, one of the very few he remembered, growing on a rockslide. There had been a large scrub tree and enough brush to shade and protect a rig from the elements, but one had to climb to get to it. From where he was located, the brush had camouflaged any semblance of a parked rig.

"It's got to be it," one side of his brain screamed. The other side of the gray matter said, "Hey, you could be wrong, probably just a mirage." Like a crazed, wounded water buffalo, with adrenalin flowing and looking to bash something, Brad charged the surrounding brush with all his remaining energy. Staggering through the thick brush with thorns ripping at his flesh, he finally broke through and slammed right up against the rig. He bounced off and then jerked open the passenger's door, looking for any water bottle available. It was all he could do to not groan with satisfaction as the tepid water splashed down his throat and neck. His right eye soon got a bath of warm water to wash away the crud and the eye began to work again.

Finally, with a deep sigh of relief, he had enough presence of mind to quietly close the rig door. He had more energy now as he staggered up the track. The camp was undisturbed. He was still very cold from the previous night until he found his lightweight bush jacket. It at least took the chill off. Brad found more water but drank sparingly this time. He knew his body would react violently if he drank too much liquid at one time. The bananas were brown from the heat, the dried beef jerky too difficult to chew, the bread moldy, and the donuts were hard as rocks. Brad opted for a couple of brown bananas to wolf down while rummaging around in the food bin before finding a couple of melted energy bars to suck on. A few minutes later, he found the inviting swag. It seemed to call to him.

Reef of Gold

He drank some more water, unrolled the bag, slid inside, and crashed face down without his pillow.

The sun eventually moved fifteen points on the compass before Brad suddenly jerked awake in a stupor.

"Where's Megan?" Brad raised his stiff body to a standing position and looked around for some sign of her presence thinking she would have made it back here at some point. That was the problem, he thought, everything looked neat and orderly with nothing disturbed. Megan hadn't been back to the camp. So, where was she, he thought, still under the rocks? She can't be, he told himself. But where was she? Brad rummaged through the frozen food box and found things still semi-frozen, so he quickly shut the lid to preserve the cold air. The red cold box containing his red backpack was still closed with eating utensils still scattered on top. Grabbing the water bottles and melted energy bars, Brad decided that the only course of action was to risk going after her to her rock hideout.

Keeping as close to the wall as possible to limit the larrikins an opportunity to spot him, Brad moved as quickly as his spasmodic legs would work, which wasn't fast. Megan needed the water and comfort now. At this late morning hour, the larrikins had to be searching again for him.

The giant-sized boulders loomed just yards in front of Brad and with a final effort, he made for a space between the second and third boulder. Gasping for breath, Brad let his sun baked eyes search the far canyon wall for any signs of movement and then scratched the ground with a bush branch, erasing any of his footprints before sliding in between the boulders and eventually disappearing into the side canyon. Megan had to be under the boulders for protection.

"Megan," Brad whispered in a horse voice, "it's me, Brad. I brought you water."

Dropping to his knees to peer under the boulders, Brad fully expected Megan to pop out with joy. He was stunned when she didn't answer. Had she been bitten by a snake and died? With some

Gary Dale

trepidation, he crawled under the rock. The shovel and screen were still in the corner, including her empty water bottles neatly placed in a row. The food wrappers were stuffed in an empty plastic bag, but no Megan. Where could she have gone? He looked for a note or sign of a struggle but came up empty handed. In the opposite corner of her cache of stuff, was the satellite phone carefully placed behind a small rock. Brad wouldn't have seen it except for the blinking low battery light casting a shadow off the back of the ceiling. He was reaching for the satellite phone when the sun shifted in its position and the blinking light reflection disappeared from the rock wall. He had been lucky to even have seen it.

Brad crawled back outside with the satellite phone, finally squatting down in a shadow of a small scrub bush. He pushed the recall button to see what phone numbers had been used the day before. He pushed a recall number. Brad closed his eyes during a moment of prayer for the phone to have enough battery power to make the connection. Hitting the send button, Brad waited for the satellites to establish the matching links, which unfortunately took their time while sucking power from the satellite phone. Finally, the links connected. The first call was to Michael. His phone sputtered before ringing and then suddenly faded away into silence. There was obviously a battery or link problem somewhere. He hit the recall for Megan's brother's cell number and punched the send button and watched the satellite phone linking do its work albeit again, very slowly.

Sweat was already pouring down his face as he was sitting in the center of this little side canyon, pretending to be a rock next to a bush to anyone who just might be scanning the area with binoculars. Unfortunately, the bush only gave enough shade for a party of ants. The satellite phone made the connection so clear Brad nearly jumped out of his skin. When Megan's brothers' cell phone clicked in voice mail mode, Brad wasn't ready to speak, as his throat wouldn't cooperate except in gagging sounds. Brad set the phone

Reef of Gold

down on the ground grabbing the water bottle with the other hand, unscrewed the cap and drank. Still mindful of the critical need for water, he unconsciously took a moment to tighten securely the cap back on the bottle.

There was a recorded message still going on at the other end when he grabbed the phone. When he finished leaving the shortest message he could give, Brad looked at the phone to hit the end of conversation button only to discover a screen saver had flashed on and then the screen went blank. Brad stared at the phone in total disbelief and mumbled a few choice words. Had the phone link somehow disconnected itself during his leaving of the message? It might have, but at what point during the conversation? Was it at the very beginning or near the end? Brad tried to reestablish the link again. The lack of power shut him down again. The satellite phone was usless.

Sticking the satellite phone into one of the multitude of safari jacket pockets, Brad grabbed his water bottles and scurried back to the rock and out of sight to decide what to do next. If Megan wasn't at the camp, then either she had been discovered and taken by the larrikins or she was still hiding. But where would she be hiding?

Loud voices from the larrikins traveled into his little box canyon. The searchers apparently weren't trying to be quiet during their search pattern. The rude comments flipping back and forth between the larrikins passed near Brad's hiding spot indicating they were searching for tracks in the main canyon rather than looking under every rock for his possible sun baked, shriveled up, dead body. Brad was ready to move.

It didn't take long for the searchers to stop near the end of the canyon and holler up to their companions on the top of the rim asking if they had flushed the quarry. With echoing of the voices going back and forth, he headed their direction. Brad kept close to the sides of the gorge, where his tracks on the hard ground wouldn't show. They were still jabbering away when Brad spotted them doubling back.

Gary Dale

Careful not to disturb any dust, Brad moved forward in a half crouch, keeping close to the canyon wall, stopping only when he had to keep from being spotted. By this time, the searchers had clumped together like a bunch of grapes as if they had found something.

Brad wasted little time moving forward gaining at least fifty yards before he snuggled out of sight in-between two boulders. He was heading for the only place left that Megan could have gone.

The frustrated searchers passed him, spreading out again and moving slower this time. Each bush and rock seemed to absorb their interest. Trying to make as little noise as possible, Brad left his rock hideout and sneaked closer towards the pond at the end of the canyon. He must have covered a few hundred yards when he heard some shouts behind him. The larrikins must have seen him from above or else they had found signs of where he had been. Ignoring the possible discovery, Brad searched for the entrance to the rock overhang. There was no immediate indication of an entrance to the ancient rock overhang and he had to carefully search for a way in as Mother Nature so cleverly disguised it. He was just too close to recognize it. He knew the entrance was there.

Pressing his back against the rock wall, Brad slid alongside each rock, scraping his safari jacket and shuffling his feet along as fast as he could. Following the contour of the boulder, Brad emerged into the tall reeds. He carefully used his hands to part the reeds, and stepped through, letting the reeds snap back into their former position. He was now invisible from the outside world. As thick as the reeds were, he was still able to find the tiny streambed and walked along its edge, until he found the rock stepping-stones to the rock overhang. Brad discovered Megan lying in a fetal position.

"Megan," he hissed. "It's me, Brad." Since that didn't work, he didn't waste any time getting to her side. Shaking her with one hand, he used the other hand to stifle any possible excessive noise erupting from her mouth. Startled, she opened her eyes and then grabbed for his neck, pulling him towards her.

Reef of Gold

"Brad, it's you. I'm so glad you are ok," she said, squeezing him even tighter. "Where have you been?"

She looked a fright, as she so often called people who hadn't taken their time to look presentable, with her hair uncombed, streaks of sweat that had run down her dirty face making little rivulets. Her lips were parched and her eyelids were swollen, almost covering the haunted look as she turned toward him. And if Brad were a betting man, he probably looked the same to her.

"Hiding like you," he whispered, answering her question of where he had been. "Want some energy bars and water?" He helped her to stand to get the blood flowing in her legs.

"Both, please," she croaked in a whisper. "I was afraid to drink the pond water unless it was the last resort." She drank the warm bottled water and chewed on the energy bar.

"They're close by aren't they?"

Brad nodded a reply.

She ripped open another energy bar, this time with wrappers flying, and literally stuffed the bar in her mouth, taking big chomps and washing some of it down with gulps of water.

It took a moment but she finally smiled, and mumbled something about not being too ladylike when eating but then again, she was hungry and thirsty. The energy food seemed to revitalize her at least enough for them to share in whispers their stories in an abbreviated fashion of the past 24 hours.

"Well, well, who do we have here?" questioned a strange voice, echoing off the wall.

Brad and Megan nearly jumped out of their skins. Brad quickly stood, facing the intruders and in the same motion, put Megan behind him.

There were two of them.

"Who are you?" Brad questioned. He tensed as one of them pulled a gun. It looked small in his big hands.

"We are the people that have been looking for you the past couple

Gary Dale

of days and would have found you sooner if you hadn't been hiding from us. You were hiding from us, were you not? asked the hired gunman.

Brad and Megan both just stood there motionless, staring.

"Brad Templeton, right?" The one with the heavy voice questioned.

Brad nodded. The only thing he could think of to do was to stall. Maybe the cavalry, with a trumpet blaring *charge* would arrive in time to save them. Brad was going to give the rescuers all the time they needed to get here provided someone received their distress messages. At least Megan's brother ought to have alerted the authorities.

"You're the one we want," suggested a new voice. The voice was a little on the shrill side and the speaker was standing in the shadows so Brad couldn't see a face. There was some movement in the background and now there were four larrikins.

"Who's the girl?" demanded the shrill voice.

Brad could feel Megan tense up and prepare to speak when Brad answered for her. The thought quickly suggested to Brad that if they didn't know who she really was, he might be able to keep her identity a secret at least for a while. It also occurred to him that the shrill voice asking the question wasn't an Aussie. An Aussie would have asked who's the Sheila.

"Her name is Alice," Brad lied. "She works with me at the company and we sort of wanted to spend some time together without starting a lot of office gossip. I thought this would be a great opportunity."

The shrill voice turned to the others and said something. They all laughed. One of them spat into the ground.

"Why are you looking for me?" Brad demanded. "Who are you?"

Taking off the baseball cap, a beautiful oriental woman in flight fatigues stepped forward, out of the shadow and into a bit of reflected

264

Reef of Gold

sunlight. She was tiny in stature and her dark hair was pulled back, exposing her jade earrings that flashed a greenish hue.

Brad caught his breath momentarily, as his mind spun the combinations to his memory bank to where he had filed away the picture of this woman. Brad had seen her before, maybe on several occasions. As she walked closer, he recognized her.

"The last time I saw you was in San Francisco," Brad exclaimed, "at a Chinese restaurant. You were with your grandfather, and we had lunch together to discuss a particular Ship Captain's Journal in my possession."

"Was that the only time we noticed each other?" she asked.

Somewhere in a stored file in Brad's brain was the answer, but he couldn't come up with it. Perhaps it was the stress.

"What do you mean?" he asked.

"We met again standing in front of the elevators at the Sterling Mining Company building. I recognized your face from the reflection from the chrome elevator doors. That's how I knew for sure you were in Perth. Of course, I didn't let you see me."

Brad blinked several times. "You still haven't answered my question. Why are you looking for me?" he demanded, still stalling for time.

"Actually, Mr. Templeton, it's not really you we are after. It's your ship captain's journal we are seeking. Tell us the location of the diary and we will let you go."

"Right," Brad snorted and pointed to the larrikin holding the gun, "Some how I don't believe you. Besides, you don't need my journal. A Wong family member was supposed to have his own version. Isn't that what you hinted to me in San Francisco?"

She hesitated for a moment. It didn't really matter to Brad if she said anything or not. He was beginning to figure out this whole scenario. Sue Wong must have been with these same larrikins that broke into his townhouse looking for his red backpack containing the ship captain's journal. The intruders had spoken with an Aussie

Gary Dale

accent with an exception of one person and these were Aussies larrikins facing him. One thing for sure, Brad was glad he paid attention to his gut feeling that he shouldn't leave the red backpack in his townhouse. Otherwise, they would have it. On the other hand, if they had the journal, they wouldn't be looking for him. The question is why do they want his version of the journal? Did someone destroy their journal? Did they lose it to someone else? So many questions.

Sue Wong started to speak, "My cousin's journal is kept at..........."

Brad couldn't help interrupting her with, "So, your relative is President Wong of Sterling Mining Company."

"Yes, he is my cousin," she answered.

Brad glanced back at Megan to see if she was understanding all of this information.

"A small world," Brad acknowledged, stalling again for time. "So why aren't you out looking for the reef of gold?"

Sue Wong stared at Brad with mounting contempt and disdain through the fierceness of her almond eyes. Hands on her hips with legs spread apart; her body language was issuing a direct challenge.

"As I was saying," she continued, "my cousin's journal is kept in his office. Our journal mentioned a map. We are unable to locate the map by researching any family journals including our ship captain's journal. There was one tiny bit of information in another family journal that mentioned that your copy specifically had a description of the reef's location. I need your journal."

"I've seen no map," Brad countered. "If I had, why would I be out here searching for gold? We both know this *isn't* the area. It's too far away from the sea."

Several of the larrikins shifted positions from boredom.

"Don't patronize me, Mr. Templeton," snapped Sue Wong. "I know why you are here. Just doing a bit of mining practice before you head up to the Northern Territories and the new claims. Right?

266

Reef of Gold

We both know that it makes sense that the reef of gold is in that area. Just as I have known about your travels in Singapore."

She could read from Brad's reaction that he hadn't figured out, until now, who had been following him and causing some of the trouble in Singapore. Sue Wong laughed at his discomfort. "We've been following you since you left San Francisco. Now where is this journal I seek?"

Brad just stared at her. It was beginning to dawn on him that these people would never give up in the quest of finding the journal and the reef of gold. Their ancestors probably have been looking for this particular ship captain's journal, currently in his possession, for five hundred years or more. "How can I fight that kind of Chinese persistence?" he asked himself. "As long as I have the journal, my future kids and their children would have to deal with this persistence." Brad quickly came to a conclusion that his choices were limited. It took him all of a few seconds to make up his mind.

Brad cleared his throat and spat into the ground. He looked defiant.

"Enough of this," shouted the husky Aussie voice. "The both of you can settle this personal dispute another day. We are wasting time. He raised his pistol."

Another larrikin smirked. "We will get him to talk another way like maybe dropping his girlfriend from the helicopter if he doesn't."

"Shut up, you wakka," said the husky voice. Pointing a deadly pistol at Brad and then waving it at him, the husky voice told him to move and start heading back to his camp.

The helicopter threat was meaningless to Brad because he had overheard their conversation with the chopper pilot. He knew the pilot wasn't coming back. They didn't know this, of course, so he didn't challenge the threat. He did realize, however, that things could get out of hand quickly. Megan's life wasn't worth losing over a journal, let alone his. On the other hand, he had no guarantee that

Gary Dale

the larrikins wouldn't leave them to die out here anyway, especially since they were out in the middle of the Outback in an unmapped canyon. It looked like he was running out of time.

Megan and Brad dutifully led the way, drinking all the water they could as they walked along the canyon floor. Brad had noticed that the larrikins had long ago finished off their water, obviously expecting to capture them quickly and be on their way. They trudged along the center of the gorge in the stifling heat taking frequent rest stops. It was Brad's idea to force a stop as often as he could, feigning heat exhaustion. He even pointed out the ancient track he had climbed to see them coming, and where he had hid. Pointing that out caused an instant internal argument among the larrikins who immediately played the blame game. While they were arguing and shouting at each other, Brad whispered to Megan through the side of his mouth that apparently they didn't know about the location of the camp, let alone the rig. Maybe they somehow could escape and double back to their camp. That was the big question.

While the argument was going on, Megan and Brad started slowly walking again. The argument was still continuing and moved with them as they walked closer to the giant sized boulders. It gave Brad an idea.

Brad whispered his improvised plan to Megan and she winked. The plan was fine with her. She drank the last bit of water in her liter bottle, dropped it to the ground and announced that she had to go to use the loo. Everyone stopped while Megan disappeared in between the huge boulders pretending to want some privacy. Brad casually leaned against the same rock all the while inching his way toward the same opening. He drank some more precious liquid. That made the larrikins' parched throats cry for some of his water as they stared at him. Brad flipped his water bottle in their direction for whoever was the thirstiest and the fastest on his feet.

The argument stopped briefly as three of the larrikins wrestled on the ground for his water bottle. Sue Wong immediately tried to stop

Reef of Gold

the altercation. There was a brief moment of cursing and grabbing efforts as to who was going to get the first drink. As the dust settled, all their eyes focused on the water bottle and the amount of water each one would be drinking. Everybody wanted a share, and they wanted it now. Brad kept waiting for the right moment to disappear, and he was rewarded when one the larrikins apparently was drinking more than his share promptly inviting a fisticuff altercation. There was a furtive glance in Brad's direction and then they were back to the argument. Since all things appeared normal, Brad disappeared.

He quickly joined Megan on the other side of the boulders, negotiating the tight turns and climbing the difficult ledge finally dropping down into the side gorge. Together, they ran to the back of the small gorge. At the far end of the side gorge, camp chair size boulders had been exposed from erosion over the eons giving them a small track to climb, eventually leading up and over the rim. They both got near the top when they heard angry shouts from the canyon.

Then the bullets began to fly, cracking against the rocks and then ricocheting off into the distance with a frightening pinging sound. Megan yelled and Brad cursed. The bullets were making more noise than they were threatening. Brad shouted hoarsely to Megan. "The shots," he said, "are only near misses. Keep going." It was as if the shooter was trying to scare them into stopping rather than hurt them. Then again, maybe the gunman was just a lousy shot.

"Go, go," Brad shouted again to Megan. "We are almost to the top."

Megan rolled over the top in a cloud of dust. Brad was right behind her. Getting to their feet, they both ran as fast as they could towards the slope leading down to the gorge entrance when they heard the sound of helicopter blades punishing the dry air.

They both stopped and looked back. Sue Wong and her larrikins had climbed out of the small gorge and were running in the opposite direction, heading for their own rig. The two helicopters began

Gary Dale

circling around the beginning of the canyon and headed directly for Brad and Megan. Sue Wong's group wasted no time retreating from the new threat by racing off in the opposite direction heading north towards Laverton from whence they came.

Megan and Brad looked at each other. The cavalry had arrived. They were going to be rescued. They hugged, shouted, and jumped around for joy. Still celebrating the excitement, they moved off in the direction of the camp knowing that the cavalry would eventually follow them.

They hadn't gone more than a hundred yards when high-powered rifle shots cracked over their heads. Instinctively, they ducked in utter amazement and shock. What was going on? What was wrong with these people? When a few shots hit the reddish dirt at their feet, they took off running, scampering down the hillside. The only thing Brad could choke out to Megan was to head for the camp. The run was arduous from their weakened condition, because their energy level had fallen off the threshold charts. They were starting to make the familiar left turn and into the gorge itself when shots splattered at their feet and a command in butchered English to stop or be killed, echoed about them. Megan and Brad stopped in their tracks.

They looked wildly around them and saw two squat looking Asians, feet apart in a shooting position, with rifles pointed in their direction. Brad looked back towards the entrance to the where their rig was hidden. They were less than fifty yards from possible safety. So close and yet so far, he thought.

The rifles, with their big bore, made a motioning signal for Brad and Megan to come back up the hill. Brad looked at Megan and the dejection on her face said it all. With their hands up, they staggered back up the steep slope only to face Yang Lee and more of his Asian henchmen.

Yang Lee stared at them with contempt. "Miss Megan, you have been quite a nemeses for us this past week. However, I expect you had some help," he said menacingly, looking towards Brad.

270

Reef of Gold

"What is it you want?" a defiant Brad asked.

"Come, come, Mr. Templeton. You mock my intelligence. The both of you know very well what I am after."

Brad asked another question, stalling for more time. "Is it the same thing that President Wong was after before you so rudely interrupted our meeting? What is your problem?"

Snorting, Yang Lee said, "President Wong is totally unaware of this effort to get back the missing disk. His only concern is with the foolish pursuit of some journal. This has nothing to do with him."

"A figure head is he?" Brad questioned. "Isn't he the president of Sterling Mining Company or has he been replaced?"

Arms folding across his chest and widening his stance, Yang Lee snarled and let it be known that in no uncertain terms, he was running the show now and Sterling Mines. His scathing glare was a direct challenge thrown at the two of them. He turned to Megan, ignoring Brad.

"Now, Miss Megan," he said threateningly, "where is the missing disk? We don't have time, as the Americans like to say, to be 'messing around'. Where is the disk?"

"I never had the missing disk. Ever!" she said angrily. "I ran because of your security guards searching my office and your people always following me."

"Somehow I don't believe you. Ah, Mr. Templeton, do you have anything to do with this? As you must know, playing games with the Triad can be very dangerous."

Brad looked down at his shoes and scuffed the desert floor. It gave him time to think. When Yang Lee indirectly mentioned his visit to the Triad headquarters, Brad was more than a little concerned for the both of them. Upsetting the Triad was an entirely different situation than upsetting Sterling Mining people. Why they were so interested in the missing disk was beyond him. Yang Lee didn't look like the conversational type, so stalling much longer would not be an option.

Gary Dale

"Yang Lee," asked Brad, "how did you find us?"

Yang Lee stared at Brad with his very cold black eyes and then he reached under his jacket. He pulled a wicked looking firearm from his shoulder holster. Yang Lee pointed the heavy looking pistol at Brad's head while walking to within three feet of him. Brad watched the tiny black hole in the gun barrel become larger and larger with each step. The big hole shook his very foundation. Brad looked for a nervous finger on the trigger knowing that a cone shaped hunk of lead could come flying out of this black hole at any moment and hit him right between the eyes with a loud smack. It would happen so fast his brain couldn't fathom the devastation.

"I'll make this quick," Yang Lee snarled, clearly disgusted with Brad's question.

Sweat began pouring off Brad's brow, and the rank smell of impending death gripped him in a vice.

"I knew you were here in the Outback," Yang Lee said smugly, "from the questions you were asking of the mining staff. You tried to be careful and not let on what you were doing but a search of several desks revealed your requests for equipment. Your exact location was a mystery because you never showed up at the caches for supplies nor did you follow any mining map. You were supposed to be in Area Five."

Yang Lee slowly flexed each finger of his right hand one at a time, re-gripping the obviously heavy pistol.

"This particular canyon," he gestured blindly with a sweep of his left hand, "was not known to us. So finding you was difficult. Michael kept me informed of your general whereabouts on a regular basis, but it wasn't until you and Miss Megan made a series of satellite phone calls using up nearly the last of the battery power. The phone automatically gave off a distress signal because of the low battery. We knew exactly where you were. Your friend Michael confirmed your final location. We flew to Kalgoorlie and picked up our mining helicopters. We had three machines but one helicopter had to return because of a malfunction. Dirt has a way of disabling a fine machine. After all, why call attention to us with a possible stranded helicopter near your location. Are you satisfied?" Brad didn't move. "Now, where is the disk?" Yang Lee demanded, taking another threatening step forward, moving closer to Brad. Yang Lee was in no mood to compromise.

Brad was stunned. No words would tumble out of his mouth. He couldn't believe what he had heard. Michael was part of this?

"I don't believe you. Michael would never give out our location to the likes of you."

"He did," smirked Yang Lee. Michael works for me. You see, his wife's parents just happen to owe the Triad a lot of money. We came to collect and since they couldn't pay, he became our eyes and ears for the first two floors of Sterling Mines. Your every move was tracked and recorded. He sniffed arrogantly. I now know about your brother Ric. When the 'little eyes' weren't able to kill him in Singapore, my Triad bosses were very upset. Michael came to my rescue with the last bit of information. The Triad knows he is in Perth. We will find this brother of yours and kill him just as I am going to do to you. Before he dies, I will laughingly tell him that I have killed you and left your body to the scavengers deep in the confines of the Outback canyon.

Brad licked his cracked lips, trying to get some moisture. He could barely breathe. Yang Lee planned to do away with the both of them very shortly regardless of the answers he and Megan would give him.

Brad looked at Megan. She looked at Brad with real fear in her eyes. Fortunately, she still had a defiant look that said she did not like Yang Lee in any sense of the word.

Finally she blurted out, "Several groups of people know we are out here, even at this precise location, and will be here soon." She glanced at Brad and then said, "We sent out several distress signals."

Gary Dale

"We are not concerned, Miss Megan. Mining rescue parties take time to set up properly with all their gear and rescue people. And you are a long ways out in the Outback. If we were to see any rescue rigs on the return trip, the Sterling Mining logos on the sides of our helicopters would seem normal out here. Now, for the last time, where is the disk?" He turned and leveled the menacing black hole at Megan's forehead this time. The moment had changed.

"We have it." Brad said quickly, "or at least we think we have it. We really don't know if it is what you are looking for."

"Brad," exploded Megan, "I thought you were not going to say anything." She turned towards him, fists clenched, like she was about ready to deck him. "What is the matter with you?"

Everyone was a little surprised by Megan's explosion of disbelief, especially Yang Lee. He had never heard a woman speak with such ferocity in front of him. He was momentarily baffled by it.

Brad bought into it. He realized Megan was deliberately picking a fight to stall a little longer. A rescue had to be close. It was their only hope. He returned Megan's accusations with a few of his own. All he had to do was think of his ex-wife and their verbal battles. The words tumbled out with venom and hand gestures to emphasize every word. Megan fired back. Their words often blocked each other's until the crescendo reached a fever pitch. Yang Lee could not stand it any longer. He physically stepped in between the two snarling combatants, shoving each one in different directions.

"Enough," shouted Yang Lee, in frustrated Chinese. The fight went out of them in an instant. Yang Lee recovered his poise and turned to Brad. A gleam of triumph sparkled in his eyes. He would have the disk. Yang Lee knew his own life hung in the balance in finding the missing disk. He must get back to his office with the computer disk.

"Get me the disk." Yang Lee commanded.

Catching his breath, Brad calculated their success in leading Yang Lee and his henchmen on a wild goose chase down in the gorge itself.

Reef of Gold

If he and Megan could break away, then they might have a chance to hide out until the real cavalry came to their rescue. They did it once before so why not again. Brad pointed towards the entrance to the gorge.

"Not far," he said. "We have our rig parked in the shade. There is a computer disk in the company laptop. We have no idea if it is your disk or not or even how it got there. We punched up the details but it was all gibberish, like some sort of code. Didn't know what it was. It was a surprise to us to even have a disk in the computer in the first place. Is it the one you are looking for?"

Yang Lee was suddenly presented with another problem. He hesitated for a moment, thinking about this turn of events. He had briefly considered someone on the inside being a traitor but the idea was so absurd until this moment.

"Show me," he said with venom in his voice. "I will tell you if it is the missing disk."

Taking long strides, Megan and Brad walked quickly down the gradual incline. This rapid movement put some initial distance between them and the Asian larrikins who finally followed them. Since they had high-powered rifles, it didn't seem to matter to them that Megan and Brad had a forty to fifty yard lead. Brad whispered to Megan about disappearing at their first opportunity once they got near the camp. If they could somehow lose the security men even for a moment, it would allow them to grab some water and food at the camp. With a little luck, they just might make it to the truck size boulders and hide out. Yang Lee would want to check the disk on the computer first before chasing them all over the place. Death, however, would be swift if they were caught.

Brad and Megan walked a little faster down the hill keeping a steady pace to gain more ground on Yang Lee. They had nearly reached the entrance of the gorge where Brad's rig had negotiated the sharp left turn so long ago, when they suddenly heard the familiar whomp, whomp, whomp of helicopter blades slapping the hot air.

275

Gary Dale

Two helicopters suddenly came roaring from the entrance of the gorge, heading right for them nearly decapitating them. They dived to the ground and rolled the last few feet to the bottom.

Brad looked back and saw Yang Lee's men diving for cover to avoid being hit by flying lead aimed at their heads. They were getting to their feet, staring in shock at the unknown helicopters, when the ungainly whirly birds of death rolled out of the dive and came roaring back for another attack.

"Run, Megan," Brad shouted over the deafening noise. He grabbed her arm dragging her to her feet, pushing her in front of him. They both ran for the entrance of the gorge. That's when a blow like a sledgehammer slammed into the back of Brad's shoulder, knocking him flat. Time seemed to stop for Brad. He lay on the ground trying to figure out what happened and why the sudden intense pain. He couldn't seem to move. His breathing was labored, coming and going in short gasps. The whole right side of his body was on fire with unbelievable pain and the agony made him want to scream. He was blinking rapidly trying to focus when Megan's face pushed against his. "Brad," she called. "Brad, do you hear me?" Megan shouted in his ear. "You've been shot by one of Yang Lee's men. We have to move. They are shooting at the helicopters now instead of us. Get up. We have to move to safety. Please Brad. I need your help. You're too heavy for me to carry you. Please Brad, get up."

Megan was shouting in his ear in between slaps to his face. It must have worked as Brad finally began to comprehend what she wanted him to do.

With Megan supporting some of Brads' weight, they staggered and stumbled over to the nearest big boulder and out of sight. The sudden increase in pain from the exertion made him collapse. His brain would clear momentarily and then would short circuit as the trauma of the rifle bullet would take over. Whenever he was momentarily lucid, he would tell Megan that they had to make for the rig and the camp.

Reef of Gold

Megan shouted in near hysteria that he was losing blood. "First aid kit," Brad mumbled. "In the rig. Back part."

"Where?" shouted Megan.

Brad struggled with his breathing. "Back, back seat. Kit," he stammered, slurring his speech.

"I'll be right back," she shouted, "and don't move."

Brad didn't argue with the moving part of her plan. He didn't want to and probably couldn't anyway. He just hoped she made it back to him in time and ease the pain.

In what seemed like an eternity, Megan was again next to him. She rolled him over onto his side and plugged the small hole in his back with gauze pads from the first aid kit and the gaping exit hole in front of his shoulder. She packed more pads to the injured area before slapping on medical tape to hold the pads in place, stopping the blood flow. She pressed herself tight against Brad to keep him from moving and loosing the medical pads.

In between jolts of intense pain, Brad asked through clenched teeth, what was going on and were they hidden well enough. His voice came out in gasps and in spasmodic words instead of sentences. Megan shouted in his ear that they were out of sight and unless the larrikins really looked in their direction, they would be fine for the moment.

She moved away from his body and checked the bandages. The gauze pads were saturated with Brad's precious blood. Megan kept adding gauze pads upon gauze pads, leaving the plug in the ugly hole. The medical situation was getting desperate.

Brad's dull brain registered more gunshots now as the whomp, whomp, noise of the helicopters had faded. The intense pain kept knocking him in and out of a semi-conscious state. Megan kept talking in a loud voice to him. Sometimes he wished she would just shut up.

The next thing Brad knew, cool water was being splashed on his face.

277

Gary Dale

"Come on mate, let's get you to the hospital," said a recognizable voice. He had heard that statement before, but where? He felt caring hands bundling him up and loading him on a helicopter. He could hear the engine noise pound into him from all sides. It was a nightmare, he concluded. It has to be.

CHAPTER 27

PERTH MEMORIAL HOSPITAL

People will tell you that waiting by someone's hospital bed for the patient to wake up is the hardest thing to do. It is a tremendous strain on the visitors knowing that the patient is fighting to stay alive. It is only a matter of time one way or the other. Patience is a must. But still, until the patient actually opens his eyes and croaks out something, there is no reason to celebrate.

As Brad slowly regained some awareness, his pain-filled body would knock him out again. He would vaguely remember a beautiful angel dressed in white floating about him. Sometimes he felt the sensation of a cold hand on his forehead and a voice saying that he would be fine.

Without any effort on Brad's part, his eyes suddenly popped open and blinked several times, trying to focus. "What were all these people doing here? And where am I?"

There was a sudden recognition from the gallery around Brad's bed with faces and voices pressing against his limited vision. He moved his tongue to wet his lips in an effort to talk. The excited celebration continued as Brad tried to figure out what all the fuss was about. There was some movement at the corner of his vision. A beautiful angel, dressed in white came into focus. She said something to Brad and he tried to talk. She smiled and gave him a tiny amount of liquid

Gary Dale

on a washcloth, which helped enormously with his cottonmouth. He could finally speak.

"Thank you," he croaked.

A big cheer went up in the room.

"Tell me where I am and what happened," Brad whispered to the angel standing by his bedside.

She leaned down close to his face and Brad recognized a vaguely familiar bouquet. He must be mistaken, he thought.

She whispered in his ear. "You are in a hospital bed in Perth after you had been wounded in the back and right shoulder area by a high velocity bullet. You were in surgery for many hours and are now recovering from a successful operation. This is your hospital room."

"Thank you," Brad whispered. His voice cracked on the word 'who', which came out like 'boo', so he had to start all over again.

"Who are all these people?" he asked hesitantly.

"Your friends," she said. "You will recognize them in time. The anesthesia will take some time to dissipate from your system. You will be more coherent in a few days. Best you get some sleep now. And don't worry about drifting off to sleep while talking with your friends. It's a common occurrence. I'll be here watching over you. Go to sleep now," his angel in white said soothingly. And he did.

At some point Brad awoke again, only this time, his eyes focused and he felt he could talk. He looked around expecting to see his angel in white and maybe some visitors but no such luck. The room was a sparkling white but sprinkled with colorful flowers surrounding his bed. The usual television was set high above his bed with its distracting and obnoxious noise. Must be a news channel, he reasoned.

Brad was propped up on his left side so he could see people coming and going along the hallway. He looked for something to ring or push to have someone come in and help him get up. He had to use the bathroom. It must have been mental telepathy as a nurse

280

Reef of Gold

suddenly appeared. To Brad, she was so beautiful that she seemed to glide over to his side of the bed. She was all smiles.

"What's your name?" he asked. She looked like the angel he had seen once before. Brad began to wonder if all the hospital nurses looked the same. He watched her move things around before she came back to his bedside. "Are you an angel?" he asked.

She smiled and her blue eyes sparkled. "Sometimes I am an angel. But today, I am your nurse. I'm Maggie. My, aren't you perky today."

"I feel much better, Maggie," Brad replied. "Can you be my nurse permanently? I'd like that if it is ok with you."

"Of course," she said sweetly. "I would be honored."

"By the way, how long have I been here?"

"Oh, a number of days since your surgery. You had a massive wound that has required some special attention. We had to fill you full of drugs to battle infections."

"Thank you. I'm just glad to be alive." Brad suddenly grasped the bed guard rails. "Nurse, I have got to use the bathroom really bad. Can you help me get to the toilet? I mean right now."

"Of course. Time to change your bandages anyway. I'll get you up in a second so the blood flow will let your numb legs work." Then she walked over to the doors, said something to someone outside and then closed them for privacy.

For Brad, the urge to go to the bathroom was now very great. Unfortunately, walking across the room two inches at a time seemed like it took forever, even with the nurse's help. When Brad finally got in the bathroom, it took a while before things started to work. Maybe it was because of the female standing next to him, holding him upright that shut things down. But finally, he could hold it no longer. The relief was so great that Brad finally concluded that it didn't matter if a nurse was with him or not.

Once the bathroom episode was over, they inched their way back to the bed. The hospital angel changed his bandages and then

281

Gary Dale

asked Brad if he thought he could sit up and lean back on propped up pillows instead of lying on his side.

"A change in body position would be helpful," he agreed.

He was just getting settled in his new position when in walked Megan. The nurse discreetly left. Megan walked over and gave Brad a kiss on the forehead. It occurred to Brad that his breath was not the kindest due to all the drugs having been pumped into his system. "You're looking so much better." She held Brad's hand for a long moment and looked deep into his eyes.

Smiling, she tenderly squeezed his hand.

"You are going to make it. That makes me happy."

They made small talk about the final hours of their adventure. She also told him that the medical staff said it would be a while before he was healed enough for some extensive physical therapy.

There was a little pause in the conversation while she found a chair and moved closer to him. They held hands again. Brad wanted to tell her how he felt about their deepening relationship and ask how she felt about him. They looked at each other for the longest time, smiling and not saying a word. Finally, Brad couldn't stand it any longer.

"Ah, Megan," he said haltingly, "I just was wondering how you felt about our budding relationship and if we could continue it during and after my recovery?"

Megan seemed to back away just a bit, giving herself a little room for a moment and then said quietly. "At the beginning, we had developed a great friendship, even a little beyond." "Maybe," she sighed, "even more than I want to admit. But now I feel it is necessary to back off for a while. Our adventure has put so much strain on us. For us to have a romantic relationship now would make it seem like a war-time romance based on adventure and not true love and commitment for the rest of our lives. I need some time, Brad, just a little more time to get used to the idea that I have fallen in love with you. After all these years of saying that I would never

Reef of Gold

get deeply involved again, you showed up in my life. I didn't expect to fall in love but I did. I do love you Brad." She smiled. "Besides, I look forward to helping you recover."

Brad smiled at the thought. Things were going to be fine. He hadn't considered her past before. In the old days, he would have offered to keep their deepening relationship going just by showing up at her apartment. Things were different now. Now he was trying to be understanding and patient. He didn't want her to get away.

There was a long pregnant pause of understanding between them when Brad finally let go of her hand. He reached out with his left arm to draw her closer for a tender moment. What stopped the both of them was a knock on the door and people bursting through. There was a lot of shouting and congratulations being passed around before the crowd came over to Brad's bedside.

"Brad, I'd like you to meet my brother, Geoffrey," said Megan.

"Hi, how are you." Brad said nodding. "Nice to put a face with a voice. For a while I thought you were a figment of her imagination."

Geoffrey laughed and then winked at Megan.

"Thanks mate, for taking good care of Megan. She is my only sister and very precious to me."

"No worries, Geoffrey. Your sister is something. She more than held her own. I would go on any adventure with her at any time."

Glancing around, Brad suddenly recognized Michael and his family, standing in the near background. They all came over, and he gave them a left hand to squeeze. Brad knew that little Melissa wanted to hug him so badly but seeing all the bandages, she held back. But her eyes sparkled with such happiness that Brad felt a warm glow. Michael told him that three other people would be here shortly, as their helicopter was on the way. Brad was puzzled because his brain told him that he didn't know anybody that would take a helicopter to a hospital just to see a patient. Michael said he would explain everything to him later.

283

Gary Dale

They all chatted about anything and everything as chairs were brought in so everyone could sit down and be more comfortable. His angel of a nurse kept checking with him to see how he was doing and asked him to let her know if all the excitement became too much. Brad told her that he wouldn't miss any of this and he would sleep later.

In the midst of their conversation, a knock on the door silenced everyone in the room.

A big smile broke out on Brad's face as the ever-cool Eurasian walked in and gave him a big welcome. It was Max.

"Ah, mate," he said. "You had me worried for a while. For some reason, I keep seeing you in hospitals and not enough socially. How about a cigar?" he asked, handing him a good Cuban.

"Not on your life," pitched in his nurse, holding out her hand for the cigar's return. Max palmed it immediately and winked at Brad.

"Brad, you gotta get out of here, he said."

"What's this 'gotta' bit?" Brad asked. "That's not British. That's American slang."

"I speak many languages, Brad. Sometimes I forget and jump into several at the same time. A promise mate, you will smoke a good cigar with me when you jump ship," laughed Max.

"Deal," agreed Brad. "Say, do you know any of these people," he asked, trying to be polite and a good host.

"Oh, yes," said Max, nodding his head to the group surrounding the bed. "I'd say we've all met on more than one occasion."

Everybody laughed at that comment. Brad must have looked a little bewildered until Max said he would explain later.

As soon as the laughter died down, Brad had the biggest shock of his life. In walked his two brothers, grinning broadly, and saying hi to everyone, shaking hands, and as usual, hugging the women. Ric was introducing brother Jon to all in the room. They finally drifted over to Brad's bedside.

Reef of Gold

"Geez, bro, you doing ok?" asked Jon, in a very concerned voice.

Before Brad could answer, Ric boomed out, "Of course he is ok. He is receiving the best treatment in the world." He looked at the nurse and winked. Brad wondered what that was all about.

"No worries, Jon. Like Ric said, I am doing much better. What about Mom and Dad? Do they know I've been hurt?"

Jon answered quickly. "They know and wish they could travel to be here. Dad wasn't feeling up to a 14 hour flight so I call them once a day to let them know about your progress and not to worry."

"That's good, Jon," said Brad, "and thanks. I didn't want them to hear from someone else. So, tell me, how did you get time off from the air force to be here and so soon?"

Brother Jon told all in the room that he had been reassigned to Australia. Since he was in-transit, he got some additional time off plus he was taking some of his accumulated leave. It couldn't have worked out any better.

Brad asked him about what his duty assignment was going to be when Jon suddenly looked questioningly at Ric. Raising his right hand to slightly touch his nose, Ric motioned him to wait before answering. Jon casually answered he didn't know yet. Someone brought in three more chairs during this exchange, so everyone was now comfortable and were circled around Brad's bed. They talked of how Jon's home might be Australia for a while and where they all might be in the next couple of years. Brad swiveled his head back and forth with the conversation.

Marge and Melissa were getting a little bored and finally said their goodbyes leaving Michael to finally say he too should go. He would return later.

"Wait in the hall way, Michael," suggested Ric. Michael nodded and left the room. Megan reluctantly excused herself, saying she had a few things to do and would be back. The door was closed and all

285

Gary Dale

eyes were facing Brad. He felt a little uncomfortable, wondering what they were going to do to him now.

"Brad," said Max, "what we are about to tell you will probably come as a shock to you but we feel we owe you some explanation of what went on. After all, you took the brunt of this mission. While it is necessary to tell you a few things that have happened to you and why, we also have to be careful not to give you too much information because you still aren't trained in this sort of thing. Also, we are one happy family here so what each of us has to say will stay here in this room. I'm serious. Deal?"

"For sure," Brad said, not knowing where Max was headed with this serious conversation.

Max took a deep breath before letting it all out. He looked at every one in the room and encouraged them to jump in the conversation at anytime. He then proceeded to tell Brad some amazing things about the Triad and their espionage efforts in Australia.

Brad lay in bed totally fixated on their comments. At first he was totally shocked by the conversation, and then he found himself finding their espionage stories incredibly fascinating. The main thing was that Michael was on their side. Yang Lee had a hold on Michael's wife, Maggie. At first, Lee didn't need Michael other than to watch things on the third floor. It was pretty quiet there on purpose. It wasn't until this disk fiasco broke loose causing Lee to hammer on Michael and his wife. Michael was able to deflect most of the bad stuff and gave us the critical information about Yang Lee's doings. He was no traitor.

Brad sighed with relief. Michael had become a best friend.

The story finally got to the part about Ric and Yang Lee's involvement. Ric didn't hesitate. "Once the Triad had figured out that I was still alive, they went after me with vengeance using the 'little eyes' organization, meaning a network of hundreds of street urchins as spies and killers, who canvassed the cities of Singapore and

286

Reef of Gold

Kuala Lumpur looking for me. The little eyes were so thorough in their search that I had to leave Southeast Asia and head for Perth."

Ric went on with the explanation that Brad's arrival in Singapore further complicated matters for him when some unknowns were also watching Brad, looking for an opportunity to get a hold of him. "It turned out to be the niece of President Wong that was looking for a journal of some kind that you had in your possession, Brad. They didn't seem dangerous to one's health, so we let them continue. Besides, their presence confused things for the Triad. They probably were going to send in some tough guys to rough you up the longer you stayed in Singapore. They wanted to send you a message."

"I know," said Brad.

Brad asked them about his encounter with a car in Singapore. "Was it an accident or was somebody aiming to do me in?"

Ric apologized for that temporary security lapse. "We did not see it coming," he explained. "Apparently a Triad rogue organization trying to make a name for themselves thought you were me and not dead as reported. One of the waiters at the restaurant recognized my last name on the guest register and reported you. It was an independent act. They were going to make sure that this 'Ric' character was really dead and claim a substantial Triad reward."

Brad shared with them his recovery experiences including mentioning his angel of a nurse. "Her perfume kept me alive." They all smiled, especially Ric. His smile was broader than anyone else's.

Max took over the conversation and enlightened Brad with more details about the Triads, probably more than he had wanted to know. Not only was this organization involved in crime and all its various and obvious forms, but also in spying on the good ole USA for the Chinese government. "The CIA and the Asian Security Forces had been unable to penetrate the inner workings of the Triad until you accidentally entered one of their nests as a courier," he explained. "At this moment, you have been the only one on our side to have seen the headquarters. Some of the mystery is gone."

Gary Dale

It was Brad's turn now to ask questions. "Ric, when I went to Perth to work for Sterling Mines, my last name seemed to startle a few people as if they had recognized it. Did you work there at one time?"

Ric told him he had briefly worked for the Sterling Mining Company. He was one of those hired to install some new computers with their specialized programs because the previous Asian installers had done a poor job. "I had secretly installed a sophisticated program in their computer system and after leaving the facilities, was electronically able to download some of the information coming into the company, especially from Singapore. That enabled the CIA to intercept and intercede in a few Triad operations causing the Triad to trace back-unidentified intrusions into their computer systems." He paused for a moment to make sure Brad was still alert.

"Computer hacking," Ric continued, "had made the Triad's security system suspect and the security lapse really showed up when some unknown hacker extorted some money from Sterling Mines for his efforts. That intrusion was the final straw. The Triad brought in a new administrator to take over the Perth operation and he immediately threw everything out and brought in new computer stuff. They had special Triad computer techs set everything up and protect it. That is why we made it easy for you to the job at Sterling Mines."

Geoffrey also explained their dilemma. "Our Aussie security people and the CIA knew that the Triad was heavily involved with Sterling Mines as a cover for a number of their operations. Many of their agents entered Australia through transfers from their Singapore office and then tried to disappear. But what we didn't know was how it all connected until one of our inside agents stole that computer disk from the third floor. That missing disk caused so much uproar within the Triad that we figured they would be forced into making some mistakes. The mistakes would allow us to figure out what they were doing."

Reef of Gold

"How did I get the Triad disk?" Brad queried.

"Well," said Ric with a shrug of his shoulders, "you really didn't get the missing Triad disk. Internal security was so tight at the mining company when they courier something to Singapore, it made slipping out the disk nearly impossible. We decided to send a fake disk out through a security exit by using a company laptop. After all, you were on a mining exploration trip, so a laptop was required equipment. Security was slightly more relaxed as mining people were always coming and going. We knew that future security investigations would turn up records showing your leaving with a company computer after the real disk showed up missing. Yang Lee didn't suspect you even then. He had made up his mind that Megan was involved and went after her. You were a back up pawn, Brad. Sorry about that."

Geoffrey smiled and explained, "Megan was a pawn as well. She was the only person really to have access to the third floor and the computers at any given time. That is why Yang Lee's suspicion fell so heavily onto her shoulders. Charlie, the slow moving custodian, is really an agent for the CIA. He was the one that lifted the disk. On Thursday, he cut his hand and had Megan and Lee's security people help stop the bleeding and bandage it up properly. Once back on the job and out of sight, he picked the lock on the courier briefcase, switched disks, unbandaged his hand, slipped in the disk, rebandaged the hand. He promptly had the third floor security guards who had bandaged his hand come down and escort him through the final check. Once through the last security check, he walked away.

Brad shifted his legs to increase the circulation. The movement gave him time to digest the stunning development. When he was ready, he nodded for someone to continue the conversation.

"Which brings us again to my sister," acknowledged Geoffrey. "The third floor people waited until Monday, a business day for the rest of the world, to courier out the vital information to Singapore.

Gary Dale

We knew the disk was important, and its loss would cause the Triad some worry."

"There was a side bar to all of this," added Ric, "which was a great piece of luck. President Wong's cousin was after your ship captain's journal, which Yang Lee could care less about, so excessive attention to you was deflected. Yang Lee concentrated his efforts on Megan except he couldn't find her."

"Then, things really heated up," continued Geoffrey, "when both parties started pulling in all their muscle to search for the two of you."

Ric cleared his throat as a signal to all that he wanted to jump into the conversation. "President Wong's people, especially his cousin, were on to you right away, Brad, when you called the office to leave a message about Megan." said Ric. "Your satellite phone battery was really used up. A distress signal was sent out. Yang Lee had picked up the same signal because of Michael. He had to tell Lee. Of course, he had told us first. We had a security team on the look out for Yang Lee's people, and could just about tell when they would make an attempt to get to you. It was a timing thing. We wanted to take him alive at the same time we rescued you. We figured that with all of our firepower, they would surrender to us. Unfortunately, they didn't surrender. Sorry about your getting shot."

"Things happen," said Brad, "but next time, try not to cut it so close." There wasn't any laughter in the room this time. It had been close.

"Can you tell me what was encrypted?" Brad asked.

Jon looked at Michael and then Ric. Ric nodded.

"My turn to jump into the conversation," said Jon. "The encryption was full of America's military secrets including messages from our embassies around Southeast Asia, our military bases, ships at sea, etc. It's going to take us a while to decrypt the entire disk. This is what I do for the air force. Encrypt and decrypt stuff. Anyway, we haven't been able to crack the entire code yet. There was just

Reef of Gold

enough information on the disk to tell us where it originated. The disk information came from our Pine Gap satellite facility near Alice Springs which was about 1,000 kilometers or 600 hundred miles from your little canyon. The general public knows about Pine Gap but few questions are asked about the internal workings.

Alice Springs is almost in the center of Australia; generally flat, desert like, no surrounding towns with their streetlights, and with beautiful uninterrupted skies for thousands of miles in any direction. This is great for our satellites to send signals to and from bases of operations all over Asia. We bounce the signals from one satellite to another and finally download the information at the Pine Gap geodesic structures, process it, organize it, interpret some of the information, share with the Australians, encrypt it again and send it to Washington DC and the appropriate intelligence agencies via other satellites. We have pretty tight security in the sky. We thought we were tight on the ground as well. I guess we weren't that secure. Brad, I hope you understand that I have to keep this information fairly general in nature?"

"That's fine," said Brad. "The concept would be all I would understand anyway. How did Yang Lee's people, and especially the Triad, get the satellite information in the first place?"

"That was the billion dollar question," chimed in Ric. "We've solved part of the puzzle a month ago, but we didn't quite have the identities of the inside men or women that were involved with stealing the encryption or how they were sending out the stolen information. Then we received an anonymous tip. We don't know who the tipster was, but he seemed to know about both ends of the spy ring. We've arrested two people within the communication system at Pine Gap. One was a radical leftist leaning woman from Seattle and the other was a man from India, who had migrated to Australia using the British Commonwealth open immigration doors policy. There are probably more spies but we haven't unearthed them

Gary Dale

yet. That will be part of Jon's job. The tipster helped to move this closure along.'

"Do you want me to continue, Brad," asked Ric.

Brad nodded.

"We were fast closing in on Yang Lee's operation any way. You, Brad, really helped us with your description of the old telegraph line with the microwave boosters every twenty miles. The idea was ingenious and so very simple. It was like skipping a stone across the water. The microwave signal would be sent from the geodesic domes, to the nearest signal box on the telegraph line, which would boost the signal to the next box twenty miles away. All the boxes had to be in a straight line to bounce the signals clear to Perth and into the Sterling Mines headquarters. Brad, when you mentioned to Megan and her brother about the old telegraph poles being in a straight line, it got us to thinking about the obvious; simple and simple. You helped us a great deal with your observation. It became only a matter of another week before we made the arrests because of their mistakes within the satellite base." Ric paused. "Feeling all right, Brad? Want to hear some more?"

"I'm all ears," Brad said, sipping some more water and changing his body position in the bed. His throat was dry and he was feeling a little tired but there was no way he was going to miss all of this. He tried to look energetic and sharp despite the pain still throbbing through his body. His pain tolerance level was fading.

"I have a question," continued Brad. "Why didn't Yang Lee and his agents just encrypt the stolen messages and send it up to one of their satellites? It would be faster."

"Good question," acknowledged Jon. "Our satellites can tell us when a burst message is sent and from what location. That wouldn't work for the Chinese. It might give away their spy network. Remember, they think in broad terms of a hundred years or more and their little spy network was created to be as simple as possible and to last a very, very long time."

292

Reef of Gold

"What happens now?" Brad asked. "Did you get Yang Lee and President Wong and all their thugs?"

"Well, not quite," spoke up Ric. "Yang Lee was wounded in our little skirmish. We saw him go down and then someone dragged him to a waiting helicopter. He got away during the excitement. Unfortunately, we can't ask him any questions. I don't think we could have taken him alive anyway. No surrendering for him. Even if he didn't tell us anything, the mere fact he was in our custody would be enough for the Triad to do him bodily harm. The million-dollar question still remains. Who was the tipster?"

"What about President Wong? How deep into this is he?" asked Brad. He must know what was going on in his company."

"Actually," said Max, "he didn't want to know about any of this spy stuff from Lee. His directives from the Triad were to put up a good front to disguise their involvement. He was told to run the mining business but let Yang Lee's people have total access and his cooperation. Since the Triad was funding Sterling Mining in its early stages, their threat to President Wong was to pull the funding and call in all the loans. They might have something else on him to keep him in line, but he didn't reveal it other than to say a relative was involved. The Triad told him to just mind his own business and to stay out of theirs. It worked. Nothing will happen to him from our end. Aussie security will still maintain a presence in his company and if you want, you will have your old job back and so will Megan. Sterling Mining has become a solid business in its own right if it doesn't expand too quickly in the Northern Territories."

It seemed to Brad that some silent signal had been given when Megan's brother Geoffrey, and Max announced it was time to leave. They said they had work to do and would see him later. As they left the room, Michael walked in, smiling.

Brad was getting noticeably tired now, but there were so many more questions he wanted to ask his talented brothers. This was only

Gary Dale

one incident in their vast security world. To him, this was the most exciting adventure he had ever had in his entire life.

Brad pointed to Ric with his one good arm and motioned for him to continue. Ric wasn't at all shy about finishing the story. He quickly added his comments. "A spy is probably still working at Pine Gap and thus very valuable to the Chinese. They will just find another way to get the encrypted files out. At this point, we really don't know how it all works. Jon will have to figure it out from the inside."

"That's going to be part of my next assignment," commented Jon. "So, I'll be around to check up on you Brad. You could do me a favor. Maybe you could set me up with some dates with a few Australian women. You must have had some time to establish yourself here in Perth."

One name immediately flashed from Brad's subconscious to the forefront of his brain, "Alice." This flash told him that he wasn't totally under the weather. She had been on the hunt for him so why not pass the Irish redhead onto his brother and watch the fireworks. That's what brothers do to each other. This could be fun and interesting. A big grin broke out on Brad's face. He told Jon that he had the perfect girl for him and to just leave it to him.

"Her name is Alice."

Ric frowned at the name. He looked at Jon and said, "Maybe." Michael stifled a laugh but gave it way when his shoulders began to shake. He couldn't help it.

Somehow Brad stayed alert long enough to share his concern for the camp and its contents in the now famous canyon. He wanted his red backpack with the ship captain's journal. He wanted to be sure the backpack was safe.

Ric quickly assured Brad that he had the red backpack safely in Michael's house. "After reading your Ship Captain's Journal, we thought you wouldn't mind if we did some exploring up in the Northern Territories on your behalf. You know, sort of get things

Reef of Gold

started while you are healing up and then you could take over the dig. Besides, the hospital staff assured us that you should pull through and that our hanging around the hospital was becoming a nuisance to everyone taking care of you. Better we leave for a week and then come back to see you. See, it all turned out fine." He winked at the other two and continued.

"Jon and I figured you would want Michael and Megan involved in this project. We all read the ship captain's journal several times, looking for clues. We found something."

"What did you find?" Brad exclaimed loudly, sitting a little straighter in his bed, wincing from a jolt of pain. He wasn't about to sleep just now. Adrenalin kicked into his system.

"Well," reasoned Jon, holding up his hand as a sign to wait a moment, "the cover of the journal had split open on the top when we were reading it in the air conditioned hotel room. Apparently, the dry air in the outback dried out the cover, and then when the humidity in the hotel room got sufficient enough to put some moisture back into the journal paper, the cover split open. I was trying to repair it when I noticed a slight bulge in the cover and took a pair of tweezers and picked out a piece of rice paper. We thought it was a map. Unfortunately, the map really wasn't a map."

Brad sat back in his bed, disappointed. After a few moments, he leaned slightly forward. "Continue," he said.

"It is really a small sketch of a Ming Dynasty vase. I'll tell you about that in a second. There was something else. There was another drawing on rice paper of, well, we think a rock." Ric held the rice paper close for Brad to see. "There's some inscription and crude landscape drawings carved into the rock showing men carrying heavy bags across their backs. We thought it might show us where the gold reef is, if we could recognize the landmarks after six hundred years. But the rock still mystified us. Who would have thought of describing the location of a gold reef on a rock?"

Brad sat back in his bed, totally stunned. The rice paper drawings

Gary Dale

were with him all this time and he never had a clue that there was even a supposed map until President Wong's niece told him. Brad smiled and then sat forward in his bed.

"That rock is probably a Runestone," he explained. "According to the Ship Captain's Journal, a Norwegian ship captain was on board a Chinese ship during this adventure and he must have carved the location into the rock. Norwegians were great explorers of their time and this is how they left their mark for other countrymen to follow. I'll bet the rock will tell of the number of crew, circumstances of the voyage, as well as the location of the reef of gold. Our only problem is finding the Runestone. Secondly, my research indicates a Ming Dynasty porcelain vase was always carried aboard a Chinese flagship. The sea captains of that era often engraved the bottoms of the vases with their various sea routes and good harbor locations marked with..." he suddenly stopped in mid-sentence.

"The vase that broke and cut the janitors hand had writing on the bottom of it. Megan told me about it but at the time, I didn't think. That was the clue I had been missing. I knew something was special about the Ming Dynasty vases in Wong's waiting room but couldn't figure it out. Look at my notes. Then go look at the bottom of a Ming Dynasty porcelain vase in Wong's conference room on the fourth floor. It is in the center of the show room in a special security pedestal. It will have the message we are looking for. I'm positive of it."

Ric and Jon both looked at each other.

Brad was animated now. "I want to remind both of you that President Wong's niece still wants the Ship Captain's Journal and the rice paper drawing. All of us need to be careful wherever we take the red back pack and its contents." Brad carefully explained his townhouse adventure, capture and the questions Sue Wong had asked. This part of the adventure had been overlooked during the excitement of Yang Lee's demise and Brad's shoulder injury.

Ric and Jon looked at each other in amazement. Their middle

Reef of Gold

brother was more like them than they had thought possible. Everyone started talking at once.

Ric held up his hand. "Ah, Brad, we read your notebook and all your research notes including hearing from Megan and her story about the broken vase. We have already looked at the bottom of the vase in Wong's special show room. Funny, but he had the reef location information all this time, right in front of him. I would bet his copy of the journal probably has the same rice paper with Runestone directions buried in the cover. He still doesn't know, and we aren't going to tell him. We were in and out of his office without him knowing it.'

Jon chuckled at the thought of their latest break in at Wong's office. "We almost blew it," he said. Megan stopped us from trying to get at Wong's copy of the 'Reef of Gold' journal. We didn't know about the extreme security until Megan warned us away."

"After a little research on Michael's part at the Perth Library special reserve section," said Ric, "he got hold of a special document that you had wanted to see. He just happens to know the curator personally, and we got access. Apparently, some thugs from Wong tried to get a hold of it while the curator was gone. The on–duty librarian was a force. She may have had legs like a pine tree back home and built like a cement truck full of concrete, but she took no prisoners and caused quite a ruckus at the library. Probably shook some dust off the bookshelves let alone the cobwebs from a few employees. The thugs never had a chance.

With that library document naming the tide flows, we knew about where the reef might be located. Michael is familiar with the Northern Territories area and the islands just off shore. Once we figured out the tide charts, the actual island was easy. That left us with the last piece of the puzzle. Finding the actual Runestone and translating the message.

"Since I learned to read a little bit of Runestone markings from Dad's compiling of Norwegian history in his library at home, I was

Gary Dale

able to understand parts of it," said Jon. "I called Dad and he filled in some gaps in my lousy translation."

Ric started laughing.

"I know," said Jon, "Dad's insistence that I know something useful paid off," he acknowledged to his brother. "We found a book at the Perth library that had Norwegian ancient writings with translations. It was painstaking work but a word here and there gave us enough information to piece things together." Ric slowly stopped chuckling at Jon's expense and became serious.

"We borrowed a company jet and eventually leased a helicopter," he said, and raced to the general area, not knowing exactly what to expect."

"Brad, we found the Runestone at low tide on a small island just off the Northern Territories of Australia. The island even had an area to land the helicopter. The Runestone gave us the direction and location of the gold reef. Without it, we probably wouldn't have looked in the right direction and most certainly wouldn't have known about the second reef. The sea had apparently risen due to global warming over the centuries of the discovery so following the directions, we ended up having to do a little scuba diving even at low tide. When diving, we found that the reef of gold sits along a ledge in fairly shallow diving water. That and extreme high tides is why no one discovered the gold reef until now. The twenty foot tide always covered up the Runestone."

"Brad, the reef is stunning," said Jon, excitedly. "Look at these underwater pictures. Great visibility, right?" Pointing to the lower half of the photo, Jon said rapidly, "See, spidery webbed gold veins leading into thick bands. This is a guesstimate, but the bands of gold seem to be fixed in coral about six feet wide from top to bottom and quite long. It will take more than our cursory search. We took our picks and loosened the coral encrusted quartz." Jon could hardly contain himself. "This ragged area, right here," he said, tapping his finger on the photo. "These are scratch marks where others,

Reef of Gold

hundreds of years before us, had mined the gold reef when the sea was lower."

Jon walked over to the door and beckoned Michael who had been quietly waiting outside, to enter. Michael opened a bag tied to his waist, reached inside, and pulled out something heavy. On the palm of his hand, he held a chuck of coral. He flipped it over to reveal the quartz backside. It was laced with thick seams of gold. Brad held it carefully.

He smiled broadly.

"We will dive together as soon as you recover," said Jon. "The physical therapist told us that diving would be good therapy for your shoulder. In the meantime, all of us have to get back to our jobs. Duty calls. The reef of gold discovery can wait. It's not going anywhere."

Brad breathed a sigh of relief knowing that all was going to be taken care of by his brothers and friends. That was enough for him. With Ric, Michael, Jon and Megan doing some of the mining, the incentive for him to heal soon was now flowing throughout his heart. He was confident his relationship with Megan would flourish. Jon and Ric were still talking when he drifted off to a well-deserved deep sleep.

His angel of a nurse would appear in his dreams again, of that he was sure. He would dream what every man dreams.

CPSIA information can be obtained at www.ICGtesting.com
Printed in the USA
LVOW06*1022060415

433449LV00001B/3/P